PAW
26/June

WITHDRAWN

Please return on or before the latest date above.
You can renew online at *www.kent.gov.uk/libs*
or by telephone 08458 247 200

CUSTOMER SERVICE EXCELLENCE

Libraries & Archives

Kent
County
Council

00884\DTP\RN\07.07   LIB 7

The Generation Game is inspired by Sophie's childhood growing up in a sweet shop in Torquay. Sophie is the winner of the 2010 Luke Bitmead Bursary and the Yeovil Literary Prize. She currently lives in Teignmouth, Devon with her husband and three children.

THE GENERATION GAME

Philippa Smith is in her forties and has a beautiful newborn baby girl. She also has no husband, and nowhere to turn. So she turns to the only place she knows: the beginning. Retracing her life, she confronts the daily obstacles that shaped her very existence. From the tragic events of her childhood abandonment, to the astonishing accomplishments of those close to her, Philippa learns of the sacrifices others chose to make, and the outcome of buried secrets. She discovers a celebration of life, love, and the golden era of television in this reflection of everyday people, in not so everyday situations.

SOPHIE DUFFY

THE GENERATION GAME

Complete and Unabridged

CHARNWOOD
Leicester

First published in Great Britain in 2011 by
Legend Press Ltd., London

First Charnwood Edition
published 2012
by arrangement with
Legend Press Ltd., London

The moral right of the author has been asserted

All characters, other than those clearly in the public
domain, and place names, other than those
well-established such as towns and cities, are
fictitious and any resemblance is purely coincidental.

British Library CIP Data

Duffy, Sophie.
  The generation game.
  1. Single mothers- -Fiction.
  2. Family secrets- -Fiction.
  3. Domestic fiction.
  4. Large type books.
  I. Title
  823.9'2–dc23

  ISBN 978–1–4448–1335–7

Published by
F. A. Thorpe (Publishing)
Anstey, Leicestershire

Set by Words & Graphics Ltd.
Anstey, Leicestershire
Printed and bound in Great Britain by
T. J. International Ltd., Padstow, Cornwall

This book is printed on acid-free paper

To my two dads:
Stephen Nigel Stenner 1933 – 1978
and
Ralph Albert Parry Pritchard 1924 – 2007

Life is the name of the game
Bruce Forsyth

Acknowledgements

Please forgive any dramatic license in the representation of the show, *The Generation Game*, which I appreciate is a national institution. I would like to offer my genuine thanks to Bruce Forsyth, Anthea Redfern, Isla St Clair and the late Larry Grayson for having a special place in my childhood. This novel, among other things, is a salute to their services to showbiz. I hope that by the time of publication Brucie will have his knighthood [and as this book first went to print, he did].

Thanks are due to the following people for their support, feedback, encouragement:

To Elaine Hanson and Tiffany Orton, Luke Bitmead's mother and sister, for their belief in me and my writing. To Legend Press for their enthusiasm and hard work. To Debbie Watkins and Liz Tait, who've been there from the start, and to Katie Glover for her later appearance. To the original Wink who introduced me to *The Generation Game*.

To my teachers, Jean Whatling, David Milnes, Jan Henley and Graham Mort. To Lancaster University MA cohort 2002-2004, in particular to Carol Anderson and Ren Powell. To Exeter Writers. To my literary godmother, Margaret James. To Louise Rattenbury for that early read. To Margaret Graham and the Yeovil Literary

Prize. To Ruth Kirkpatrick for that trip to Bulgaria for research that had nothing to do with this book. To my house groups past and present. To Teignmouth Library Bookseekers.

To my mum for her love, support and vacuuming. To my children, Johnny, Eddy and Izzy, for putting up with a distracted mother and her lack of vacuuming. To Niall for being with me all the way.

2006

Oh dear. How did that happen?

Last time I looked, I only had myself to worry about. Now I've got you. Another person. Yesterday you were hidden away, tucked up inside me, completely oblivious to what lay ahead. Now here you are, floppy and exhausted, the biggest, scariest journey of your life over and done with. All screamed-out and sleeping the way babies are supposed to on a good day.

So what now? Where do we go from here, you and I? Backwards, I suppose. To the beginning. While you are quiet and still and here in my arms. Before they chuck us out and send us home.

Home.

But where to start? Where is the beginning exactly?

Long before the bags I packed full of nappies and cream and teeny-weeny babygros. Before the hairy ride in the taxi over the speed bumps of East Dulwich banging my head on the roof while the Irish cabbie recited his Hail Marys. The tracks I played on my iPod, full blast to drown out the noise I couldn't help making. The Best of The Monkees. Hearing those voices and tambourines took me back to a time when I had

1

a best friend in all the world who I thought I was going to marry. Who I thought would be there forever. Who taught me that everything changes. (A Monkees compilation was as far as your father got involved in your birth. That and the quick leg-over that was lost somewhere amongst the ravages of my fortieth birthday.)

Long before then. Right back at the beginning, my beginning, way back when I was held for the first time in my mother's arms.

Were my fingers ever that small? My toenails? Was my skin ever that smooth and wrinkled at the same time? My hair that fluffy? My grip that tight? My nose that squashed?

Did my mother hold me and wonder these very same things?

I can't answer these questions.

And try as I might, I can't tell you everything that went before. Everyone I could've gone to for help, for answers, has gone, is lost — in one way or another. But I'll tell you what I can. I'll tell you about the people who loved me. Who brought me up somehow, against all odds.

I'll tell you about Lucas, the boy I was going to marry.

I'll tell you about your father (though I'd rather not).

And I'll tell you about a little fat girl called Philippa.

I'll tell you my story. Our story. Because there's nothing worse than wondering. Knowing is always better.

1

1965

Family Fortunes

On the 29th day of July, 1965 I arrive in the world — a brightly-lit poky delivery room high up in St Thomas' Hospital — amid a flurry of noise. The doctor is shouting at the midwife, the midwife is shouting at my mother and my mother is shouting so loudly, her screams can probably be heard across the Thames by the honourable gentlemen in the Palace of Westminster, possibly even by the Prime Minister himself, if they weren't on their holidays. In fact, my mother is so busy screaming, she doesn't seem to have noticed that I am already here. But I am. I have arrived in style, waving a banner, heralding my birth. I am happy to be here even if she isn't so sure. I'd put up some bunting and have jelly and ice cream if I could.

(It is years later before I find out the truth: that I am in actual fact yanked out of my mother with a sucker clamped to my head, her (ineffective) coil clenched in my tiny fist. I am lucky to be here at all.)

I spend the first week being manhandled by stout nurses in starchy uniforms. They poke me and prod me and tip me upside down for no

3

apparent reason. They bring me to my mother every four hours ('Baby's feed, Mrs Smith! Left side first!') and whisk me away again to be comprehensively winded and gripe-watered before I've even had the chance to take a good look at her or to have loving words whispered in my newborn ears. Instead I have to lie on my tummy in a little tank in a large room. I am one of many. The others cry a lot. I give up and join in.

When I am seven days old, I am brought to my mother's bed. It is empty. She is sitting in a chair next to it, reading a magazine. She looks quite different fully clothed. She has long legs and red lips and green eyes and smells of something other than the usual milk. The nurse hands me over hesitantly, as if I might explode in the wrong hands. But these are the right hands. My mother's hands.

'Time to go,' she whispers to me after the young nurse has gone. 'You've been here long enough.' And she embarks on her plan to smuggle the pair of us out of St Thomas', swaddling me in a yellow blanket despite the sweltering August heat ('Always keep Baby warm, Mrs Smith!'). Not an easy operation as the sergeant major of a sister is of the belief that new mothers are incapable of doing anything more strenuous than painting their fingernails.

But my mother, I am already discovering, is a skilful liar. She convinces a stranger in a pinstripe suit — lost on his way to visit an elderly aunt — that his time would be better spent posing as her husband and my father (the first in a number of such attempts). He is only too happy to oblige and, at a carefully chosen moment when Sister is making tea, the young nurse relinquishes Mother and I into his control. We follow meekly behind him, down squeaky corridors and ancient lifts until at last we are out through the front doors and into my first gulp of fresh air (well, semi-fresh, this is London after all).

Mother gives the poor chap a cheery wave and a dazzling smile that makes it quite clear his assistance is no longer required and makes for Westminster Bridge, in her Jackie Kennedy sunglasses and killer stilettos, clutching me to her breast, like a fragile parcel she has to post. She hails a black cab all too easily and bundles me into the back of it while the cabbie deals with all our worldly belongings: a Harrod's bag full of nappies and, more importantly, my mother's vanity case.

Inside the Cab we are bumped and swayed along the London streets at unbelievable velocity. It is not as comfortable as my little tank. Or indeed my mother's womb where I was safe and happy, swimming about in her amniotic fluid sucking my thumb, listening to the drum beat of her heart, not a care in the world.

At last we come to rest at Paddington Station. My short life as a Londoner is almost over.

Some time later, I lie in my mother's awkward arms on the train, hot and fidgety. We have a carriage to ourselves. She is feeding me from a bottle. I preferred it when she fed me with her own milk which tasted of grapes and hospital

5

food, each time slightly different. It is all the same out of these bottles and I keep leaving pools of curdled cream on her shoulder as she pats me rather too vigorously on the back ('Come on, give me a good one, pleeeasse,'). I have the hiccups and tummy ache. Doesn't she know I am too young to be on the bottle? Doesn't she know that breast is best? My mother tuts, wiping her eyes with her sleeve. Maybe she is a hay fever sufferer. I know so little about her. This is the first time we have been on our own together.

Over her shoulder the world whizzes past the window so fast it hurts my little eyes, spins my tiny head. Maybe I am drunk. Maybe she's given me too much gripe water to try and staunch the crying. She could probably do with a gin and tonic herself.

After a fitful sleep the train jolts me awake as we pull into a hazy greyness otherwise known as Reading. Heavy doors bang and crash but we stay where we are, trapped together in our carriage. Mother's green-lidded eyes are closed but it is unlikely that she is sleeping as her fingers appear to be playing an invisible piano. The journey continues as does the winding and the curdling and the sniffing.

We do not get off at Swindon either, a new town with new hope. We carry on, via Bristol, heading south through Somerset and into Devon until we reach the coast. Sandy beaches, coves, and palm trees. The English Riviera. Torquay.

'Our new home, Philippa.'

My mother sighs — whether from relief or

regret is anyone's guess — before lugging me and the bags out of the carriage and onto the platform, where she stands for a moment looking wistfully back up the track. Then she turns her face to the sun and lets the warm breeze brush over her. She sighs again, taking in this new air. Air that will thankfully make me sleepy over the weeks to come.

'Right then, Philippa, let's go.'

I don't know where we are going. Of course, I don't. It could be to one of the hotels on the cliffs or to one of the painted Victorian villas overlooking the Bay. Our lives are all set out before us and we could do anything. I could be destined to attend the Girl's Grammar. To have tennis lessons. Elocution lessons. Cello lessons. I could be part of a happy family . . .

Unfortunately it is 1965 and my mother is unmarried.

So my first home turns out to be two rooms above a garage. Nothing flash — not Rolls or Daimler or Jaguar. No. The cars in the showroom below aren't even new. There isn't a showroom to speak of. Just a 'Lot' out the front, full of second-hand cars run by a bloke called Bernie from Wolverhampton. 'Sheila and me came on our holidays here in 1960 and fell in love,' he informs my mother, with a misty sheen to his eyes as he holds open our shabby front door to show us into our home. 'We've never looked back.'

Advice we should all take on board.

(Too late, too late, I've started so I'll finish.)

★ ★ ★

My second birthday. Mother (otherwise known as Helena) has baked me a cake in her Baby Belling oven in the kitchenette of our flat above Bernie's Motors. The cake is big and chocolate and covered with spiky mint icing. It feels lovely when I smear it all over my highchair. I spend a lot of time in my highchair. Three times a day I am strapped into it for approximately one hour. Less if I manage to eat all my vegetables without throwing them at Andy, our kitten. I am not clever enough yet to hide them in my pockets but before the year is out I will cotton onto this trick. But so will my mother as she is the one who has to laboriously wash all of our clothes in the sink.

Today, as a concession to my birthday, I am allowed to forgo my greens and am presented with a slab of cake. For all her airs and graces my mother lets me eat like a savage. She doesn't allow me to use cutlery as this has previously resulted in minor injuries to both myself and Andy. I put my face into the cake. It is very sticky.

Mother is not particularly house-proud but she shrieks when she sees me. Gripping her cigarette tightly between her red lips, she hoiks me out, depositing me at arms' length into the sink. The rubber shower attachment makes light work of my face. It is unpleasant. The water keeps going hot and cold. 'The boiler's on the blink again,' my mother wails, as if she was back in London. Not that she'd have spoken like a

8

Cockney in Dulwich Village. For that is where she grew up, the posh bit south of the Thames. As for my father (I use this term in the vaguest of senses), I'm not sure where he came from. But I do know he was a dandy in a sharp suit and should probably have been avoided at all costs.

My mother is a sucker for a fancy dresser and let this man take her to the pictures to see *Goldfinger*. They enjoyed it so much they went again the next night. And for several more nights. With each subsequent screening she let his gold fingers travel a little further until *Bingo*! she is pregnant (despite her posing as a married woman to get herself fitted with the aforementioned, new-fangled and ineffective coil). Not the best move considering she was only eighteen and my grandfather was a judge with a reputation to keep. And not helped by the fact that my grandmother was recently diagnosed with an unmentionable cancer. Before Helena made up her mind whether to tell my father, it was too late. He was gone. A one way ticket to Peru.

So that is why we left the capital and all the possibilities it held in the Swinging Sixties. That is why we ended up in two rooms above Bernie's Motors in Torquay.

Torquay was the only place my mother knew outside London. She had spent a fortnight's holiday there as a child. She and her parents had stayed in the Palace Hotel. The judge spent his days sampling the local golf courses. My grandmother Elizabeth and little Helena spent their days doing all the things holiday-makers do: sandcastles and gritty ice creams, a show at the Princess Theatre, a coach trip to Widecombe-in-the-moor. My mother fell in love at the age of eight. This time with a place, rather than a man.

But now it is my birthday. *I* am the centre of her attention. Once I am cleaned up, she sings me Happy Birthday in a husky voice (for by this time she is smoking at least forty Consulate a day.) I clap my hands and smile a toothy smile. She laughs and flashes the camera in my face. I wish she wouldn't do that. It always makes me cry. And that is usually enough to set her off. For Mother, tears are always waiting around the next corner.

★　★　★

A warm and windy day. Mother and I are going to the beach. She has bought me a windmill and stuck it to my pram — a Silver Cross chariot that is her pride and joy. But despite its size I am too big for it. Mother insists on using it even though my knees are approaching my chin. I should be encouraged to walk. I wouldn't mind having reins but Mother says I am not a pet poodle. A Bull Mastiff, perhaps. Old ladies make comments like: 'What a bonny girl,'. Or: 'Isn't she a strapping maid?' Mother says I'm big for my age. But really I am overweight. Mother still feeds me countless bottles of milk even though I have a fine set of teeth and should long since have been on a trainer cup. Mother is clueless. She hasn't read Dr Spock. She doesn't have a mother of her own to talk to. The only contact she has with the outside world is the old ladies on the street. And Bernie.

Bernie has taken to coming upstairs of an evening. Mother puts me to bed at some ridiculously early hour. Six o'clock! Practically the afternoon. Now it is summer, it stays light forever. I have to entertain myself in my cot until sleep eventually takes over. My favourite pastime is chewing the pink (lead) paint off the bars of my prison. I also listen to the birds. I can distinguish between a seagull, a blue tit and a wood pigeon though of course I don't have the words for them yet. But I do know what they look like as Mother has pointed them out to me on occasions when she is feeling educationally inclined. There are seagulls everywhere in Torquay. I've seen them attacking pensioners on the prom, those who are a little slapdash with their chips. I once had an ice cream whipped right out of my hand. I watched my mother throw her handbag at the gull in question and I was so shocked at this act of solidarity that I didn't make a sound.

Today the seagulls are more interested in a trawler at large in the Bay so they leave us alone. We find a patch of red sand for ourselves and Mother spreads out a tartan rug for our picnic. Hard-boiled eggs, tomatoes, cheese rolls, apples. Standard picnic fare for 1967. I am wearing a tight-fitting bathing suit. It cuts into the top of my white legs and pinches me under the arms. I am lathered in sun cream ('because of your skin,

Philippa') and crowned with a cricket hat picked up in a jumble.

Helena is modelling a bikini. Her smooth skin is as brown as strongly brewed Typhoo from afternoons sitting out in the sun at the back of Bernie's Lot while I play with a washing-up bowl of water and a wooden spoon. Not a stretch mark to be seen on her flat stomach. You'd never know she had a baby if it weren't for the evidence sitting next to her on the rug. Though even that could be disputed — we hardly look like mother and daughter.

'Fancy a dip, Philippa?' She grabs my hand and steers me down the beach, in and out of clustered families, all on tartan rugs, eating the same food as us.

The water is warm but it stings my legs. A wave almost bowls me over but Helena reaches out and catches me in the nick of time. She is a good mother. She loves me.

★　★　★

Bed time again. If I could count beyond the fingers of one hand, I could work out from the bells of St Bartholomew's that it is seven o'clock. But I am too busy concentrating on the safety pin of my nappy to worry about practising my counting. Surely I should be toilet trained by now? Despite my concentration, I can make out Bernie's voice. And Helena's fake giggles. I imagine Bernie as a bird. A fat preening wood pigeon. I do not like Bernie. He has a red face and smells wet. Like my nappies in the morning.

I want to wear knickers like a big girl.

Success! I have finally opened the safety pin. I pull off the (dry) nappy and throw it over the side onto the floor. I am naked! What a glorious feeling! It makes me want to bounce up and down but my joy is cut short when something pricks my foot. The safety (!) pin has punctured my skin. My screams hurt my ears but nothing hurts as much as my little foot.

The door is flung open and Mother is suddenly here, leaning over the cot, her mouth open but nothing coming out of it though tears are spouting from the corners of her eyes. Another face appears beside her. I don't want to look at that great big face but it is even worse further down where a hairy stomach presses itself against the bars. One of Bernie's nylon shirt buttons has popped open. So I look back up at his face which is redder than usual, his Bobby Charlton comb-over out to one side as if he is standing in a wind tunnel. His mouth is moving too, like Mother's, but I can't hear what either of them is saying. I must be deaf. But my mother has now started to wail so loudly that she stops me in my tracks.

'Pick her up, Helena,' Bernie urges.

My mother is inert so Bernie bends forward with some difficulty and scoops me out. I can hear his heavy breathing as if he has been running the hundred yard dash — though it's unlikely Bernie ever runs anywhere.

'What's the matter little one?' he coos (fat pigeon), wrapping an abandoned towel around me.

I rub my nose on his orange shirt, leaving a number eleven on his shoulder. I feel better for that but my mother has spotted a drop of blood on the cot sheet and the shiny pin lying next to it and for once puts two and two together correctly.

Bernie realises what is going on too. He isn't a hotshot-car-wheeler-dealer for nothing.

'Isn't it about time she was out of nappies, Hell?' Bernie dares to ask.

My mother doesn't say yes, I suppose you're onto something there, Bernie. Instead she makes a lunge and wrestles me out of his beefy arms.

'Don't ever tell me how to look after my own child!' she shrieks at him.

'Alright, Hell, calm down, I was only saying. Our Terry and Toni were out of 'em at two and a half. Just the odd wet night but Sheila put a rubber sheet on the mattresses — '

'Don't talk to me about ruddy Sheila,' Mother snaps.

'I was only saying.'

'Well, don't.'

Bernie leaves soon after that. He tries to hold my mother but she won't have it. Bernie realises he isn't going to get anywhere tonight and disappears back to Sheila.

For once I wish Mother had listened to Bernie. He was only looking out for me. But anyway, I never wear a nappy again. It saves Helena heaps of washing and gallons of Milton. The next day she proudly takes me shopping and buys me a pack of knickers — one for every day of the week (which helps my counting no end).

14

And she doesn't even have to bother with a rubber sheet — which is one in the eye for ruddy Sheila.

'This isn't a boarding school,' Mother tells me as she puts me to bed. (She knows all about boarding schools having been incarcerated in one in the middle of Wales for nearly a decade.) 'You're not destined to be one of life's bed-wetters.'

Oh dear. What if I let her down?

2006

I'll probably let you down. I won't mean to. I'll try my hardest not to. But Life gets out of control and bulldozes best intentions.

Then there's Adrian, the man you're supposed to call 'Daddy'. He and I dressed up in uncomfortable clothes and said vows in front of our raggedy collection of friends and family (those that would come) and I do believe he sincerely meant those vows on that day, in that register office. Maybe. But his good intentions flew out the window, fell by the wayside (etc, etc), when he decided I wasn't quite enough for him. He omitted to tell me this for a while, seeing as I was cultivating varicose veins and stretch marks on your behalf. But eventually, one evening, a few weeks ago, as I was slumped at the kitchen sink, glugging down the Gaviscon, after much huffing and puffing and beating around the bush, he pointed out to me that Someone Else was more than happy to fill in the gaps, step into my boots, take over the helm (etc, etc).

Do we blame that on Life? Or on him? I'm not actually sure. All I know is I never want him back. I don't want you to get used to him being around only to disappear one day. I know too

16

much about disappearing acts.

Here I am. Left again. Left holding the baby, as they say.

And a lovely baby you are, you are. And a lovely baby you are.

2

1969

Dragon's Den

Fast forward to a windy Monday morning in September two years later when my rickety sash window rattles me awake. Or maybe it is Mother crashing about downstairs. We have a Downstairs now as well as an Upstairs. I have my own sash window and my own bedroom. We have moved from Above Bernie's Motors to a little two-up-two-down in a Better Area. Bernie can't 'pop up' anymore after work. In fact he doesn't visit at all. Not since Mother has become friends with Sheila.

I am wondering if it is safe to get up when I notice something on the back of my closed door: some funny clothes hanging stiffly on metal hangers. A navy blue pinafore and matching cardy. When Mother breezes into the room the hangers make a jangle that cuts right through me, ominously. This is not a normal day. No playing with a washing-up bowl of water and a wooden spoon. No trips to the beach. No buckets and spade. No ice cream.

'Come on, Philippa. Wakey wakey, rise and shine.'

Oh dear. Why the fake cheeriness? Usually

18

Mother is silent until her third cup of coffee of the morning. And she is already dressed rather than doing her shuffling-around-in-her-dressing-gown-clutching-her-head routine. In fact she is dressed up to the nines. Her best red frock and matching red lips. She looks pretty. 'Dynamite,' Bernie would say. But there is only me and all I can do is stare at her as she reaches up for the funny clothes on the back of my door and I realise that the time has come to wear them.

It is my Uniform. I am going to School.

Unfortunately Mother has underestimated my waistline and there is a struggle squeezing me into the pinafore.

'I should have splashed out on a new one,' Mother says. 'Toni's a petite little thing. I should've known it would be too small.'

Yes, Toni. Our Toni. Bernie and Sheila's Toni. Mother is now such good friends with Sheila that she is happy to receive hand-me-downs from her. Toni, who is now in her first year at Torquay Girls' Grammar. Sheila has kept her school clothes all these years wrapped up in tissue paper in the attic waiting for a suitable little girl to have them. Though only four years of age, I am not little by any stretch of the imagination. What was Sheila thinking when she offered them to Mother?

Mother attends Sheila's Coffee Mornings every week without fail. At last she has friends in Torquay. A circle of friends. Sheila's friends. Much to Bernie's horror.

'What do you want to be friends with them old bags for?'

'What's wrong with them? They're a nice crowd. They've welcomed me with open arms.'

'What about my arms? They used to be big enough for you, Hell.'

'It's friends I need Bernie. Not you.'

And that was the last time Bernie was allowed upstairs. Soon after this frank exchange Mother moved us to our new house. She borrowed enough money for the deposit and a month's rent and a small refrigerator — from somewhere or other — on the promise of her new Job which she is going to start on this historic day. She is a Free Woman now I am starting School.

School.

I don't know if it is the tight pinafore or the boiled egg ('you need a proper breakfast, Philippa,') or if it is the way Mother tugs my unruly hair back into pigtails liberally applying Harmony hairspray in an effort to keep the frizz at bay or if it is the walk itself, the windy walk to School that makes me feel so sick. Nothing usually makes me feel sick. Too much cake. Too much ice cream. Too many greens. A ride in One of Bernie's cars round Devon country lanes. Nothing.

Something is most definitely Up.

The short walk to School is over in a flash. All too soon we are heading through the gates into the playground. It is pandemonium. Screaming children everywhere you look. Barking dogs running round in circles and in an out of legs. Weeping mothers with hankies held to their noses. Mothers looking as scared as their children. Not a father to be seen. Perhaps all families are like mine after all. Perhaps the families in the books I am allowed to borrow from the library when Mother remembers my Education are the exception. The ones with the mummy and the daddy, a boy called Peter and a girl called Susan. (I have yet to see the books in my new classroom which will soon wither this blossoming hope.)

I look up at Mother. She is the only mother without a soggy hanky. Quite dry-eyed. And the prettiest, by far. It isn't just her dress and her lipstick and her heels. It is something about the way she holds herself. The way she walks as if she was on stage. A tilt of the hips, the shoulders. The curvy but perfectly trim figure. Her youth.

All the other mothers take time away from their grief to notice her. To turn their heads away from their precious children and stare. And does Helena enjoy it? Does she even notice it at all?

Either way, Mother will come to hate the Playground. She will despise these other mothers. The idle chitchat at the gates. The gossip. The fierce maternal protectiveness and pride that they wear like essential accessories. She will prefer the company of Sheila's cronies. Established women whose children are now at secondary, who've moved on from child-talk and speak instead of money and houses and husbands. (Of which Mother is still in short supply.)

Today she starts off as she means to go on. She takes me as far as the classroom door, handing me over trustingly to my new teacher, a woman neither of us has ever met before. Helena

21

can't wait to get out of there, leaving me as soon as possible. (Too soon Mummy! I hate it here! It smells of cabbages and dirty bottoms!) I do my best to detain her, to make her behave like the other mothers who fuss around their darlings, helping them find their seats, running a last comb through their hair. Begging makes no inroads on her so I start to howl instead. But it is no use. My misery is nothing to her.

'You'll soon get used to it, Philippa. Your grandparents dumped me in the back end of Wales for a decade. This is nothing. I'll be back for you at three o'clock. It's only six hours.'

Six hours! Mother has no idea what those slow crawling six hours will entail. She knows nothing of Christopher Bennett who licks his bogies and smells of bonfires. Nothing of Mandy Denning who cries her eyes out when I fall off my chair so that she wrestles all the attention from the teacher. She knows nothing of the humiliation of PE when we are forced to strip to our pants and vest and pretend to be as small as mice. She knows nothing of the endless dinner-time when we are chucked into the throng of the playground to be bumped and barged by really big boys and girls all of whom like calling me Fatty.

Instead.

She plants a rare kiss on the top of my head, grimacing at the taste of hairspray.

'Must dash, Philippa. Mustn't be late for work.'

And she is gone.

I am hot and squashed on the Carpet, one of a multitude trying to 'sit on our bottoms with legs crossed nicely', extremely tricky with plump legs like mine. I manage to dodge Christopher Bennett who is fidgeting in a Special Place at Miss Hitchcock's feet, craftily untying the laces of her man-shoes (I caught Mother scowling at them this morning during the brief moment she was in Miss Hitchcock's orbit). Instead, I am wedged between Mandy Denning with the blonde hair and doll-sized hands (do her eyelids click shut when she lies down?) and a quiet boy with messy hair and skin the colour and smoothness of duck eggs, who quite possibly might crack open if he falls in the playground he looks so fragile. Maybe that is why he spent Break playing on his own in a (miraculously) quiet corner, gently moving his arms up and down, side to side and round and round in some kind of balletic rain dance.

Miss Hitchcock sits on her chair reading from a book with funny pictures. It is about two children with absentee parents and I warm to it straightaway, especially when a cat sporting a rather nice hat turns up, causing mayhem. (Why isn't this book in the library?) Just as we think things can't possibly get any messier, the cat introduces his two friends, Thing One and Thing Two, Chaos! But not to worry: the cat tidies up before Mother gets home. All we catch of her as she opens the front door is a glimpse of red coat and high heels (and even if they do have laces like Miss Hitchcock's shoes, I just know she is wearing lipstick like Helena).

By the time the bell rings at Hometime, I am feeling better. I've done it. I've been to school. I am a Big Girl now. We surge for the cloakroom, a riot of shuffling feet and flailing arms, freedom beckoning. So it comes as something of a shock when Miss Hitchcock's booming voice cuts through the hullabaloo: 'Don't forget to bring your dinner money tomorrow, Christopher Bennett.' We all look at each other, horrified.

Tomorrow?

★ ★ ★

'Yes, tomorrow, Philippa.' Helena hands me a tissue at the school gate. 'I thought I'd explained. School is every day.'

'Everyday?'

'Except Saturdays and Sundays. And the school holidays.' She buttons me into my coat. 'But you've got weeks before those start,' she adds, finding it hard to disguise the relief in her voice. Then she manoeuvres me deftly through the swarm of reunited mothers and children, and strides off along the pavement as fast as she can in her heels, pulling me along in her wake.

How long is a week? I look up at Helena — focused straight ahead — but no further information is forthcoming. All I know for sure is the length of six hours: an eternity filled with bogies and bonfires.

Eventually we Halt at the Kerb around the corner (I am a fully-fledged Tufty Club

24

member). 'Look right, look left, Philippa,' Mother commands. 'And look right again.' I am still not sure which is which so I watch Helena out of the corner of my eye. 'If all clear, quick march.' And we are off.

Helena is fervent about road safety, preparing me for later life when I will have to cross roads on my own, knowing there is little hope that cars will stop for me in the same way they stop for her (with a screech of brakes and a funny whistle). So I take it seriously too and know my Kerb Drill by heart.

Things lighten up, however, when Helena stops at a newsagents, one we have never visited before, presumably because this school route has taken us out of our usual environment. She peers with some interest at the window display of tobacco and pipes before scanning the little hand-written notices by the door. Then she smiles down at me and I notice for the first time that her face is funny: blotchy and mottled. Has she been crying?

'Are you all right, Mummy?' I enquire politely. But this just sets her off again.

'Oh, Philippa,' she says, sniffing. 'I wish you were a boy.'

A boy? This is awful. Has she no idea?

'But boys pick their noses, Mummy,' I inform her, a prickle to my pride.

She laughs then, blowing her own pretty red nose before pushing me through that door into the shop, whispering the magic words: 'Sweetie Time.'

It is an Aladdin's cave inside. Glass jar upon

glass jar filled with rubies and emeralds and diamonds and amethysts and gold and silver and pearls. Sherbet Lemons, Acid Drops, Aniseed Twist, Toffee Bon Bons. And all the rest of the names I can't yet read but know by heart from the shapes and colours and smells.

'You can have a quarter of whatever you like,' she says to me. Then she too is lost in her own world of comfort, the lines of neatly stacked cigarette packets beckoning her from behind the counter, where a man has looked up from his newspaper at the sound of Mother's voice.

'Afternoon, madam,' he says. 'And what can I do for you?'

I am far too absorbed in making my decision and distracted by the rows of comics at my feet to hear what she says in reply. It is sometime later that we find ourselves back outside on the pavement (a paper bag of wine gums clutched in one of my hands, a copy of *Twinkle* cherished in the other) and Mother is telling me that the Nice Man has offered her a Job.

'But you already have a Job, Mother. Do you need two Jobs? Are we very poor?'

'That other Job was a Bad Job.' She tears open a fresh packet of Consulate with some venom at the memory of this Bad Job. This one will be a Lovely Job, Philippa. A Proper Job as they say Down Here. (Down Here being the only place I've ever known but still a foreign land to Helena.)

'Just think, Philippa,' she says. 'Think of all those sweets!' And she plants a (second of the

26

day) kiss on the top of my head that I wouldn't swap for all the sweets in the shop.

★   ★   ★

It is Saturday at last. Hurray! No uniform today. No Christopher Bennett. No Miss Hitchcock with her man-shoes and voice of doom. But Mother has her Job to do and so I have to go to Auntie Sheila's for the morning with my duffle bag of 'things to keep me quiet'.

I like going to Auntie Sheila's — as long as Bernie is at the Lot. Terry ignores me as he has recently become a teenager. He spends his time in the garage attempting his Guitar Riffs and playing darts. Toni treats me like the pony she's never been allowed to have because Sheila thinks riding will give her bandy legs, which are of no use for ballet. Toni battles with my frizzy hair, trying to train it into French plaits, pulling my scalp and making my eyes water. But it is worth it for the pretty ribbons she weaves through them. Toni makes obstacle courses in the garden and I have to gallop-and-trot and leap over bamboo canes pilfered from Bernie's neglected greenhouse.

This morning I have been awarded a blue rosette that Toni pins to my jumper (another of her hand-me-downs). She made it from an old cornflakes packet and strips of neatly-cut crêpe paper. 'What do you think, Philly?' she asks, arms folded, beaming at her handiwork. 'I saw Valerie Singleton do it on *Blue Peter* last week.'

I have no idea who Valerie Singleton is as we

do not have Television at home. But I know I want this beautiful hand-crafted rosette.

'Can I keep it, Toni?' I ask in my sweetest voice.

'Course,' she says. And she pats me on the head and produces a sugar lump from her pocket which she offers to me in the palm of her hand.

I wish Toni was my big sister. My only hope is for Mother to give me a baby sister but when I asked her one time, she spat her tea across the kitchen table with such force it hit the far wall, so I don't hold out much hope.

'Let's go and ask Mum for a Nesquik. It'll help keep your coat all shiny.'

And with a click-click of her tongue and a tug on the reins (one of Bernie's best polyester ties), we walk on to the kitchen.

Auntie Sheila is baking a cake. She has a smut of flour on her rouged cheek (she is almost as glamorous as Mother — but it has been a long time since Helena has done any baking). She pops the cake in the oven and dabs at her face with a tea towel. We sit down and watch her make two chocolate milkshakes and — with a finger to her lips as Mother has modified my dairy intake — she sets one of them on the table in front of me.

★　★　★

That night, my (slightly crumpled) uniform hangs on the back of the bedroom door, waiting for Mother to wash it, moving like a ghost in the draught from the window. My rosette is pinned to my pyjama top.

It is daylight still (of course) but I don't really mind. I am so tired after my first week of school and a day of gymkhanas that it takes just a few minutes of trying to work out the pattern in my curtains before sleep takes me off to dream of a horse in a hat being ridden by a boy with messy hair and skin like egg shell.

2006

The pattern in these hospital curtains is disturbing. Laura Ashley slash IKEA. It's using up all my energy when I should be conserving it for the job in hand — Motherhood — which is probably going to be even trickier than I thought.

I could have trouble bonding with you, Fran says, my over-friendly midwife. She's worried that you will remind me of your 'father' (who she is yet to meet but has heard all about) and that will inevitably lead to resentment. I think resentment is the least of my worries. Resentment is a bit of a luxury I wish I had more time for.

My friends have never liked Adrian. They think he is patronising and insincere. They are right. But then I don't particularly mind those qualities in him. It is the Casanova stuff I'm not so keen on. Or the golf. Or the mother. Or the cocaine habit that he promised he'd left behind in the 90s along with the Spice Girls and the Teletubbies. But then his promises have proved to be empty words.

So there's just you and me, Baby. And you smell divine. I could breathe in your scent forever.

The boy I was going to marry smelt of currant buns.

3

1969

New Faces

The boy's name is Lucas Jones. Although he lives in the next street, I've never seen him before, not until that fateful day when School brings us together. By the end of the second week of term Mother has discovered the reason for this: he's only recently moved to Torquay from London with his mother who had a Divorce from his father — which means they don't like each other anymore. My mother likes his mother however, because now she doesn't feel so bad about leaving the capital behind, knowing she isn't alone in such recklessness.

She'd like to ask Lucas and Mrs Jones to tea but she can't possibly let them see the Squalor we live in so she arranges for us all to meet in a teashop in town one Saturday afternoon after Mother's stint at the newsagents. She makes me wear white gloves and a flowery dress that shows off my chubby knees. She unravels this week's French plaits and tries to brush out the kinks in my hair. 'A hundred brushes a day, Philippa ... fifty-nine, sixty ... If I've taught you nothing, I've taught you that ... sixty-two, sixty-three ... '

31

The tearoom is full of genteel ladies nibbling cream cakes and sipping tea from bone china cups. Lucas and I are each given psychedelic orange squash with a straw and an iced bun. Helena and Mrs Jones order Earl Grey with no milk, throwing the uniformed waitress into a flurry.

The conversation is a little awkward at first but our mothers soon get into their stride:

'Don't slurp, Lucas.'

'Take your gloves off, Philippa. They'll get sticky.'

'Don't chew with your mouth open, Lucas.'

'Sit up, Philippa. You look like a sack of potatoes.'

'Don't put your elbows on the table, Lucas.'

'Slow down, Philippa. You'll choke if you're not careful.'

And so on.

After a few minutes, when they realise that they went to neighbouring preparatory schools (pre-Wales) and had mutual friends, they forget all about us and we can slouch and slurp as much as we like. Then I decide it is my turn to get the conversation going with Lucas.

'D'you like Miss Pitchfork?' I ask him.

'No,' he says.

(Hurrah!)

'D'you like Christopher Bennett?'

'No.'

(Hurrah!)

'D'you like Mandy Denning?'

'She's alright.'

(Boo!)

At least Lucas shrugs his shoulders when he says this so I suppose he isn't particularly bothered one way or the other about Mandy Denning. It is in that moment, seeing that gesture, that I determine I will become his friend. When someone asks Lucas Jones if they like Philippa Smith, he will say: 'Yes. She is my best friend.'

★　★　★

When we've finished our tea, Mrs Jones asks, 'How about a stroll along the seafront and maybe an ice cream?' She looks at Helena for reassurance that this is acceptable (I noticed her taking in my knees as I tried to hide them under the table-cloth).

'Good idea,' says Mother.

We bob up and down, gathering together hats and gloves, while Mother counts out coins, insisting it is her shout although, confusingly, she says this in her normal husky way. As we shuffle in and out of tables, heading for the door, Lucas is the one who suddenly shouts out in a real shouty voice, 'All scream for ice cream!'

And every one of the genteel ladies turns to stare at our party. They tut-tut and stir their cups ferociously. Mrs Jones says, 'Lucas!' in a way I will come to hear many times — a sort of growly hiss, a cross between a mother bear and a snake. Then she slaps his thigh, leaving a handprint the colour of raspberry ripple on his shell-skin.

I want to marry this boy.

33

School is more bearable now I have Lucas for a friend. He might only be small and thin but he has a voice that even Miss Pitchfork must envy. A voice like a crow having a bad day. A voice he uses sparingly, for greater effect.

Lucas and I soon settle into a shared routine that gets us through the six hour long haul. We play together at break in our corner. We pick each other for teams in gym. I save a place for him on the carpet. He saves a place for me in the hall at lunchtime where I give him my greens in exchange for potatoes. (He is a boy of mystery.)

We see each other after school too. When I am invited to play at Lucas' — a bigger house than ours, almost on a par with Auntie Sheila's in terms of tidiness — Mother is spurred on to tackle our grotty terrace, starting with the little front room that Helena refers to as the Parlour. She buys cheap magnolia paint and I am allowed to help her slap it over the walls. Luckily we have no carpet, only bare boards so our inexpert approach doesn't much matter. We paint the floor too. A dark green. And she swaps a pair of earrings for a Persian rug at the junk shop on Belgrave Road, along with a couple of prints of city life that send Helena into a daydream.

Finally, after she's blitzed the kitchen with Ajax and scrubbed the downstairs bathroom with so much Vim her eyes are watering, she is happy to ask Lucas back to play.

The big day arrives. Mrs Jones has coffee with Mother while Lucas and I build a den upstairs in my bedroom using blankets, an umbrella, the clothes horse and some imagination. I am Thing One and Lucas Thing Two. We try putting my bobble hat on Andy but he isn't having any of it, so we use a teddy instead, with a sock stuffed full of hankies for a tail. Lucas wants to tidy up after a while as he feels uneasy about the mess.

'Let's go out in the backyard,' I suggest when we are done, skipping across my forgotten carpet, visible once more.

'All right,' he says.

'You can see a Magical Land through a hole in the fence,' I tell him.

'You mustn't fib,' he says.

'I'm not fibbing. Just you wait and see.'

To add to the sense of mystery, I tell him it is a secret and we mustn't let our mothers know in case they spoil things. We tiptoe downstairs — I am pretty deft at tiptoeing despite my weight as I've had plenty of practice pretending I'm not there when Helena is in one of her Moods. We can hear enraptured voices coming from the Parlour and so it is easy to sneak down the passage and out through the kitchen door into the backyard. Helena prefers to call it a courtyard and she's stuck pots of red geraniums around it because they remind her of Italy and Sofia Loren films. The courtyard is let down by the old outside lavatory that I am not allowed to use but where I store my treasures (a gold button, a lock of hair, three shells and one of Andy's whiskers). One day I will divulge my booty to Lucas. But today I am going to show him the Magical Land.

'There, Lucas.'

I point over at the fence. It looks like a giant rabbit has burrowed its way through the bottom in the corner. Before you can twitch your nose, Lucas is down on his hands and knees, peeking through to the other side.

'Wow,' he says, in wonder. 'You're right.'

For on the other side of our backyard, through this tatty old fence, is a land of giant gnarly trees, hidden pathways, stone pillars and angels and temples adorned with flowers. And a sharp tang that Lucas says is fox pee. He used to have a family of foxes in his garden in London, lucky thing. All we've got in our yard are big fat seagulls at which Mother actively encourages me to throw stones. And sometimes Andy puts in an appearance when he can be bothered to venture outside on a summer's day for a spot of sunbathing, baring his tiger stripes next to Helena's flat brown stomach.

'Let's go in,' Lucas says.

I can't possibly love him anymore than I do at this moment. His sheer courage swipes my breath away.

'After you,' I manage to say.

So I follow his scrawny legs through the fence, squeezing myself as fast as I can because he is already up and running down a stony path, shrinking into the distance. When I eventually catch up with him, my chest is on fire and I have to bend over for some minutes to cool it down. Lucas is oblivious to my pain. He is totally absorbed in examining one of the stones. It is a huge cross — I know that much from Auntie Sheila who wears a gold one on a chain around her neck. On a Sunday, while Bernie fiddles with his cars and his accounts, Sheila takes Terry and Toni to church for bread and wine (which I reckon must have something to do with her famous cheese and wine parties). But I have no idea what the cross is for. And I have no idea at all how symbolic this moment will become one day.

I watch Lucas' lips move. He is reading in his head in a way I can only wonder at. I can barely read my own name (it will be a long, long time before I can spell it — what was Mother thinking when she chose it?). His skin looks even paler than usual. His eyes dark and sad.

'What's wrong, Lucas?'

'It's a dead boy.'

'Where?'

I look around me frantically, thinking we've stumbled upon a tragedy (which in a way, of course, we have).

Lucas says, 'No, silly,' and goes on to explain about tombs and headstones and graveyards. Apparently that is what my Magical Land has turned out to be: the graveyard of St Bartholomew's where — beneath the very ground we are standing on — dead people are buried.

I do know about dead people; I am not completely naïve. Virtually all my grandparents are dead. Even my father is presumed dead having got lost while exploring the jungles of South America. I clutch onto the hope that he's just been mislaid like my white gloves (actually they are shoved up the chimney in my bedroom because they are such hateful things) and that he will turn up again one day. I am constantly worried that my mother will die before this miracle happens and I will have to go and live in an orphanage and I will never be chosen by a nice family because I don't have doll-hands like Mandy Denning. So I do know a bit about death (though not as much as I will in time — which is true for everybody). But, like Lucas, I am intrigued by the stone and I ask him to read the mossy old writing on it. (I am not in The Slow Readers for nothing.)

He takes a big breath and I am expecting the Voice but instead all that comes out is a hoarse whisper:

'ALBERT MORRIS, DIED AGED 7. SUFFER LITTLE CHILDREN, AND FORBID THEM NOT, TO COME UNTO ME: FOR OF SUCH IS THE KINGDOM OF HEAVEN.'

And a single perfect tear drop rolls down his shell-cheek. I reach out to him and wipe it away with the tips of my fingers.

'Pooh, Philippa,' he shouts, his Voice back. 'Your hands stink!'

So I chuck mud at him and he pushes me over (he is stronger than he looks, my Lucas). Then we hear voices . . . someone is coming! We run and run as fast as we can — in case it is the dead boy at our heels — back down the stony path and through the rabbit-hole into the yard. We slink into the bathroom and clean ourselves up with wet cotton wool before Helena or Mrs Jones has even noticed we are gone. Though it is all I can do to keep our secret when Mother interrogates me later over the mud stains on her Vim-cleaned basin. So I do what I always do. I blame the cat.

★ ★ ★

Another Saturday. Only this one is going to be different. Auntie Sheila is excused babysitting duties as she has to accompany Toni to a ballet exam (Grade 4 — she is a proper little Margot Fonteyn). Mother's other option, Mrs Jones, is also unavailable as she has taken Lucas to London for a few days to stay with his grandparents (lucky Thing Two). He is going to the Planetarium and the Changing of the Guard. (I am not sure what the guard is changing into. A clean uniform, perhaps?) But there is excitement of a different kind in store for me: a whole morning in the sweet shop with my Quiet Bag, sitting out of the way, in the back room.

The nice man who gave Mother the Job is called Bob (which rhymes — Miss Pitchfork is getting through to me at long last). His proper name is Mr Sugar which makes Lucas roll over with laughter when I tell him. I think it is a lovely name. Much nicer than Smith. Mr Sugar is as nice as his name and lets me choose a comic. I opt for *Twinkle* again as you can't go wrong there. He also lets me fill a bag with penny chews and throws in a packet of colouring pencils from his stationery sideline.

'Take this as well,' he says then. And he balances a colouring book entitled *Picturesque Devon* on top of the heap of goodies in my arms so I stagger about like a contestant on *Crackerjack's* Double or Drop. (I have seen this at Toni's and I am beginning to get a taste for popular culture.) Mother is too busy tidying the cigarette shelves to notice this act of kindness so I draw on my reserves of politeness and utter a thank-you-very-much-Mr-Sugar.

Out the back, I settle down at the desk, clearing a space amongst the invoices and receipts before making a start on a liquorice shoelace and a picture of a Devon pixie. I have not yet ruled out the possibility of the existence of pixies. I had hoped to see one in the Magical Land but now realise I will have to widen my search to a place that doesn't contain dead bodies as I don't think they attract pixies. Only angels. (Is my father an angel? Maybe he is in the graveyard? I will consult Lucas on his return.)

I am halfway through the pixie's toadstool when Mr Sugar pops his head round the door.

'You alright, Philippa?' he asks and he lobs a packet of Salt 'n' Shake onto the desk. Then he winks. Not a creepy wink. Not the sort of wink the ironmonger throws at Helena when she is forced to go in his smelly shop for nails and things because she has 'no man about the place'. (Is that why she wishes I were a boy? So I could change a plug and unblock a drain?) This is more like the wink I've seen Bernie give Toni when he's done something he knows Sheila won't approve of, such as putting his dirty great clodhoppers on her Ercol coffee table.

'Thank you, Mr Sugar,' I say politely.

'Call me Bob,' he says.

I must look shocked at this show of friendliness so he says, 'I'm pretty sure it's my name.' And he checks inside the collar of his shirt, looking for an imaginary name tag. 'Yes. Definitely, Bob. Short for Robert.'

Then he fills the kettle and puts it on the little stove like the one we used to have Above the Lot. The bell goes in the shop but Mr Sugar stays put, leaning against the mug-rimmed Formica worktop. He obviously trusts my mother to deal with customers in his absence.

'Cup of tea, Philippa?'

I've never been asked that before but I don't let on. 'Yes please,' I say as casually as I can. (I don't want Lucas being the only one to have new experiences this weekend.)

He starts chatting away to me about school. He says he hated school but he wishes he'd stuck it out. He left with no qualifications and ended up being a waiter at one of the big hotels until he was bequeathed some money and bought the shop.

'But what could be better?' I am flabbergasted at the way he sighs when he recounts his disappointing career.

He laughs, 'Do you know what, Philippa? You could be right. It's not a bad little shop is it?'

The kettle whistles on cue and he pours water into the pot. While we wait for it to brew (there is a lot of waiting involved in tea-making), we can clearly hear a woman's raised voice out in the shop. The customer is shouting at Mother. Why is she doing that? Has Helena made a mistake with the Mint Imperials? Given her the wrong cigarettes? Short-changed her? I look at Bob who shrugs. Then he peeks his head round the door into the shop, briefly, before withdrawing it again.

'Nothing to worry about,' he says, all cheerful, walking back to the worktop. 'Just one of your mother's friends. A little tiff. Something or nothing.'

I carry on with the colouring, more restrained now, my ears pricked to the conversation outside. Bob cuts in when the volume increases once more, this time my mother joining in.

'So,' he says, pouring the tea from a great height into three mugs, two of which are chipped. 'Does your mother have a gentleman caller?'

'Excuse me?'

'A . . . ' he coughs, his cheeks flushing red ' . . . a boyfriend?'

I consider this, chewing the end of my new pencil, trying not to listen to the noise outside. 'There's Lucas,' I suggest helpfully. He is a boy. But he is my friend. Is that what he means?

'What's he like, this Lucas?' Bob asks, carefully placing a mug in front of me.

'He's got lovely hair and egg-skin and he's this much shorter than me.' I indicate a hand span, the way Toni measures me when I am her pony. Bob looks puzzled.

42

'How old is he exactly?'

'Five.'

'Ah,' he says, relieved. 'That kind of boyfriend.'

'What other kind is there?' I ask, confused.

But Bob doesn't answer. By now there is a full scale row going on in the shop. I hear phrases like, *you filthy harlot* and *you disgusting slut*. I know Mother is a little lackadaisical with her housework but I don't know why this woman is so cross about that. And why is Bob doing nothing? It is his shop after all and Mother obviously can't be trusted on her own.

I look at Bob. He ignores my look entirely and instead helps me colour in the pixie's cuffs which are particularly challenging. He shows me how to stay within the lines which is another of life's mysteries solved. Despite — or maybe because of — his reluctance to sort out my mother, I want Mr Bob Robert Sugar to marry her. (My own father will jolly well have to learn to share if he ever makes his way out of that jungle.)

Finally the shop door is slammed with such force that a pane of glass tinkles to the floor. This is enough to make Bob abandon the pixie cuff and hurry out to see what is going on. I follow him.

There is Helena, quite still, standing amongst the broken glass, lighting a cigarette, staring after a woman who is striding down the street with a girl in tow. Mother is not crying, though crying is not far off. (I can make out the telltale signs of patchy skin.) But when I look again, through the jagged glass of the door, down the street, it is my own eyes that fill with tears. The girl who is galloping after her mother has her hair scraped back neatly in a bun. A little Margot Fonteyn.

★ ★ ★

Lucas did have new experiences in London. His grandparents took him to the Planetarium where he saw the birth of Earth amongst other things. They took him to the Changing of the Guard (apparently there were lots of guards and they'd all kept their clothes on which was a little disappointing but I didn't tell Lucas that as I didn't want to spoil his memories). Then Mrs Jones took him to see a Special List in a hospital. I wonder what was on this Special List — names of good children, perhaps? And why was it in a hospital? When I ask Mother she is vague and fails to light her cigarette on the first strike of a match which is strange as she is an expert.

So, when Lucas comes round with Mrs Jones to help us pack (we are moving again), I ask him.

'It's a man,' he says. 'A doctor.'

'He's on the list?'

'There is no list.'

'Oh.'

'He's called a Specialist because he's the best doctor.'

'Is your mother poorly?' I ask, horrified. His mother always looks as immaculate as mine and I can't imagine her lying pale and sick in bed.

'No,' he says.

'Oh, good.'

'No. It's me. I'm poorly.'

44

And somehow when he says this, I know he doesn't mean a cold or tonsillitis. I know it is something beyond my understanding. Why else would they go all the way to London? Why else would Helena's hand be shaking? Why else would she have held me so fiercely when she tucked me in last night?

But everything is suddenly hectic this morning. I don't have time to ask any more questions (not that I'd get any answers anyway.) Mother and I must pack up all our things in our little house (goodbye giant rabbit hole!). We must move out because the landlord doesn't want us here anymore.

There is a silver lining, however (must it always be silver?). We are moving in with Mrs Jones and Lucas who have a spare room. Lucas will be my landlord!

'We'll stay until we find somewhere else,' Helena says.

'Please,' urges Mrs Jones, 'stay as long as you like.'

And they both steal a Look at Lucas, lying on the sofa sipping Lucozade, watching *Blue Peter* with eyes like pebbles washed up on the beach.

I am not sure what that Look means exactly, though I can see it is full and heavy. But at least I know who Valerie Singleton is now.

2006

I'm supposed to go home today. Home is not two rooms over a Lot or any of the other various places I lived as a child. It is a very expensive Victorian house in the over-priced trendiness of East Dulwich where we were going to play small-but-happy families.

You and I can't go anywhere yet though — not until the doctor has been to check us over. I'm an old mother and could fall apart at any moment apparently. It's not me I'm worried about; I always seem to scrape through whatever challenges Life arranges. It's you that concerns me. I won't feel happy until I am told by someone with years of medical training that you are as you should be. All present and correct. You may look absolutely fine but who knows what's going on in that little body of yours that can't be seen? Appearances can be deceptive, I should know that.

'It's perfectly normal to worry', Fran says. 'You're a mother now. It's your job.'

I don't remember it being in my own mother's job description but I plan to be more conscientious.

'Who's going to take you home?'

Good question. I don't have anyone to take us

home. I don't even have a car seat contraption thing. I wanted the most expensive one Mothercare had to offer but that idea flew out the window, along with 'Daddy's' hastily-packed suitcase.

Fran has a muslin square swathed over one shoulder where she is rocking you like the old pro she is, while I finish off my hospital shepherd's pie which brings back memories of school dinners shared with my brown-eyed boy. It is the weight and consistency of concrete and would sink a dead body but I'm famished so needs must. 'That's breastfeeding for you,' says Fran, 'you can never get enough food inside you.' She changes position and is now cradling you, examining you closely, a concentrated look in her eye, holding you up to the light at the window, checking for jaundice. You do have a slight yellow tinge. Or is it blue? Duck egg blue like Lucas. Whatever colour it is, you don't look quite right, even to my inexpert eyes. But there's probably a perfectly simple explanation.

'What do you reckon, then?' I ask.

She sighs. 'She's lovely.'

(You are, you are.)

Then she hands you over, my baby-with-no-name, saying it's my turn.

'Whoever did your stitches made a good job of it,' Fran announces. 'Which is one less thing to worry about.'

Indeed.

4

1971

This is Your Life

The following months are a mixed, confusing time stuffed with emotion of one sort or another. Life has become that infamous roller-coaster when once it was a rusty old roundabout. Lucas and I never know what to expect of our mothers. We don't know if we are coming or going or what is round the next corner (etc, etc).

Sometimes Lucas and I are given complete and utter freedom, freedom that would never be contemplated these days for six-year-olds without serious concerns for their health and safety. We like to wander the local streets. We like to go down the road to Toy Town with our pocket money to add to our growing collection of Dinky TV tie-ins. We like to call in to see Mr Bob Sugar who stocks us up with goodies and sometimes lets us play with the pipe display. And although we no longer have the giant rabbit hole at our disposal, it is just a quick walk to Albert Morris' graveyard where we like to spend hours playing Hide-and-Seek amongst the crosses and angels or Guess-the-Animal-Poo amongst the shrubs and undergrowth. But the time I am happiest in the Bone Yard is when Lucas helps me with my reading. I have mastered several Biblical verses and all the old family names of Torquay. He is a good teacher.

At other times our freedom is stripped and we are imprisoned inside the house. We are not even allowed to go in the little garden and fiddle with the snails. But as long as Lucas and I are together there is always something to do. We can play on the old piano in the dining room. We can listen to The Monkees on Mrs Jones' record player. We can make our way through the games in the sideboard: Battleships, Tiddlywinks, Draughts and (my favourite) Happy Families. And, when we are feeling imaginative, we can play Sweet Shops (where I am Mr Sugar and Lucas is the paperboy) or Schools (where Lucas is almost as strict as Miss Pitchfork but much easier to fathom) or even Vets (when Andy is in a compliant mood).

Sometimes Mrs Jones — or Auntie Nina as I am now allowed to call her — is the cheeriest person imaginable (after Father Christmas). She has a wide-stretched smile that shows off her silver fillings. Mother too is trying her best to be a ray of sunshine and to avoid dipping into her Moods — tricky for her as she is still harbouring resentment over the Eviction. I am beginning to suspect the Eviction had something to do with Auntie Sheila as I haven't been to play with Toni in a long time (I am really out of practice on my dressage).

At other times Auntie Nina is swaddled in anger. I watch her in the garden, snipping the slugs in half with the kitchen scissors, pruning the rose bushes aggressively until all that remains is a row of miserable-looking stumps. And she spends a lot of time simply staring. She will walk into a room and suddenly stop, forgetting what she has come in for. She carries on standing there for some considerable time, staring into nothingness. I wonder if that is exactly why she came into a room in this way: just to stare and transport herself to another place where she doesn't have to worry anymore.

Worry is taking its toll on Auntie Nina. She no longer looks the immaculate creature that first grasped my mother's attention across a crowded playground. Even Mother sometimes fails to coordinate her shoes and bags these days. They are worried about Lucas. He has a disease with a name that could've been made for him. He doesn't have to go to school because he must go to the hospital an awful lot where they give him medicine that makes him sick. 'Go to bed,' Auntie Nina urges her son on their return. But he doesn't want to miss his favourite pro-grammes so she lets him stay downstairs on the sofa, cocooned in a green blanket. Underneath the blanket I know he is as thin as our class stick insect, Graham. And he lies as still as Graham does on his twig of privet so that every now and then I have to poke Lucas. Just to check.

★   ★   ★

Lucas has another trip to London to stay with his grandparents. This time they take him to the Tower of London and St Paul's Cathedral and a

50

Very Important Doctor in Harley Street. Lucas is exhausted on his return and doesn't even want to watch *The Monkees* with me. He takes to his bed for three (endless) days while I have to go to the shop with Mother after school to give him some Peace and Quiet. I help Mr Bob Sugar with the stock-taking. He says I am a natural and I can feel my cheeks burning up just like Lucas' do from time to time.

★ ★ ★

Lucas starts wearing a hat. A Torquay United bobble hat. Blue and yellow like the Swedish flag (according to his Book of Flags). Lucas doesn't like football but Mr Bob Sugar says every Torquay boy must have one of these bobble hats. What about every Torquay girl? That's what I want to know. But I don't say anything. I know this isn't about me.

★ ★ ★

Lucas still hasn't returned to school. 'I want him to have Happy Times,' I hear Auntie Nina tell Mother. 'We're going to have Days Out.'

After weeks of Days Out in the museums and castles and country houses of the West Country, Lucas begs to be allowed back to school.

'But why?' Auntie Nina protests.

'Because I like school.'

Shock, horror. But it is true.

So Lucas goes back to school with special dispensation to wear his bobble hat, only

51

— lucky Thing Two — he doesn't have to do PE! Instead, while the rest of us strip to our pants and vest, he goes into the class next door with his copy of *Stig of the Dump*.

Lucas is happy. And that's what counts.

* * *

I am not happy. We are not allowed to play in the Bone Yard anymore. And I don't think this is because we come back caked in red mud which isn't hygienic for Lucas who has to keep very clean in case he catches Germs (little tiny alien life forms that no-one can see).

It is more than that. It has something to do with Albert Morris, the dead boy.

* * *

A strange man turns up on our doorstep. He is short for a man. Much shorter than Bob and Bernie but with a familiar look about him — pale skin and dark eyes. Mother invites him in for a cup of tea and sits him down in the dining room. Auntie Nina is out at the chemist's fetching a prescription.

'Stop following me round like a seagull, Philippa,' Mother snaps.

I follow her to the kitchen where she fills the kettle.

'Who is that man?'

'Mr Jones.' She will not look at me.

'Mr Jones?'

'Yes. Mr Jones.' She lights the gas stove and

puts on the kettle before adding in a quiet voice, 'Lucas' father.'

'Father?'

'Yes, father,' she whispers loudly, her green eyes flashing up at the ceiling above where we can hear Lucas' mouse-steps patter across the floor boards, busy on his Secret Project.

'I don't know what Nina will say,' Helena adds, sparking up a cigarette at the back door.

And then I remember the Divorce. Lucas' mother and father do not like each other anymore.

'She won't be very happy to see him, will she Mummy?'

'No, Philippa,' she says. 'But the least I can do is make the poor man a cup of tea.'

While we wait for the kettle to boil, music floats in from the dining room. Mr Jones must be playing the piano. It is a tad off-key but you can tell he is a good musician. The tune is far more sophisticated than Chopsticks which is as much as Lucas and I can manage. A little while later we also hear mouse-steps on the stairs. Mother quickly pours the tea and the cup rattles on the saucer as she carries it through to Mr Jones, me at her (high) heels.

And there is Lucas. Standing by the piano, watching the man's pale hands as they flutter over the black and white keys like a swarm of moths. The man doesn't need to look at the music or at the piano. He can play by heart, by touch. Instead he looks at Lucas.

And there we stand, Helena and I, in the doorway, watching this tableau: Mr Jones

53

studying his son; Lucas studying his father's hands. They don't even notice we are there.

My throat hurts so much because I am trying not to cry. I am trying hard to be cheerful because I know that is what I must do, though I can't stop myself from saying: 'Don't take him away.'

But I don't know who it is I am pleading with.

★ ★ ★

After his second cup of tea, Mr Jones says he must go. He is staying at the Imperial but will call back again in the morning as he wants a Word with Nina before he catches the Paddington train. (I think that Word is most probably 'Lucas'.) Lucas begs him for one more tune on the piano but he never gets the chance; none of us have heard the front door. None of us have noticed Auntie Nina come in the dining room to find us huddled round the piano.

'Lucas. Go to your room,' she says, taking us back to the days when he had the energy to be naughty.

'Yes, come along, children,' Helena says, all Joyce Grenfell. And she wafts us out of the room, like a bad smell, closing the door behind her. They might be solid Victorian doors in this house, but we can still make out the drama unfolding in the dining room beyond.

Auntie Nina: How did you find us?

Mr Jones: Your parents thought I should know what's been going on.

Auntie Nina (repetitively): My parents? What's been going on?

Mr Jones (simply): Lucas.

After that, we don't hear anymore as we are shunted upstairs where Helena manages to get us into our pyjamas and supervise teeth-brushing. She smokes out of the bathroom window while Lucas and I sit at the top of the stairs waiting for his parents to emerge from the dining room.

Five minutes later the door opens and Mr Jones follows the woman he used to love into the hallway. He looks up briefly and smiles at his son, a pixie in a bobble hat, and in that moment I see an expression of longing never to be forgotten.

★ ★ ★

The next morning is Saturday. Mother goes to the shop and Lucas and I wait for Mr Jones to turn up. But he doesn't.

'He must've been called back urgently to work,' says Auntie Nina.

'What does he do?' I ask to fill an awkward (and dangerously deep) gap.

'He's a dentist.'

I imagine all those teeth in London waiting for Mr Jones' return and am unsure why they can't wait until the weekend is over. (I haven't even had a wobbly tooth yet, let alone tooth ache so can't possibly appreciate the severity of a dental emergency.)

When it is clear that Mr Jones is not coming

back, Lucas goes to his room to continue work on the Project. Auntie Nina skewers a family of snails before pruning the buddleia (poor butterflies — they will be homeless next summer). I wonder if all families are like mine. But only briefly, as I know they aren't. I have seen the books to prove it. I've even read some of them, thanks to Lucas.

★　★　★

Lucas stops going to school. I have to survive on my own again. There is no-one to save me a place in the dinner hall. I have no-one to save a place for on the carpet. But at least no-one calls me Fatty now. Maybe this is because Miss Pitchfork has told them to be kind to me. Or maybe they've noticed that I am not actually fat anymore.

★　★　★

Lucas goes to hospital. I am allowed to visit him tucked away in a corner of the ward with strict instructions not to get him excited — though I don't see how I can possibly get him excited in such a dreary place. The only difference between this and the other wards are the tiles on the walls, depicting nursery rhymes. Above Lucas' over-sized metal bed — where Auntie Nina has tied a Torquay United scarf knitted by Bob's neighbour — stands Dick Whittington on his way to London fully expecting to find the streets paved with gold (rather than dog mess).

It is a bit like my first day at school. All the other children are being fussed over by their tearful mothers; I feel completely lost. While Auntie Nina talks to the doctor, I sit with Lucas. His eyes are closed but I know they are as dark as can be under those duck egg lids.

'Will you finish my Project,' he asks, his eyes still tight shut.

'Yes, Lucas,' I promise solemnly, feeling the burden of the world on my shoulders.

He opens his eyes briefly and smiles a smile that scorches my heart. Is this what they mean by heartburn?

'Thank you, Philippa,' he says.

I have no idea what the Project is as I have been banned from Lucas' room ever since he embarked upon it. I only hope that I am capable of finishing it. Lucas is the cleverest boy in all the world and I am just Stupid Philippa in the Slow Readers (though at least I'm not Stupid Fat Philippa anymore).

★　★　★

I don't have much time to prepare for my task. Two days later, Auntie Nina comes home from the hospital and heads straight into the garden where she hurls an old chair at the baby gulls and then massacres the forsythia hedge that will never bloom again. Helena watches from the back door, smoking cigarette after cigarette. In the end she can stand it no more. She goes to her friend and gently prises the shears from her hand. Then she wraps her arms around her in

57

the evening sun, trying to offer what comfort she can, knowing it is futile. Auntie Nina's tears will never stop.

Lucas — the boy I was going to marry, my best friend, my Thing Two — has gone. He is not mislaid, or even lost. He is as dead as Albert Morris.

2006

Fran is back, banging on again about you being underweight even though you were well over-cooked and should have put in an appearance last week. I was surprised myself when I caught sight of you, when I held your little damp body in my arms. I'd been sure you were going to be a nine-pounder. My skin was stretched so tight, you could've seen your reflection in it if you'd been on the other side. But you turned up looking like a doll. The sort of baby Amanda Denning would have. The sort of baby Helena must've been expecting when she got lumbered with me.

But here I am, mother to a petite little thing.

Fran doesn't want you to stay petite. She is concerned about your latching on. It seems you're a little off centre and that's why it feels like you were born with a set of teeth already in place. She squeezes and manipulates my breasts as if they are made of Miss Pitchfork's play dough, desperately trying to get more of them into your tiny mouth but you have lost interest, your little body twitching as you drift back towards sleep.

'We may need to take you down to the ward after all,' Fran says.

'I thought I was going home.'

'It's probably best you stay in overnight. Just so we can make sure the feeding's up and running.'

'Oh.'

Fran scribbles in my stack of notes.

'When's the doctor coming?'

'He's doing the rounds as we speak,' Fran pats me sympathetically on the shoulder as she notices the tears spring to my eyes.

'He has a right to be told,' she says.

'The doctor?'

'Your husband.'

'I thought you said he was letting me down.'

'It doesn't matter what I think of him,' she says. 'It doesn't change what's right.'

It is quite clear that there's no arguing with Fran when she sets her mind to something and I'm far too tired to argue. You have to be on the ball to argue with her. She's just like Lucas in that way.

My Lucas.

And then she's gone, leaving the smell of latex gloves behind her.

And we're on our own.

5

1971

Shooting Stars

It is a very hot day. Holiday-makers flood to the seafront and the beach armed with rubber rings and parasols. Mother and I, on the other hand, have something less frivolous to do.

I was supposed to spend the afternoon at the newsagents but in the end it is decided I should be allowed to go with the grownups. Bob shuts up shop and comes along too, with his neighbour, Mrs Gracie, the one who made Lucas' scarf. It is quite a gathering in the end, but not a nice end, a fair end.

They say things are never black and white but on this day, as we shuffle into the cool church, they quite clearly are. The flowers in St Bartholomew's are all white: in the porch, at the end of each pew, at the front where the vicar appears like a magician in his long dress and sombre face amid a puff of smoke. In contrast, everyone is wearing black: black suits, black skirts, black jackets. And all the ladies have black hats. Auntie Nina has a smart pill box with a veil. Mother has a wide-brimmed hat like Audrey Hepburn in the film where she wants diamonds and sings a song on her window ledge. Mrs

61

Gracie is weighted down by an old lady straw hat, a sprig of berries attached to the side with a lethal-looking pin. I am wearing a floppy woolly beret that makes my head itchy the way it did when I had head lice one time (another reason not to get too close to Christopher Bennett).

I am put between Mother and Bob. Mrs Gracie sits on the end so she can stick her gammy leg out into the aisle. Auntie Nina is sitting with her mother and father in the pew in front of us, staring at the little box where her son is hidden. I keep expecting him to lift off the lid, like he is the magician's assistant, spilling the white roses onto the flagstones in a theatrical gesture. To sit up and shout: 'All scream for ice cream!' But Lucas is quiet and still and dead.

We sing a song I know from school, one of our assembly hymns called 'Abide with me'. Bob has a good voice, clear and loud and unembarrassed, in a way his normal, everyday voice can never hope to be. Mrs Gracie sings like all old ladies — a high warble that suggests a bygone era: the War, gas masks, men in uniform on trains smoking roll-ups and the white cliffs of Dover (which are hard to imagine, ours being so red).

The vicar coughs for our attention the way Miss Pitchfork does. Then he chants a tuneless song in a language I don't know, but that tells of ancient times in musty monasteries on wind-swept hills. He asks us to please be seated and Auntie Nina slumps onto the pew between her parents. A child, their child. Her dead child. And another man's child, not just her own: Mr Jones, who has left his own parents behind in London, while he mourns alone, to one side, his fingers still, dead moths in his lap.

Lucas would have liked it here. His family. His friends. It isn't fair. He is hidden away in a place from which he'll never be able to escape. Maybe he can hear us from there, singing 'Abide with me'. He liked that song. He had the voice of a choirboy and got countless house points for piping up when no-one else knew the words (it helps when you can read).

Maybe he is knocking on the door of his box with his pale little hand, only no-one can hear him because we are too busy singing.

Or maybe he isn't really in there at all. Maybe he's fooled everyone and just run away. Maybe he'll slip in quietly at the back and listen to the words of the vicar, the musty chants, the warbles and the tears.

Or maybe not. Maybe I'll never see him again as long or as short as I live.

My Lucas.

My huckleberry friend.

★   ★   ★

That night I lie awake in bed. It has been an eventful day to say the least. Not only have I lost Lucas forever but I have also lost my first tooth. I've had plenty of time lately for wobbling and it has only been a matter of days from the first looseness to the final extraction and I've accomplished this milestone all on my own, with no fuss. I don't bother telling Helena as she has her mind on other things, mainly comforting

Auntie Nina and keeping us fed and watered (lots of hard-boiled eggs and ham salads. I am wasting away and no-one has noticed). I examine the little yellow tooth (too many sweets on tap, what would Mr Jones think?) before wrapping it up in a tissue and sliding it under my pillow. Then I wait for the tooth fairy.

No-one has remembered to draw my curtains. I can watch the moon which is small and round and might bounce away like a ping-pong ball if the residents of Torquay all breathed out at the same time. I wonder if Lucas is up there somewhere, a speck of stardust that Auntie Sheila would hoover up if she were an angel on cleaning duty. I decide not to get out of bed and close my curtains, in case he is watching me, lonely up there without Auntie Nina or Mr Jones.

Sleep comes eventually and shakes itself over me, pouring dreams into my ear. There is the smell of Palmolive. A splash of water. A whisper that mentions a father and a son and (scarily) a holey ghost. Then suddenly it is morning and, after hunting high and low, it is apparent that the tooth fairy hasn't put in an appearance. Later that day I find out why: Helena has scared her off. I know it was Helena because I overhear her telling Bob when he calls round with a box of Milk Tray. I am sitting at the top of the stairs (I've spent a lot of time there lately) and eavesdrop on their conversation in the kitchen below.

'Are you all right, Helena?'

'Well, no, actually, seeing as you've asked. I

think I'm slowly going mad. In some horrible way I feel jealous of Nina.'

'What do you mean?' Bob asks, flabbergasted.

'I know it sounds horrid but nothing can ever happen to her again that will make her feel like this. The worst is over.'

Bob doesn't say anything but I hear his heavy sigh.

Then Helena goes on: 'You'll never guess what I did last night.'

And no, Bob can't guess, so Helena tells him.

'I baptised Philippa. I crept in her room in the middle of the night and I sprinkled water on her forehead and said those magic words.'

'Oh,' says Bob. 'Well, that makes sense, I suppose. You could always do it properly, you know, in church.'

'It's done now,' states Helena before excusing herself, saying she must shop for more eggs and ham.

I watch her show Bob out. When he's gone, she stops in front of the hall mirror and sighs at her reflection. 'Yes, I know. I'm old before my time,' she agrees with the woman she sees there. Then she looks up, feeling me watching her, and I can see that the woman in the mirror is lying to Helena; she is so young, barely a woman. She smiles and I see my own face reflected in hers and I know she doesn't want me to die. But in case I do, she wants protection. She wants to know I won't become a speck of stardust destined to be sucked up by a cosmic vacuum cleaner.

She is a good mother. She loves me.

But she is wrong about Auntie Nina. Surely the worst is only just beginning.

★　★　★

Auntie Nina has gone. The Movers have been in and packed up all of her things in tea chests and carried them away in a big lorry, back to London. She always planned to go home eventually but she never expected it to be on her own.

Poor Auntie Nina.

And poor us. Mother and I must move out too as the house is being sold. I wish we could buy it so that we could stay on. So that I could pretend Lucas was still pit-pattering overhead in his room. Unfortunately there is no chance of that. Mother might be able to find the money for shoes and lipstick and handbags but not for a house.

We pack our own things in cardboard boxes with the help of Mrs Gracie who is becoming as much a part of everyday life now as Lucas used to be, though in a completely different way.

'Call me Wink,' she says.

'Why?' I ask.

'It's my name,' she says, rolling one of Mother's few ornaments up in newspaper.

I can't think what mother would call her child 'Wink'. Then again, I can't imagine Wink ever having a mother because she looks like she's always been an old lady. Wink seems to know what I am thinking.

'I'm only sixty-two,' she says. As if this were

66

young. (Six is young, I know that for sure.)

'People think I'm much older,' she goes on, placing the ornament in an orange box from the International. 'Because of my ruddy Multiple Wotsit.'

Multiple Wotsit is a disease Wink has, a disease which takes it out of her, makes it harder for her to get about and do all the things she used to do like gardening and shopping and the hokey-cokey. I hope the disease is not lethal like Lucas'.

★ ★ ★

On the final afternoon, as the sun is heating up the house so it feels like I am going to bake like one of Auntie Sheila's Victoria Sandwiches, I kneel on the bare boards of the dining room amongst the dust and forgotten marbles and hairgrips, staring at the place where Mr Jones' fingers travelled up and down the piano keys. I remember Lucas watching him. I remember my promise. Or rather, Mother reminds me.

'This is yours,' she says. 'Auntie Nina left it for you . . . Well, Lucas did.' And she has to take out her hanky and give her nose a good blow, before handing over a Quality Street tin.

She lights a cigarette as I take off the lid to reveal, not chocolates, but the contents of the Secret Project. It isn't quite what I imagined. I pictured all sorts of things in the weeks leading up to Lucas' death and then I forgot all about it. Now here it is in my hands. Here I am, taking off the lid . . .

Inside, Lucas has lined the tin with familiar flowery material.

'That's where my Laura Ashley blouse got to,' Mother says. She is almost cross, for a second, but she soon smiles a sad smile and then inhales deeply on her Consulate.

I slowly pull back the cloth like I am detonating a bomb. And it *is* a bomb of some sort. A time bomb ready to go off at some unknown point in the distant future, one we can only guess at. I realise what it is even before I read Lucas' instructions. It is a time capsule, like the one that John Noakes and Peter Purvis and Valerie Singleton buried on *Blue Peter*. Of course, I should have realised that's what Lucas was up to. He was fascinated when we watched it together and saw them pack up a *Blue Peter* annual, some photographs and a set of decimal coins (whose introduction has been tricky for Bob and his sweets, but trickier still for old ladies like Wink who still hark back to rationing coupons).

I open the instructions which are sealed inside a brown envelope with my name in bubble writing on the front. This is what the letter says:

Dear Philippa,
    Sorry I had to go and leave you. I wanted us to have more days together in the Bone Yard. But do not forget to visit me there. (Maybe I will be near Albert Morris.) Tell me about Miss Pitchfork and Bob. Tell me what

68

you are reading. Tell me what happens in *Doctor Who*. Tell me anything you want. Even when you become a grown-up. Please keep on telling me. And please find somewhere good to bury the Time Capsule. Then come back and open it when you have children of your own. Bring them with you and tell them about me.
   Your (best) friend,
   Lucas. xxx

For the first time in weeks I feel happy. Tear drops are falling onto the paper but they are happy ones. Lucas is still my best friend even though I can't see him or touch him or breathe in his currant bun smell.

★ ★ ★

The next day Mother and I (and a disgruntled Andy) move into the Shop. Bob has insisted that this is the solution to our accommodation problem. He has plenty of space in the maisonette above and he'd appreciate the company. So while he and mother and Wink do their best to make this new arrangement work, I sit in the yard with Lucas' tin and contemplate where to bury it. The most obvious place is the Bone Yard but how can I be sure the box won't get dug up to make room for new residents? So I decide here is as good a place as any. Here in Bob's backyard. I add one or two of my own items to Lucas' precious collection — my booty from the outside lav — before foraging in Bob's lean-to for a trowel. I find the perfect spot in a corner under his one and only unidentifiable shrub.

Now I just have to sit back and wait until I am grown up.

2006

So now we're on the ward, babies either side of us, opposite us, screaming, feeding, sleeping. You, on the other hand, are lying sweetly in your plastic crib. No murmur, no cry. Surely you must be hungry by now?

Fran has this funny look in her eye that she's trying to hide from me by scribbling frantically in your notes which are growing more and more copious by the minute, like a barrister off to defend some beyond-hope criminal from a life sentence.

'Everything alright, Fran?' I ask.

'Time to take your blood pressure,' she says and wraps that vicious Velcro thing round my arm, squeezing it in a Chinese burn — the type that Terry would give me if I set foot in his garage looking for Toni's roller skates.

I want to breastfeed you. Fran doesn't care what I do as long as we get something inside your little body. There's been whispers of feeding tubes if you don't get on with it sharpish. You don't really seem that bothered. I don't know why they don't just let you sleep. That's what you're supposed to do isn't it, when you're this tiny? I'd know if you were starving, wouldn't I? Isn't that the sort of thing mothers intuitively know? Did Helena know? She plied me with a constant stream of bottles. That's why I was so 'bonny'. You don't look 'bonny'. You look scrawny and pale. Dark-eyed and small like Lucas. Maybe Fran's right. I don't know.

What would Helena do?

6

1972

Saturday Night Takeaway

Mother now looks less like Audrey Hepburn and more like Carole King. She has relaxed her make-up and fashion standards in the interests of comfort (it gets hot and clammy in the shop in summer and she likes to go bare-footed). She has also become proficient at sweet-serving, stock-taking and being polite to old ladies, and performs all these duties (and countless others) in her stride. Bob says he doesn't know how he ever managed without her. Mother reminds him that he probably didn't.

Bob and Mother are becoming a partnership. They move around the shop — and each other — with ease. When one of them bends down to retrieve a sweet wrapper from the floor, the other will reach over them to restack a shelf. However their paths cross, however busy it gets — and it can get very busy, especially on half-day closing when the whole neighbourhood wants their pools coupons — they never bump or crash into each other. Their movements are slick and smooth. It is a choreographed dance. A double act. But that is what time does. It makes you find your place, slot in. Mother and I have slotted

73

into the shop. It has been nearly a year after all. And now this is most definitely Home.

But Mother is lonely. She misses Auntie Nina so much that she contacts Auntie Sheila. Auntie Sheila is so upset about Lucas that she forgives Helena. Mother and Sheila soon slip back into their old friendship. They go shopping together, to the theatre together, sip gin and orange on a fine summer evening together. Mother is welcomed back into her old circle of friends because the situation looks somewhat different now. And it isn't just Lucas and Nina's departure that has changed things. It is Bernie that has done that.

Bernie has been up to his old tricks. This means that Helena is no longer the slut Sheila believed her to be. It is far more likely that Bernie is to blame.

'It wasn't your fault, Helena. It was ruddy Bernard. He's moved in with that Welsh woman who runs the antique shop in St Mary's church.'

'I know, I heard.'

'She's welcome to him.'

'She'll soon get fed up.'

'He's not crawling back to me when she does.'

Sheila often pops into the shop for the Western Morning News or a packet of Extra Strong Mints, an excuse for a cup of tea and a natter with Helena. If Helena isn't there, Bob is only too happy to oblige and put the kettle on.

'Do you take sugar, Mrs Siney?'

'I shouldn't but I do.' She taps her tummy. 'And please call me Sheila.'

'You don't need to worry on that count,

74

Sheila,' Bob says, the Bobby Dazzler.

And Sheila giggles in a way that makes my heart miss a double beat. My hopes are being dashed before my very eyes.

Then one day another man walks into the shop — and into Mother's life — and dashes all my hopes. Forever.

★ ★ ★

Now I can go back round to play with Toni. Only things have changed here too. Toni is too old to play ponies anymore. Instead she likes to lock the door of her bedroom and practise make-up skills with her friends from the Grammar. I am allowed into this inner sanctuary not because I am one of the Chosen Few but because they like to practise on me. I am a living, breathing Girl's World. I go home with glittery eye shadow and red cheeks that takes all Mother's elbow grease to scrub off (and a layer of my skin).

I don't *have* to go to Auntie Sheila's on a Saturday morning anymore but I like being in her house with all those teenagers hanging around. I don't even especially mind Terry and his long-haired mates who congregate in Bernie's double garage (that never houses any of his cars). They meet there, allegedly to play darts and bar billiards but really to smoke and swear and snigger about Birds. Sometimes, if they are a man down, they let me join in with a tournament just so as I will make them look good.

But I prefer to spend my time watching Toni and her more refined friends who pretend to be

75

Pan's People from *Top of the Pops*, wearing floaty nighties and leaping across Sheila's sitting room in practised formations with whimsical expressions on their faces. I like being there, amongst the bustling chaos that was once Sheila's pristine show home. I like being there because then I can forget I don't have Lucas anymore.

Though of course I do have Wink.

★　★　★

Wink, remember, is Bob's neighbour. She lives on her own, two doors down from the shop. Her husband, Mr Gracie, died a long time ago. There is a picture of him in a polished silver frame on top of her black and white television set. She catches me looking at him one day.

'You're not to worry, duck,' she says. 'I'm not lonely. I've got my Captain.'

She points her stick over at her parrot, perched on top of the telly, her three prized possessions together.

'And don't forget Bruce,' I remind her.

'No, dear,' she says. 'How could I forget Bruce?'

Wink has a slightly unhealthy addiction to a new game show on the BBC hosted by Bruce Forsyth and the lovely Anthea Redfern (our very own local girl made good). It is a Family Show and I always watch it with Wink on a Saturday evening. Usually Mother and Bob come over too and we have a fish and chip supper on our laps in Wink's front room.

Wink's front room stinks of bird pee but you soon get used to it. At first I wanted to be sick as soon as I got through the door. The only way I could eat my supper was to smother it in vinegar and ketchup to help block up my senses.

'It's not Wink's fault,' Mother said, the first time, as Wink struggled off to the kitchen to make us a cup of tea. 'She can't get about like she used to. Cleaning is tricky.'

We ducked, as Captain — to prove her point — swooped overhead and splatted the television screen, covering Frank Bough's face with war paint.

Now, I can hardly smell Captain. I am too busy playing with him, trying to teach him new phrases such as 'Nice to see you, to see you, nice.' It isn't easy. He prefers to stick to his tried and tested ones like 'Up The Gulls' and 'Keep your hair on.'

'Give him time,' says Wink. 'He's got to be in the mood.'

Now, coming over the road for a fish and chip supper and *The Generation Game* is part of our Saturday routine. I even start to look forward to it. I feel a warmth towards Wink that started when she knitted the scarf for Lucas and grew when she sat in the church with her gammy leg in the aisle, tears sliding down her overly-rouged cheeks (perhaps Toni had been practising on her too). She is one of those people that you can't help liking despite the smell of her place. She is a survivor who has survived on her tough sweetness so that although she is widowed and disabled, she manages to get by quite nicely thank you very much. Even Helena takes a shine to Wink. It is an unlikely friendship as Wink is neither stylish nor able to go shopping at any given opportunity but she is kind to Helena in a way that possibly puts her in mind of her mother (though as a judge's wife she probably wouldn't have been too pleased with the comparison as Wink has a criminal record for a breach of the peace that she will tell me about one day when I am old enough. I hope Wink lives to see me old enough as this disease of hers can be a Bugger).

You don't really notice the differences in Wink because they happen so slowly. But if you were to think about it, you'd realise that Wink is doing less. That she's started to get Mother or Bob to put on the kettle or do bits of shopping.

Wink gets me to do jobs too.

'Cover up Captain,' she tells me one Saturday. 'It's nearly time for Bruce.'

So I reach up with the travel rug and smother Captain in darkness. We all know what will happen if I don't. As soon as Bruce appears and strikes up *Life is the Name of the Game*, there are feathers everywhere and squawking like the cries of a newborn that can't be ignored. Captain doesn't share Wink's love of Bruce. He is most probably jealous.

Tonight it is just Wink, Bob and me (and Captain, Bruce and Anthea). Helena has gone out with Auntie Sheila to the pictures to see *The Poseidon Adventure* after an early evening supper at the (ironically named) Berni Inn. By the time Bob brings in the fish and chips all plated up, Anthea has already given us a twirl

78

and the contestants are spinning plates to the audience's hilarity. Wink and I are in stitches as the plates come crashing to the ground. The programme whizzes by in its usual fashion and before long we are sitting with huge expectation for the finale of the show.

'I'd love to be one of them contestants, Philippa,' Wink says. 'What I wouldn't give to be sat at that conveyor belt.'

And I have to agree. It is the height of sophistication — the music, the tension, the wonderful electrical goods that seem to come from an ideal home of the future. But while we shout out the names of the objects we have committed to memory — 'Fondue set! Vanity case! Picnic hamper!' — I have this niggling feeling that shakes the sparkle off the excitement and turns it to dust.

Will I ever live in an ideal home?

What is an ideal home?

I thought it was Sheila and Bernie's but it turns out that their supposedly stable foundations have been built on nothing but sand.

★ ★ ★

I am old enough to walk home from school on my own now. Sometimes I imagine Lucas beside me as I trudge the familiar route, laden with my satchel and shoe-bag. But mostly I simply relish the freedom after a day cooped up with my new teacher Miss Turnbull. The shop bell always rings in the same half-hearted way as I fall in the door, looking like an unmade bed in my rucked-up uniform. And there is Mother, as smart as a smoothed counterpane. An expression of surprise on her face as if she's forgotten she ever had a daughter.

Today Mother isn't there. Bob is assisted by Auntie Sheila who says she has rolled her sleeves up to lend a helping hand — which is two cliches packed into one sentence which would impress Miss Mothball, who is keen on cliches and encourages us to use one at every given opportunity as they are a great time saver. (She is not a fan of imagination.)

'Where's Mother?' I ask.

Sheila does a shifty double-take to Bob who turns and fiddles with the boxes of Panini stickers.

'She's nipped out, sweetheart,' Sheila says, cheerily.

'Where?'

'Down the town.'

'Who with?' (But I already know who with. I just know.)

'A gentleman,' she says.

'A gentleman?'

'A man from Canada. He's on his holidays.'

Canada. I know about Canada. It is a big splodge of pink in Lucas' Atlas that Auntie Nina left me, along with his Book of Flags. So I also know that the Canadian flag is red and white with a big leaf on it. And I know that the Canadian policemen ride horses and wear comedy trousers. There are also grizzly bears and racoons and Red Indians and maple syrup and lots of mountains and gigantic lakes and the biggest waterfall that makes a roar so mighty you can't hear yourself think. Why would someone leave a country like that to come on their holidays to Torbay? (Even if we do have palm trees and Agatha Christie.)

'Is it the very tall man?' I ask, to be sure. 'The one who smokes the French cigarettes?'

'I suppose he is quite tall,' says Bob, turning back and straightening up to his full five foot nine and a half inches. 'And yes, he seems to think he's Sacha Distel. He's not even a French Canadian. His family come from Torbay, he reckons.'

As I thought. I know this Canadian. I saw him for the first time a few days ago, coming into the shop to buy a postcard to send the folks back home in Labrador. Tall and dark and handsome, he gave my mother a smile that she hasn't seen in a long time. Bob has been trying for two years to give her a smile like that but they come out all wrong. Mother has no idea that Bob is in love with her. Or at least she pretends she has no idea. Bob would walk to the ends of the earth and back again for Mother, but she won't even let him walk her along the seafront in case people get the wrong idea. That is exactly the idea Bob has in mind but Mother can't see it. Even though he took us in when we were homeless yet again, even though he looks after me and teaches me football, even though he loves Mother with every single thrown-together part of him, she can't see it. All she can see is his bald patch and baggy cardigans. All she can see is that Bob is Bob and that is that. Their

81

partnership will never be any more than a shop dance.

And now there is the Canadian. And Auntie Sheila.

'Cheer up, Philippa,' Auntie Sheila says now. 'Have an Orange Maid on me. You look all hot and bothered.'

She plunges her arm into the freezer and produces my favourite lolly so that I am glad she and Mother are friends again. But my hopes for Bob being my new dad have gone down the Swanney (one of Wink's favourite phrases — maybe I should try sticking it in one of my stories, see what Miss Mothball makes of that).

★ ★ ★

The Canadian was supposed to stay in Torquay for three days but he has extended his holiday for three weeks. He's come to do some family research on behalf of his mother who lives in another Torbay, on the eastern tip of the island of Newfoundland (next stop the British Isles). She wants him to try and find a connection somewhere. In that time my mother has seen him every day and has discovered much information about him all of which she recounts to Bob and Sheila (and me from my stakeout behind the door).

The Canadian is called Orville Tupper and whereas I expected him to be a farmer or a mounted policeman, he is in actual fact a male model who has moved from his island and crossed the Gulf of St Lawrence to tread the long, long road to Fame and Fortune in the big city of Toronto. It has been a tricky road, full of the Bumps of Knock-back and the Potholes of Disappointment so that Orville Tupper has not yet become the sort of model who poses mysteriously and makes women swoon, but Auntie Sheila is impressed, nonetheless.

'Ooh, what's he done?' she asks, positively glowing at the prospect of some glamour in her life.

'An advert or something,' Helena says, dismissively.

But Sheila won't let this drop. 'What for?' she asks. 'What for?'

'Vicks Sinex,' Helena says, though I could be mistaken, as she murmurs this rather too quietly for me to hear from behind the door and at that moment the shop bell pings.

I come out from the back and join Bob and Sheila behind the counter. All three of us stand there looking at Orville Tupper, dressed in his cream suit and panama.

'Good morning.' He nods at his reception committee, before briefly forcing himself to pick me out for his special attention, like the Queen: 'How's it going, kid?'

He calls me 'kid' when he is trying to impress Helena but really he can't remember my name. He doesn't wait for my answer, turning to my mother instead.

'Ready, Helena?' he asks, holding out his muscley arm for her, as if she is suddenly incapable of walking, which possibly she is in those new six inch heels of hers (where *does* she

83

get the money from?).

Mother puffs out her smoke, reapplies her lipstick and says in her finest English accent, 'Yes, Orville, ready.' And she accepts his arm.

'Let's vamoose,' he says. Then he adds: 'See ya, kid.' But he isn't looking at me when he says this. There is only one person he is interested in. My mother.

'Philippa,' I whisper. 'My name is Philippa.'

But it is too late; they are gone.

★　★　★

In spite of the pharmaceutical turn down his career path, Orville does take care of his appearance — unlike Bob who thinks waving a comb at his hair and buttoning up his cardy is all that is required of male grooming.

But seeing Orville Tupper swagger into his shop every morning and every evening makes Bob take a good long look at himself in the bathroom mirror. He goes up to Exeter on half-day closing and forks out on a leather jacket and that very night starts growing sideburns. He should've looked a bit longer in that mirror because now he has the appearance of a dodgy private detective — and there are plenty of them on the television, in all shapes and sizes. But there is no-one quite as unkempt or kind-hearted as Bob. Not that it matters; Helena only has eyes for Orville.

So Bob turns his attention to Sheila, waiting patiently in the wings.

Sheila is only too happy to accept Bob's

84

attention as it has been quite some considerable time since Bernie has thrown any her way. She has never forgotten what it is to be a woman and always dresses accordingly in frocks and skirts and blouses — the finest St Michael's has to offer. This is partly what attracted Mother to Sheila, though of course Sheila is not in Nina's league as far as Style is concerned. But Sheila is the best of Torquay women of distinction. And Sheila is the best Bob can aspire to. They form a new partnership of sorts. Companionship with a twist of romance, enough to make them both feel they are real. That they will not blow away on a gust of wind.

Over the next fortnight, while Helena and Orville go-a-courting (where exactly, I have no idea, for they never ask me to go along with them as I am somewhat of a passion-killer), Bob and Sheila muddle along, slightly gauche, slightly clumsy, completely alive again (and a hideous embarrassment to Toni and Terry who can't bear to think of their mother as having the same surging hormones as them). Until the Welsh woman from the antique shop in St Mary's church turns up at the newsagents as Bob puts Sheila's cup of tea on the counter where she is pricing up the sandcastle flags. (Lucas would have loved a packet of those.)

'It's Bernie,' the woman says. 'He's in Torbay Hospital.' And, seeing Sheila's face, she adds: 'Don't worry he's not dead — it's been a close shave, mind. A heart attack, I'm afraid. A big heart attack.'

She waits a few moments, letting her news

sink in, surreptitiously casting an eye over the magazines on display.

'He's been asking for you,' she goes on. 'And to be quite honest, he needs you more than me. He needs his family.'

She moves towards the door and, before leaving, turns and says: 'This is a bit awkward, you see. I'm going back to the Bay. Tiger Bay. I've had enough of this one. I'm sorry. It was a bit of a mistake, really.'

Then she exits the shop, the half-hearted bell tolling her departure.

★ ★ ★

I do not like Orville Tupper. He hardly notices my presence at all, rarely bothering to look down from his dizzying height to the land where I live. I don't matter one iota to him. And I don't matter to Helena either, for late one Saturday afternoon, when I return from the Bone Yard, falling into the shop in my normal Philippa way, Helena isn't there. Helena has gone. She has vanished. Vamoosed.

I call up the stairs for her. I look in her room, the one next to mine. It is unusually tidy and I can see straightaway that she isn't there either. I even look in Bob's room in the attic, where he relocated after we moved in so we could have our own floor. There is an assortment of cardies lurking in his wardrobe, but not my mother. She is nowhere to be seen.

She has gone. But she is not lost. She is not even mislaid. She has flown away, not on a cloud to Heaven like Lucas, but on a Boeing 747 to Canada, according to Bob who has to break the news to this seven-year-old girl. 'Maybe she's been kidnapped by Orville Tupper?' I ask, hopefully. But Bob says nothing which tells me everything. Instead, he pats me gently on the head and gives me a packet of Opal Fruits which I do not have the stomach to eat.

★ ★ ★

I will never buy Vicks Sinex again. Not as long as I live. However blocked up and full of cold I become, I will not be reminded of the man who stole my mother.

2006

We have been removed to a side room. To give us some peace and quiet because it's mayhem on the ward. Too many breasts and babies and bemused-looking men. And I'm an old mother. Old.

'Please can we go home?' I beg Fran.

'All in good time,' she says before going home herself for a well-deserved sleep (what about my sleep, haven't I deserved one?).

And now he's here. Outside in the corridor. I can hear him pacing up and down the lino, his footsteps squeaking like an injured animal. I know it's him though I haven't actually seen him. A nameless nurse pops her head round the door, primed by Fran, to inform me that my husband has turned up with a teddy bear. Yes, a teddy bear. For you. He won't get around me that easily. I will not be bribed.

That name, label — 'husband' — attaches Adrian to me in a way that makes me feel sick. All those images conjured up by that word, tumbling round my stomach, surging through my blood, tingeing my milk with a nasty taste so that I am petrified you will never want it.

To have and to hold. Where was he when I was pushing you out? *To love and to cherish.*

Where was he when he was supposed to be with me? *Till death us do part.* I feel like killing him right now. *Forsaking all others.* Yeah, right.

'Tell him to go home,' I bark at the nurse the next time she dodges in, and I get an angelic sympathetic smile in return.

'Are you sure?'

'Quite sure.'

So he leaves, my husband, quietly. A squeak that grows faint and then the distant thud of a door closing. He doesn't even bother to kick up a fuss.

I don't know where he's gone. Not to our home. But I have you and your home is with me.

7

1972

The Apprentice

These days I would be taken in by Social Services and fostered out to a family with a clutch of other abandoned children. But at this moment in time there is no question of that; I stay on at the shop with Bob. Neither of us really believes this arrangement will continue forever. Surely Helena will come back and resume her rightful place at the counter at some point in the near future? Maybe she's just gone on holiday and forgotten to mention it in all the dizzy rush of packing and organising a foreign trip. Maybe she'll send me a postcard of a Mountie sitting proudly on his horse and bring me back a racoon's tail hat (á la Davy Crockett) as a souvenir.

But it isn't a postcard that flutters through the shop letterbox onto the Embassy doormat. It is an airmail letter with a row of stamps Lucas would have spent his pocket money on. It arrives one Saturday morning a few weeks after Helena's departure. I am on my way to Auntie Sheila's when the postman hands it over to me in such a gingerly fashion that I wonder if it is one of those letter bombs. My name is on the front in

Helena's school girl handwriting (which is much neater than my school girl handwriting as she spent several hours a day practising it in her boarding school in Wales and Miss Mothball isn't particularly bothered how neat our writing is as long as we 'get on with it quietly'). I peel open the seal very carefully and unfold the tissue-thin letter, catching the faintest whiff of Helena's perfume-mixed-with-cigarettes.

My reading has suffered without the benefit of Lucas' tuition. So I hand the letter over to Bob, lurking nearby, shuffling some packets of tic tacs on their stand. He coughs dramatically (for this is most definitely a dramatic moment, my future hanging there amongst the Sherbet Dib Dabs and *Daily Mails*) and then begins:

Dear Philippa
I hope you are well and being a good girl for Bob. I am sorry I didn't say goodbye. Orville asked me to marry him and I said yes. There is no room for you at the moment in his condominium (flat) in Toronto. He is very busy with his work and I am also busy looking for work so that we can buy a bigger condominium and there will be room for you. I think you are better off at the shop for now. You can go to school and see your old friends and Bob is the best father you could ever hope for.

(At this point Bob chokes up and has to blow his nose.)

Please don't be cross with Mummy.
All my love
Helena.

91

And there it is: the truth of it, there in that name, Helena. I see that she is as confused as I am. She has never been a fully-fledged Mummy. There has always been such a strong part that has remained Helena. And that is the part she is now embracing in Orville Tupper's small condominium (flat) in Toronto, while the Mummy part is kept at arms' length. Kept over the ocean.

Bob smiles at me with that smile which completely passed my mother by.

'She thought she was doing the right thing by you,' he says. 'She thought you'd be better off here, with me.'

He looks as bemused as I feel, his hands searching inside the pockets of his baggy cardigan as if he'll find the answer in there. But somewhere deep down, that niggle returns. Maybe Helena is right. Maybe I am better off with Bob.

* * *

Bernie toes the line now he is invalided by the weak heart that over-exerted itself one too many times in his philandering days. He can pay more attention to matters closer to home including why all his bamboo canes are missing from his dilapidated greenhouse. He doesn't dare exert himself these days. He doesn't dare do anything more strenuous than a bit of pottering about the garden, weeding the alpine rockery and dead heading the roses. He's given up his Lot. There was a retirement party at (appropriately) the Berni Inn where men in greasy ties made feeble jokes about dodgy tickers and faulty starter motors. But the biggest change in his lifestyle is his avoidance of women. On the cusp of his twentieth wedding anniversary, he has at long last forsaken all others.

Sheila can't give up Bob though. She still hankers after him, his good heart and his warm smile that came out all wrong when he aimed it at the true woman of his dreams (Helena/Mummy). Sheila comes into the shop, like the old days, under the pretence of purchasing a *Western Morning News* or a packet of Extra Strong Mints, but really to be with Bob, to check up on me and to keep an eye on Patty.

Patty is a school leaver that Bob has procured to roll up her sleeves and lend a helping hand, though Patty does it in return for a paltry wage that she spends on clothes and make-up. It is these clothes and make-up that worry Sheila because when Patty is kitted out in them she could easily be mistaken for a member of Pan's People (to Toni's annoyance). Patty has giraffe-length legs and a Marie Osmond smile. Sheila needn't worry though. Bob is quite oblivious to Patty's charms; he is relieved to have her cheap and efficient labour. And as for me, Patty is another longed for big sister, the other one being Toni of course — which is just as well because unfortunately I am soon to lose Toni. All that ballet practice has led to her being accepted by the Royal Ballet School. She is leaving for London next week (lucky thing).

I am invited along on a final shopping trip to Tip Taps, a dance shop in Paignton. It is a small shop packed out with pink tights and leotards of every shade you can think of. Some of the costumes look like they've been hanging there since before the War. The elderly gentleman who owns Tip Taps is less like a dancer than you could possibly imagine with his thick-set frame, Dennis Healey eyebrows, handlebar moustache and Harris Tweed. He'd be more at home in the cockpit of a Spitfire. Sheila hands over the list she's been sent from the ballet school and each time Toni pirouettes out of the changing room — a flimsy curtain in the corner behind a stack of shoeboxes — Auntie Sheila has to reach for a fresh hanky (she's come well prepared) and the elderly gentlemen blushes the colour of the red ballet shoes hanging above the counter. Toni has sprouted into womanhood and no-one has noticed until we are brought face to face with it in this small corner of Paignton. She is a woman and she is going to London and poor Auntie Sheila is beside herself. But I do not feel sorry for her. I feel cross and angry and worried that there will be no-one to fret over me when it is my time to up and leave. Or maybe I am destined to stay forever by the seaside.

★ ★ ★

Two years on and the situation has changed very little (apart from a new *Doctor Who*). I still have no mother but I do at least belong to a gaggle of girls at school. I am officially accepted into their circle — though perhaps somewhat on the circumference — mainly because they are short of some muscle when it comes to confrontations with the boys who rule the playground with their football and their spit. I am no longer Poor Lucas' Friend. Somehow I have swallowed Lucas up into my persona and give off the aura of quiet strength that he had. I am Philippa, the Tough Nut.

I also have a badge of honour: Library Monitor. This is somewhat ironic considering my illiterate beginnings but all that hard work in the Bone Yard amongst the tombstones must have finally paid off and I am at long last reading like a veteran. I have read so many books that I can help the little ones with their book choice and try to steer them away from the B section (Blyton) and towards such modern books as *Stig of the Dump* or *James and the Giant Peach*. For those who haven't yet mastered the mysteries of reading there is always Dr Seuss further down by the leaking beanbag.

I am not left alone in my duties. Miss Parry, who looks like she could have been a Tudor queen in a former life, is the archetypal librarian: she is stern and quiet and knows her books inside out. She defends the Dewey Decimal system to within an inch of her life and would burn heretics at the stake in the defence and upkeep of the library rules. The library rules — NO TALKING, NO RUNNING, NO EATING, NO DRINKING — are pinned up in bold print at several prominent points in the small library so there is no excuses for them not to be known off by heart by anyone passing through (except of course if you can't read which

95

is where the rules usually fall down).

'Philippa, please can you deal with C section. The infants have been on the rampage again.'

'Yes, Miss Parry,' I nod like an eager Jack Russell, an image of little savages with woad smeared across their cheeks running bare-chested across the dangerously-polished boards of the library spurring me on.

And I have to agree with Miss Parry here. The infants are a disgrace when it comes to filing. Ca's and Co's and Ci's all over the shop (as Wink would say).

And then I see it. *The Penguin History of Canada*, a single red maple leaf fluttering on the cover as I flick through this grown-up book that has somehow made its way into the school library. And I feel my legs weaken, all my strength sapping away like tapped Maple syrup.

'Philippa, are you all right?' Miss Parry rushes over to me in an unprecedented fashion and touches the back of her cool hand against my forehead. 'Low blood sugar,' she diagnoses with confidence. 'Deep breaths, Philippa,' she urges, as if the Armada are attacking. 'Don't move,' she orders, sitting me down on the library's one and only comfy chair, 'I'll be two ticks.' And she disappears, leaving me alone with my head in my woollen skirt, listening to the distant thud of children being let out to play, little feet storm-trooping down the corridor and out onto the tarmac beyond. The shriek of scattering seagulls. A teacher's whistle. A heavy door closing with finality. Then all sound stops and it is just me, alone, in the musty library, the smell

96

of old books and beeswax. The warmth of the chair beneath my legs, my head upside down, the sickness in my stomach, a pain in my chest, feelings inside me that have been gurgling for so long, ignored and unnamed, but that are now set to explode. *Canada . . . Orville Tupper . . . Helena.*

'Sit up now, Philippa.' Miss Parry shouts across the room, rushing over with a half-full glass of milk and a Rich Tea biscuit that she has procured from an unknown source (thereby contravening all the golden rules in one fell swoop, the whole gamut of library law smashed to smithereens by this Tudor queen). When I've nibbled at the biscuit and sipped at the milk, I look at her face trying to find a trace of motherhood. She clearly finds this awkward, examining her wristwatch as if she's forgotten how to tell the time.

'Thank you, Miss Parry. I feel better now.'

She cracks open a smile and her war mask slips, revealing the woman beneath.

'Do you have children, Miss Parry?' I ask. She is almost as surprised as I am at this sudden question.

'Well, no, Philippa, actually I don't. You see, Mr Parry died soon after we were married so no, I don't have children, I'm sorry to say.' And in that sentence I learn so much about Miss Parry. She was actually Mrs Parry. She was married. A whole other life. The love of her life lost. She wanted children but never met another man to match Mr Parry. She will never be a mother now, not with all that grey hair and the look of war in her eye.

'But I have my cats, Philippa. And my nieces and nephews. And all of you children.' As she says this, the whistle blows in the playground and there is a surge for the heavy front door which bashes open under the tide of storm-troopers. Quiet conversation is no longer possible and Miss Parry raises her eyes heavenward. I do the same. And she smiles.

'And what about you, Philippa? Have you heard from your mother?'

My cheeks burn at the mention of my mother. Tears swarm into my eyes but I beat them back, biting my lip. Miss Parry might have the body of a weak and feeble woman but she has the heart and stomach of a librarian and there is no way I am going to let the side down by crying.

'She's in Canada, Miss Parry. She's going to send for me when she has a bigger place.'

'I see,' she says, like she can indeed see all the way over the Atlantic Ocean. 'And are you happy living in that sweet shop of yours?'

No-one has actually asked this question of me before so I take a few deep breaths to consider the state of my happiness. And yes, I have to say, I am happy. Happy enough.

'Yes, Miss Parry.'

She laughs then. A surprisingly girlish laugh and offers another Rich Tea. 'Watch the crumbs or we'll be in trouble.' She winks at me.

Ten minutes later I am back in class squashed next to Christopher Bennett on the carpet as we learn about high and low sounds. I listen to the voices around me. You can tell a lot about someone from the sound of their voice. A mother's voice should be as sweet and comforting as raspberry jam. I can't clearly remember my mother's voice — only the occasional echo that I catch on waking up in the early morning, the same way I hear the gulls call or the waves break on the red sand of my town: you have to really listen to hear it. Wink has a voice that sounds like she must've been a sword swallower at some point in her long and varied career. Bob has a hesitant voice — a cough in the middle of a sentence, a subordinate clause, a get-out clause. Mandy Denning has a high voice like a baby bird. Christopher Bennett has the low gritty voice of a northern comedian on *Opportunity Knocks*. But Miss Parry has the perfect voice, quiet and forceful and full of knowledge and tragedy. I try to recall her parting words to me outside the classroom door, where I had to leave her behind in order to go and sit cross-legged on the carpet and endure the tumult of a badly-orchestrated music lesson. Her words: 'I only come into school a few hours a week, you know. To keep things in check or there'd be anarchy. Come and see me in the town centre library. That's where I do my proper job. It's about time you joined up and got your own library tickets.'

And then I remember Mother taking me there before I started school. When she felt educationally inclined. I remember Susan and Peter and Pat the dog who entered my literary world long before Thing One and Thing Two. But I can't remember if I was ever a member or where my library tickets could possibly be. In a secret corner? In the bin? Over the ocean in a small condominium (flat) in Toronto, tucked up all forgotten about in my mother's never-quite-empty purse?

So that's what I do after school, while all the other children queue up on the corner for Mr Whippy ice cream. Patty minds the shop while I drag Bob down town with me and we both join the library. I am beside myself with excitement to see so many books in one place and now I have the key to reading them all. And if I turn it, I might be able to make sense of my life. I might be able to work out how to get my mother back.

2006

Fran is back, a sheepish look on her rosy face because she's the one who phoned him. Is she really allowed to do that? For all she knows, he could be a violent man. Not just an idiot.

'He came,' I tell her.

'Did he?' she says, surprised. 'I didn't think he would. I mean, it sounded like he wanted to give you some space.'

'The Pacific Ocean wouldn't be enough space.'

'Oh?' Fran says. 'What's happened now? I thought the baby would bring a truce.'

'Nothing happened. I didn't see him. We didn't see him. I just told him to go. Well, the nurse told him to go. I wanted to spit in his face.'

'Oh,' she said again. 'Maybe tomorrow then.' And she looks at you lying there asleep in your crib. 'You *should* let him see the baby.'

'Why?'

'He's the father.'

'Maybe.'

'What do you mean, maybe?'

'I mean, maybe I will. But not yet. Not till I've

sorted this feeding out. I can't face him right now. I just can't.'

And for once she's beaten and says no more. But not for long, knowing Fran.

8

1975

Come Dancing

I am ten-years-old and, seeing as Helena is still adrift on another continent, it is left to Bob to celebrate the survival of my first decade, which he does in Bob-style by giving me the present I most crave (a pogo stick) and hosting a thrown-together party for me at the shop.

My circle of friends has remained pretty much the same and they are all invited. They arrive bearing gifts of talcum powder and Avon soap-on-a-rope, dressed head-to-toe like Agnetha and Frida. Here we are dancing to the Bay City Rollers in the living room. Bob hands out limeade and Twiglets, while Wink hogs the armchair over in the corner, knitting a wonky jumper, waiting for *Jim'll Fix It* to come on. (She's taken to watching our telly on a Saturday evening as we have colour and it is worth the trek up our stairs to see her two-dimensional heroes in their full glory.)

The closest I have to a best friend is Cheryl who moved down from Solihull the summer before. She brought me some cherry flavour lip gloss which we apply extravagantly in the bathroom every ten minutes.

'So how come your mum's not here?' she asks, during one such application. 'Is she still away?'

For although Cheryl is the girl I feel closest to, I don't feel close enough to tell her about Helena's disappearing act. Or the fact that I've only had five letters in three years. So I've told her that my mother had to go away to care for a sick relative in Canada. It's easier that way.

'Yes, I say. She's still away.'

Cheryl is nice because she never pushes any further than I want her to and she smells of Parma Violets. And because she asks me round to her house once a week for tea where we have normal family suppers of goulash around the dining room table with her younger brother Darryl and her mum and dad. Her dad is normal and tousles my hair in a non-annoying way and has an accent like Bernie's. Somehow this makes me warm to Bernie so he and Auntie Sheila have also been invited to my party.

Auntie Sheila has drunk one too many gin and oranges and when Cheryl and I make our way back into the fray, we witness her pulling Bob onto the makeshift dance floor (the slightly-tacky Axminster carpet) for a smooch to David Essex. Bernie breathes heavily on the sofa, his face slowly turning the colour of Sheila's smudged red lipstick. As his wife wraps her arms around Bob's girth a little too tightly, Bernie struggles to his feet and cuts in. Only Sheila won't have it.

'Leave me alone,' she slurs.

Bob immediately lets go of his dancing partner, throwing his hands up in the air as if this were a stick-up.

'You've had enough, Sheila,' Bernie announces in an authoritative manner so that Wink looks up from her knitting and the circle of friends stop dancing to David.

'Yes, Bernie, you're right,' Auntie Sheila says, surprisingly. 'I have had enough. Enough of this marriage. I'm in love with Bob and I want a divorce.'

I haven't thought about divorce in a long time but suddenly I remember a short man in a smart suit, with dark eyes and long fingers that fluttered over the keys of Lucas' piano. Surely Auntie Sheila doesn't mean it? And I have this longing for Toni to come back from London (where she's finished with ballet and taken up tea-making in an estate agents in Hampstead). I even think sympathetically towards Terry for one brief moment until I remember he's never had a kind word or deed for me. Where are they now? They should be here, doing something to save their parents' marriage.

I am slightly mortified as my fragile circle is staring open-mouthed at the *Play for Today* unravelling in front of them. Will their parents ever let them come here again?

Meanwhile Bob has gone green and sickly-looking like the time we caught the Dartmouth ferry. He didn't anticipate this turn of events when he heard David Essex crooning (appropriately) *Hold Me Close* only a few minutes before. Bernie looks like he might be about to embark on his second heart attack and I consider dialling 999 and asking for an ambulance quick smart.

Wink, on the other hand, is more concerned

that *Jim'll Fix It* is about to start.

'Take it somewhere else,' she barks, echoing earlier days of being a barmaid in Catford. And with that, someone switches off the record player and people scatter from the room to different parts of the maisonette.

'This is what I call a party,' says Cheryl, downing the last of her limeade and instantly deepening our friendship. A friendship I hope will carry me through my teenage years. I am going to need it.

★   ★   ★

That night, lying in bed, I have lots of scenes to replay in my head. Lots of possible repercussions to think about. I feel I am on the cusp of the next stage of my life. Maybe Bob will marry Auntie Sheila thereby making Toni some kind of step-sister. Maybe Bernie's heart will finally get the better of him. Or maybe he'll give his heart a second chance and lose some weight (weight that he's piled on since giving up the fags and booze and women). Maybe Bernie and Sheila will make a concerted effort to reach their silver wedding anniversary. Maybe Wink will learn some manners. Maybe I will become the most popular girl at school, renowned for throwing the best parties. Maybe I will find my own happy family, a normal family like Cheryl's (though I could do without the younger brother). Or maybe, just maybe, despite the smallness of her condominium (flat) or the unwillingness of Orville Tupper, Helena will reclaim me. (I've given up

106

hope that my father will ever learn to read a map.)

In fact this is the last we see of Auntie Sheila for quite some time. She no longer calls in at the shop. Bob seems quite relieved at this outcome — as does Patty who's never got used to having Sheila's beady eye on her. I miss Auntie Sheila. But I have Bob and Wink and Patty.

Patty has a boyfriend called Lugsy. He is very handsome despite his big ears. Fortunately for him he's grown his hair long, like every young man in Torquay and on *Top of the Pops*, so that his legendary ears are almost hidden and only a gust of wind reminds people why he collected his nickname.

Lugsy is the type of boyfriend I would like but I am only ten and boyfriends are a long way off. All the boys I know my age are only interested in Kevin Keegan and Choppers. I much prefer my pogo stick because I can stay in the backyard with it and keep away from the holiday-makers who are currently clogging up the Bay. Cheryl and I steer clear of the boys in our class, though this isn't always possible as Christopher Bennett occasionally comes into the shop to buy cigarettes for his mum. He's lost the green crust from his nostrils but there is still something distasteful about him. Possibly the ridiculous hairstyle he's recently acquired thanks to his mum's Carmen rollers.

Lugsy has a motorbike and he picks up Patty

from work everyday. Wink says they are living in Sin. I have no idea where that is, somewhere in Paignton maybe, but she sounds disapproving when she says this. Surely Paignton isn't that bad? And why Wink should disapprove of anyone with her colourful past is beyond me.

Now it is the summer holidays, Bob and Patty are so busy that even Lugsy comes in to roll up his (cheesecloth) sleeves and lend a helping (nicotine-stained) hand. Lugsy is probably Bob's only male friend in the world and, when there is a lull in the quest for *Herald Expresses*, they go out the back to smoke roll-ups together even though Bob doesn't officially smoke.

I usually hang around the shop doing word searches or practising my pogo-ing in the yard while I wait for Cheryl's mum to drop her off. We spend every day of the holidays together. Neither of us go away because when you live in a seaside resort you tend to stay put all year round. Especially if you have a shop that does its best business in the season.

So we go to the pool at the Rainbow Hotel or down to the shops to look for cheap clothes. Or we make our way over to Cheryl's for a Soda Stream and a game of Swingball. Now I have Cheryl, Lucas seems a long way off. A little boy from a fairy tale. A speck of stardust.

★   ★   ★

The long days of summer are finally over and Patty takes me to BHS to kit me out with new school uniform. I've had a growth spurt, mainly upwards. No sign of the old puppy fat (hurrah!) or of a reason to buy a bra (boo!).

I am to be a fourth year junior, the oldest in our school. Bob fills my new Adidas bag with his finest stationery and waves me off on a warm September morning.

Our new teacher, Miss Mills, is the most on-the-ball we've ever had. She is actually a friend of Miss (Mrs) Parry and she might well have ruled Scotland in a former life, beating the English at Bannockburn on her way. She tells us this is the most important year of our lives so far (oh dear). In a few weeks we will sit the Eleven plus (which is a bit unfair as I am still only ten). Those who pass will go up to the Grammar. Those who fail . . . well, they will have to go down to the Secondary Modern which isn't as modern as it sounds but is definitely secondary to the Grammar. One short exam that will divide our class forever into winners and losers, high achievers and drop-outs.

What if Cheryl passes and I fail? Cheryl is clever and comes from a family with educational aspirations. Cheryl's mum and dad met at university. Cheryl's mum has a part time job, teaching French at evening classes. Bob wants me to do well because he did so badly at school but he doesn't really know how to ensure I'll pass. He just reminds me to do my homework and pins up the times tables in the outside loo which has by now been done up so it is useable and no longer the forbidden place it was in Helena's time.

Now it is becoming more and more clear that

that was a different time entirely. A time when I had a mother who loved me.

* * *

The big morning comes and Bob makes me a Full English breakfast and sends me off with a packet of Dextrose so I am high on sugar and fat. Fortunately these dietary excesses get me through the verbal and non-verbal reasoning and even the maths. So it is a huge relief and the proudest moment of my life when I discover sometime later, once Christmas has come and gone, that I have passed. And so too has Cheryl.

The circle of friends will disintegrate by the end of the year which is no great surprise when you think of it. But there are two shocks to come out of all this: Mandy Denning, of the doll hands and clicking eyelashes, has failed. And, more extraordinarily, Christopher Bennett is to be a Grammar School Boy. It seems that all that surplus energy he harboured was a result of being bored and he has in actual fact a very high IQ. Who would have thought it of the Bogey Boy? He becomes more unbearable than ever, snatching all the credit for his academic achievement when really he has Miss Mills to thank for discovering and nurturing his talents when all her predecessors wrote him off as a naughty boy (which he still is, deep down, as far as I am concerned).

But I am Clever Philippa. Grammar School Philippa. I am going places. One day I will leave Torquay to seek my fortune. I will go to London.

110

I will fly across the ocean and track down Helena and release her from the clutches of Orville Tupper. I will enlist the help of the British High Commissioner if I have to. I will get her back. Because now I have power at my fingertips. I have knowledge in my heart and in my brain. I have the whole wide world at my feet.

2006

Power and Knowledge have both run off and deserted me. I have to trust those who are here. Fran and the doctor.

The doctor comes and checks you over, though she can't possibly have years of medical training; she looks like a sixth former on a careers day out. But she has a proficient pair of hands and you are a floppy doll in them. She looks at your eyes, listens to your heart, holds your little hand in hers as if she is reading your palm, telling your fortune.

It seems she is a little concerned. She would like to do a blood test. I can't really concentrate on what she's saying. I must be hearing things because there is nothing wrong with you. Nothing serious. My initial instincts that all was not as it should be was a little premature in a way that you were not. That was a gut reaction. A mother's worry. Looking at you now, I'd know if there was a real problem. You're just a slow feeder. A little pale. A sleepy baby. I probably should interrogate the doctor further (What are you doing this for? How? Why? etc, etc) but how can I be expected to focus on all her words when I'm so tired. So consumed.

You are not happy about this turn of events.

Neither am I for that matter. It wasn't quite what I had in mind when I first saw that little blue line in that little plastic window. I thought this was my chance to be what Helena wasn't. I didn't expect a nurse to be rubbing magic cream on your hand. I didn't expect the waiting around wondering what the hell is going on. Or the needle pricking your little vein. The drops of blood in a tube being sent down to the lab. I didn't expect to be dealing with this on my own. I didn't expect your father to be in love with Someone Else.

I will find out who she is. I will find out and I will kill her.

9

1977

Summertime Special

Two years later and I've only got as far as the Third Year, where I am conscientiously working my way up through the streams to try and join Cheryl at the very top. Unfortunately for me I've chosen a best friend who is cleverer than me (bringing back memories of my Lucas) and there are days, not so good days, when I wish I could shine above her — and everyone else for that matter.

Bob, in his own 1970s-man blundering way, understands something of my self-esteem issues and tells me that I am the best shop assistant he's ever had. But I can see through his weak attempt and know he is just being nice in a way that makes me want to both kiss and hit him at the same time (I am virtually a teenager, after all). It is quite obvious to anyone who steps inside our little shop that no-one comes close to Patty. Patty, who can weigh out sweets, do a stock take and make a cup of tea at the same time, whilst being able to sing the whole of the Top Twenty off by heart.

Punk Rock elbowed its way into the Top Twenty quite some time ago but it has only recently made it down to Torquay. Lugsy now sports a half-hearted snot-green Mohican which, with his renowned ears, makes him look like a gonk and riles Captain the parrot when Lugsy calls in with fish and chips for Wink. Captain thinks it is some kind of giant tropical bird come to take over his place at the helm of Wink's home. The Mohican doesn't last long as it is too high maintenance for someone who has to get up at the crack of dawn and deliver milk. It also scares too many old ladies and most of the neighbourhood dogs who, between them, cause a cacophony to rival the seagulls of a morning. The Dairy says he has to change his hairstyle or face the sack. So Lugsy gets a number one and becomes a skinhead instead.

Despite this fickleness, he sticks by Patty (he knows which side his bread is buttered) and saves up for a nice engagement ring which he presents to her on her 21st birthday at (where else?) the Berni Inn. Unfortunately for Lugsy, this doesn't go down too well with Patty who murmurs a firm No. So he has to make do with yet more living in sin. And of course now I am virtually a teenager, I know that Sin isn't a place but rather an action.

I have discovered one or two other sins:

1. Smoking: which I've always known a lot about, having lived in a tobacconists for much of my life and also clinging memories of Helena who always had a cigarette in hand. I don't know what all the fuss is about.

2. Drinking: I've raided Bob's drinks cabinet on a few occasions and found that Babycham is

the best he has to offer. All the others make my eyes water and my throat burn.

3. Boys: I know what boys and girls do but there is no way I am ever going to do it. (Bob delegated the little chat about the birds and the bees and the Curse to Wink, who took on the task with some relish — and far too much X-rated detail — thereby putting me off ever wanting to become a woman.)

Bob's love life and therefore sinfulness has taken a turn for the better (or worse, depending on which way you look at it). For two months he's been going out with a stationery rep from Newton Abbot called Linda who is a divorcee and mother of a young lad in the navy. Bob is smitten with her Farrah Fawcett hair and smart trouser suits. And she seems to have fallen for the Bob-smile that never quite worked on Helena.

If I were still a child I would already be thinking of bridesmaids dresses and resisting the urge to call Linda 'Mummy'. But now I am virtually a teenager, I have become a cynic. If even my own mother could fly thousands of miles to get away from me, why would someone with no blood ties want to take me on? So I keep Linda at arms' length. Bob on the other hand, tries to keep her as close as possible. I think he is quite possibly a sex maniac.

Despite my sometimes Ice Princess demeanour, Linda does make an effort. She even puts herself out to come and watch *The Generation Game* one Saturday. She convinces us to forgo our usual fish and chip supper and opt for a Chinese

116

takeaway meal. Wink is won over by the prawn balls. 'Why have you never got this before, Bob?' she asks, accusingly, oil glistening on her lips so I wonder if she's been at my cherry lip gloss.

But Linda's finest achievement is about to dawn when she suggests something that — no matter how many times we've thought, fantasised and dreamt about it — no-one has ever dared say out loud.

'You should apply for *The Generation Game*, Wink,' she says. Just like that.

It's as if Linda has whipped off all her clothes and done a cart-wheel across Wink's filthy rug for all we can do is stare at her, open-mouthed at this shock-horror advice. But really we are mortified at ourselves for never plucking up the courage to do what she has done.

Bob breaks the moment and says: 'Brilliant!'

I take his lead and murmur words to that effect. Only Wink sits quietly in her chair. For a few moments it's like all her Christmases have come at once and no-one loves Christmas as much as Wink because she can drink as much sherry as she wants and therefore it is the only time of the year she can sleep painlessly. But it is precisely because of this pain, because of her Multiple Sclerosis that she is sitting so quietly. For those few brief moments she is spinning plates, icing cakes and acting the buffoon in a farce while Bruce writes notes to himself in his little book. But then reality hits at her like a wet towel across the face.

'But I'm just a sick old woman. Why would they choose me?' She takes a gulp of brown ale.

117

'And I don't even have a son to make up a team. All I've got is this lousy old parrot.'

At this, Captain takes offence, his feathers visibly drooping.

But Linda strikes again: 'What about Bob? Bob could do it. He could be your son.'

Wink looks at Bob, perched on the pouf, scooping up the remains of his radioactive sweet and sour with a prawn cracker.

'Bob?' she says, bewildered. But it isn't clear if her bewilderment stems from her inability to imagine Bob as her son or her inability to imagine him on her telly.

Meanwhile Bob splutters on his cracker and Linda has to bash him on the back.

'Well, I think it's got to be worth a try.'

Wink snorts at this latest from Linda.

But Linda has really got me excited (and it isn't just the effects of the heady monosodium glutamate). I can't let Wink pass up this opportunity. I know exactly how to win her round.

'Think of the conveyor belt, Wink,' I say. 'Close your eyes and think of the electric blankets, the sets of knives, the Thermos flasks. Think of it, Wink. Think!'

And Wink does. She shuts her eyes and she thinks of all the wonderful electric goods and new-fangled household gadgets passing before her eyes. She thinks of Bruce urging her on. The audience shouting out items. The pile of luxury goods that she'll bring home to her stinky house in Torquay. The chance of a lifetime.

118

'Go on then, Bob,' she says. 'Let's do it. Let's write to the BBC.'

A wave of near-euphoria passes round the room, drenching us in Wink's sudden enthusiasm. But the tide soon goes out. 'They'll probably turn us down anyway,' she says.

But nothing can dampen Bob's ardour for the lady in his life. He smiles at Linda and she smiles back at him (a little smugly, it has to be said). Then he takes her hand lovingly in his own before addressing the room.

'They probably will turn us down, Wink,' he says. 'But nothing ventured . . . '

$\star$ $\star$ $\star$

Unfortunately a few Saturdays later, the unimaginable happens: it is Bruce's last show and Wink is devastated. We all rally round and try to make the best of it. We are back to our usual cod and chips, but Bob splashes out on some mushy peas and pickled eggs. Then, as the tears roll down Wink's cheeks at the final conveyor belt, and spurred on by Linda's bolshiness (though of course these days it would be seen as assertiveness), Bob makes his own suggestion. All year the country has been building up to a certain day: June 7th, when all of us British subjects are expected to celebrate our Majesty's silver jubilee. She's been Queen for twenty-five years and, according to Bob, she is doing a bloody good job — despite a wave of general unrest gathering on the horizon.

Bob is a surprisingly keen monarchist. If he

119

was smarter and more dashing he could been mistaken for Tim Brook-Taylor on *The Goodies* because he stands to attention whenever he hears the National Anthem and even knows all five verses of it. There is a Union Jack in the outside toilet, a collection of coronation cups hanging from hooks on a high shelf in the kitchenette and, somewhere in the depths of the sideboard, a jigsaw puzzle of Henry VIII and his six wives (definitely a sex maniac). One of the strangest things Bob once said to me, in the months following Helena's departure, was: 'At least she chose Canada, part of the Empire, I mean, Commonwealth.' I had no idea what he was going on about at the time, but in all the current royal furore, I can see what he was trying to say, in his own Bob-way.

And right now, Bob is trying to take Wink's mind off the end of an era and the crushing of her hopes to be on Bruce's show. A party to end all parties might just do that.

★　★　★

Fortunately for Bob — and the rest of the street — Linda takes it upon herself to do the bulk of the organisation, enlisting Patty's help. Bob and Lugsy lend their (relative) muscle when required but it is quite clear that their respective girlfriends have it all under control.

They organise raffles, coffee mornings, bring and buy sales in order to scrape enough money together to make her Majesty proud and to give the residents of our street a day to remember.

120

There is party food to be made, trestle tables to be borrowed, bunting to be hung. There is a bonnet competition, a tug of war, a beautiful baby contest and a talent show to be organised. But most of all what we need is sunshine and sunshine is what we get.

It is evident from the moment the seagulls wake us that it is going to be a scorcher. We have to be up bright and early to help cleanse the street of dog dirt and fag ends. I am part of the cleaning brigade, led by Lugsy who is used to early starts.

'Not glamorous, I know, Philippa,' Linda says, 'but essential. Without the cleaning team this party would be a disaster. Can you imagine the tug of war taking place on a road full of seagull splats and last night's grockle vomit?'

Linda can be disparaging of the tourists that the locals call 'grockles'. She conveniently forgets that the town relies on them. But, no, I don't want to imagine this scenario and so, in an effort to please her Majesty (and Linda), I put in some elbow grease. Linda eventually passes our efforts before moving us on to the next task: blowing up red, white and blue balloons. This takes some time. Just as I am about to pass out, we use up all of Bob's extensive stock and, finally, I am excused from further duties so that I can add the finishing touches to my jubilee bonnet. This is one competition where I am determined to shine.

I've been working on my bonnet for weeks. The basis of my bonnet is an old boater of Auntie Nina's that she left behind in her hurry to leave Torquay. I've kept it all these years in the bottom of my wardrobe, for dressing up. I don't dress up anymore as I am far too old for such childish malarkey. But I can't bring myself to chuck it out because of the memories of Lucas that ripple through me whenever I look at it (and because I never tidy the bottom of my wardrobe).

The colour scheme has been easy to choose: red, white and blue, obviously. But finding a novel way of displaying these colours has taken some thinking. I've thought about it a lot. And then it comes to me, one night staring at the pattern in the curtains (that I've decided looks like a Cavalier, quite possibly Charles I — which reminds me of a painting I've seen in an art book in the library called *And when did you last see your father?* A question I often ask myself.). It comes to me: Winning the bonnet competition rests on the judges. And who are the judges? Mainly old ladies from the street. And what do old ladies like? Flowers, of course.

A few weeks earlier, I asked Wink to help me out. Being an old lady, (but unfortunately not a bonnet-judge as she's already accepted the honour of tug of war adjudicator) she has a whole stash of fake flowers and has given me free rein to select the best. 'I never go out now, duck,' she says, with a faraway look in her eye. 'The only airing they get is funerals.' That puts a dampener on things as we both remember the black and white church and the little coffin and Wink with her gammy leg out in the aisle.

122

'If I could win first prize,' I muse, 'that would be something.'

'Yes,' she says. 'It blinking well would.'

After the marathon cleaning operation and balloon blowing effort, I nip down to the florists with a pound note that Linda has given me for doing such a proper job and buy a bunch of cornflowers, several sprigs of gypsophila and a single red rose. I carefully walk home with them, the scent making my nose twitch, the cellophane crackling with excitement. Forget the Queen, this is going to be my day. I will be holding the coveted fiver in my hand in a few hours if I pull this off.

In my room, I sit back and admire my efforts so far: the silk and paper flowers arranged delicately around the rim of the boater and across the top. The neatly tied (red, white and blue) ribbons. The selection of sequins to add that bit of sparkle (it is a celebration after all). Now all I have to do is attach the fresh flowers as best I can and then, in the middle of the boater, sticking out the top, place a Union Jack from a set of Bob's paper sandcastle flags.

There. This is it. Not only will it appeal to old ladies but it also smells nice. A multi-sensory bonnet that is sure to win me that fiver and do her Majesty (and Bob and Wink) proud.

I should've known by now that things never turn out the way you plan them.

All day long I look forward to the bonnet parade. It is hot and sweaty in the tank top that Wink has knitted me from a pattern in *Woman's Realm*. (Red, white and blue again, but with the added motif of a row of crowns around the bottom.) I have to sit through the knobbly knees of the street. Lugsy's are surprisingly knobbly but not as knobbly as Mr Taylor from number thirty-two whose wife is extremely proud of his accomplishment, brandishing the winning voucher for 'a Take-away for Two' donated by the Chinese as if it were a Golden Ticket for Willy Wonka's chocolate factory.

Then there is the beautiful baby competition. Let it be noted that babies are not especially beautiful when they scream which is what every last one of them does as the judge — the Catholic priest of all people — tickles them under the chin. What a noise! There are only four entries (and to my knowledge only one of them lives on our street) but there could be a whole midget-choir of them for the racket they're producing.

Once the mothers have ssshh-ed the babies and the runners-up sulk over the winner (a Benny Hill look-a-like), it is time for the Bonnet Parade. A makeshift stage has been fashioned out of planks and milk crates 'on loan' from Lugsy's dairy. The contestants are told by Linda, who's been chained to a megaphone for most of the day, to line up on the catwalk. Straightaway I am at a disadvantage as I am squeezed, in a way that I haven't been for a long time, next to Christopher Bennett who completely over-shadows my creation with his own. Christopher Bennett has put even more effort and planning into his hat than I have into mine; his eyes have been on that five pound note for far longer. He will shine brighter and bigger and . . . shinier than I could ever hope to in a million years. Whatever was I thinking? He's got to the heart of the matter:

Q: What do old ladies like more than flowers?
A: The Queen. Her Majesty. HRH. Elizabeth II. That's who.

Christopher Bennett has engineered a bonnet Isambard Kingdom Brunel could only dream about. Christopher Bennett's construction is something else. It is at least two feet tall, like a chimney. But it isn't just the size that matters. It is the painstaking effort he's put into decorating it. Every last quarter of an inch is covered in photos or drawings of the Queen in her various ages. There is Baby Princess Elizabeth in her golden curls sitting on her mother's lap. Girl Princess Elizabeth with her little sister Princess Margaret toddling by her side. Bride Elizabeth with her groom, Prince Philip and the Coronation Elizabeth weighed down with her massive crown and orb and sceptre. There is Mother Elizabeth with her four children and there is Colourful Elizabeth in all her various hats and coats and handbags that she's coordinated over the years in a way that must have impressed even Helena over the Ocean who still shares the very same monarch as me. (Who even now, if she is awake, could be celebrating at her very own Canadian street party amongst the Mounties and raccoons, Orville Tupper on her arm, pouting at the little people around them.)

This Queen montage, manipulatively manu-factured by Christopher Bennett, earns respect from the three old lady judges who bestow the crisp five pound note on the Bogey Boy, who I know will put it to ill use on sneaky cigarettes and slot machines when he should really spend it on a jolly good barber.

It is a disaster. All my best laid plans squashed and flicked away like one of his greenies. But things are about to get even worse. Christopher Bennett talks to me.

'Hard luck, Smithy. Better luck next time . . . like, in twenty-five years, if the old bat lasts that long.'

Trust my luck for these traitorous mutterings to go undetected by any other witnesses. If Bob heard his Republican views, Christopher would be out of this street before you could whistle God Save the Queen (the traditional version, not the new one by that Punk Rocker band). He would be blackballed by the shop, never to return for a packet of fags 'for his mother' ever again.

And why can I never think of a witty put-down when I need one?

'Oh, get lost, Bogey Boy,' is what I eventually come up with.

He laughs and shoots one out of his left nostril across the pavement in a way that I can't help but admire. The boy is a pro, it has to be said, if a little uncouth.

'Fancy a bag of chips, then, Smithy, or what?'

And before I can stop myself, and because Cheryl has gone back to Solihull for the week and there is no-one else of my age to moan to about the grown-ups, I say, 'all right then, go on.'

And on things go, queuing up at the Jolly Roger Fish Bar, a roaring trade, despite the jubilations and the abundance of sausage rolls and scotch eggs to be had on every other street in Torquay. Too much salt and vinegar giving me a thirst so I don't mind having a swig out of Christopher's hip flask, his mum's Pomagne with all the fizz gone so it tastes like one of Bob's pear drops (oh-Bob-if-you-could-see-me-now).

Another swig and another swig and suddenly we are in the Bone Yard, near the big angel, two rows down from Albert Morris. And Christopher Bennett decides now is the time and place to try it on with me. One rancid kiss later and Philippa Smith wallops him across his curly bonce and then legs it as fast as possible down and up the once-so-familiar rows until she can no longer hear his curses. Until she finds herself face to face with her old friend, her best friend, her Lucas.

Lucas.

It has been a long time. Long enough to make me feel guilty when I remember his letter to me:

Please keep on telling me.

*   *   *

I haven't kept on telling him. I used to come every day at first. Then maybe twice a week. Then it dwindled to once in a while. I stopped keeping on telling him because it felt like he wasn't there anymore. Like he was off somewhere else, Heaven most probably. And now it has been too long. It isn't like I haven't

127

thought about him. I think about him all the time. I think about him more than I think about Helena. Because he never wanted to leave me. He never chose to leave me. He just went. 'Life's unfair,' Wink likes to tell me. That's why Lucas went. But her philosophy doesn't explain Helena's departure. It didn't just happen. Helena *meant* to go. She caught a plane and she flew across the ocean to a country of ice and snow and mountains and giant crashing waterfalls. And I am still waiting for her to find that big condominium (flat) with the extra bedroom for me, Philippa, her daughter.

And, yet again, for the second time in a day, I can't think of suitable words to say so I simply whisper: 'I'm sorry, Lucas.'

But I do have something for him. Something that every school child has been given. Something that has been burning a hole in my pocket ever since I received it, knowing that Lucas would've appreciated it far more than I ever would: a jubilee commemorative coin.

I search for a stick and start digging a hole. Only a small one as I don't want to be accused of grave-robbing (though in actual fact this is more like grave-giving). Only a little hole at the base of his headstone, big enough to bury the coin.

'There you go, Lucas. I haven't forgotten you.'

* * *

Night isn't far off now though it is still just about light in the Bone Yard despite the bell recently

128

tolling nine times. The party sounds like it is in full throw and is set to go on indefinitely — which it can thanks to Linda's organisation of coloured outdoor bulbs that hang back and forth across the street, like the ones along the seafront.

Lucas and I have had a heart-to-heart. He quite obviously doesn't approve of my snog with Christopher Bennett or my first over-indulgence of alcohol. If Lucas were here he would also be a Grammar Boy, but he would shine above the likes of Christopher Bennett. He would be the proud owner of that crisp five pound note. He would be a responsible citizen. A studious student. A rock for me to lean on. But he isn't here. He is a headstone. A memory. A speck of stardust.

The music has stopped. The Bone Yard is in darkness. I'm not scared. It is a safe place. All the people here are dead. I'm not scared of the dead. It is the living that does all the hurting. (This is some years before Michael Jackson's *Thriller* and the possibility of zombies.)

I make a bed for myself, a nest, curled up like Andy, next to Lucas in the uncut grass. The smell of soil and dry leaves. An owl tooting in a tree nearby. I could stay here all night. I am so tired, I can't move. When I do move, my head hurts, the cells fizzing from alco-pear-drops.

'Goodnight, Lucas.'

★   ★   ★

Much later. A bright light in my face. Is it Heaven? Will I see Lucas dressed up to the nines in his white robe, his feather wings folded neatly behind him, his halo polished and gleaming?

''Ello, 'ello, what've we got here, then?'

Oh dear. It is like an episode of *Dixon of Dock Green*, a kindly officer of the law, trying to ascertain if I have a home to go to.

'Yes,' I tell him, politely. 'I live at Bob's News.'

'Ah,' he says, bending in a plié Toni would be proud of, his whiskered face inches from my own. 'You'd be Bob's daughter, then.'

'Yes, sir, that's me,' I say. 'Bob's daughter.'

Well, you shouldn't argue with a man in uniform.

★　★　★

Later, in my own bed, my warm, dry, comfy bed, I know I'll never get to sleep. The tiredness — and the after-effects of the Pomagne — evaporated the moment that torch beamed in my face. And now the Cavalier is laughing at me in the way that Cavaliers do — haughty, flouncy and not really laughing at all. I am an idiot. I had my first kiss with Christopher Bennett and then fell asleep at the grave of the boy who should've had that honour.

Still, the Queen must be proud of her subjects. She's had a whole lot of riotous, jubilant behaviour going on up and down her land, all over the kingdom, and far across the oceans, from Botswana to Jamaica, from Australia to Canada, all in the name of her twenty-five years as our Queen. I'm not so sure what she'd make of my own conduct.

Bob isn't too impressed. He's had the whole street out looking for me once they'd packed up and swept up and realised I was nowhere to be seen. But he doesn't show it. He just says a quiet thank you to the policeman and gives me a hug. As he holds me in his arms I pray he can't smell anything illicit clinging to my woolly tank top or my hedge-backwards hair.

I can smell something on him though. He reeks. Not of cider or bitter or Pina Coladas. But of desperation and . . . yes, something else, something much stronger: Love.

Bob is my father. Bob loves me.

★　★　★

Summer comes and goes as do the grockles and the hosepipe bans. It has been a time of bright celebration for our Queen, the last days of loyalty and innocence, only dimmed by the advent of the Sex Pistols banging on about a fascist regime. But on August 16th the Queen is eclipsed by the passing of the King. Elvis is dead. Half of Torquay is thrown into despair. There are tributes everywhere; his songs on the radio in every shop you go into; his white cat suit and big sunglasses on the telly every time you switch it on. The other half of Torquay are less bothered. They spend their Saturday nights down the town in the new discotheques that have sprung up with glitter balls and lit-up dance floors. There is a new king on the block: John Travolta, King of the Disco. Times, they are a-changing.

Well, they are certainly going to in our neck of

131

the woods. It appears that Bob and Wink were wrong to be pessimistic on that Saturday evening over the prawn balls; the BBC didn't turn them down. It has taken a while but sometime the following year, a letter arrives from a research assistant, inviting Wink and her son to come to London for an audition. Apparently it isn't the end of *The Generation Game*. There is to be a new host, Larry Grayson and a new assistant, Isla St Clair. Bob has to find a new suit, a new name, and a whole new persona if he is to have his fifteen minutes of Fame and if Wink is to have her cuddly toy.

2006

I thought Adrian/Daddy would venture back again today but he hasn't bothered. And your grandmother hasn't bothered to come either. Not Helena. She is still unaware that she is now a granny (ha!). No, your other grandmother. Adrian's mother. The old mother-in-law-hippopotamus-dragon. So we'll have to make do with our own company. For now. Until I get up the nerve to call for reinforcements.

Right now I could do with an ice cream. Yes, an ice cream. Not your Häagen-Dazs or your Ben and Jerry's, but a proper Devon cornet with a dollop of clotted cream and a flake perched on the top. Or a Mr Whippy from the van on the front. Greensleeves and Mind That Child. Being pushed around the harbour in my Silver Cross chariot, watching my windmill spin, the seagulls dive-bombing the pensioners, Helena above me, strutting with that pout, that tilt, those heels, those beautiful eyes fixed on the horizon, across the bay and over the seas.

Helena. Grandmother, Grandma, Granny, Gran, Nanny, Nana, Nan.

She should be here.

10

1978

Gladiators

Times they are indeed a-changing. It isn't just the cultural manifestations of the Punk Rockers or of the Discotheques; the Winter of Discontent is beckoning. But despite the prospect of overflowing dustbins and funeral parlours, it is an exciting winter as far as I am concerned. Bob and Wink by some fluke of Fate have wangled their way through the audition and so we are completely absorbed with preparations for the forthcoming game show. What little spare time is left over is spent playing with matches during the frequent power cuts. (Bob could well have been an arsonist in a former life, perhaps Guy Fawkes or the French chap who built the funeral pyre for Joan of Arc. I've seen the film with Ingrid Bergman and it doesn't make happy viewing.)

Our preparations mainly involve testing Wink's memory which is probably the part of her that works the best. 'Things can always be improved,' she says, eyeing up Bob's hairline. Every day after school I set up a tea tray with twenty small items borrowed from the shop for her failing eyes to scan briefly before covering it over with one of her (rather grey) tea towels. Then she has to reel off the items she can remember ('a pencil sharpener! a packet of Rizlas!'). She is becoming proficient and we are all confident that if she gets to the fabled conveyor belt we'll be coming home with a car load. The problem is getting her to this coveted position. She's been struggling to walk lately and pooh-poohs the idea of a wheel chair. How will she manage plate-spinning or other such dexterous activities?

'I'll smash all the plates,' Wink complains.

'That's the whole point,' Linda says. (Linda is cynically post-modern before her time.)

Most of the neighbourhood know about Bob and Wink's impending rise to stardom and every last one of its residents, it seems, is keen to be involved in their training. Mr Taylor (of the first class knobbly knees) has a part-time job as a pottery teacher at the technical college where he has access to a wheel. He offers to take Wink there for a spin. She comes back beaming, showing off her creation to anyone she comes into contact with. It looks like some kind of nuclear meltdown but it is a priceless work of art as far as Wink is concerned and takes pride of place over the gas fire in her front room.

Miss Goddard from number nine does amateur dramatics and teaches Bob and Wink about voice projection — not that Wink needs any encouragement but Bob's cough-voice certainly requires attention. They disappear inside the murky depths of Miss Goddard's house — unchanged since the war — and spend an afternoon reciting Kipling and Longfellow.

'Bugger Hiawatha,' Wink says, on her return

home. 'Give me Pam Ayres any day.'

Then there is Christopher Bennett. Christopher Bennett has a secret talent that he's been hiding under his big mop of hair and from the likes of me. Christopher Bennett can ballroom dance! When Wink gleans this information from Christopher's gran who lets it slip at the bingo, she grabs hold of him and will not let go until he promises to impart some of his skill to her. You'd think that Wink could already do her Ginger Rogers bit, being a member of the generation that frequented tea dances and the like. But she can't. She has two (not very useful) left feet and is unable to tell the difference between a foxtrot and a quickstep.

Christopher agrees to help out but at a cost. He won't charge for his tutoring but he knows how to get what he wants. Christopher is now thirteen and legally allowed to earn some money. To my indignation he manages to manipulate Bob into offering him a job as a paperboy. I've wanted this job for myself but unfortunately I won't officially be a teenager until the summer. Christopher is a good actor and can be pleasant when he wants to be so I shouldn't blame Bob for his gullibility though, it has to be said, this is probably his worst character defect. I toy with the idea of informing Bob of his new recruit's Republican tendencies but I opt to keep quiet as he might delve into the how's and why's of my knowledge of this. I don't particularly want to be reminded of that evening. However, it means I have to keep out of the way in the early mornings in case I come into Christopher's stratosphere. I don't really mind. Now I am virtually a teenager, I love my bed and can spend whole days at a time in it, wrapped up inside my new continental quilt that Wink ordered me from one of Bob's *Sunday Telegraph* colour supplements. 'Seeing as you've got no-one to make up your bed for you.' (She means well).

So between Mr Taylor, Miss Goddard and Christopher Bennett, Wink and her new son, Bob, are as ready as they'll ever be.

$$\star \quad \star \quad \star$$

One chilly November day, the long-awaited trip to BBC Television Centre is at last about to commence. The hotel has been booked, our bags packed, a London A to Z purchased, and Bob's new suit pressed. Linda and I will make up the entourage and the four of us set off at the crack of dawn in Linda's Austin Maxi. She's been delegated to drive as Bob's nerves are in shreds and he would be a hazard on the M4, besides the fact that his Ford Cortina is on its last legs. Linda, being a stationery rep and a former stock car racing enthusiast, grasps every opportunity to put her Highway Code to the test. She is especially keen to tackle the legendary North Circular (for which we will have to make a slight detour), as she's heard all about its challenging obstacles and hurdles from fellow reps. Linda is all for challenging obstacles and hurdles and puts me in mind of her namesake, Lynda Carter a.k.a. Wonder Woman.

After a hearty and heart-stopping breakfast at

137

the Gordano services outside Bristol, we pass the smoke clouds and metal monsters of Avonmouth, the Severn Bridge in the distance, the aircraft hangars at Filton, and head down the M4. I haven't been to London since I left it twelve years ago with Helena, a small bundle in a yellow shawl.

London: a place that conjures up so many faces, so many associations, so much of my history that didn't happen in Devon. A mystical place of otherness, of family, of Helena, of Auntie Nina and Lucas, my grandparents, the Changing of the Guard, the Planetarium, Special Lists, the Queen, Bruce and Anthea, Larry and Isla.

★ ★ ★

It is hard to tell where London begins. The fields gradually disappear and the landscape takes on a different colour. No more red earth, no more sea, no more narrow lanes and high hedges, brambles hitting the car and deer peering at you through the trees. Instead we find ourselves driving past sprawls of towns and high rises, the traffic slowing as the roads begin to clog up with cars, people everywhere, shops and buses and noise and greyness. Presumably this is now London, though there is no welcoming sign anywhere to be seen like the one we have in Devon with the picture of the ship and the caption: WELCOME TO DEVON. TAKE A BREAK. TIREDNESS CAN KILL.

The streets are quite clearly not paved with

gold (obviously), but are instead scattered with rubbish (though nothing like the debris which we would be witnessing if we were to make this journey in a couple of months time with the bin men out on strike). But I am taken aback by the pockets of bleakness, the dirty buildings, the closed-down markets and soggy paper spilling across the pavements. I half expect to see Ralph McTell's old man wandering about with his worn-out shoes.

Despite this abundance of trash (as I like to think Helena would call it after all those years in North America), I am surprised to see so many trees and parks tangled throughout the city. So much green mixed in with the grey. Helena used to tell me about the park where she lived, where her nanny took her sometimes to feed the ducks. Dulwich Park with its famous rhododendrons and boating lake. Is that near here? It is hard to imagine nannies wheeling babies past rhododendrons in Acton.

Linda is in her element. Bob is wielding the A to Z to no great effect but this isn't a problem for Linda who was possibly a cabbie in a former life because she manages to cut up the Granadas and the Capris and the Jags and the Mercs, moving in and out of lanes like she is on a slalom run. Her eyes dart between the road and her mirrors, her hands gripping the wheel so her knuckles are bony. She sings along to Radio One quite unashamedly, as if she were Patty (who's been left, with a little help from Lugsy, to run the shop and keep her vigilant eye on the paperboys who are all in love with her — none as much as the deluded Christopher Bennett).

Wink and I sit side by side in the back, contemplating all our other lives. The one Wink left behind when her husband died. The one I could have had if Helena hadn't decided to leave the capital and move to the sticks . . .

. . . I must've drifted off because suddenly the engine has stopped and we've been plunged into darkness. It takes me a few disorientated seconds to work out that we are in an underground car park belonging to the hotel.

'This is it,' Linda announces dramatically as if our whole lives have been building up to this moment — which is quite possibly true in Wink's case.

Bob hauls Wink out of the Maxi.

'Come on, Mother,' he says. 'Let's get you settled in.'

And the look she gives him is enough in itself to make the trip worthwhile. If she had her stick to hand she might well use it imaginatively.

★ ★ ★

The hotel compares favourably to the only hotel I am familiar with, the Rainbow in Torquay where Cheryl and I go swimming. In fact, as far as I am concerned, this hotel is a palace because we don't have to pay for it and because there is such a thing as a mini-bar in each of the inter-connecting bedrooms and also — the height of sophistication — an avocado bidet in the en-suite (I am already learning a whole host of new words) where Bob gives his feet a thorough wash with the doll-sized complimentary soap (that would be perfect for Mandy Denning).

Wink and I are to share a twin room, Bob and Linda a risqué double. Bob is spending a duplicitous couple of days, not only posing as Wink's son (well, son-in-law, it has been decided, as this avoids the problem of them not sharing a surname), but also as Linda's husband (which means she's had to change her surname temporarily, as she isn't as liberal as she likes to make out).

Once we've unpacked and freshened up, we make our way downstairs to the lobby where we meet the three other couples — and their entourages — taking part in the show. The other contestants all look really nervous. But not as nervous as Bob (who knows he is a fake son) or Wink (who knows she has to convince the powers that be that she is the picture of health and not likely to flake out on prime time television). Everyone makes rubbish small talk and laughs too much.

Then two researchers appear with their clipboards and trendy London clothes and whisk the couples off in order to run them through tomorrow's proceedings. The rest of us — a collection of sons and daughters, wives and mothers, brothers and lovers — are left, redundant and forsaken, to entertain ourselves.

'Sod it,' Linda mutters to me. 'Let's go out.'

I shrug because I'm not sure what she wants me to say to this, but that doesn't put Linda off as she is (ahead of her time once again) not for turning.

'We're in London, Philippa. Where do you want to go?'

'The Changing of the Guard?'

'We've missed it.'

'Madame Tussaud's?'

'Too late.'

'Alright, then . . . the Underground.'

'The Underground? Where to?'

'Nowhere. I just want to go on the Underground.'

The only public transport we have in Torquay is the odd bus, the train line to Exeter and the funicular railway down to Babbacombe beach so I know I shouldn't pass up this opportunity.

Before either of us wobble, we stride out into the fresh dusk and head for the nearest tube station. I am very excited by this excursion into the subterranean world of our capital city. I love the long, long wooden escalators and the smell of smoke and hot bodies. I love the posters and the buskers and the maps. I love the static crackle of the tracks in the moments before the train emerged like a worm from its hole. The whoosh of warm air that hits you in the face. The swish of the doors and the holding on for dear life to the hand straps, still warm from somebody else's hand. Somebody you might cross paths with at some other moment in time, and never even know it. (But that's London for you.)

'Have you had enough yet, Philippa?' Linda asks, after several stops. She is sitting next to a rather smelly tramp (possibly another one of

Ralph McTell's) and is relieved when I suggest we go back to the hotel for some tea.

'Supper,' Linda corrects me.

I decide Linda is quite possibly a snob.

★   ★   ★

The two trendy researchers have gone. The contestants are swapping their life stories in the dining room and hardly notice our arrival, except for Bob who gives me a diluted smile before turning his attention to Linda, squeezing her hand so tight she gives a little yelp.

'Nervous?' she whispers, bending down to kiss the top of his head, right on his (increasingly) bald spot.

'A little,' he lies.

Wink, on the other hand, is in her element, her nerves quite gone, a captive audience plus the prospect of meeting Larry the next day. She is telling them all how Larry has remained a man of the people despite his success. How he still likes to eat fish and chips out of the newspaper — he even keeps salt and vinegar in the glove compartment of his white Rolls. Looking at her, sitting there on the plush dining chair, far away from her whiffy terrace, you'd never know she was ill, she blends in so well with this new world. She is a chameleon. She could be anyone. She could be Bob's mother. She could be my grandmother.

★   ★   ★

Wink sleeps like a baby that night, not that babies snore quite so loudly to my knowledge — which is limited. You'd think she'd be restless but nothing keeps her awake. She'd sleep through the storming of the Bastille, most probably. Or a Black Sabbath concert. Bob, on the other hand, looks terrible the next morning at breakfast and rejects the bounteous buffet on display to feast on black coffee alone.

Bob is infected with a life-threatening fear that he will make an idiot of himself on television. He worries that his customers will come into the shop for ever after and remind him of his embarrassing moments. That Linda will see him in a new objective light and switch off his life support.

'Why on earth did you bloody agree to be on the show if you're so worried?' Wink asks, a little unsympathetically. 'It's not *Panorama*. It's meant to be embarrassing. We're meant to copy the professionals and get it arse-over-wotsit.' With that she swoops off in admirable fashion to get her hair done in the hotel salon.

Linda offers to give Bob a massage. This suggestion perks him up somewhat and they disappear, quick as you like, into the depths of the lift. I am left alone with a boy called Raymond from Preston. He is the same age and height as me, which puts him into a whole new category of boys as all my male contemporaries back home only come up to my chin. This spurs me on to a moment of recklessness.

'Do you want to come with me on the

Underground?' I ask.

'Alright,' Raymond says.

★　★　★

Raymond hasn't been on the Underground before, though he has seen the Changing of the Guard (and can also confirm that he didn't so much as change a light bulb).

Raymond is a boy of few words and those he does mumble are quite different to the ones I've grown up with. But we get by.

We only travel a few stops, then we come back again (is this all I am destined to do here?) and surface into the busy morning of Londoners going about their focused business. We go halves on a Coke from a news stand. Raymond is quite happy to share the bottle and doesn't even bother wiping the germs off the top — a strangely moving gesture, full of intimacy and awakening sexual tension.

'C'mon,' he says. 'Let's get back. Me mam'll be wondering where I am by now.'

Not only is he tall, he is considerate. Just my luck he lives hundreds of miles away, up north — and me, a West Country girl.

We make our way to the hotel, bumping and dodging the crowds, early Christmas shoppers, secretaries and businessmen, two provincial almost-teenagers holding their own in the big city.

'Your gran's alright,' he says as we turn the corner to the hotel. 'Your dad looks dead nervous though.'

145

'Yeah, he is,' I agree. 'What about your mum? Is she looking forward to the show?'

''Course. She loves Larry. Thinks he's the best thing ever. Wishes he were her dad, or summat.'

'Doesn't she have a dad?'

'Yeah.'

'Oh.'

And I picture this nameless, faceless dad/granddad and wonder why he isn't up to the mark. Why he isn't here. It has been a long time since I've wondered about my own dad, now I've commandeered my own Bob-one. But I do get a quick flash of him hacking his way through the Amazon jungle with a white shock of hair and a beard like Methuselah.

'What about your brother?'

'Robbie?'

'Is he worried about tomorrow?'

'Nah, nowt worries Robbie.'

I can believe this confident assertion. Robbie is much older than Raymond; he must be in his twenties, born when his mam was too young to be worrying about nappies. He swaggers around the hotel, eyeing up the receptionist and 'anything in a skirt,' according to Wink so I imagine being on the telly is the sort of thing he'll take in his stride (swagger).

'Robbie loves Isla. He reckons she's — '

But I don't get to hear what Isla is exactly, in Robbie's expert opinion, because a red double-decker — I don't even have time to make out the number — zooms past us at terrifyingly close quarters.

'Bugger,' says Raymond, using one of Wink's favourite words, which goes to show we do share the same language after all. 'That were close.'

★ ★ ★

We slip into the hotel before either his 'mam' or my 'dad' has even noticed we've gone. Bob is presumably still having his massage. Raymond's mam is propping up the bar along with her firstborn, Robbie, and the father/daughter combo from Littlehampton.

'Bugger,' says Raymond again. 'I don't think they should be doing that. Them researchers said they had to take it easy on the bevvies.'

Call me selfish, but I feel a certain something when I see the red faces of Raymond's family and the Littlehampton pair. At least my family will be sober.

This can only stand them in good stead when it comes to the recording later this evening. It is the couple from Inverness I am worried about. They are inscrutable.

★ ★ ★

The researchers are back in a different set of trendy clothes but with the same gusto. They are called Imogen and Amber, like characters from a Jilly Cooper novel, and both of them speak the way I remember Helena and Auntie Nina speaking. The way Helena would've made me speak if she'd stuck around to enhance my elocution. They encourage the contestants to

147

overcome their butterflies and eat a 'good lunch' from the buffet in the dining room. They don't practise what they preach, pecking at their sausage rolls like malnourished baby birds. Captain would have them for breakfast.

★ ★ ★

Two hours later Linda and I are sat in the studio audience listening to the warm-up act, an extremely tall man with bendy legs and an annoying way of talking. Still, he does the job and we are now completely ready to be a fantastic audience — though those of us who have a loved one as a contestant are also all of a quiver. My stomach is crying out for a share of the packet of Rennie in Bob's pocket, so I have no idea how he and Wink — my family — are feeling right now. They've spent this afternoon going through the schedule with Imogen and Amber and having make-up done (to Bob's shame). There have been no rehearsals because the show's success relies on spontaneity (or *humiliation* according to our cynical Linda).
Are they really ready for this?

There is a sudden change in the air. A wave of something or other, excitement most probably or the dispersing gas in Bob's dodgy stomach. Anyway, every one of us in the audience is sitting up, hands clasped to the seat or leaning forward in expectation. We are in the presence of a light entertaining legend: Larry Grayson.

Larry speaks to us in an unassuming way, as if he's just walked into Bob's News and asked for a quarter of sherbet pips. He talks about his imaginary friends Pop-it-in-Pete and Everard. We laugh and laugh because we are near hysteria at being in Larry's confidence. Even Linda can't help herself; she is now well and truly entranced by the world of Saturday Night Television.

Larry goes on to introduce the charming Isla St Clare. Though not in Anthea's league in the glamour stakes, Isla shines in her own wholesome, intelligent glow. Before they leave to prepare for the recording, Larry reminds us that we need to be a great audience so the people at home can enjoy the show even more when it is transmitted on Saturday night (maybe he knows there is trouble brewing here at the BBC and before long they'll be lucky to get any viewers at all). Not that we need any encouragement. As soon as the music starts, Linda and I go crazy, clapping till our hands hurt and whooping like wild things, (in a way that will be commonplace on the television of the future).

Then my heart does a double-take. I feel a surge of worry for my Bob-Sugar, out there in the limelight, supporting his mother-in-law, the pressure of performing, the full horror of being watched by millions — though not half as many as in a year's time when the Beeb's trouble will pass to the Dark Side where there'll be nothing but a blue screen with a white caption apologising for the lack of programmes.

149

But still. This is now. No going back. This is it . . .

. . . and it all passes in a dream-like, surreal-type, hazy-blur kind of thing. The next fifty-five minutes are condensed into but a fuzzy few moments . . .

And 3-2-1, action.
> *Cue opening number:*
> *Shut that door and en-joy The Generation Game*
> *What's in store? The best of relations*
> *Here's our aim.*
> *Larry Grayson is here to play so . . .*
> *Shut that door.*

Then . . . *Larry in his cream suit and brown tie, Isla in her dress (nothing flash like Anthea, more girl-next-door). Larry: Let's meet the eight who are going to generate. And there they are, paired up and perched on their chairs: the father/daughter combo from Littlehampton, Robbie and his mam from Preston, the Inscrutables from Inverness, Bob and Wink from Torquay. And soon it's . . . Round 1: Littlehampton v. Inscrutables in 'Ice that Cake'. The four contestants watch the professional at work, smoothing royal icing over a fruit cake with a perfect knife action and a flawless finish. Cue Robbie and his mam making a complete hash of it, Larry joining in, rolling his sleeves up and lending a helping hand and making even more of a pig's ear of it in the process, the audience*

150

beside themselves. Meanwhile the Inscrutables from Inverness are almost as good as the professional. Larry (covered in icing): What are the scores on the doors, Isla? Isla: The names in the frames are Robbie and Beryl 4, Jackie and Donald, 9. And then, Round 2: Name that Dog where the four contestants battle it out again. Robbie and his mam know almost nothing about dogs, whereas the Inscrutables must have been dog breeders in a former life. They have streaked into the lead, guaranteeing themselves a place in the final. Robbie and his mam shrug it off light-heartedly, they are on the telly and will live off this night down the pub for some years to come, and Raymond is relieved not to have to sit through yet more embarrassment. So now it's the father/daughter combo from Littlehampton v. Bob and Wink. Round 3: Yes, it's pottery-throwing. Wink is full of confidence, you can see the spark in her eye, though I suspect her confidence is ill-founded judging by the effort above her gas fire at home. Bob — in his smart new suit — looks like he's on the verge of fainting and Larry is doing his best to prop him up. The professional crafts the perfect pot and now the contestants are having a go, Larry joining in, getting covered in sludge-like clay, the audience shrieking. The father/daughter combo from Littlehampton make the usual lop-sided versions and the professional gives them each a respectable 6 out of 10. Bob's creation looks like a drunk has tried to copy the leaning tower of Pisa. As Larry looks at it from all angles the tower suddenly leans dangerously and then keels over in a way that Larry can infuse with maximum innuendo. To counterbalance this amazing lack of skill, Wink's creation is almost on a par with Clarice Cliff. It's as if she's been invested with special powers (maybe from mystic vibes generated from Wonder Woman sitting next to me, biting her nails). Wink scores a whopping 9 out of 10 and Bob, who could only realistically hope for a 4, earns an extra point for 'trying so hard'. Then, Round 4: Name the Famous Baby. Bob finds his niche. Being a newsagent he has seen virtually all of these photos before and those he hasn't, he makes accurate guesses at. They score full marks whilst the Littlehampton duo scores a dismal 5. Wink and her son-in-law are through to the final against the Inscrutables ... not a play but a dance; this is going to be tricky as Wink must surely be tiring by now. Luckily it's not a quick step but a slow tango, not with a partner but with a dummy. The Inscrutables perform the steps, demonstrated and judged by a celebrity from Come Dancing, in a perfectly good imitation, in time to the music but it has to be said with precision rather than passion. And it is this passion that carries Bob and Wink, carries them all the way, because it's certainly not their timing or their grace or any sense of balance as at one stage Bob falls over on top of his dummy to the delight of Larry and the hilarity of the audience who have a clear favourite — as does the judge who, spurred on by Larry, gives our Bob and Wink the higher mark. That's it. They've done it. They move, Wink and Bob, into position, one each side of Larry for the play-off, one question that will put the winner through, and of course the first to answer correctly is Wink, and it doesn't matter whether Bob let her win or not, though it seems unlikely as Wink has that killer look in her eyes compared to the terror in Bob's and so now there is one last hurdle to perform, one last dream to enact. We can't believe this is actually happening! We are waiting for the futuristic, sparkly doors to mechanically pull back to reveal our very own Wink sitting behind them like a cashier at the Co-op. Her chance of a lifetime. The conveyor belt starts up, Larry standing to one side announcing the luxury goods that seem to whizz past at breakneck speed. All too quickly the buzzer goes, the objects are out of sight and Wink is left, under the spotlight, her face perfectly calm. Larry: You have forty-five seconds starting . . . now. And Wink reels them off, the pencil sharpener and the packet of Rizlas replaced by the bigger more expensive items that have been watched over all day by a security guard. Wink (to the accompaniment of the audience): Suitcases! Golf clubs! Radio Alarm Clock! Dinner service! Coffee percolator! Teas-maid! Electric blanket! Toaster! Canteen of cutlery! Basket of fruit! Champagne! A tiger! She doesn't even use the opportunity to say 'cuddly toy!' on national television. She is above all that. She is Wink, TV star. She is our Wink.

Once Bob's make-up has been removed, he looks older and when he bends down to tie up his shoe lace, I notice his shiny patch has visibly grown. But Wink is a new woman. You'd think all the strain and excitement would be too much for her but tonight, when the after-show party has finished, snaps taken of the contestants with Larry and Isla, and the car has taken us back to the hotel, along with all the prizes, Wink walks straight-backed and with a skip in her step into the lobby where she orders nightcaps all round (except for the Inscrutables who've vanished, presumably back to Inverness, never to be seen again).

It is only when we get home, back home to Torquay, that catastrophe comes looking for us.

★ ★ ★

The next morning, Raymond and I share one last bottle of Coke.

'We could be pen friends,' I suggest, regretting it immediately as he looks like I've offered myself to him in marriage. His horror gradually dissipates after a slug of Coke and he manages to pull himself together.

'Alright,' he says.

I hand him a beer mat procured as a souvenir while the barman is busy filling up the optics. He produces a pen (also procured with sleight of hand from the hotel reception desk) and scrawls his address. A street and a town that might as well be in a foreign country. That might as well be in Manitoba or Alberta or Inverness.

And I write down my address for him. Bob's News. My home.

I am leaving London again, this time in a car. I've merely sniffed at all that lies in store in the capital; it has been snatched away too quickly from under my nose, for a second time.

Wink is full of it, regaling yet more Larry Facts she's gleaned from Amber and Imogen. How Larry was born out of wedlock. Put up for adoption. Brought up in a foster home. She looks at me as she is telling us all this, partly because I am the one stuck in the back of the car with her gammy leg on top of my lap. But I wonder if she is making comparisons with my life. After all, I was born out of wedlock too. Unfortunately there the similarity ends as I've never been put up for adoption. Where would I be now if I had? Not on my way home from BBC Television Centre that's for sure, so I should be grateful for my unofficial foster home (but I am almost a teenager and gratitude is not in my repertoire).

Eventually Wink shuts up and I am able to sleep, the tiger in my arms, dreaming of a tall boy called Raymond. My pen pal. Another friend I've had to relinquish all too soon, as Linda's Maxi speeds me away, back to the likes of Christopher Bennett and Terry Siney. Not that I've seen Terry in a long time though I've heard he is now known as T-J. However, something tells me we'll be seeing something of Auntie Sheila in the not-too-distant future if she switches on her television set on Saturday evening.

We arrive home to find Torquay in the midst of another power cut. Wink says I can keep the tiger in return for all my supportive shouting. She says she could pick my voice out from the audience and it had kept her going, which surprises me as Wink looked the picture of self-containment. But then you never know what's going on inside someone else, as Wink's always telling me.

She also gives Bob and Linda the golf clubs ('something for you to take up together, all that massaging can't be healthy') and the bottle of Champagne because it gives her heartburn something chronic. She tells us she is going to give the toaster to Miss Goddard who still makes do with a grill (someone should tell her the Japanese have surrendered) and Mr Taylor has earned himself the set of suitcases so he can take his proud wife and his knobbly knees on a second honeymoon. Christopher Bennett will get the digital alarm clock so he has no excuse for being late for his paper round. His time-keeping is shocking and Bob is possibly beginning to see through his flimsy veneer of Nice Young Man.

This will leave Wink with enough luxury goods to keep her happy for a long time to come — though something about the way she is so keen to hand out the prizes makes me dread she hasn't got as long as I'd like. Surely she isn't trying to tell us something?

★　★　★

The next morning we get a wake-up call, early, even before the paperboys arrive. Bob is still in his dressing gown as he lets himself out into the frosty morning where there is a commotion going on in the street. I am a deeper sleeper than Bob and it is only the sound of sirens that wake me up. In those first few seconds I try to calculate which emergency service it is. I am sure I'll see an ambulance as I draw back the curtains, the Cavalier sneering at me before I yank him to one side. But it isn't. It is the fire brigade, busy at work outside Wink's house, where thick orange-black flames swarm around her bedroom window. I can almost kid myself I'm watching television but for the now unmistakeable crackle and smell of smoke and the heat I can feel as I push up the window, scanning the people outside . . . but there's no sign of Wink. Wink, who can sleep through anything, even fire. Even fire!

'Wink!'

No-one hears me screaming. There's too much noise going on. I sprint from my room, leap down the stairs three at a time and am outside, out on the street in my pyjamas, running to her house when a fireman grabs hold of me.

'Oh no you don't,' he says. 'It's hot in there.'

And as I find myself on the floor, the scene of the street party, the tug of war that Wink judged, there are familiar arms helping me up again.

'It's alright . . . ' Bob coughs ' . . . Captain got her out.'

157

Thank God for the Fire Captain! He must've rescued her in a fireman's lift, down a ladder, out of that blackening fire. I love the Fire Captain. I want to kiss him and thank him but Bob is leading me away from the fire crew, taking me round the corner, where there is indeed an ambulance parked up, a dirty old lady sitting inside with a blanket wrapped round her as if she hadn't got hot enough inside her burning house, an oxygen mask over her face. And a parrot perched on her shoulder.

Captain got her out.

★ ★ ★

So Wink's chance of a lifetime goes up in flames though somewhere there could be a recording of her and Bob unless it has been taped over by someone in the Corporation. All she has left is a charred photo of Larry with his arm around her. Otherwise it could all too easily have been a dream. It could never have happened.

But I have proof of it. I have the tiger which I offer to give back to her but she won't have it. So, he goes everywhere with me.

Bob offers her something too. 'Come and stay with us, Wink. Stay as long as you like.' So that's what she does. She stays as long as she likes. In fact she never leaves.

'Just don't go playing with matches,' he has the nerve to say that first evening. 'Next time there's a power cut, use a torch.'

And this time she does have her walking stick to hand.

158

2006

Fran is back to check on us. Does she pay every new mother this much attention or am I in the maternity equivalent of the Slow Readers? She whisks you away, ordering me to get my head down. Do I look that hideous? That old?

So I am actually alone, completely alone, when the doctor tells me. The young doctor with the proficient hands. Pianist's hands. Surgeon's hands. Hands that can suture and examine and deftly poke and prod. A simple wedding band shines on the appropriate finger and I want to ask her if she has children because for some reason I need to know that she understands. That she can realistically put herself in my shoes (well, in my Totes Toasties).

'Are you sure you don't want your husband here?' she asks. I swat that idea away. 'Alright, then,' she says. 'I've got the results of the blood test. I hurried them along because I know what agony waiting can be.'

(She does! She does understand!)

'Thank you,' I say politely but, from the grim expression on her face, somehow I don't think I'll be thanking her in a minute.

'It's her heart,' she says.

Her heart. My beating heart.

159

11

1980

Blind Date

I am right about Auntie Sheila. That Saturday evening she does switch on her television set instead of going and doing something less boring instead. And there he is. The man who was once almost a significant part of her life. The almost-man: Bob. Acting the buffoon in front of the nation. But it is her Bob. My Bob. And watching him do that tango, she imagines it is her in his arms, not the dummy.

So, a week after the fire, when Wink has filled Helena's old wardrobe with a new set of nylon clothes from Newton Abbot market and Captain is once again beginning to pass comment, Sheila turns up at the shop. She is allegedly after a *Western Morning News* and a packet of Extra Strong Mints but really I know she wants to see Bob. And, as her luck would have it, there he is, propping up the counter.

'Sheila!' he says, genuinely thrilled to see her again. 'You look well.'

Yes, Sheila does look well. A slick haircut and a slim line body that makes Bob straighten his spine and pull in his stomach.

Linda is out, on the road, flogging stationery,

160

and so Bob makes Sheila a cup of tea. One cup of tea leads to another and before you know it Sheila is once again ensconced back in our lives, rolling up her sleeves and lending a helping hand.

★　★　★

Two years on and the situation is largely the same. At school, I've crawled my way to the top stream but one. Cheryl continues to shine above me but has the good grace never to mention it. We are still best friends but can't spend as much time together in the way that we'd like, memorising the pop lyrics in *Smash Hits* and crimping each other's hair, as we have revision for our mocks. (If only the events of the Industrial Revolution would stick in my brain as firmly as the words to *Ant Music*.)

At home, it's hard to remember a time when I didn't live with Bob and Wink and Andy and Captain. Linda is still on the scene though since her promotion to area manager she's on the road even more than ever. Over the next decade she will become one of those women inspired by Margaret Thatcher and Alexis Carrington into wearing power suits with shoulder pads that Captain could roost on. But, for the time being, she settles for Lady Di ruffs and flicky hair. In fact, Linda is so keen on Lady Di, hoping fervently for the engagement to be officially announced, that she uses 'Princess' as her CB handle. She's become obsessed with her CB radio and whiles away the hours motoring all over the south west, imagining she is in *Convoy*. Driving, for Linda, is now a greater pleasure than ever.

★ ★ ★

One Saturday evening, Auntie Sheila asks us all round to a dinner party. Bernie, who is still behaving himself, will be there. Terry (T-J), who still lives at home, might or might not be there, depending on his 'plans' (primitive plans involving pints and pubs and mates). Toni, on the other hand, is still in Hampstead, working her way up through the rank and file of the estate agents and has bought herself 'a nice little flat' in Belsize Park where she sometimes has her mother to stay so they can 'take in a show'. I remember my trip to London where I barely got above ground level and feel overwhelmed briefly by jealousy. Toni may not have become a member of Pan's People but she does have her own flat in London and can take her mother to see *Evita*, when I have to make do yet again with taking Wink to the pantomime at the Princess Theatre.

At the last minute Linda has a crisis at work and calls Bob from the office to say she can't make it. So there is a spare chair at the table which T-J is persuaded to fill before going down town. Unfortunately the spare chair is situated next to mine and so I am not looking forward to the meal although Auntie Sheila has pushed the boat out and done steak and chips followed by Arctic Roll. I am even allowed half a glass of Chianti as I am fifteen and well-and-truly a teenager and should be given the opportunity to learn how to handle alcohol in a responsible manner. (Little do they know I've already learnt the hard way.)

T-J and Bernie have lager, as wine is for wimps. Wink joins them but Bob risks being branded a lesser man as this is favourable to Auntie Sheila necking back the entire bottle of Chianti (bar my measly half a glass) all on her own. He obviously hasn't managed to blank the whole sorry David-Essex-Hold-Me-Close fiasco. Unfortunately this isn't the only bottle of Chianti; it turns out there's a whole cellar full of the stuff thanks to Auntie Sheila's wine club.

The evening drags by and I have to sit listening to T-J chew his steak that could still possibly be breathing it's so rare. (I must've been a vegetarian in a former life.) Auntie Sheila has tried. She's got out the best dinner service and cut glass and has painstakingly polished the cutlery. She's even concertina-ed the napkins into fans which impresses Wink no end though T-J leaves his on the table in preference for his sleeve. I wonder how anyone as sophisticated as Auntie Sheila could have brought up a philistine like him. But then I look at Bernie chewing his medium-rare with his mouth open.

The conversation isn't flowing as freely as either the wine or the lager. Auntie Sheila does her best to kick start things.

'How's Linda?' she asks Bob through gritted teeth.

'Oh, you know, busy,' says Bob.

'Poor Bob,' says Auntie Sheila as if he's announced that Linda has run off with one of the paperboys. She puts her hand over his hand and leaves it there. Bob looks at it, as if it might spontaneously combust. Bernie takes a slug of his lager, and undoes the button of his Farah slacks, oblivious to his wife's treachery. After gallons of Italian vino, Auntie Sheila's skills as a hostess (and wife) have gone awry.

T-J, meanwhile, is also untuned to the radar of his mother's attentions. He's spent the first half of the meal looking at his watch and the second half looking at my chest. My chest has grown somewhat since I last saw him (hurrah!) and it is finally dawning on him that I am well-and-truly a teenager now. He even attempts to make conversation with me. But what is more surprising is that his sudden interest is not unappealing. I find myself talking in a strange voice and feeling strange things. The draw of the pub is too great, however, and as soon as T-J has finished his last shovelful of Arctic Roll, he is splashing Brut all over and heading for the door, shrugging into his leather jacket and shouting a cursory see you later over his shoulder, which it has to be said is quite a nice shoulder.

'He's thinking about moving up to London, you know, to stay with Toni,' Sheila says as the front door bangs. 'There's a chance of a job working in her office. Delivery boy or something.'

'He's hardly a boy,' Wink points out. (She's noticed too.)

'He's only twenty-four,' says Sheila.

'He's a bloody sponger,' says Bernie.

'We should be encouraging him then, shouldn't we?'

And with that note on parental guidance, Auntie Sheila swans off to fetch the cheese and biscuits, leaving an awkward silence in the candle-lit dining room which no-one has the heart to fill. I could, if I tried, but I am too busy thinking of T-J. Terry, of the Chinese burns and obnoxious friends. Terry of the pools and bar billiards. Terry, who is moving away to stay with his sister who can take him to see *Evita* (not that he'd thank her). Terry (T-J), who — after half a measly glass of Chianti — I quite fancy.

Midway through the after dinner mints the door bell chimes. It is Linda — who's been heavy-handed with the make-up and over-generous with the cleavage — carrying a bottle of Blue Nun that Auntie Sheila winces at, being a wine connoisseur.

'It's all they had in the off-licence,' says Linda, flushing as red as T-J's sirloin, on the verge of battering her smug hostess over the head with the embarrassing bottle. It is clear that for whatever reason Linda has decided to turn up at this point in the evening, it would've been better all round if she'd gone straight home from work, put on a little Manhattan Transfer and had a bath.

Linda is jealous, that is the reason. But she is in good company as Sheila is jealous too. Bernie, oblivious to the heavy emotion at large in the room, skulks off to watch the snooker. Wink skulks off with him, being partial to men in black tie. Bob is left with Sheila and Linda all to himself. But he is also left feeling bemused. He can't understand anyone committing the sin of jealousy over him. There is no use for me here, other than Peace Maker, but I'm not in the mood for negotiations. I am quite possibly infatuated with someone I shouldn't be.

'I need the loo,' I announce. No-one hears me despite the silence hovering over the dinner table.

I take the opportunity to have a quick snoop around upstairs. Toni's bedroom, where I used to be a dummy for her friends' crude make-up skills, has been preserved like a museum piece: Room of a 1970s Teenager. Pink shagpile, pink woodchip, a huge paper lampshade swelling from an Artexed ceiling painted with clouds. A pair of pink ballet shoes hanging by their pink ribbons from her bedknobs-and-broomstick bed frame. Her ballet exam certificates framed along one wall. A tutu strung up from the picture rail. And I bet if I were to look in her wardrobe I'd find her Pan's People floaty nightie doing a ghostly dance.

I don't dare go in Sheila and Bernie's room but I make myself peek inside their son's, which I am fully expecting to look like a crime scene ripe with forensic evidence. But I am shocked. Despite the obligatory Athena tennis girl on his wall (the one who forgot to put on her knickers), I see a room where everything is in its place.

There are no dirty socks strewn on the floor. No mouldy mugs or crisp packets scattered about. The bed is made. The carpet hoovered. It even smells pleasant. A mixture of soap and toothpaste and Shake 'n' Vac. The type of room Lucas might've kept though he would have had more books and refrained from displaying pictures of naked lady bottoms on his walls. Maybe Auntie Sheila is responsible for this meticulousness, though somehow I doubt it — these days, although she can find the time for napkin origami when the occasion requires it, she is too busy to uphold her former housekeeping standards. Maybe I've underestimated T-J. Maybe he's never let me set foot in his room all these years because he knows what a slob I am. Maybe it is remembering Lucas that makes me soften towards the boy who used to call me Porkchops.

Being in T-J's bedroom reveals how very little I know about him but, even without this glimpse into his private world, I know two things which really should be all I need:

1. He is twenty-four.
2. He is leaving for London.

However, there's been no-one of any note since Raymond. Christopher Bennett is just a bad memory though he can still be found in our shop in the early mornings. Lucas is just a speck of stardust. And I am well-and-truly a teenager with hormones — to quote Helena — 'on the blink'.

When I arrive back downstairs, Bob is bundling Linda and her cleavage back into her

Dannimac and Wink is shouting at Terry Griffiths to get a move on. It is clearly time to go before we outstay our welcome.

Bernie has dragged himself away from the snooker and stands next to his wife who forces a smile as she sees us out, her new hairdo a little dishevelled. While Bob shepherds Linda and Wink into the night, I linger on the doorstep, dragging my heels (flat heels, unlike Helena as I don't want to add any extra inches to my height). I'm not exactly relishing the drive home in the company of this threesome. Sheila pecks me on the cheek and disappears into the kitchen. Bernie and I remain, static on the threshold, listening to his wife lobbing her best china into the dishwasher. Then he looks at me. I feel awkward but I don't know why.

'Do you miss her?' he asks, out of the blue.

'Who?' I say but I know exactly who he means. I want him to say her name. I never hear her name anymore. It is as if she's never existed.

'Your . . . mother,' he says. 'Helena.'

'Why should I miss her?' I ask, defiantly. 'When I have such a loving family.'

We stand and look at my family displaying their love on Bernie's driveway: Bob and Linda and Wink, the three of them battling it out over who is going to drive the Maxi, my argument faltering a tad.

'Honestly, I'm fine.' I assure him. 'But thanks for asking Uncle Bernie.'

And he gives me a wink, one of the special ones from the collection he keeps for his Toni.

Lying in bed that night, the Cavalier shuns me. Maybe he knows my heart lies elsewhere. I think about what I told Bernie. I *am* fine. But I'm not sure if that is because of my new passion or whether I am in actual fact 'fine'. And I let myself think of my mother. She is a real person, someone Bernie has known in every sense of the word. A living breathing woman, not a figment of my imagination as I sometimes wonder these days. Because why wouldn't I wonder? It has been so long. And would a real mother do what she did? A few short letters and a handful of birthday cards?

* * *

Christmas comes and goes without a word from Helena, surprise, surprise, elusive as Father Christmas. It is a new year: 1981. Unfortunately it begins with me making a mockery of my mocks. I do alright in both English Language and English Literature, seeing as I've been an active member of the library all these years (though I am rather heavily influenced by the photo stories in *Jackie*). But as for the rest, maths makes me feel faint-hearted, despite all that practice in the shop when I've had to roll up my sleeves and lend a helping hand. All I know for sure about geography is that Canada is a long way away across the ocean. I should never have chosen art because my skills have never progressed much beyond colouring in pixie cuffs. French is double Dutch. And as for history, I seem to confuse fact with fiction.

★ ★ ★

But all my efforts pale into insignificance a few weeks later, on a cold February morning, when there is a genuinely historical event: Charles and Diana announce their engagement. When asked in an interview when the marriage is likely to take place, Charles says sometime at the end of July. But I know the date before it is decided. I just know it will be July the 29th. My sixteenth birthday.

While Diana, four years my senior, moves into Clarence House and prepares to marry her prince, I remain in my bedroom, revising and singing along to Madness. As the blossom falls off the trees and the first baby gulls begin their slow, tortuous flying lessons, we are nearly there. The next few months will be a trial to be endured but I know that whatever happens, however many O-levels I do or do not get, there are the long summer holidays, my sixteenth birthday and a royal wedding to look forward to at the end of it. But the biggest surprise of all is that we will not be enjoying this latest royal milestone in Torquay. Bob has arranged with Sheila for us to go and stay with Toni in her flat in Belsize Park. We will all be witnesses to prove that this is not just a fairytale wedding, a thing of fiction. It is real.

★ ★ ★

Two days before I am sixteen we leave in convoy. The excitement for Linda is only tempered by the fact Sheila doesn't have a CB radio in the Volvo estate that she's banned Bernie from driving. Instead we have to communicate by hand gestures and flashing lights.

The M4 whizzes by, not as fast as Linda would like as Sheila takes road safety seriously (she is a Volvo owner after all). But once we hit London, Linda is in control and makes sure we enjoy a longer stretch of the North Circular than we did the last time. Cheryl and I count how many Union Jacks we can see lining the roads and flapping from tower blocks. We give up after a while as it is clear that the numbers are far too overwhelming to even contemplate. The whole of London is wedding crazy.

And I don't know why but I have a feeling this will all end in tears. Something holds me back from completely enjoying myself, from completely letting go into the arms of the holiday spirit. Maybe it is just because Wink has been left behind with Patty and Lugsy. They'll have to make do with the colour television in the living room to witness Saturday's nuptials.

Maybe that is all it is. Wink.

$$\star \quad \star \quad \star$$

Toni isn't as house proud as her mother or as obsessive-compulsively tidy as her brother. While T-J keeps the living room, bathroom and his bedroom army-clean and orderly, Toni can't even manage her own room which looks like it has been burgled. Sheila is on the verge of phoning the police when Toni has to put her right. So while the rest of us have a cup of tea and some ginger cake, Sheila dons her rubber gloves (metaphorically as Toni doesn't own a pair of Marigold's) and gets the bedroom ship-shape, to her daughter's exasperation.

'Mother!'

'Well, you can't possibly expect Bob and Linda to sleep in here with your discarded smalls all over the mucky carpet,' Sheila points out.

'What about T-J's room?'

'It's far too small to offer to guests. Bernie and I will have to go in there.'

'Really, Mother,' says Toni. 'It's 'bijou'.'

I'm not sure how Bernie will cope with the box size of his nightly surroundings, but Cheryl and I will get along fine, in the lounge, on put-you-ups. As for T and T, they'll be staying with friends nearby so everyone has a bed for the night and some notion of privacy, though the flat is a cheap conversion with partition walls that could be blown over by the big bad wolf if he tried hard enough. (I am of course too old now for such imaginings. And I know without a shadow of a doubt that after tomorrow's fairy tale, that will be it. My childhood over.)

★ ★ ★

We decide to give the fireworks in Hyde Park a miss so that we can better conserve our energy for the big day. The plan is for Toni to order an Indian takeaway (poor Wink, missing out on this

172

culinary adventure), then an early night. We need as much sleep as we can forage, as we are to leave the flat at the crack of dawn to hunt out the perfect spot on the procession route, where we can stand and cheer and wave our flags.

Toni is packing her overnight bag, waiting for Terry to escort her to their friends' flat as she has a fear of being mugged since the riots. As the grown-ups tuck into a bottle of brandy, I prick up my ears like a cat as a key goes in the lock. I am horrified to find my stomach contracting in emotion of one kind or another all because I know that in two seconds time I'll be seeing Terry/T-J/Whatever-he-is-now-called. Oh dear.

'Wotcha,' he says, stumbling through the door, slightly coy, everybody witnessing his mother's passionate embraces.

'Terry, love,' she croons. 'How are you?'

'Fine, Mum.' He backs away a little and then manages to throw a half-smile in the direction of his dad who says: 'Alright, son?'

The three of them have reverted to their Brummie roots, though Toni, who went to the Grammar, speaks almost as well as the bride-to-be, Diana. (Not that the Grammar had that effect on me. My accent defies categorisation, a result of my mixed 'parenting', presumably.)

T-J has now found his feet, saying hello to Cheryl, asking how she's done in her exams. This is astonishing! He's always thought my friends to be nothing but stupid kids. And now he is talking to Cheryl (who's also reverted to her Solihull upbringing) like he cares about what she is saying. I think I might possibly be experiencing the grip of the green-eyed monster that so often digs its talons into Sheila. But I soon realise that T-J is just being polite. I soon realise that he looks at me in a completely different way. Straight in the face. I am his equal (in as far as that's possible for a man of twenty-five and a teenager of sixteen-minus-a-day). I am no longer a school girl in his eyes. I am Philippa. And he fancies me, I just know it!

He leaves me alone with these romantic musings to go and pack his overnight bag. The rest of the occupants of Toni's lounge hum away at their conversations. I catch the odd word . . . spicy . . . carriage . . . sandwiches . . . shop . . . brandy . . . but what I am thinking is far more important. It is the only thought in the world of any worth. And my extreme happiness is only tainted by the knowledge that Terry is now packing a bag to go and sleep around the corner, instead of under the same roof as me.

But there is some consolation. As he goes out the door, he slips me a piece of paper. I clutch it tightly without anyone seeing and smuggle it into the coffin of a bathroom, feeling like a glamorous Russian spy from a Bond film. On the piece of paper, in T-J's un-joined-up hand, it says:

Happy Birthday Sweet Sixteen. x

Some might say you can't read an awful lot into this. But I manage to. I am quite possibly going to die with longing.

Lying on the camp bed soon after this, teeth brushed extra carefully, hair combed one hundred times, the way Helena instructed me all those years ago, I stare, not at curtains, but at a Habitat roller blind. Behind the blind, the trees move like shadow puppets, acting out their own drama in the orange of the street lights. I imagine the tree-figures as all of the romantic couplings I know: Romeo and Juliet . . . Cathy and Heathcliff . . . Charles and Diana . . . John and Yoko . . . Bruce and Anthea . . . even my mother and father, lost across the Ocean, in the snowscapes of Canada and the tropical rainforests of the Amazon. But best of all, I imagine T-J's puppet moving mysteriously against mine. If only the Cavalier could see me now. He would feel the green-eyed monster tugging at his long curly hair.

Is Diana as in love as this? Is she as excited about seeing Charles tomorrow as I am about seeing T-J? What future can the princess-to-be see in her curtains? Or does she feel the same niggle of doubt creeping up on her from behind, in the dead of night, trying to put a dampener on things. Or maybe that is Bernie's phlegmy cough emanating through the flimsy excuse of a wall.

★ ★ ★

Linda has taken over the organisation of the big day. Her travel alarm pings off sometime in the middle of the night. It is still dark when Cheryl

175

and I are prodded awake with a cup of tea that is completely inappropriate when sleep is all that should be required of our bodies. But as the seconds tick by on Linda's travel alarm that she's left considerately by my ear, in the midst of my haze of sleepiness, the excitement muscles its way through: Diana and Charles.

And then the excitement hits me full whack: T-J!

'Happy birthday, Phil,' murmurs Cheryl, her eyes glued together with the generous deposits of the Sand Man.

'Thanks,' I say but I am hardly bothered by my birthday. My birthday is just the icing on the cake. (Though I do have time to wonder if there will be an actual cake.)

Cheryl delves in her duffle-bag and produces a small box tied up with ribbon. It looks promising.

'It's from me, Mum and Dad and our Darryl as well,' she says as I open the box and find inside, nestling amongst the shocking pink tissue paper, a silver bracelet with a 'P' on it. And I remember Miss Pitchfork who was the one to point out my name didn't begin with an 'F' — which was about the extent of her teaching that year.

'Cheryl, it's lovely, thanks. Thanks a lot.' And I hug my best friend so hard she starts complaining.

Now, I am pleased it's my birthday. Everyone is keen to acknowledge the importance of being sixteen. It is a milestone. A bridge I have crossed. A gateway I have entered into (etc, etc). Not quite a grown-up but certainly no longer a child. I can tell this by the way Auntie Sheila and Uncle Bernie refrain from the usual summer dress, and give me instead a card with a ten pound note tucked inside. The way Linda looks at me anew, as if seeing me as Philippa, not just Bob's daughter. And Bob himself has tears in his eyes as he hands over a present that I wasn't expecting in a whole century of birthdays. He's given me a small box, so like Cheryl's that I wonder if it is a matching bracelet. But no. It is a ring. A gold ring with a fairly decent-sized opal set in it. I've seen it before.

I look at Bob.

'It was Helena's,' he says. 'She left it for you.'

'Why have you waited so long to give it to me?'

'She said to wait till the time was right. I always thought she'd be back to give it you herself but . . . '

He runs out of words though they are obvious enough. Instead, he slips the ring on my finger. Well, not so much slip as shove, my fingers not being as slender as Helena's.

'Does this mean she's not coming back?' I say them, the obvious words, because suddenly they need to be said. Suddenly I am a little girl again.

'I don't know Philippa,' he shrugs. 'I wish I did.'

Then he plants a kiss on top of my head. My Mr Bob-Sugar. And I believe I know why he's never asked Linda to marry him.

★ ★ ★

You'd imagine that getting up at three o'clock in the morning would've guaranteed front row seats as it were, but when we arrive at the Mall — the destination of Linda's choosing — we find it already filling up with half the Commonwealth. Linda's organisation and determination secure us a spot a good long way down the Mall, almost at the Queen Victoria Memorial with its soaring gold Victory, a cake decoration of the gods. And there, in front of us, impressive against the clear blue sky, is the huge, ugly, outrageous Buckingham Palace. We put down our picnic bags and rugs and settle in. We have a long wait.

★ ★ ★

By breakfast time, the streets of London (yes, those again) are bulging. Despite the lack of space there is a euphoric atmosphere and we find a happy place amongst it: Linda and Bob hold each other's hands, like teenagers, the impending marriage casting its spell over them, bathing them in a glow of romance that has been missing of late. Cheryl and I recite songs from the Top Twenty, chew Hubba Bubba and plait each other's hair in an attempt to make ourselves into Bo Derek. Poor Cheryl has her work cut out. My hair still frizzes around my shoulders as it has always done, never to be tamed by mere mortals. I have greater success with Cheryl's long glossy chestnut hair but she would score more points at a gymkhana than on a film set. Those long ago Saturdays spent masquerading as a pony, with Toni as my groom, haven't gone to waste.

178

Toni has gone off with work friends somewhere near St Paul's. T-J is down his local (one of them). Bernie at the last minute decided he wasn't up to the crowds and the long day and has stayed behind in bed.

'Don't forget my ticker, Sheila,' he said.

'How could I?' she replied.

I think Auntie Sheila is secretly glad not to have Bernie to worry about. She has other things on her mind, not least getting the snap of a lifetime. She is convinced the bride and groom are going to kiss in public and she wants to be ready for that moment. If Bernie were here she'd no doubt miss it as she would be otherwise engaged pandering to his needs, topping up his tea from the Thermos or tying up his shoelaces as he has difficulty bending down.

But she didn't tell him this. She said, 'Really, Bernie you might as well have stayed in Torquay and watched it on the box.'

'Well,' he said. 'I wanted to see our Toni, didn't I.'

When she glared at him, he added: 'And our Terry.'

I realise there is a third reason any relationship with T-J is doomed: Auntie Sheila. Auntie Sheila, like Luke Skywalker (or Darth Vader on her darker days), is a force to be reckoned with. I know she has a soft side that Bob (and even Bernie on occasion) can tap into. She's always shown this side to me and of course to her Terry and Toni. But I remember the time at the shop, waiting for my first cup of tea. I remember the tinkle of breaking glass. I remember Helena's blotchy face as she realised her one and only friend was walking away from her. And she was a friend, Sheila. She came round eventually, only to be let down by Helena again. (But then weren't we all.)

I've seen Auntie Sheila protecting her family with a fierceness I can only envy. She wants the best for her Terry. And that won't be me. To Auntie Sheila, I am the poor girl with no mother. The girl who needs help from time to time: choosing clothes, trips to the hairdressers, a slab of Victoria sandwich on a wet Saturday afternoon.

The thought of a wet afternoon is quite appealing right now. It is getting hot and sticky and it is barely half past ten. The ceremony doesn't start for half an hour at least and who knows how long it will go on for (apart from the Archbishop of Canterbury and Linda). But we are happy to wait for our fair share of history, our first hand experience that we can pass down the generations. For although Toni will be one of the privileged few to see Diana pick her way up the red carpeted steps of St Paul's, dragging a train as long as the Penzance to Paddington, we are experiencing the joy of a nation all around us, in this most historical of backdrops.

Time passes quickly, people offering round sandwiches, strangers swapping crisps and KitKats and Silk Cut. Before long, Diana will have married someone called Philip Charles Arthur George (and an unexpected third person to be made known to us in the years to come).

Kiri Te Kanawa, a bird of paradise, will have belted out a song that captures Bernie's (weak) heart as he slouches indoors eating his daughter out of house and home. Even Terry will have found time, at some point during his fourth pint, to comment on the shocking state of Diana's creases.

Time doesn't quite pass quickly enough for Cheryl though, who starts to burn under the ferocious midday sun just as the bridal carriage, escorted by the Household Cavalry, is sweeping Charles and Diana along the procession route lined with flowers and every police officer in the country (apart from the ones otherwise engaged trying to stop rioters in any way possible). Nearer and nearer, sweeping down Fleet Street, along the Strand, through Admiralty Arch and finally into the Mall. Linda won't relinquish her place to get Cheryl into the shade so she shrouds her in a wedding tea towel that she brought in the picnic hamper, like a bridal veil. She looks no less ridiculous than half the crowd who are likewise draped in Union Jacks.

'Not long now,' says Bob, slurping his tea. 'Then we can go home for a lie down.'

'I don't think I'll ever be able to sleep again,' says Linda, as the carriage looms into view, the roar of the crowd swallowing her words and carrying them off somewhere over our glorious capital city. The place that Helena loved. My birthplace.

We catch a glimpse of the bride, Diana in a halo of sunshine, waving in our direction and then all too soon she's passed by with her new

181

husband, closely followed by the Queen and Earl Spencer and behind them, Prince Philip and Mrs Shand-Kydd, then Prince Andrew and his gran.

'That's a convoy and a half,' Linda gushes as the royal party disappear into the forecourt of the palace and away to the wedding breakfast inside. We hold our collective breath, knowing they'll reappear before long, for all to see, out on the balcony, in the glittering sunshine, then there is a surge, a rush to fill the Mall, the crowd urging itself forward, those at the front pressing against the railings of the palace, the best view in the land.

And they do. All the royals you could ever hope for, gathered together in one family grouping (an ideal situation, if you were a monarchist or a member of the Paparazzi or an assassin). But unfortunately Auntie Sheila misses the magic moment of the predicted Kiss — a chaste, embarrassed peck on the lips rather than a fully-blown snog — because something else has grabbed her attention. Or rather someone. Auntie Sheila finds herself drawn to Linda. Linda who's taken this opportunity to get down on bended knee, in front of the nation and indeed the Queen herself, and ask Bob for his hand in marriage.

★ ★ ★

Several hours later we are congregated back at Toni's flat with tales of royal sightings and wedding stories that will go down in folklore.

And with a double celebration of the wedding and an engagement to be endured. Oh, and my birthday which has been completely bypassed. Still, the Champagne (well, Asti Spumante) is flowing and who am I to complain? Especially as any minute now a certain someone's due to come in that front door.

But we are also waiting for another guest. Linda's son Clive (the sailor) is on leave and, with Bob's connivance, has arranged to turn up at the flat as a surprise for his mother. Only he is the one in for a surprise when he discovers he is to have a new father. (Bob is still reeling from the shock himself, though he has managed a strangled 'Yes' to his now-fiancée.)

While we wait, there is music — a toxic mixture of Toni's Duran Duran records and Bob's Elvis tapes. It isn't the cool party most sixteen-year-olds hope for but then again I am more mature than most sixteen-year-olds (in some ways anyhow) and realise I am not the centre of the universe and never have been. Plus, I know things will pick up once T-J has torn himself away from the pub. My greatest concern is that he'll end up staying till closing time. That he'll be too drunk to remember who I am. To remember that I am that sweet sixteen.

★ ★ ★

Just as I am cutting the cake (yes, Linda remembered and got Auntie Sheila to bake one of her finest), the door goes and my heart rate doubles so I know what it must be like for Uncle

Bernie. But it is Clive, looking dapper in his uniform, though more like a sea cadet than a fully-fledged member of Her Majesty's Royal Navy. Linda is in tears of rapture but soon pulls herself together to tell him off for not letting her know he would be on leave. Then she breaks the news to him, a little red-faced because she knows how much Clive thinks of his dad. And so the evening progresses, Duran Duran being completely usurped by the dead king, though we have gone from the *Hound Dogs* to the *Love Me Tenders* of Bob's extensive collection.

Until. The door again. And this time it is. T-J. Looking ever-so-slightly-worse-for-wear but looking right at me. I feel like everyone in the room must know but actually they are all too involved with reminiscing, with cake, with brandy, with reunions, with plans, with sunstroke. Yes, poor old Cheryl has had to go to bed early. But it is alright, the party doesn't have to end. There is now a bedroom going spare and she can lie down in it without impeding our celebrations. The spare bedroom is a result of the other surprise of the day: Linda has booked her and Bob into a five star hotel using her well-earned commission. After an hour or so they disappear, leaving a bemused Clive to make his own arrangements.

'Well, nobody told me,' says Linda who hates surprises, being a control freak. 'I'm not wasting the hotel room.'

Bob agrees and shepherds his fiancée out of the flat before she changes her mind, the prospect of a five star massage over-whelming

184

any fears he might have of impending marriage.

So, poor over-heated Cheryl has T-J's tiny room as Sheila can't stand another night cooped up in such close quarters with Bernie. Especially as she won't get an ounce of sleep fretting over the latest engagement. They move into Toni's room. And I'll be on my own in the living room. Only that leaves Clive. No-one seems to have a problem with him sleeping on Cheryl's vacated put-you-up, alone in the living room, with me. They obviously trust him because he's in the navy and a respected citizen. But surely that is exactly why they should be worried. Surely I will be too much for him to resist after all those weeks at sea. Why can't they see this? Do they think I am a child after all? Does no-one care about my virtue?

Yes. Someone does. T-J. Though whether he cares about me or whether he is getting a touch of the green-eyed monster himself, I can only guess at. T-J decides against going back with Toni to her mates, much to her annoyance.

'You'll never forgive yourself if I get mugged,' she says coldly to her brother.

So Clive steps in like a gent (or an opportunist, depending on which way you look at it) and offers to walk her to her friends' place round the corner. And that gives T-J his chance.

But before he grabs it, the telephone rings. I sense that no-one else in the flat is in the mood for phone calls and so I answer it.

'Hello, Philippa,' a tiny voice says.

No, it isn't Helena's voice, crackling down the Atlantic airwaves. It is my Wink.

'Happy Birthday, duck.'

And I tell her about our day and she says she spotted me on the telly which I am sure is a complete fabrication. Apart from the fact there were over half a million people out there today on those legendary Streets of London, Wink's eyesight is by no means capable of picking out one individual.

'Why did Cheryl have a tea towel on her head?' she asks, surprising me yet again.

We chat on for a while, T-J mooching round the lounge, picking up napkins and sweeping up cake crumbs. I want to marry him (sorry Lucas).

Just as I am wondering why Wink is telling me about Andy's latest mouse cull, she suddenly comes out with the one thing she's been holding back. The one piece of information I've also been trying to keep at bay all day. Helena hasn't forgotten my birthday. Sixteen is important in her eyes too.

'She sent you a card.'

Silence.

'Shall I open it for you? Or do you want to wait?'

I could easily wait. I am an expert in that area. But for once, I feel life pressing its urgency on me. I am sixteen. I want to live a life that is more than waiting.

'Yes, open it.'

I can visualise Wink with the letter opener, hear her slice the envelope. I can smell Helena's perfume-mixed-with-smoke coming off the air-mail paper inside. I can touch her beautiful school girl handwriting.

186

'Well, it's short and to the point.'

She describes the picture on the front, a clapboarded house with a white picket fence and a big maple tree out the front, a Canadian Waltonesque scene that is quite perverse coming from Helena. Maybe subconsciously she is telling me something, though I can't for the life of me imagine what.

Wink continues to read out the message that has been inscribed on the inside:

Dear Philippa,
Happy birthday. I wish I had a photo so I could see you all grown up. I know I've been hopeless but that doesn't mean I don't love you the way I should. One day I hope you will understand. Give Bob and Wink a kiss from me. And have a big one for yourself.
I hope to see you soon.
All my love
Helena x

Neither of us can think of much to say after that so she tells me to keep my pecker up (another skill of mine) and then she is gone, back to her world of sleeping pills and pain killers and parrots that go squawk in the night.

Meanwhile everyone bar T-J has gone to bed, leaving it to me to check on Cheryl. For all we know she could be dead and we are supposed to be looking after her. I feel her forehead which seems to have cooled down thanks to the frozen peas. Then I shut the window, blocking out the London traffic and alcohol-related activities.

187

Talking of which, I've only managed a couple of glasses of Asti and T-J has somehow completely sobered up.

'Do you want to go in the bathroom first?' he asks when I am back in the living room, sending a charge of sexual tension through my body, stronger than anything I felt with Raymond and the shared bottle of Coke. Stronger and more serious because now I am virtually a grown-up.

'Thanks,' I say.

Though I don't need to thank him. I don't need to be grateful to him for what is about to happen. If anything it should be the other way round. I am, after all, offering him a priceless gift for nothing. Though actually, in return, he'll give me something that is quite precious. He'll give me his undivided attention, his experience, a tenderness I've only read about in Wink's growing collection of Danielle Steel's. He'll give me a private kiss, unwatched by the nation, that is far from chaste, far from embarrassed and that will move me into unchartered territory, land that is as undiscovered as my father's route out of the Amazon. Terry will give me the chance to succeed where Cheryl has failed. The chance to shine.

Oh dear.

2006

'Would you like someone to talk to? Your husband perhaps? Or your mother?'

She has no idea, this young doctor with the hands. And all I can think about right now is how I can make her feel better, stop the tears crowding her eyes. She'll never make it if she doesn't toughen up.

'Maybe you've got a leaflet or something. That might help. I do know something about heart problems but there's always more to learn.'

'I'll see what I can do,' she says. 'I'll get back to you soon.'

And she leaves us, blowing her nose because she understands a mother's worry.

Yes, I know a bit about heart break. But I have no idea how they can be mended. Am I up to this? On my own?

Here comes Fran. 'Your husband's here. Shall I show him in?'

I feel a surge of maternal power, heating up my blood, my milk. Boiling up my bones. Sterilising all the feelings I've ever had for him. All the good ones and even most of the bad ones. So I don't care anymore. I don't care about anything except you. I am wiped clean of him and I WILL NOT LET HIM HURT YOU.

'Tell him to get lost.'

'You really should be with someone,' she insists.

She doesn't get it, does she? I've got you. What more could I possibly want?

'We're fine,' I tell her. 'Just fine.'

I am horrified to find myself crying. I can't hear it or feel it but I must be doing it on autopilot because, when I reach up to my face, there is the wet, soggy evidence.

'Please, Philippa. Talk to me.' Fran looks kindly at me. I look at you, lying there in my arms, checking you're still breathing, the way I used to do all those years ago, creeping up on tiptoes and kneeling down beside a pale, still boy, curled up like a caterpillar on the sofa. Watching for the rise and fall while he watched Valerie Singleton.

Oh dear.

12

1981

Bullseye

Over the next few weeks I catch myself smiling at odd moments. At home I can be doing something simple — going down the stairs, running a bath, squeezing my spots — when an image of a shoulder, or a look, will float into view. At school, drinking coffee in the sixth form common room, reading from a Shakespeare text, sketching a bowl of flowers, watching a slideshow on the rise of the Third Reich in a darkened classroom, or hanging around the hockey net, fat and heavy with protective gear, my head will float off to that other place of love and lust and passion.

I've made it through to the other side of my O-levels with a cunning combination of wits, blagging and short-term memory. To my great relief, I get the two predicted A grades in my English exams. But the big surprise is the other results: Bs in Art and History and Cs in all the rest. Not bad for Philippa who started off her school life dumbfounded in the Slow Readers. Who would have thought she'd become Grammar School Philippa, Sixth

Form Philippa, Hopefully-University-But-More-Likely-Polytechnic Philippa? And after that, well . . . there is a whole world out there.

★ ★ ★

One day after school, as the conkers are falling from the tree outside the shop and the palms on the seafront brace themselves for stormy times ahead, I make my way to the Bone Yard. I tell Lucas about T-J. I tell him that I'm not especially bothered I don't see him very often. I was wrong about being in love with him. I was wrong about wanting to marry him. I want to be independent like Jane Eyre or Princess Leia (who both have hair as ridiculous as mine). Now I am a sixth former, I am encouraged to think for myself. I spend a lot of time thinking for myself and have come to the conclusion that I don't need a man — surprising, perhaps, given my role models: Auntie Sheila always chasing Bob when she has a Bernie of her own, Wink drooling over Bruce Forsyth, Helena following Orville Tupper across the ocean without so much as a backward glance. But what about all those other women who've influenced me over the years? All those spinsters like Miss Parry, the librarian and Miss Mills, the visionary teacher who'd pushed Christopher Bennett and me through the Eleven Plus. I'll never forget their battle cry.

I don't feel the need to cling to T-J because I know now that there will be other men in my life. If I want them. If I can be bothered.

'You were the first,' I tell Lucas. 'And the most special.'

I don't tell him *everything* about T-J who was also the first in another way. I certainly don't tell him about Christopher Bennett who has also had his small part to play; that would be admitting to treachery of the highest order. I can't tell him these things because, really, Lucas is still just seven-years-old. But I am sixteen. I am growing up.

Looking at Lucas' grave, I realise it has been a decade since he left me. Ten years that I've had to make do with talking to a headstone. And that knowledge somehow justifies my need to be close to another human being. To T-J. To Christopher Bennett who got me drunk again, only this time on Merrydown. To Clive, back on leave, and with a girl in every port (including Torquay). And now, although I am not in a particular hurry, I am looking around for the next one — though they aren't exactly beating down my door, queuing up round the block, or doing any other clichéd nonsense in response to my newly-discovered feminine wiles. (I spurn cliches now I am a free thinker and like to push my imagination to its limits.) But I am not a sex maniac. I am not a tart or a slut. I am simply alive.

★   ★   ★

While I am being something of a free spirit, Cheryl is more conventional and has managed to get herself a steadier boyfriend, Doug, from Torquay Tech. He is doing something science-y for his A-levels so I have little in common with him, as I like to think of myself as the artistic sort. However, he has a car and is happy for me to tag along with him and Cheryl at the weekends as this means he can pair me off with his best mate, Nathan, a fellow scientist who can do the Rubik's cube in less than a minute. I put up with Nathan and he puts up with me, though we are anything but a pair. Despite having completely separate interests, we enjoy philosophical debates in the back of Doug's Mini as well as chips and chocolate.

Today we are on our way back from a drive to Brixham and have had plenty of time to indulge in our latest topic for debate, which is less philosophical than usual, revolving round the question: Who shot JR?

Despite being an avid *Dallas* fan thanks to Wink's encouragement, my heart isn't in it tonight. We are supposed to be heading back to Cheryl's to watch the long-awaited episode which will at last reveal the culprit. But I am tired and have eaten too much chocolate and too many sweets.

'Can you drop me home first, Doug?' I ask. 'I've got homework to finish.'

Seeing as I always have homework to finish they don't question my excuse, just moan at me for not being as organised as them.

'That's what I'm trying to do now,' I say, a little curtly and immediately feel guilty. It isn't their fault I'm having an off day.

Everything goes quiet. I've spoilt our camaraderie. Popped our bubble of friendship. Doug switches on Radio 3 and we pretend to listen appreciatively to Bach or Beethoven or whoever it is until at last we reach Bob's News.

'Enjoy the programme, I force myself to say. You'd better tell me all about it tomorrow.'

I get out the car. They each stare at me through the steamed-up windows. I stand for a second looking back at their cloudy faces as they drive off and have a bad feeling that I should've gone with them. There might not be many more times like this.

*   *   *

Cheryl has been put on the Pill by her mother in consultation with the doctor at the family planning clinic (is there really such a thing?). Cheryl's mother is the sensible, practical sort of mother that Helena could never have aspired to be (or Bob). All those hormones make Cheryl gain quite a bit of weight so she now looks as voluptuous as Marilyn Monroe. I too am piling on the pounds but that has more to do with the amount of chips and chocolate consumed in the back of Doug's Mini. And I, it has to be said, look nothing like a Hollywood legend. I will never be on an Athena poster with my dress blowing up all around me — or playing tennis without knickers for that matter. But I have reached the point where I don't especially care. I have power at my fingertips. I have knowledge in my heart and in my brain. I have the whole wide world at my feet.

★ ★ ★

Unfortunately by the time the conkers outside have all been secreted by squirrels and little boys and the Christmas lights are twinkling all over Torquay town, I have to rethink those bold statements. For I have used my power without thought for its consequences. I have buried my knowledge in the chambers of my heart and the craters of my brain. I have put my foot through the crack in the bottom of the world and slipped through it.

I am Stupid Philippa. I am Fat Philippa. I am Pregnant Philippa.

Oh bugger.

★ ★ ★

The worst of it is I don't know exactly how pregnant I am. What clues I have (a lost waistline, no morning sickness, forgotten dates) don't help me whatsoever in trying to pin down a particular time or place. Not that there have been that many times or that many places but there has been a certain amount of carelessness by all parties concerned. And surely it only takes the once. However many times I examine the finer details of the last few months, I am no clearer. I have no evidence. But instinct tells me what I can't possibly know for sure.

Where do I go from here? I don't have a

vigilant mother like Cheryl's watching over me (I wouldn't be in this position if I did). Nobody has a clue. Who shall I tell? I feel like a child again. Seven-years-old again. I don't know anything. I don't know my own body, my own mind. I am being invaded by an unwelcome task force, an invisible but overwhelming alien presence. I want to jump in the sea and swim and swim and swim across the bay, into the Channel and out into the wilds of the Atlantic, until I can swim no more. Or until I can find my mother. For surely this is how Helena must have felt when she discovered I was tumbling around inside her. Frightened. Confused. And it shouldn't have happened to her; somehow she got hold of a coil — according to Wink in her X-rated version of the Birds and the Bees. Helena told her once that I was born clutching it in my hand. Wink said you could never rely on contraception because that would be to underestimate the power of nature. The only safe way was to keep your legs crossed at all times. Well, I didn't do that. And now I am just like Helena. Poor Helena. Finally I know how she felt. Alone. No-one to turn to. Her father was a judge, remember . . . and her own mother was dying. She only had me.

I resort to crying. A flood I can't hold back however hard I bite my lip and dig my nails in my palms. I am crying for Helena. I am crying for Philippa. I am crying for this poor baby who can't possibly be real. But, according to the chemist somewhere on the other side of Torquay, most-definitely-one-hundred-percent *is* real and can no longer be ignored.

You would think it would be Wink or Bob that I turn to in the end, when I realise I can't do this alone. After all, they love me no matter what. But somehow I can't. Bob is happily engaged and caught up in his future life with Wonder Woman. Wink is going steadily downhill and even poor old Andy can be too much for her lap these days, and Captain too loud. There is the possibility of Linda or Auntie Sheila, but if I confide in one, the other will be offended. So I make my way down to the library one lunch time, on a day when I know my Tudor queen will be there. Miss Parry takes one look at me as I sidle up to the desk and whisks me off to a store room stuffed with books that almost distracts me from my mission impossible for a moment.

She sits me down on a chair, gives me a glass of water and I am back in the school library, the smell of polish and the feet of mini storm-troopers marching out to play. But I am not a little girl. I am most definitely not seven-years-old. I am a woman and I have to take responsibility. So I tell Miss Parry my barely-concealed secret and she doesn't tut or chide. She pats my hand and says, 'dear, dear'. I've done my part and from now on she seizes control, handing it over to doctors and teachers and finally to Bob who looks like he's discovered the world isn't the place he thought it was. Which, of course, is true for all of us at some point in our lives.

The end of term comes and goes without me taking part in the usual festivities or merry-making. At home, if I walk in a room, I catch a look between Bob and Wink that I am unable to fathom. I hear whisperings behind closed door, sometimes a raised voice, and I know that I have created this tense atmosphere that has never existed here before. Everything is changing and it is all my stupid fault. The relief of telling my family is spoilt with shame and guilt and knowledge.

And there is no escape. No release. I can't lie cocooned on the sofa like Lucas; I am not ill. I can't go out with Cheryl; I can't do any of the things a girl of my age should be doing. No more sitting in the back of Doug's Mini sharing chips and chocolate with Nathan. No more swimming in the Rainbow Hotel. No more hair crimping or *Smash Hits*. I can't even tell Cheryl, the closest I have to a best friend. I don't want to see her. I don't want to see anyone. So I stay in my room, not listening to music, not reading, not able to sleep.

I dread the return to school after the holidays. What's the point? I'll be having the baby in a few months.

'She should be able to stay at home,' Wink tells Bob. 'There's no sense packing her off to school in her condition.'

'She should go to school for as long as she can,' Bob insists, for once the stern father, putting both his feet down firmly. 'Her education's important. More important than ever.'

Maybe he is right but I sense he is trying to punish me in some way, whether he means to or not. I've let him down. And however many times they ask me who the father of the baby is, I never tell them. So he gets none of the blame. That privilege is all mine.

★   ★   ★

In the end, it is all for nothing. On Christmas Eve, I wake up early with the breath snatched out of me. I've been kicked in the guts from an unseen boot. And then again. And again. The pain is real, more real than anything that has happened so far in my life, but the pain is somehow not happening to me. I've stepped outside of my body and float up and away somewhere. Somewhere by the window where the curtains flicker in the draught. I've become someone else. Someone familiar and yet someone who's always lurked on the edge of my consciousness. I've become the Cavalier. I see through his steely eyes. I see a young woman curled up on the bed, hugging her stomach, cradling her unseen child that is trying for all its worth to be born early, too soon. I hear this young woman's screams. Watch her father run into the room, panic in his eyes, arms flailing, holding his daughter who looks impossibly young, though this is a grown-up's pain, a grownup's horror. She is left alone and then sometime later there's the sound of a siren screeching, footsteps on the stairs. The Cavalier floats alongside the girl as she is carried downstairs by two men in uniform, out the back way and into the ambulance, all the while sobbing with pain, with inevitability. The Cavalier covers her with a blanket, gives her oxygen, holds a sick bowl for her to vomit into, and carries her across Torquay in a whirr of noise and light. He pushes her through heavy metal doors, bumps her along corridors, distracts her from the squeak of lino, the splatters of sick. Then he leaves her. And Bob's face is there instead, holding her hand. Then nothing. There is nothing.

This baby has gone. It will never be. It is lost to the world. As lost as Helena. As lost as Lucas. As dead as Albert Morris.

★ ★ ★

I wake up, empty. It is over. I am just Philippa again. I am told I've had a lucky escape. I am told my life has been saved by the men in uniform and the doctors and nurses at the hospital.

I don't feel lucky. My baby has gone before it ever really got going. It has never breathed a breath or cried a cry. But then what do I know about babies? I know nothing. And how could I possibly be a mother when I have no mother of my own. Maybe it is a lucky escape after all.

I am technically still a child, the doctors and nurses make that perfectly clear. I should be kept on the children's ward but, given the sensitive

201

circumstances, I am shunted into a side room. After an immeasurable length of time, I am allowed out of bed to walk to the loo, a challenge in itself. After this Herculean task is accomplished, I shuffle back down the corridor to my room, but take a wrong turning, though maybe someone makes me go that way, who am I to say, she-who-knows-nothing.

My wrong turning brings me into the children's ward, the place they've been trying to keep me from. There are children of all shapes and sizes and illnesses, sitting, lying, eating, sleeping in beds livened up with shiny tinsel and glittery stars in an attempt at Yuletide celebrations. I stop at the foot of the bed where Dick Whittington once stood over Lucas, on his way to London. (He'd have more luck in the city than Helena, Lucas or me. I never want to go there again.)

Now there is a small girl in Lucas' place, her leg strung up and a mass of cards hanging all around her. Get Well Soon, they instruct her. And she will get well soon, no doubt. Her leg will heal and she'll go home and run around and live a happy life, and grow up and get herself a husband and bear children of her own one day in the future.

Lucas didn't get well. He was taken from that bed to the mortuary and then to his grave. I don't know where they put my baby. I don't want to think about that.

★　★　★

I am brought back to a home stripped of Christmas. It has been and gone and passed me by completely. A new term is approaching but I can't go back to school. Not yet. Bob listens to Wink and doesn't push me into it.

'Next week, Philippa,' he says. 'You mustn't leave it too long.'

'Maybe,' says Wink. 'See how you go.'

I lie silently on the sofa, the telly on, a blanket covering me. I can't face my room. My bed. For when night comes and I close the curtains, who knows what I'll be able to see? Then a *Blue Peter* special comes on and I cry again. I cry so much that Bob wonders if he should call the doctor. But Wink gives me a shot of her brandy instead and then somehow manages to scoop up old Andy from the hearth and place him gently beside me on the sofa, so I can cuddle him, listen to him purr, feel his thick, wiry fur on my face.

★   ★   ★

Days pass. The sun rises and sets in a muddle of time that has no meaning except for when the television is on to guide me. Some days I eat a little of what Bob puts in front of me. Sometimes it goes cold and congealed and is only fit for the bin. Sometimes I can sleep. Sometimes all I can do for a whole day is cry. But I have at least ventured into my room. Which is as it has always been. It if weren't for the gaping hole inside me, I could almost make myself believe nothing happened to me. It happened to someone else. Like it was something off the telly. On an

203

episode of *Angels*. A news item. Though I don't kid myself this is an important event in the grand scheme of things. But television helps. Television is more real than life at the moment. I can see why Lucas was so transfixed by it. His eyes like pebbles washed up on the beach.

★   ★   ★

I am grateful for Bob for never saying it was for the best. Maybe it was, but we'll never know that for sure. Instead, what he does is show me the love of a father. The love of a parent who feels his child's pain as sharply as if it were his own. He drops the whole school thing and tells the Head I'll be back in September to repeat my lower sixth. And he pops down to the travel agent in Castle Circus and buys two plane tickets. One for himself and one for me. We are going to Canada. We are going to hunt down my mother and . . . well, we don't know what. But we know it is something that has to be done at long last.

'What about Linda?' I ask, as we prop up the counter together during a quiet run in the shop.

He looks sheepish.

'She's too busy with work,' he comes up with eventually.

And I don't ask any more. It doesn't matter. I look round Bob's News and try to capture in my head the place where I've spent so much of my life: the shelves of papers and magazines and comics that bank one side of the shop; the cigarettes and tobacco — and everything you could possibly need to make a hobby out of smoking — displayed behind the counter; the chocolate and chewing gum and cough sweets; the grockle souvenirs, including those paper flags that wrench my heart from its mooring, set me adrift, whenever I see a child buy a packet with their pocket money; the local maps; the batteries; the plasters and safety pins and emergency sewing kits; the Mills and Boon rack that you can whizz round so all you see is a blur of petticoats and brunettes; the bell that pings every single time the door opens; the sound of the kettle boiling from the kitchenette out the back; the smell of print and sugar and old rain; the jars of sweets glittering like jewels, the first thing I ever set eyes on in here. A treasure trove. My home.

But still.

We are going to Canada!

2006

You made it. You made it this far and I will make sure you carry on all the way. You may only be small — like Lucas — but you have filled that gap, that empty space left by all those people I have lost. You have filled the minutes in the day when I used to stare, in the manner of Auntie Nina, into the middle distance and pretend I was Someone Else. The hours at night when I used to lose myself in the pattern of my curtains. You have filled me with emotion, worry and love, so that there is not room for much more right now. But they tell me you are a special baby for a different reason. You are on the Special List. A man has been down to see you, sent by Dr Standing (Auntie Cheryl to you) who I spoke to yesterday on the phone. 'I know the man for the job,' she said. 'If there's anything wrong, he'll find it and he'll put it right.' And here he is, poking and prodding and adding to your canon of notes, listening to your heart beat through a stethoscope. Your little heart that doesn't quite beat to the rhythm of my own.

You have a murmur. A possible hole in the heart. He says they can fix it. But I know without a shadow of a doubt that if anything happens to you, it is my own heart that will be broken beyond repair.

13

1982

Have I Got News For You

Three weeks later, I am feeling much stronger and I am in my bedroom packing an old suitcase with clean underwear plus all of my warm clothes, which include a new parka purchased by Linda especially for the trip. The chill that she is anticipating in Canada can't be anything like as cold as the atmosphere in a room when both she and Bob are in it at the same time — not that that is very often these days. Linda is always busy-busy, always driving from A to B and right through to the end of the alphabet and back, checking up on her underlings who can never hope to be as efficient as their boss. But she isn't efficient as far as Bob is concerned. He is always left in her pending tray, never quite got around to. Massages and Chinese takeaways have become a rare event indeed.

Still, Linda has made an effort to help me out on this trip. She thinks seeing my mother will help me get over not being a mother myself. I can't think clearly enough to decide whether she is right or not but I am grateful for the packing checklist which I've almost got through when I hear Bob's cough-shout

207

making its way up the stairs.

'Someone to see you,' it says. 'I'm sending them up.'

For a moment I wonder if it is. But it isn't. The footsteps are too light and determined. I am nonetheless very pleased to see Miss Parry pop her head round the door. She's brought me a book from the library. It has a maple leaf on the front.

'It's most comprehensive,' she says, handing it over. Then she gives me a smile that inspires valour and courage and the desire to step forth across the Atlantic and discover all the how's and why's of my mother's disappearance. Now is the time for answers.

'Send me a postcard.'

Then she is gone, leaving the Cavalier fluttering his eyelashes in the breeze created by her departure. I hope she's left some of her strength of character behind, just a little so that I can pack it in my suitcase and tick it off my checklist.

★ ★ ★

Two days later, after another stay at Toni's flat (her brother nowhere to be seen) and a taxi ride to Heathrow that Linda would have loved, Bob and I wait to board our plane. He buys us both a cup of tea and, to everyone around us, we must look like any other father and daughter going on holiday. But you never know what's going on with other people. You never know.

After a turbulent plane journey that takes us through a never-ending night from all that is familiar to all that isn't, we eventually touch down on Canadian soil. We collect baggage and stagger through customs, Bob proudly wielding his British passport as if this makes him superior in some way. And that is almost how we are treated, as English cousins from the posh side of the family (if only they knew). Everyone is so nice. They ask us if we've had a good flight, if we are staying long, if we know their cousin Doris who lives somewhere in the Greater Manchester area. Finally they insist we visit Niagara Falls (as if you could stop us) and impress on us the need to enjoy our trip, eh.

It is dark and foggy as we make our way outside Toronto airport, into the chill of the January night. I have little sense of this new country but feel sick with excitement and longing amongst other unnamed emotions. This is where Helena lives and breathes! She is probably sleeping in her bed, maybe minutes away from where we are standing right now, dreaming away an everyday sort of night, completely oblivious to our arrival.

Yes, oblivious. For Bob has only just admitted he hasn't told her we are coming. I'm not sure why he hasn't told her we are coming. Perhaps it's because he wanted to make sure she didn't run away again. But this does throw up all sorts of traumatic questions: What if she isn't there? What if she's gone on her holidays? What if she's moved? What if all this has been for nothing?

'She'll be there,' says Bob, the mind reader. 'Don't fret.'

And with this new-found confidence, he manages to grab us a taxi in a way that would impress both Helena and Linda. We are driven along the wrong side of the road with all its signs in English and French and metric, past skyscrapers we can't see the top of, down vast multi-lane highways and across back-to-front intersections, to our motel (a motel!).

Our motel isn't anything like the accommodation we stayed at in London with the avocado en-suite. Nor anything like Toni's flat in Belsize Park. We collect our key from a very nice man called Ed. Ed looks like he's been employed by the Canadian tourist board to satisfy our English expectations, in his checked shirt and deer stalker, as if he's about to set out and fell a giant tree. In the meantime he's watching an over-sized television in his little office.

'What's on?' Bob asks in an attempt at male-bonding.

'Hockey,' Ed says, immediately perking up.

It's nothing like the hockey I play at school. This hockey is played by huge men with crates on their heads zooming around on ice. The only men I've previously seen on ice have been of the Robin Cousins ilk, dressed in spangly costumes with too much blusher. I can see this will be the first of many cultural differences between our two countries.

Once Ed has enquired about our flight, our length of stay, his old school buddy, Ken in

210

Cirencester, and impressed upon us the need to enjoy our trip, we bid him goodnight and he points us in the direction of our home-from-home.

'Be sure to come and ask if you need anything,' he calls after us. 'I'll be right here, eh.'

Fortunately we don't have far to struggle with our luggage and the cold. We are soon inside our basic, to say the least, accommodation. Basic and not authentically Canadian accommodation; there isn't a racoon's tail or a picture of a Mountie to be seen. We make a (very) brief tour — twin beds, a small fridge, a two ring cooker, an ancient telly, a tiny bathroom (washroom) with only a shower, a loo, and a basin — and then unpack our night clothes and wash bags.

'Which bed do you want?' Bob asks.

I look at them both, with their overhead lights in the fake wooden headboards and indicate the one by the window which doesn't appear to sag as much as the other as far as the eye can tell. (I am recuperating from a near death experience, remember.)

'I'll get changed in the bathroom,' Bob says.

I listen to the noises he makes through the bathroom door and realise that I've never watched him brush his teeth or shave or do any of those things I might have witnessed if he were my real father. But this is not the time for regrets. He has brought me here after all. No-one else in the world would have done that.

He re-appears after several minutes in his Marks and Sparks striped pyjamas and towelling dressing gown.

'It's all yours.'

I wish it wasn't. It's grim inside. There's something about the shower curtain that brings Norman Bates to mind. Maybe it'll be less horrifying in daylight. But unfortunately there's no window, so presumably not.

Once I've brushed my teeth and got into my own familiar pyjamas, I feel better. It doesn't matter where we stay. All I want is a bed. And the bed isn't so bad. It is good enough to lure me towards sleep, to soften all visions of a psycho lurking in the shadows. I turn on my side and gaze at the window, the orange curtains. And I blow a kiss at the Cavalier who's stowed away in my suitcase and followed me across the ocean in the hold of the plane and is right at this moment settling himself down for the night, getting ready to watch over me.

★ ★ ★

It is late morning when we finally surface into a fug of jet lag. After a shower (a very brief shower due to the cold and the haunting violin shrieks), we have a complimentary cup of coffee. Then we sit on our beds and stare at each other.

'Let's get some breakfast,' says Bob. 'That's the best place to start.'

So he puts on his sheepskin coat that makes him look like a thinner version of Bernie and I put on my parka. He eases open the front door and we step into our first day in Canada. We promptly go straight back indoors. It's freezing out there! A thick layer of snow covers the

212

over-night cars in the parking lot and we realise that even Linda hasn't prepared us for this.

'We need proper boots,' Bob decides. 'And maybe a hire car.'

'How about we order a taxi instead,' I suggest. 'That way you don't have to worry about driving in all this.' I sweep my hand in a grand gesture at the vista through our window. On the wrong side of the road.

Bob is about to object but then he gives in. He knows I'm right.

'We need to get breakfast first,' he says. 'According to this,' — he brandishes a curled up leaflet from a selection on the bedside cabinet — 'there's a diner called Sally Ann's round the corner. Reckon we can make it that far?'

'Yes,' I say. 'We can make it.' We are Polar explorers on the verge of venturing out into the undiscovered wild (though someone has always been there before you. Just because you stake your claim, doesn't mean you're the first one).

We spend the next few minutes scrambling into gloves and scarves and coats. Finally I zip up my hood which means I have to survive from now on with limited tunnel vision. Bob dons a flat cap which might cover the bald patch but which makes him look twenty years older (and he's getting on a bit, somewhere in that vague, indistinguishable region of Middle Age).

'Are you sure you want to wear that?' I can't help asking. After all, he might be seeing my mother later today, the love of his life. Doesn't he want to impress her?

'It's all I've got,' he says forlornly. 'Linda

forgot to buy me a proper hat. Whatever a proper hat is for these occasions.'

'We'll have to get you something else after breakfast then,' I decide. 'We'll know when we see it.'

He doesn't argue. He picks up his wallet, secures it inside the deep pocket of his coat and then taps it, treating it like the precious object it is. For I know the wallet contains all our Canadian dollars and travellers cheques but also, and most importantly, the wallet contains Helena's address and telephone number.

This time we are slightly more prepared for the cold that assaults us on every front as we set foot back outside, a sharp wind quickly numbing any available skin. I track behind Bob across the parking lot, following the tail of his coat, Scott and Oates, into the unknown, down the road (highway), looking for somewhere authentically Canadian to eat. We pass a gas station and a restaurant called Tim Hortons which sells every type of doughnut (donut) you could possibly imagine and which I like the look of.

'We need a proper breakfast,' Bob says. 'Not cakes.'

On we go, past smart shops and offices, another gas station, a school, and more exotic-looking fast food outlets (of which we've only heard rumours in Torquay, like some kind of urban myth that has some truth in it after all). Ten minutes later we are still not there, at our authentic Canadian diner.

'I thought you said it was round the corner.'

'It is,' says Bob. 'That's what the leaflet said.'

It's becoming apparent that being a pedestrian in a country where size is on a different scale altogether to ours back home isn't going to be easy, particularly when snow is fluttering into the equation. Just as we are beginning to lose all sense of reason, and any feeling in our extremities, we find it: Sally Ann's.

Inside Sally Ann's is a warm welcome in every sense of the word. We are able to take off our coats before being shown to a booth by a waitress who looks like she enjoys her job and says, 'Welcome to the Great White North,' when she spots our red noses.

We both order as close to a full English as we can: eggs (sunny side up), bacon, fried tomatoes, toast and a bottomless cup of fresh coffee which is a far cry from the Mellow Birds we're used to at home. The food when it comes is only spoilt by the apprehension gurgling away in the complicated workings of my insides (and in Bob's too by the sounds of it).

'Are you going to phone her?' I indicate the wallet which Bob has laid carefully in the centre of the table, secure between the two of us and a wall of napkins (serviettes). He rubs his bare head, possibly trying to warm it up, maybe trying to get his brain into gear.

'I think we should leave it for today.' He rubs a little harder when he notices my raised eyebrow. 'You look far too tired for any excitement. We could do some shopping, go back to the motel, watch some Canadian TV, read a book, have an early night. That way we'll be on the ball tomorrow.' He replaces the flat cap on his head,

215

even though he's always been adamant it's rude to eat with your hat on.

And why this mention of books? I can't remember the last time I saw Bob read a book. He's quite possibly stalling. But I don't object and exclaim: *No, Bob, let's do it today! Let's go hunt down my mother!* I just mumble a quiet 'alright.' Even after a second refill of coffee, I am shockingly tired. And I am most definitely stalling.

* * *

Once we've wrapped up well again, we locate a department store and purchase a hat called a tuque or a toque or something like that, which is apparently what all Canadians wear in winter, apart from Ed who over the next two weeks will never be seen in anything but his deer stalker that brings Michael Landon to mind in *Little House on the Prairie* (rather than Sherlock Holmes). Tuques (or toques) are not particularly attractive, being basically a bobble hat without the distraction of a bobble. It seems Canadians are more bothered about function than appearance which suits Bob down to the ground. Though I can't help wishing the tuque (or toque) suited Bob down to the ground. Still, at least his bald patch is covered up.

We then find a grocery store near the motel and gather essentials to see us through the remainder of the day so that we can hibernate till morning. For the morning should bring us more excitement and trepidation than today. It should bring us my mother.

★ ★ ★

When I wake up, daylight has scared off the Cavalier. This is it then: morning. I sit up and look over at Bob's bed. Bob's empty bed. For a second I wonder if he's taken off, scared to face up to his responsibilities for once in his life. But then I hear the shower and Bob's morning ablutions.

Bob will never let me down. That's the job of other people, namely my mother (and that hopeless father of mine, running in circles in the jungle, most probably shacked up with some Amazonian woman with a whole tribe of children of his own).

Perhaps I should feel more excited at the prospect of seeing Helena but actually I feel very little that is good. I feel sick, sad, scared by all the different scenarios. What if her condominium is bigger than she's always maintained? What if Orville Tupper still calls me 'kid'? Even though I'll be closer to his dizzying heights than a decade ago (though much closer than I could actually have guessed). What if Helena doesn't know who I am? What if she slams the door in my face? What if she cries? What if she doesn't cry? What if, on seeing me again, she hot foots it to the Soviet Union, to Australia, to outer space? And this time, like Lucas, her disappearance will be for good. Forever. Which, when all is said and done, is a very long time.

Bob escapes the clutches of Norman Bates and has scrubbed up well despite sharing a shower with a psychopath. Hopefully Helena won't be too shocked at how much he's aged over the last ten years. He's softened the edges a little with soap and Brylcreem and something less obvious, possibly hope. But then of course Helena has got older too. I still think of her as young but she'll be in her thirties now, in her prime. Will she really want Bob and me turning up on her doorstep with all our baggage?

After a half-hearted breakfast we wash up and brush our teeth. Then there's really nothing left to do.

'Ready, Philippa?' he asks.

'As I'll ever be.' I put on my most courageous smile, drawing on the vibes of Miss Parry, my Virgin Queen back across the ocean.

★ ★ ★

The address we have for Helena is only a few blocks away according to Ed but a fair old distance by our standards. Ed orders us a cab and invites us to sit down and watch some American soap opera with him while we wait. The soap opera is made up of over-tanned, long-legged, almost-beautiful people who've never seen the inside of a drama school. The programme is thankfully relieved at frequent intervals with many adverts for things I've never heard of, mainly medication of some description. I add these cultural differences to the ones I've already absorbed and am in a far off daydream, far away from the here and now when Bob taps me on the shoulder and tells me it's time to go.

'Have a nice day, eh,' says Ed. And then, as we are about to leave him alone with his TV, he adds: 'Did you know Toronto is the Mohawk word for 'meeting place'?'

I didn't know that. And I have no idea why Ed has decided to tell me this right now. But I am pleased to hear it nonetheless. After all, it's about time I met my mother.

★ ★ ★

'Here you go,' says the driver. 'This building right here. Real nice condos.' He whistles to illustrate just how nice these 'condos' are.

And they are nice. A far cry from the Upstairs of Bernie's Lot. Several notches up from our two-up-two-down. A different league altogether from the maisonette above the shop that we've left back in Britain, further away than all the miles we've travelled to get here. Helena's home is somewhere in there, somewhere inside the impressive building that looms above us. Soon I'll get out the taxi, enter the lobby, or whatever they call it in this country, and quite possibly be reunited with my mother. Any minute now.

'Philippa?' Bob says. 'Are you coming?'

Bob has paid the driver and is holding out his gloved hand to help me because I am incapable of voluntary movement. He guides me towards the towering darkened glass doors and has to take my hand to get me through them.

'This is a bad idea,' I tell him.

'Have you got a better one?' he asks.

I let him lead me towards the lift or elevator or whatever and watch his finger push the button that lights up a number 6 and then we're inside, Bob and I, the smell of stale smoke and air freshener, going up, up, nearer and nearer our destination, until we're almost at the home that has never had quite enough room for me, that I was expecting to be small and poky and a bit of a hovel but that I now suspect is going to be rather grander, bigger, than I've ever pictured on all those lonely nights, staring at my curtains, trying to conjure up my mother.

There is a jolt, a ting-a-ling, the quiet swoosh of the lift doors like in *Star Trek*, soft carpet underfoot down the long corridor, brass numbers on front doors, looking for the right one, the one that's waiting at the far end with the name TUPPER written in neat schoolgirl handwriting on the label below the bell. A bell that Bob presses with determination mustered from somewhere or other. A door that will open to reveal . . .

. . . a boy? . . .

A school boy of maybe nine or ten.

'Hi,' he says. 'Who are you?'

I feel like saying the same thing only I can't speak. I can't say anything, anything at all. Bob has to kick-start his own voice with a cough.

'I'm Bob,' he says. 'I'm a friend of Helena's.' When the boy doesn't respond, he adds: 'Have we got the right address?'

'Uh-huh,' the boy says. But it is me he is

looking at. Me, he is interested in.

'This is Philippa,' Bob says.

'Philippa.' The boy rolls my name around his mouth, tasting it, like a Revel, wondering what flavour it will turn out to be, if it is one he'll like. Or one he'll want to spit out in disgust. (My metaphors are coming on no end since being in the sixth form, even with all that time off.)

The boy stands very still but there is a slight flicker in his eyes that suggests his brain is doing something, making connections.

'You mean Aunt Philippa?'

His brain is quite clearly not working properly and Bob has to put him right because my brain isn't working at all.

'No,' he laughs. 'Philippa's only sixteen. Philippa . . . Helena . . . well . . . '

As Bob stutters, falters, can find no way of introducing me to this unknown boy staring up at us, he is saved by a man's voice from deep within the condo.

'Wes,' it says. 'Who is it, kid?'

If I were asthmatic this is when I'd reach for my inhaler but unfortunately I have no such crutch and have to ride it out, this wave of memory that is earnestly trying to drown me, to squeeze the air into my lungs and not let it out again.

'It's Bob and Philippa, Dad,' the boy calls out. 'Shall I show them in?'

There is a gap, a black hole of silence.

'Sure,' the voice says eventually. 'Bring them on in.'

'Follow me,' Wes says and I am compelled to

do as this boy instructs, even though I'd far rather retrace my steps, get back in the lift, back in the taxi, back to the motel where I can settle down in front of the adverts with Ed.

Wes ushers us into the hospital-warmth and shuts the door behind us. We are standing in a wide long hallway on a glossy wooden floor. There are black and white photographs all around us on the walls. Landscapes. Mountains. Prairies. Lakes. Forests. That sort of Canada thing. A single-stemmed orchid blossoms in a glass pot, tall and slender, its roots on show, seeking out the light, its scarlet red flower a shock against the white walls, the black and white photos. I can't smell the flower . . . but I can pick out the lingering remains of Helena's cigarette smoke and perfume. I'd know that anywhere.

'This way,' Wes says when we've put our coats and winter-wear on the hallstand. We follow him down the hallway, past several doors, all closed, all possibly hiding Helena.

'Through here.' We reach the end and Wes disappears into a room which, when we step in behind him, turns out to be some sort of living room/office. There is a big red sofa beneath the picture window which overlooks a tree-filled park, all white and dramatic. There are more photographs in here, row upon row of black and white framed portraits. Handsome chiselled men — the sort that pose mysteriously and make women swoon. Over in the corner stands an ornate bureau above which hangs a cork notice board with messages and lists pinned to it, most of them written in the loops and curls that I've never quite managed to forget. And then the centrepiece of the room: a vast table covered in papers and magazines and photos and general mess, behind which sits Orville Tupper. All he needs is a fluffy white cat.

'Bob,' he says. 'It's been a while.'

I don't hear Bob's reply. I can only stare at Orville Tupper sitting there, making no effort to get up, showing no signs of pleasure at seeing us. Waiting for him to notice me, to speak to me.

'Hi Philippa,' he says on cue. 'You've grown up.'

This is the first time I've heard my mother's husband say my name. Somehow I wish he'd stuck with 'kid' because my name is the one thing he cannot take away from me. I want him to keep his hands off it. It is mine.

Bob answers for me.

'Children have a tendency to do that,' he says. And I could kiss him for those words, for sticking up for me.

Orville doesn't notice this dig — or ignores it — and takes Bob at his word.

'They sure do. Seems like only yesterday Wes was in diapers.'

'Is he . . . your son?' Bob blushes as he asks this question which, given the circumstances, is rather personal and obtrusive.

'Sure,' Orville says. And when there's more silence than anyone can bear, he adds: 'And Helena's too, of course.'

Of course. I knew this the moment Wes opened the door. I knew he was Helena's son, though strangely it was the one scenario I've never played out. I've never in a million years imagined her having other children, not when she tried so hard to keep her first born at ocean's length.

'Wes, can you go get some pop for our guests. Or would you like coffee?'

'Coffee,' I manage to say, my first word. I don't want Orville thinking I want pop. Like he said, I am grown up. I drink coffee.

'Do you need a hand?' I ask Wes.

'No, I'm alright,' he says. 'I do it all the time.'

Orville waits for Wes to go and then he speaks in a quiet voice. 'Wes is very helpful. He's had to grow up fast and help out around the place. You know, since the accident.'

'Accident?' Bob asks.

It is then that we are told. We realise why Orville didn't get up. He isn't being rude. He is stuck in that position. Always stuck in that position. In a wheelchair. Paralysed from the waist down after a car crash five years before.

I hear Orville Tupper explaining all this. I hear it and I am pleased. Not because I've had my revenge already done for me. But because it goes some way to giving me a reason, a real reason, why Helena hasn't called for me. She must have had Wes unexpectedly and then, just as he was old enough and she thought she could send for me at last, there was the accident. Orville in a wheelchair and no longer able to earn money as a model. That was what happened. She did love me. She does.

I slump onto a chair next to Bob who's already

224

taken up Orville on his offer of a seat. If I don't sit down I could quite possibly faint with the excitement of it all. The shock. The relief.

Orville is now on a level with me. Across the table I can see his hands that once might have appeared in adverts for Canada's equivalent to Ratner's. Now they have calluses and look rough and raw from doing the work his legs used to.

'I guess we never quite got round to you, Philippa,' he says. 'I'm sorry.'

And it is that word, sorry, that makes me cry.

Bob hands me his hanky and after a few minutes I am calm enough to notice the mug of coffee on the table in front of me. The boy next to me, offering me a donut.

'Thanks, Wes.' I am suddenly ravenous and sugar is what I need. A cake. A comfort.

'You're welcome,' he says.

'Why did you call me Aunt Philippa?' I ask him, after a few mouthfuls, while Bob and Orville talk about unimportant things like the state of the Canadian health service and education system. But Orville is still half-tuned into our conversation and cuts in.

'It's my sister's name too,' Orville says. 'My kid sister, back home in Labrador. Wes has never met her but she's around your age. Funny, eh? Two Philippas Wes has never met.'

We make half-hearted smiles and murmurs. Then I ask the question no-one has asked.

'Where is Helena?'

'At work,' Orville says with a note of longing. 'In a book store down town. She's not home till six.' He checks his watch. 'Wes, you need to get back to school.'

'Sure, Dad,' he says, getting up, not needing to be asked twice, going round the table and then bending and kissing him on his still-lush fine head of hair. 'It was nice meeting you,' he calls over his shoulder as he leaves, already putting on gloves and a toque of his own (which, it has to be said, isn't any better on him than on Bob).

'He's a good kid,' Orville says. 'Comes home everyday for lunch just so's I'm not on my own.'

We listen to this good kid retreat down the hall, close the front door and we all wish he was still here, a distraction. I concentrate on Helena's ring on my finger, twiddling it round and round in an attempt to loosen it.

'I could call her if you want,' Orville suggests after an awkward pause. 'I'm sure she could make an excuse to come back. Her boss is real considerate.'

'Helena always has considerate bosses,' I say and Bob flushes the colour of prawns for sale on a hot summer's day in Torquay harbour.

'That would be good,' Bob agrees. 'I mean, we could come back another time. Or maybe we could go and see her.'

'Sure, why don't you do that? I can call you guys a cab if you want?'

Orville looks relieved to be able to hand over responsibility for us to his wife. He looks relieved at the prospect of our imminent departure from his home. But he doesn't look like he hates us, which is what I've always assumed. Instead he seems a little embarrassed, guilty perhaps, even sad. Maybe his accident has taught him that life is capable of changing in a second. A lesson I learned a long time ago.

★ ★ ★

We are back inside another taxi, shuttling us for ten minutes or so from Helena's home to Helena's place of work. It drops us right outside Jabberwocky, a small second-hand bookshop in a back street downtown, old-fashioned but respectable and, for all her longings to be modern and with-it, I can see this is the sort of place Helena would love to spend her days. As I would. For unlike Bob, my mother and I love to be surrounded by books.

Bob hands over more Canadian dollars and then we are left standing in the cold, snow whistling around us, weighing down the branches of the trees that line this quaint avenue that is so far from Bob's News.

'Come on,' he says. 'This is it.'

As if I need telling.

This time I take the lead. I stand for a few moments studying the shop window with its rather clever display of Agatha Christie's before I push open the door. I keep my head down until Bob is inside too, shutting the weather out, standing next to me, stamping his boots on the mat.

There are rows of books in here (obviously, being a book store) but they are packed so tight, so high, that you can't see through them, beyond them. You have to walk around the stacks and down the rows to get a feel for the layout, to find your way around, to make your way past the counter, the ancient till, the man writing in a ledger, looking up and smiling a welcome, saying, 'Hello, can I help you?'

You have to strain yourself to hear Bob's reply as his voice is now almost all cough. But you still can't see anyone else, no other customers, no woman who can pass for your mother. No woman in her prime with smart clothes and accessories. No lipstick. No high heels. But if you turn the corner at the back of the shop, you can at last see someone who might pass for her, but she is obscured by the trolley of books beside her, so you can't be certain. There is a copy of *Madame Bovary* in her hand, which she is about to push into its place on the shelf. There are glasses perched on the end of her nose. Her fine dark hair, no hint of grey, is piled on top of her head. You will see her look up at the sound of footsteps. A double-take. Eyes opened wide in wonder. A jaw dropped. *Madame Bovary* crashing to the floor, the pages rippling open.

'Philippa? Is that you?'

Her voice is deeper than I remember. Years of countless cigarettes. I want to make my own voice loud and clear. I want it to ring out across the battlefields but all I can manage is a mouse-like: 'Yes, it's me, Philippa.'

She pushes her glasses up onto her head, takes a step towards me, puncturing *Madame Bovary* with her heel. Then she stops and takes a deep breath before reaching out for me. I go to her. I am in her arms and the smell of her — perfume and smoke — turns back the clock, wipes away the last decade, shrinks me back to a little girl again. A little fat girl with ribbons in my hair. *A hundred brushes a day.*

I shut my eyes and feel her holding me, awkward and tense but strong and firm. Then she lets go. I hear her give out a small gasp. I turn to the place her eyes are now focused and there is Bob. I don't know how long he's been standing there but he can see as clearly as I can that Helena is crying.

'You brought her,' she says, breathing hard to try and control the sobs. 'I always hoped you would.'

Bob stays still, stays firm.

'You could've come back, Helena,' he says. 'It wasn't up to me.'

'I know . . . I'm sorry . . . I couldn't . . . '

The considerate boss is now also crammed into the row of books with Helena, Bob and myself.

'Would you care to take your friends out the back, Helena?' he enquires softly, handing her a hanky. 'I'll make you all tea.'

She smiles at him, grateful, and I can see that Helena has tried her hardest to replace Bob. But we both know — Mother and me — that that is quite impossible.

★ ★ ★

Half an hour later we've drunk tea, we've explained our visit to Orville. She's smoked two cigarettes whilst explaining Wes. And it is as I expected. She found out she was pregnant with Wes soon after arriving in Canada. She'd had a difficult time with him, as he was a sickly child. Orville was away most of the time, modelling. And then, as she was getting on top of things, she had a visit from the police late one night, informing her that Orville had been in a near-fatal car crash out in New York State.

'I'm sorry, Philippa.' She takes my hand, squeezes it tight. 'I should've told you. I was stupid not to . . . I suppose I thought it was best this way. You had Bob.'

She smiles at him. The lines around her mouth disappear.

'You had Bob and I thought you were better off with him. I still think that. Really.' She squeezes my hand even tighter so I think she might crush it, break my fingers. But it is somehow a comfort to feel the ring she left for me all those years before dig into my skin. I know I am really here, in this moment. 'I can't tell you how happy I am to see you.' She says this so quietly I hope I'm not imagining it.

She *does* look happy. She's lost that edginess she used to carry around with her, along with her Consulates and lipstick. The edginess that she could pull out of her handbag at any given moment. I'm not stupid enough to think she's only just discovered happiness now, having finally seen me after all these years. I am not confusing happiness with relief. Helena's state goes deeper than relief. Far deeper. It is a contentment with her life in Canada, despite the accident and the changes that it must have brought them all. Despite the fact she never sent for me.

And I think of all the things I could be saying. All the things I could be shouting. But it doesn't matter. I am here with Helena when she could so easily have been killed in that car crash that took away the use of Orville's legs. When for all I know she could've been as dead as Albert Morris or Lucas. As dead as my baby that never was. Helena is alive and living a life without me. And, knowing that, seeing that for myself, is alright. I don't want to ask if I can move into the condo and play big sister to Wes. I want to have my holiday, go to Niagara, spend some time with my mother and then leave her here while I go back home with Bob. Back home to Wink and Andy and Captain. I want to see Cheryl. I want to see Auntie Sheila and Linda. I even want to see Bernie. And, now the memory is beginning to fade, a little, I want to see Terry and Clive and even Christopher Bennett because they are part of my life. My home. So I have nothing else to say. I only want to listen to her talk about Toronto, to Bob recounting tales of Torquay and its residents that make Helena smile wistfully. That is enough.

At last, when Helena has stubbed out her third cigarette, she says she'd best get back to work, though I like to think she would have stayed much, much longer, talking, listening. Bob and I go through the rigmarole of hats and gloves and coats all over again and then Helena walks us back through the shop, to the door.

'How long did you say you were here for?' She

brushes the drips from my shoulders, without thinking what she is doing.

'Just a week,' Bob says. 'There's the shop . . . and Wink . . . '

At Wink's name, Helena has to blow her nose again. But then she forces some deep breaths on herself, conjures up the strength of her old friend across the ocean, strong despite her wheelchair and her hastening decline, and makes herself say difficult words.

'Why now?' she asks. 'I mean, why did you decide to come now?'

Bob looks at me, waiting to see if I'll answer this question. But I don't feel the need to tell Helena. I might be happy to see her, happy to hear why she's been absent from my life, but I don't feel the need to tell her about my latest loss. That experience belongs to Bob and me. He is the one that will pick up the pieces.

'Bob thought it was time,' I say,

'Thank you,' she says, turning her attention to him. She lightly touches his arm and his face melts in a way that it has never done with Linda.

★   ★   ★

That night I banish all thoughts of Norman Bates and my Cavalier. I focus on Wes and Orville and Helena. I am back in their living room that overlooks the tree-filled park, sitting on the sofa, reading the lists pinned on the notice board, picking up the papers strewn across the table, breathing the cigarettes and perfume of Helena. My mother.

We've arranged to see Helena again the next day for lunch but our plans are going to have to change. Bob is having a bad night, swinging between vomiting and heavy bouts on the toilet. I give up trying to ignore the disgusting noises in the end and turn on the radio which I've only just discovered, also built into the headboard along with the light (what other gadgets are hidden in there?).

When Bob too realises he'll never manage any sleep, he says: 'I don't think I'm going to make it to see Helena today.' He looks miserable. Forlorn. Like the bottom has fallen out of his world (when actually the world has fallen out of his bottom).

'You can still go,' he says. 'Ed'll put you in a cab.'

Yes, I could still go but it won't be the same without Bob there beside me.

★ ★ ★

And I do go. I am put in a taxi by Ed, I have lunch with Helena in a diner round the corner from Jabberwocky and she tells me about Wes, she tells me about Orville's new business (he runs a kind of male model agency from home) and I tell her about school, about the shop, about what I hope to do in the future. But I don't tell her everything. And she probably holds things back from me too. But I can't help feeling a sense of history. Just the two of us. After all

233

these years. It was never easy then. Somehow it is easier now.

Afterwards, she gives me a hundred dollars (*A hundred dollars? Think of it as pocket money back payment.*) and tells me to go shopping. To have fun and give Bob a chance to rest. She'd come with me only she has to go back to work. She points out the best shops within walking distance and gives me details of a bus that will take me all the way back to the motel when I am done (presumably because she still has little confidence I'll be able to stop a taxi dead in its tracks the way she can).

I have a surprisingly good time on my own, feeling much more adventurous than when I went to London and rode the tube with Raymond — though I don't actually manage to spend more than a few dollars on souvenirs, including a must-have racoon's tail and some postcards, one of which will be for Miss Parry. When I eventually return to the motel, there is a note from Bob pinned to the door, telling me to sit with Ed for a bit while he catches up on sleep. So I spend the next few hours with Ed, hat on his head, Labatt's in his hand, watching the hockey and the bad American actors. And of course, my favourite, the ads, wondering if there might be an old one of Orville's.

★ ★ ★

Bob is up and about the next day but looking ashen and wiped-out so we don't go far. We can't see Helena as she has to take Orville for a

234

hospital check-up. But we do make it to a travel agents where we book a coach ride and an overnight stay in a hotel. We are going to Niagara!

★　★　★

The following day we visit a museum and traipse through a shopping mall where every other shop sells ice hockey gear. Later, Helena and Wes join us for afternoon tea in a hotel lounge. I remember the white gloves she used to make me wear. The ones I mislaid up the chimney. I remember Lucas shouting, 'All scream for ice cream!' She must remember too because she catches my eye. But we don't mention his name for that would open a box of memories that have been hidden in the attic for far too long.

Then we say our goodbyes and arrange to meet one more time, after our tourist trip, before we head back to Britain.

★　★　★

I've seen pictures of Niagara in books. I've watched the film with Marilyn Monroe. And — perhaps because I've grown up beside the sea and know what water can do — the unstoppable power of the Falls has always frightened me. But not enough to prevent me from witnessing this sight myself. I used to imagine the almost-deafening crash of the Falls from one great lake to another. The spray hovering above like great billowing clouds of smoke. The thundering water. But I am not prepared for seeing it — this wonder of the world — in winter.

Bob and I stand at the rails, staring in awe. The water still continues to fall on and on like it has done for thousands of years. But at the edges, there are frozen formations like monsters trapped in ice. There is even a bridge of ice that you can imagine stepping onto and walking across the river, crossing from Canada to America. But it is enough to stand there, to see the weird ice-shapes, the water crashing, the frozen spray clinging to the trees and lampposts all around us.

'Did you know in 1848 the residents of Niagara woke up to a deafening silence?' Bob is reading from a guide book, loudly, so he can be heard above the boom of the water, and through the parka covering my ears. 'The falls had dried up by some freak of nature. Further upstream the Niagara River had frozen and prevented the falls from working properly. When the ice began to thaw, the falls once again thundered and the residents could breathe easy again.'

Bob gives up on the guidebook after this; the wind howls off the river and the snow hits us horizontally in the face. But it is more than the impossible weather; he is speechless. So am I. We will never see anything like this again.

★   ★   ★

Our final morning. We are getting ready to meet Helena for a last coffee in yet another diner, the Lakeside Grill, somewhere near the CN Tower (which Bob and I have yet to see the top of, as it has so far been enveloped in clouds). Just as we are putting on our boots, there's a knock on the door.

'It's probably Ed,' I say. But when I open the door it quite clearly isn't.

'Hello,' Helena says. 'I thought I'd better come now in case I lost my nerve later.'

'Lost your nerve?'

'I wanted to make sure I said goodbye properly this time.'

She comes in and then fumbles in her handbag for something — hopefully not her old edginess. Probably her cigarettes.

'I got you this,' she says.

She hands over a book. But not any old book she could've plucked off the shelf at work. I sit on the bed and savour the present for a moment. I can't remember ever opening presents from Helena though I must've done at some point when I was little. Those memories have been replaced with memories of Bob's presents. Wink's presents. Cheryl's and Linda's and Auntie Sheila's. I can only ever remember the handful of cards and letters from Helena. They are kept in my top drawer, wrapped in a yellow baby shawl, every curl and loop memorised.

'Go on, Philippa, open it.'

She is sitting on the bed next to me. So close I can feel the cold coming off her coat. I can hear a slight crackle and wheeze as she breathes in and out. I can smell her cigarettes and perfume.

I carefully unwrap the tissue paper, peeling back the Sellotape so I won't rip it. I think I am

237

about to lose my grip that has been so tight the last few days when I see what is inside: the best book in the world: *The Cat in the Hat* by Dr Seuss.

'It's a first edition,' Helena says. 'I picked it up during a house clearance, years ago. I always knew I wanted you to have it.'

'Thanks,' I say. I look up at her green eyes, her red lips. 'I wish I had something to give you.'

'Don't be silly,' she says. 'You don't owe me anything . . .'

Her tears are just waiting round that corner.

' . . . Everything I've ever done . . . however awful things might appear . . . it was . . . it was because I loved you . . . even if it hasn't always seemed that way.'

You can say that again, is what I think. But I don't say it. There is no point. I've flown across the ocean and now I know I don't want Helena back. She hasn't been kidnapped or held against her will. I don't need to enrol the help of the British High Commissioner. She doesn't need to be rescued. Helena is staying here. And Bob and I are going home.

★   ★   ★

We settle our bill with Ed who takes it upon himself to give me a (grizzly) bear hug.

'Take care of yourself, Philippa, eh.'

Then he turns to Bob. 'And don't forget . . . if you're ever in the Cirencester area, be sure to look up Ken. Tell him he owes me a beer.'

He thumps Bob on the back so hard I think he

might topple over, felled like a giant tree. After the Falls, Ed is quite possibly the closest we'll get to the Canada of my dreams.

* * *

Bob and I are back in Torquay the following night. As Linda drives us along the front, the lights remind me of Niagara, but only slightly as Niagara is far more like Blackpool than our sedate town. They remind me how far away Canada is. How pleased I am to be home. To know where Helena is. To know she loves me even though she hasn't exactly shown it. I might never quite get to the bottom of it but I am just about old enough to know I am not going to keep looking back. And wise enough to realise this will be unavoidable.

Linda picks us up from the station. She looks washed-out and — I am not sure if it is the shoulder pads — more than a little tense.

'Hard day at the office, dear?' Bob asks, trying to cheer her up, presumably hoping for a welcome home massage.

'Don't,' she says, in a way that suggests absence hasn't made her heart grow fonder.

* * *

When Linda leaves us at the shop that night, we don't see her again. It turns out Princess has been having an affair with some bloke she's got to know over the airwaves. The engagement is off, though I am ever hopeful things can be

239

patched up between her and Bob. In April, this dim hope shines a little brighter. A British task force that includes Linda's son, Clive, sets sail on a 7,500 mile journey to liberate a small group of islands we've never heard of; Linda might need Bob again. But that would be to underestimate Linda, a woman of substance. She doesn't ask for Bob's comforting arms. And Bob doesn't offer them. There is only one woman he wants to hold. And that is not Linda.

April is also a trying time for the Queen. While her boys are off defending an outpost of her empire, she is in Ottawa, proclaiming an Act of Parliament that will sever all remaining constitutional and legislative ties between Britain and Canada. This is the last straw for Bob who sinks into the wet sands of depression that only Valium and long walks across Dartmoor can pull him out of. So it is just as well I am not going back to school until September. Someone has to help Patty. Someone has to get up at the crack of dawn and sort out the papers (and paperboys). Someone — me — has to grow up. But I am not sure I am quite ready for that yet.

2006

I'm the grown-up now. I'm the mother. But I still need reassurance. The cardiologist does his best to do that and he has now left us alone. I feel a wave of peace lapping at my ankles, enough to know it is there, a possibility.

The cardiologist has confirmed there is a problem with your heart. They need to do some further investigations but he suggests it will be a condition that may sort itself out. If not, the doctors will fix the hole in your heart. As for the one in mine, you are the one who can mend that. Which is probably too much to ask of you. Too much for any mother to ask of her child.

It will mean more hospitals. More doctors. More treatment. And I've been there before. And not just for Lucas.

But right now I need power and knowledge. So I read the leaflet that has been left for me.

A person with a hole in the heart is born with it — this is called a congenital condition. Most of the time it's not known why the person has the hole in the heart. It happens when a baby's heart does not develop normally in the womb.

There is no specific cause for this condition, but some things increase your risk of being born with the problem. For example, if the mother had German measles or toxoplasmosis (an infection that is passed through contact with cat faeces) during pregnancy, or if she has diabetes, or if someone else in your family was born with a heart complaint.

Is it me? Did I have German measles and not know it? Was it the cats, Valerie and Leslie? Or is someone else to blame for passing this on?

14

1984

University Challenge

The end of the world hasn't come so far but two momentous events do occur during this potentially apocryphal year. One day in the spring, our old arthritic Andy curls up for the last time under the bush in the backyard. Lugsy is out there having a fag break when he discovers him. He carries poor Andy inside, tears in his eyes, and I am the strong one who has to decide what to do.

'Get Bob,' I tell him. 'And a cardboard box.' Then I disappear upstairs and fetch my yellow baby shawl. I'll have to find somewhere else to keep Helena's letters.

When I come back into the kitchenette, Wink is handing out brandy all round. I have a slug and then prise Andy from Patty's arms and wrap him up in my shawl. Bob pulls himself together and gently takes Andy from me and lays him in the box, tucking in the shawl, making him comfortable.

Wink, Patty and I watch from the window while he and Lugsy dig a hole under the canopy of the unidentifiable bush. It is a warm day and you can see the sweat glistening on Bob's head, on Lugsy's forearms. Then they suddenly stop. Bob reaches into the hole for something. When he straightens up, I can see a smaller box in his hand. A chocolate tin.

'Don't!' I scream.

'He's got to,' soothes Wink, patting my arm. 'Andy's gone.'

'No, it's Lucas.'

There is a stunned silence.

'Lucas?' Wink whispers.

But I've gone into the yard and am at Bob's side, snatching the tin from him. It takes all my courage to stop myself, as I have just stopped Bob, from taking the lid off. It is too soon.

'We can't open it yet. Not for a long time. Not till I have children.'

At this point, I remember no more. Nothing till I wake up inside on the sofa. Till I am told that the tin is safe once again in its place, near Andy, a rose bush planted above him so he'll live on.

★　★　★

The next event is slightly happier and a lot more unexpected. A few months later, I pass my A-levels and, though not the best grades, they are good enough for me to get into Portsmouth Poly.

Cheryl left a year ago, to go to Bristol University to study medicine. She wants to be a doctor! The very thought of all that blood and guts makes me want to spew. But I can't help admiring her and feeling slightly ashamed of my desire to study English Literature, though there's been one or two occasions when books have saved my life.

Cheryl will be in a different world to mine, her days filled with papers on medical advancements and the latest in scientific knowledge. Her week will revolve around doctors and nurses and patients and the substance of the Hippocratic oath. She will be conscientious about attending lectures and seminars and tutorials. In her spare time (what little of it there is) she will attend balls and charity dos and push hospital beds down and up the steep hills of Bristol whilst swaddled in bandages like an Egyptian mummy on loan from the museum.

I, on the other hand, will only have a few compulsory hours of education a week; the rest is up to me to put into some kind of responsible structure which I manage with only limited success. I do spend a fair amount of time reading, as students of literature should of course do. But more often than not I can be found listening to The Smiths on the jukebox, along with the other sweet and tender hooligans, down in the Student Union.

The Student Union is a whole new world. I've never been in a place with so many young people, not even when I was at school (where they were all girls anyway). They talk in accents that I've heard enough times in the Bay in the summer months but it is somehow different here and now, all of them muddled together, one babbling mass of youth dressed in slogan T-shirts and denim.

The Student Union also contains a bar. Alcohol has fortunately lost its allure for me and cigarettes contain too many memories as well as tar and nicotine and goodness knows what other chemicals, probably ground-up glass and arsenic for all I know and I know quite a lot about them. So I stick to pool and darts — my time spent in Bernie's garage paying off — and within weeks I'm on a team for both.

During an early match in my darts career, down in the Union, I am pitted against Adele who looks more suited to glamour modelling than bar sports but who has drawn quite a crowd as she's decided to leave her bra at home. Despite this distraction, I manage to get down to a double first. But unfortunately the burden of winning is closing over me, causing my hand to shake and scuppering my chance to shine. As the arrow leaves my hand I know I am way off target, not just my nerves but because I've been barged into by a bladdered philosophy student from Worthing. The dart quivers through the air, watched in slow motion by everyone in the bar, except the one person that it is aiming for: the big strapping lad wearing a donkey jacket, decorated with a vast and colourful array of badges which — as luck would have it — form a barrier as effective as a bullet proof vest and prevent the arrow from piercing his heart.

Instead, the arrow bounces off his chest as if it were made of rubber and lands by his Doctor Martens. He is so immersed in his own world that it only just dawns on him that he has nearly been stabbed by a girl from Torquay who is currently offering to buy him a pint as recompense whilst being shrieked at by her team mates to get on with the game in hand.

'Another day,' he says, bending down to retrieve the arrow. 'I'm on my way to a meeting.'

'Tomorrow, then?'

'Alright,' he says. 'I'll meet you here, same time. But try not to kill me, alright? You should take up a less dangerous sport . . . crocodile wrestling perhaps, not that I'd condone it. It's cruel.' And he smiles a cheeky grin that makes it clear to both of us we will only ever be friends.

He is there the next night, same time, same place. He leaves his group of weird-looking mates to come over to me and let me buy him a pint of lemonade. We find a couple of chairs in the corner and by the end of the evening we've traded much of our histories and eaten our way through four packets of Wotsits, a mound of KP nuts and a Curly Wurly. His name is Joe and he is studying Social Policy. He is a few years older than me, having had time out of education working, among other things, as a truck driver. He has an HGV licence, an attainment that is much more impressive than knowing your way around a cash register. Joe tells me he comes from Penge (Beckenham borders actually, but he tries to play that down) which he pronounces as if he is French (ironically, of course) which gives a little aura of the exotic to an otherwise drab London suburb.

At last orders he offers to drive me home — he can borrow a car off a comrade. He can't quite believe I've been stuck over on the Paulsgrove

247

estate, miles from all the other students. He seems quite keen to see the place so I say thanks a lot, that'd be great.

As he drops me off he says he'll be in the bar the next night. There is going to be a meeting for something or other I don't quite get the gist of. I can tag along if I want.

'Or we could just get some chips afterwards,' he suggests, sussing I am probably happier sticking to darts.

'Game on,' I say.

It is nice having a friend again. A friend who also happens to be a boy. He even reminds me slightly of Lucas — which is odd as he is tall and chunky and dirty-blond. Not that Lucas would have been a card-carrying member of NOLS (the National Organisation of Labour Students). As if that isn't enough, Joe is also a member of SSIN (Socialist Students in NOLS) which isn't half as exciting as the name suggests. (The politics of the Student Left are puzzling.) Lucas wouldn't have known anything about SSIN — or sin for that matter. And the only card he'd have carried would be a library one which he would've kept guarded in his wallet whilst walking dreamily amongst the glittering spires of Oxford. For Lucas would surely have left me behind eventually — whereas there is something about Joe and I that is similar, other than our mutual love of bar snacks. Maybe he was also in the Slow Readers at school — though he certainly has a way with words now, particularly evocative catchy phrases such as 'Smash the Tories!'.

By the end of the evening he is on his way to becoming my new best friend which is such a relief as I don't want a boyfriend. I don't want to kiss him or go out with him or have him say slushy things to me. I'd rather sit in the bar, matching my pints to his lemonades, listening to this charming man.

Over the next few weeks, Joe tries to persuade me to use my political conscience but I am not actually sure I've got one. While my Jiminy Cricket is off collecting money in a bucket for the miners outside his local Spar in Southsea, I am left behind at the Union, trying to double the black ball in the middle pocket.

I spend a lot of time in the Union which, although it resembles a barracks left over from some war or other, makes a welcome break from the at-times-oppressive atmosphere of my digs. There are not enough places in halls of residence for first years and being one of the youngest they decide to lump me in with Mr and Mrs Raby.

Mr and Mrs Raby relocated from London some years before (like me!) and have somehow ended up in a post-war council house on the aforementioned Paulsgrove Estate. They take in students to supplement their pension. As well as me, they've also managed to squeeze in Susannah from somewhere-in-the-Cotswolds. Susannah doesn't even make it to the end of Freshers Week.

I, on the other hand, am used to sharing my life (and the bathroom) with people from all walks of life. I actually quite like Mr and Mrs Raby but not enough to also share my free time with them even if their house does have a garden and a view of the Isle of Wight on a good day. They eat their dinner at three o'clock in the afternoon because Mr Raby used to be a boatman on the Thames and has never got out of the habit of eating when he got off shift (or should that be watch?) in the middle of the afternoon when most people are still digesting their lunch and only just beginning to think about having a cup of tea. Mrs Raby keeps my food warm in the oven till I get home at around six. It is always meat of indeterminate origin with some combination of tinned veg coated with a thick layer of congealed Bisto, unless Mrs Raby is in a creative mood in which case it would be a thick layer of congealed cheese sauce.

When Joe calls round to see me one evening, having braved the journey out of town and across the motorway, he pretends to be quite at home in these working class surroundings but I notice the brief look of despair when Mrs Raby offers him a Scotch egg (he is a vegetarian) and when Mr Raby offers him a pale ale (he only drinks at weddings and tries to avoid such patriarchal celebrations wherever possible — unless absolutely forced into it by his mother). It takes all his NOLS/SSIN training to fit in, though I've primed him not to mention his far left views as, true to their roots, Mr and Mrs Raby wouldn't dream of voting anything other than Tory. They love Mrs Thatcher almost as much as they love their Queen and Country. If they only knew what Joe said about the Prime Minister ('Maggie-Maggie-Maggie! Out-Out-Out!'), they would feel completely justified in chucking him in the Solent.

'So, Joe, what do you do at the polytechnic? Is it English like Philippa?' asks Mrs Raby, in her pleased-to-meet-you voice.

'No, Social Policy.'

'Oh . . . that must be interesting.'

Mr Raby looks up from his copy of *The Sun* and says, 'I hope they're not teaching you any of that Commie filth.'

Mrs Raby is standing in her apron, arms folded, looking down on Joe and I, perched side by side on the grubby couch which is at an awkward angle to Mr Raby, sitting in his chair by the window with its glorious view of Pompey laid out before him (where you can see what a mess has been made by a succession of town planners trying to clear up after the Luftwaffe). I have to call on all my psychic powers to try to stop Joe responding in his usual way.

'No, Mr Raby,' he says cricking his neck to try and make some sort of eye contact. 'They offer a balanced curriculum.'

Mr Raby is unsure of this answer, suspecting a subversive message in there somewhere. He suspects Joe could quite possibly be the enemy within. He suspects — quite rightly — he has a Trot in his home. A Trot in league with the devil himself, aka Arthur Scargill, leader of the National Union of Mineworkers. But there is nothing he can do without entering into a full-scale confrontation and Mr Raby would

251

rather go back to the television page. He likes to highlight all the programmes he and Mrs Raby could have watched during the day but were too busy watching other ones instead. A man after Wink's heart if ever there was one.

'Have a sausage roll,' offers Mrs Raby.

'No thanks,' says Joe. 'I've just eaten my tea.'

'I'm sure you could manage one, a big lad like you,' she says, amazed at Joe's restraint.

And Joe is restrained. He could've informed Mrs Raby that meat is murder but it will be a few months yet before we hear Morrissey sing these words at the Guildhall. Thus he spares Mrs Raby's feelings and avoids a conflict which normally he'd thrive on.

Joe is most definitely becoming my best friend. It takes a special someone to know when to speak out and when to shut up. But what I like most about him is his humanity which is somehow more profound than his political persuasions. When he paints statements onto placards to hold up on marches, feeling like a soldier with his banner riding into battle, he believes in COAL NOT DOLE and THATCHER STOLE THEIR MILK NOW SHE'S STEALING THEIR BREAD. He believes in every heckle he shouts from the back of the hall during union meetings. Joe even believes in every last word of Billy Bragg's protest songs. But it is more than words. Actions do speak a lot louder as far as he is concerned.

This becomes clear to me one day when we are sitting in the Union. He is reading the *Morning Star* when he comes across a photograph of a boy, the same age or thereabouts as his little brother Michael who is a sixer in his local cub pack and likes to collect first day covers.

'Look at this,' he says, nudging me out of the depths of *Middlemarch*. 'Can you see what this kid has been forced into by this government?'

I look at the picture and can see that this boy has other things on his mind than woggles and stamps. Other things that he has to do. He is crouching on a tip, sifting coal through the grill of a shopping basket to take home to his mum to put on the fire, to do his bit to help keep his family warm through the long, hard winter ahead, with a dad out on strike and a community struggling to hold itself together.

'I'm gonna do something, Phil,' he says.

And he does. He gets up early one morning the following week to drive to south Wales in a comrade's truck, the back of it filled up with food donated by fellow students and activists.

I love him for doing this. And I love him even more for not asking me to go with him — because he doesn't want to hear me say no. Though I do give him a tin of baked beans and the fiver I won from my latest pool contest. I want to do my bit but I am sort of fed up with always being expected to help elsewhere. Looking round Portsmouth, I think quite a bit of help is actually needed right here. It isn't called the northern town of the south for nothing.

Joe likes to think of himself as a man of the

253

people, but he has more affinity with the miners of South Wales than with the locals; he dislikes the way they apparently cling to the glories of the Falklands. (It isn't their fault there's a whacking great naval base on their doorstep.) If it weren't for Mr and Mrs Raby, Joe could pass most of his time at the Poly without interacting with any genuine Pompey inhabitants apart from those who shout abuse at him as he shakes a bucket outside their pub.

Joe's heart always seems to lie elsewhere. But he does have a heart and that is what I love about him. When the bomb goes off in the Grand Hotel further along the south coast, he isn't pleased or impressed by this action, as one might've wrongly assumed he would be. Being a pacifist, he is full of horror at the idea of people wanting to kill other people. Even Margaret Thatcher.

But he doesn't have long to dwell on this. Soon after, he is round at mine, the Raby's out for the evening at the working men's club. A quiet evening watching telly, eating biscuits, when the news comes on. We are not prepared for what we see. If I'd have been warned, I might've switched off the television and taken Joe to the club to experience a true Pompey night out with the Raby's. We could've gone to the pub, the Union, gone anywhere except the place where Michael Buerk transports us. A country in Africa . . . a country I remember from school . . . Abyssinia . . . Haile Selassie and Rastafarians. We are taken to Ethiopia where a

254

famine of biblical proportions is desiccating the nation while we sit in our comfy chairs, an empty packet of Hobnobs on the table, watching in silence the sickening images . . . tiny starving children clinging to their dying mothers . . . the skeletons of cattle lying in the dust . . . brown, dead earth . . .

Big Joe is in tears and that starts me off. I grab one of Mrs Raby's tissues and offer the box to Joe but he waves it away, sniffs, and demands some paper.

'Paper?'

'I've got to write a letter, Phil. I've got to do something.'

So he writes to Mrs Thatcher, still no doubt reeling from the shock of the bomb. A short-and-to-the-point letter which he leaves me in the front room to go and post in the box round the corner, possibly even before Bob Geldof has got off the phone to Midge Ure.

Joe is no fool. He knows words will not be enough. And he knows he will not ever be able to collect enough tins to feed the world. But this doesn't stop him trying.

'We've got to do something, Philippa,' he says. 'We've got to do something.'

It is a mantra of his I will hear many times during our friendship over the years. My Jiminy Cricket nudging me to get off my arse and stop reading about the plight of downtrodden Victorian women. And do something.

★ ★ ★

Term ends all too quickly and I go home to a Christmas that is the first in living memory without Andy. In honour of my return, Bob and Wink kill the fatted calf (which would horrify Joe). They also stockpile a sickening amount of presents under the tree which makes me feel even worse for the famine victims who won't be getting so much as a bowl of rice or a cup of fresh water. Who won't even know it is Christmas.

Still, it is lovely to be back, to help out in the shop, filling the sweetie jars and stacking the stationery shelves, to sit with Wink in front of the telly and watch all the Christmas specials, to share a box of Quality Street and argue over who gets the last green triangle, to throw the travel rug over Captain's cage as he has decided to grow old disgracefully. But I worry about her. She is smaller than I remember. More frail. Her eyesight so bad she has to sit closer to the screen and ask me to tell her what is going on every few minutes.

'You got yourself a boyfriend yet?' she interrogates me one evening. Wink won't be happy till she knows I have a man to look after me as Bob can't do it forever.

'No,' I say. 'I'm too busy.'

She almost chokes on her tea.

'You? Busy? Busy drinking cheap beer, I suppose.'

I feel an almighty blush coming on and for once am thankful her eyesight is not refined enough to see it.

I get three Christmas cards in the post. The first from Cheryl, apologising for not coming home for Christmas. She's chucked Doug and moved in with a final year medical student in Fishponds. The second is from my mother who this year is at least honest and signs it with love from Helena, Orville and Wesley. The third is from Mr and Mrs Raby, apologising for not being in the flat on my return as they'll be off on a cruise on the proceeds of a five horse accumulator at William Hill's. Will I be all right on my own? And will I water Mr Raby's assortment of African violets? Plus will I buy the *Radio* and *TV Times* every week — so they know what they'll have missed on their return. There is some money in a jam jar in the boiler cupboard.

At last. Independence.

★ ★ ★

On the eve of my return, I wander out into the backyard of the shop. If I were a proper student I'd be puffing on a roll-up but I have no desire to smoke as smoking has far too many associations for me. Lugsy, however, has no such worries and gets through as many fags per hour as Helena, though she probably wouldn't be too impressed by the liquorice Rizlas.

'So, is it like being in *The Young Ones*, where you live?' he asks.

I don't like to let him down, so I skim over Mr and Mrs Raby and their plated-up meals.

'Yeah, it could be based on my life.'

I am not completely lying. I get an image of Joe and his donkey jacket and Docs and try not to compare him to Rik Mayall.

When Lugsy goes back into the shop, I notice the slight stoop to his shoulders.

'She'll say yes, one day,' I call after him.

He turns back and shrugs.

'I don't think so. But what can you do?'

It seems that everyone is asking themselves this exact same question. Only some of us are more prepared to try than others.

I stay outside a little while longer. The new rose bush has established itself, Andy's bones feeding it well. I don't have time to get melancholy because Lugsy has reappeared.

'Phone,' he calls from the door. 'It's your mate, Joe.'

I've been trying to get hold of him for days. As has his poor mother.

'Where've you been?' I demand.

'Up in London.'

'What, to see the Queen?'

'Organising my passport,' he says sombrely, not nipping at the bait. 'I've got onto VSO. I'm going to Africa.'

'But I thought they only needed doctors and nurses.'

'They need truck drivers too. Someone's got to get the food there.'

So Joe is going away. Far away. Not for the day, with a carload of beans. But for as long as it takes. My third best friend, snatched away from me. Only this time, as much as I want to, I can't complain.

* * *

Bob drives me back to the Raby's after Christmas. He helps me unpack and gives me a bag of fifty pence pieces for the meter. He makes me a cup of tea, the latest in a long line that he's brewed me over the years, the first still being the most memorable — the tinkle of glass on the shop floor and little Margot Fonteyn trotting down the road after her mother.

'Have you seen Auntie Sheila?' I've been meaning to ask that all Christmas but I've been waiting for Bob to mention her name first. The very fact he's kept quiet fills me with worry for him.

'Yes, I have, funnily enough,' he says.

I am not surprised. I knew she'd be back once she heard about the departure of Linda. But I am surprised it has taken her this long. Poor old Bernie. I am actually beginning to feel sorry for him. And there is someone else of course that springs to mind.

'And Toni and T-J? What's the latest with them?'

'Oh, well, Toni's moved in with some chap from her office, some estate agent or other . . . Anthony . . . Aidan' . . . I can't remember.'

'What's he like, this bloke?'

'Sheila's none too keen. And Bernie hates the sight of him apparently.'

259

No-one will ever be good enough for his Toni.

'And T-J?' I have to prompt Bob to continue with his news update because he's got distracted, hunting for the watering can in order to see to the drying-out African violets.

'Oh, Terry, ah . . . let me see . . . he's somehow managed to get himself a girlfriend. Swedish or Danish or is it Norwegian? Tall and blonde by all accounts. Very attractive. Works for a travel magazine . . . something trendy like that . . . gets all these free flights and things. Sheila can't quite believe he's landed on his feet. Bernie certainly can't.'

It is quite a struggle to control the tornado of jealousy twisting about inside me right at that moment but I must have managed it somehow because Bob is quite oblivious to my stormy emotions.

'Have they got any Baby Bio?' he asks, searching in the cupboard under the sink, giving me a bird's eye view of his pink scalp. 'By the way,' he says, straightening up and clutching the bottle of plant food in his hand, 'he's not called T-J anymore.'

'Has he gone back to Terry?'

'No, he's using his other initial, the J.'

'What does that stand for? I've often wondered.'

'Justin.' Bob notices a look of surprise on my face. 'I know,' he says. 'He doesn't really seem like a Justin, does he? But he's gone all London now. An estate agent living with a leggy Swede in Camden Town. Who'd've thought it?'

Not Bernie that's for sure. Not me either.

'Why's he gone and changed his name again?'

'Something to do with Captain Kirk apparently.'

'Captain Kirk?'

'You know, the Starship Enterprise.'

'Sorry, you've lost me.'

'Well, not Captain Kirk exactly. William Whatsit, who plays him.'

'William Shatner?'

'Yes, that's it.'

'Why doesn't he want to be associated with William Shatner?'

'It's his other programme, the one where he's a police officer or a private detective, that sort of thing.'

'Do you mean T-J Hooker?'

'Oh, you know it?'

Yes, I know all about that telly programme. Between Wink and Mr and Mrs Raby and Ed in his deerstalker (and of course Lucas who started me off all those years ago) I have a pretty thorough knowledge of television programmes on both sides of the Atlantic.

But I don't care if he is Terry or T-J or Justin. He's got what he's always wanted. A bird. A beautiful woman. Not plain old frizzy-haired Philippa. Not me.

After Bob has stopped faffing, he goes into the bathroom and because of the appallingly thin walls, even thinner than those of our Canadian motel which from here seems like a dream, a telly programme I once watched long ago, I hear the rattle of a bottle of pills, a telltale sign that he is still on the Valium.

'Do you want to stay here the night?' I ask him when he reappears. 'You look tired.'

'The shop,' he says automatically. 'I can't leave the shop.'

'Don't be daft. Call Patty. She'll take care of things.'

'What about Wink?'

'Patty and Lugsy can stay over. I'm sure they won't mind if you explain.'

'It's only a three hour drive,' he protests. 'I'll be fine.'

Three hours driving that shouldn't happen. Not with those pills kicking round his blood system. I need another excuse.

'Please stay with me. Just till I get settled. Till the morning. I'm lonely without Joe.'

It is true; I will miss Joe. But I'll find someone else. Someone else always turns up in the nick of time.

Bob smiles. A genuine beam. Because he believes I still need him. More than the shop. More than Wink. More than anyone in the whole wide world.

★ ★ ★

Bob goes home the next morning and I don't see him again till the Easter holidays because I am so wrapped up in my new life, my independence, that I can't bring myself to get the train back home and see my Bob and Wink needing me as much as I used to need them. I may live in Portsmouth, but I have the

262

whole world of literature at my command. I can go anywhere, be anyone — all from the (comparative) comfort of my little box room, huddled under my duvet with George Eliot, the orange street lights shut out by the purple velour curtains that Mrs Raby was so proud of when she first showed me into my new accommodation. No sign of the Cavalier.

2006

No more classic novels. No more Agatha Christie. It is all baby manuals and heart leaflets.

Some holes are so small that they cause no problem, and are left alone. Some holes in small babies may close by themselves: if the cardiologist thinks this is likely, he will not close it immediately, but wait for some time to see if it has closed by itself, by repeating an echo. Other holes must be closed, either because they are already a problem, or because they will cause a problem in the future. There are two ways to do this. The first way is via an operation . . .

No, please, no.

15

1987

Jeopardy!

Three years later I've left Portsmouth Poly with a respectable enough 2:2 in English but with no real idea of what I want to do now I am officially an adult. So I manage to get on the PGCE course at Rolle College in Exmouth. I think I'd quite like to be a teacher. After all, I can't do as badly as the Mothballs and Pitchforks of the profession. And Exmouth is the ideal place to study. As much as I enjoyed my time away, I hanker after Devon. And Wink is now so ill — and Bob so dependent on tranquilisers — I don't want to be too far away. Just in case.

By having a part-time job in the Union bar, I managed to pay for driving lessons and passed my test on the first attempt, thanks to my well-developed road sense born of the Tufty Club and Linda. So I can live at home and drive in to college every day in Bob's still-limping-on Cortina. I can also drive up to Bristol to see Cheryl (now married to her doctor). I can go anywhere I want, though it tends to be nowhere.

But it is good to be home. I like to walk through the shop and complain at Bob when I notice any changes.

'Where's the pipe display gone?'

'No-one smokes pipes anymore.'

He is right of course. When was the last time I saw anyone puffing on a pipe? But I like my shop to be the same. The same as when Helena left. Though maybe I can take this as a positive sign. A sign that Bob has somehow managed to move on. To look to the future. To go with the times.

'When did you decide to sell potpourri?'

'Sheila suggested it.'

'Sheila?'

'She popped in a while back. To buy the *Western Morning News*. And to see how Wink was doing. She'd heard she wasn't too good.'

I suspect ulterior motives but it is sadly true that Wink isn't too good. But the old girl has done well so far; she was never expected to live this long. She's kept going mainly thanks to Bob, not an easy burden what with all the early hours, getting up for the papers.

'Sheila could see for herself the deterioration,' Bob goes on. 'She suggested a home.'

'A home? What's it got to do with her?'

'Well . . . she's worried about me.' He does his cough-thing. 'I told her I'm not sure how much longer I can go on.'

He reaches for his bottle and washes down another tablet with his afternoon cuppa, then cracks open a Twix, offering me a half but I've lost my appetite. Wink can't possibly go in a home.

'I could help out more.'

'No.'

'I don't mind.'

'No. You need to stick at college. Wink would want you to get that qualification.'

'Wink wants me to get married.'

'She wants you to be happy.'

'I am happy.'

'Are you?'

'Yes, pretty much. I'm just worried about you and Wink. I don't care about teaching. I'm not sure I even like children.'

'Does that matter?'

'I should think so, yes.'

Despite my protestations, Bob wins in the end. He persuades me to carry on with college and agrees to up the home help's hours.

So the following week, I'm back at school, only this time I am not hot and squashed on the carpet, I am allowed the privilege of a chair as a student teacher and I am referred to as Miss Smith by Mr Donnelly, the class teacher, a young keen man — though more keen on chatting me up than on teaching. I can feel his eyes every time my back is turned, every time I bend down to re-tie a rogue shoelace (of which there are several thousand). Mr Donnelly gives me the creeps. He must give the children the creeps too because this is the quietest class I've ever been in. All those six-year-olds doing what they are supposed to be doing. Spooky.

At the end of the day, Mr Donnelly leaves me to read them a story. I choose *Where the Wild Things Are*, hoping to give this subdued bunch of children a bit of imagination.

It is an ill-fated plan. This meek and mild class mutate into a group of hooligans and I hear my voice warbling like Wink's but sadly it lacks any of her authority. After half an hour of this torture, I am fighting back the tears as well as the little hands that grip my ankles like octopuses' tentacles. Mr Donnelly strolls back in with his mug of tea, as I was contemplating giving screaming a go. I've tried everything else.

'It's the wind,' he says, shrugging his shoulders. 'The wind always whips them up into a frenzy.'

I look out the window onto the empty playground where leaves and crisp packets are bowling across the patched-up tarmac. He grabs the book from me and rereads it. He is a magician, a mesmerist. A hypnotist. Every pair of eyes focuses on the pages of the book, every pair of ears listens to the story. I will never make a teacher. I do not like children, especially in large numbers. I want to work in the shop. I want to take care of Wink. I just have to persuade Bob.

After the bell has gone, Mr Donnelly stands outside the door to the playground, pairing each child off with the (hopefully) correct adult. He is proficient and the pandemonium of my school days only serve to remind me that it needn't be like that — which it would be with me in charge.

The wind blows into the class scattering worksheets and sugar paper. I've just finished piling them up again when he nips back inside, pulling the door closed behind him, face flushed and hair messed up.

'It's really getting up out there. I don't think we should hang around long tonight. I can give you a lift home if you want.'

I am relieved not to stay one moment longer than I have to now that I've reached this decision. But not desperate enough to accept a lift off this randy young man who'd try any excuse to get me into a confined space with him. I am not having any of it. For the last few years I've embraced celibacy and I don't intend letting go any time soon. That part of life in which most students over-indulge, makes my stomach turn when I think of all the consequences. The maybe's and the what-if's. It is all too complicated. Too difficult.

'It's fine. I can get the train.'

'No, you can't,' he says, triumphant. 'It could be dangerous. Trees on the track.'

You don't even have to look out the window to see there's a storm brewing. There is a change in the light, the beginnings of a low howl washing over the sea towards us. But it isn't that bad.

'It's hardly a hurricane,' I tell him, gathering my things and preparing to leave.

'Let me drop you at the station,' he insists. 'It's cold.'

It is cold and I want to get home.

'Alright, then.' I give in, my mind changeable as the weather. Five more minutes and I'll never have to see him again, (so long as I can persuade Bob this job isn't for me). I needn't worry; Mr Donnelly is a teacher after all, a respectable member of the community — if a little creepy. And I have a good right hook if push comes to shove. What harm can one little lift do?

I follow him to the car park. His car is by far the most battered and un-roadworthy. I probably

269

have more to fear from his Triumph Dolomite than from his roving eye. Though when he judders out of the car park and into the road, I see it is his driving that should be giving me the most cause for concern.

He switches on his decrepit cassette player and a burst of Irene Cara's *What a Feeling* fills the Dolomite, which briefly takes my mind off the nasty smell that I know to be Eau de Dirty Children, having been one of them myself from time to time (and having sat next to Christopher Bennett on many occasions). If it wasn't so cold outside, I would open a window — though I'm not sure the handle would be that effective judging by the amount of electrical tape wrapped around it.

The source of the smell emanates from the junk piled up on the back seat.

'Don't mind that lot,' he says, noticing me looking at it. 'It's marking and stuff. I haven't got round to it. There's so many other things to do.'

Yeah, like the pub and womanising and listening to dodgy music.

As he pulls into the station I can breathe easy again. He hasn't attacked me or propositioned me or anything like that. He is just a teacher who has to go home to a load of work and then go back to class again tomorrow, and the next day and the next. I definitely do not want to do this.

'Thanks, then,' I tell him, holding my skirt as I get out the car in case the wind flings it over my head.

'See you tomorrow,' he says.

But I've already started to shut the door and

don't have to reply to this.

He judders off, nearly knocking over a cyclist. I dart into the station so the cyclist doesn't come after me. And that is when I see him.

He is sitting on a bench, presumably waiting for the same train back to Torre station as me. He hasn't noticed my arrival yet because he is busy trying to keep his *Herald* from blowing away, the very same paper he used to deliver for Bob. Christopher Bennett. He must hear me thinking his name because he looks up and grins.

'Smithy!' he shouts. 'What are you up to?'

I have to force down the urge to shout back *Mind your own!* as I'm not a teenager anymore. I am an adult.

He's up on his feet now, walking towards me, the wind pushing his hair back so I can see his face which he's finally grown into. No crusts around the nostrils. No frown lines on the horizon.

'You alright?' he asks, in front of me now, smiling, offering me a cigarette.

I shake my head at the packet and tell him I'm fine, fine. I tell him about Mr Donnelly, the children and then he says his name: Lucas.

'Do you remember your friend, Lucas?'

''Course I do.'

He tries to light his cigarette but it's a losing battle with the wind, which is whooshing up the tracks.

'He was a smart kid,' he goes on, nostalgic. 'You'd be alright if they were all like that. Maybe you'd stick it out then.'

'They're more like you, Chris.'

271

'No-one's like me,' he flirts.

'Cut it out, Christopher.'

'What've I done?' he asks, pretend-offended.

Then our train pulls in, blasting our words away. But there is no escape; I have to sit with him all the way back to Torquay.

'You're looking good, he says once we've found our seats. You going out with anyone?'

'Mind your own.' There. It's out before I can stop it.

'I'm engaged,' he announces, out the blue, sounding slightly bewildered.

But not as bewildered as me. When I've managed to recover myself, I ask a flabbergasted: 'Who to?'

'Mandy,' he says. 'You know, Mandy Denning.'

'Really?'

Mandy Denning of the doll hands and china blue eyes.

'We're getting married next month so I'm sorry, Smithy . . . you missed the Bennett boat.'

'I'm crushed.'

'You wish,' he says, pretending to jump on top of me.

'Cut it out, Christopher.'

I shove him back on his seat, flushing as everyone is staring at us, tutting. I've had a lucky escape. Poor Mandy. I hope she's toughened up.

* * *

It is quiet back at the shop. Not one customer. They must all be staying indoors, in the warm.

Patty is getting ready to close up.

'Where's Bob?' I ask.

'Cash and Carry. He should be back soon.'

So I tell Patty about my day as Bob isn't there to listen. She doesn't say much but then she is a woman of action not words (a female Joe). Perhaps Wink will be more sympathetic. I find her in her usual place, sitting by the fire with a woolly blanket over her gammy legs, watching *Blue Peter*. She's never got over the vandalism of the *Blue Peter* garden and never misses a programme out of solidarity (and maybe as a nod to Lucas).

At the sound of the closing hornpipe, she switches her attention to me. Or rather to the weather, which is beating a persistent rhythm at the window.

'Time to batten down the hatches,' she warns, with the wisdom of old mariners and their wives. 'It's coming in.'

Wink refers to the weather as 'It', as if it is a person of many disguises. Today the weather is to trick us all. Apart from maybe Wink who has sniffed 'It' out. Or maybe it is Captain. Maybe he harks back to the monsoons of the Congo, where, in his youth, he swooped through the trees of the equatorial rainforests. He is certainly restless tonight and snatches any possibility of Wink's attention for himself so there isn't much point in bringing up my future career prospects.

'Shall I get the tea on?'

'Why don't you pop out and get fish and chips. I fancy fish and chips.' She gets a fiver out her bag. 'Get some mushy peas and all. And the

273

scrapings for Bob. He likes the scrapings.'

The fish and chip shop is empty too so I am back before long but there is still no sign of Bob.

'Plate his up and put it in the oven,' Wink suggests.

I do as I am told, feeling like Mrs Raby. Then Wink and I eat off our laps in the living room, in front of the telly, John Craven's *Newsround*, the same way we used to all those years ago over the road in Wink's old place, watching *The Generation Game*.

'I miss Bruce,' she says, eyeing up John's jumper. Then she looks at me. 'But probably not half as much as you miss Helena.'

I am not sure how I feel. I keep on eating my cod.

'I miss Andy,' I say eventually. And I do. At this moment I miss him more than Helena.

'Don't be too hard on her,' Wink says. 'One day you'll understand.'

'What is there to understand?'

'More than you think,' she says enigmatically. 'Most probably,' she adds.

When I've finished washing up and poured Wink a sherry, I open Captain's cage. But he doesn't want to come out. 'Shut that door,' he says in his campest voice.

'Poor love,' says Wink. 'He's sickening for something.' He does look odd. Head down and a bit droopy-feathered.

'But I am more worried about Bob. He's never this late — not without due warning.'

'Don't worry,' says Wink. '*Top of the Pops* is on soon.'

'I'm going to have a bath,' I say. 'Some of those kids were filthy.'

'Oh, Philippa,' she says. 'I never asked, did I? I never asked how you got on.'

'Not so good, Wink. Looks like I'll have to fall back on that other plan.'

'Which one's that?'

'Your plan. The one where I find a husband.'

'Don't be daft. What do you want one of them for? You're alright on your own for now. You don't want to go thinking about that. There's plenty of time.'

'Yes, I've always had lots of that: time. More than enough to go round.'

'You can always get a parrot,' she says. 'They'll outlast any husband. Captain certainly has.'

She reaches out to him and he edges out the cage door, then swoops and lands on her shoulder, nuzzling into her curly white hair.

★ ★ ★

Once I've scrubbed away the grime of school, I decide it is late enough to put on my pyjamas and dressing gown and make a mug of Ovaltine for Wink and myself even though *Tomorrow's World* is still on and most people my age are out and about as the night is still much too young, except for Cheryl who'll most likely be up all night trudging the wards learning about the latest medical advancements from her husband among other people. I have to make do with *Tomorrow's World's* Maggie Philbin.

Only the most dedicated of young people will

be out in this though. The wind is now rattling the windows but you can make out the motorway-drone of the sea in the distance. Captain has retreated to his cage. Wink is out like a light. But Bob is still not back. And, like Captain, I can feel it in my bones: 'It' is coming in.

★ ★ ★

He is still not back by the time the news has finished. Then there is the weather to sit through. Wink likes watching the weather, presumably because she likes to know what 'It' is getting up to. So I tap her shoulder gently to wake her up. When that doesn't work, I tap a little harder, bringing her back to life.

'Oh good,' she says. 'It's Michael.'

Michael Fish is her favourite weather forecaster. She struggles to lean forward in her chair all the better to see and hear him.

Michael tells us to 'batten down the hatches, there is some really stormy weather on the way', which gets Wink's nod of approval. Perhaps she was a meteorologist in a former life as she's already predicted this herself.

I get up and check behind the curtains, looking out into the dark street where the chestnut tree is getting rather uptight.

'Don't worry, duck,' says Wink. 'He'll be fine. He's most probably run into an old friend.'

Perhaps that's what I am worried about. There is only one old friend of Bob's who would purposefully run into him.

At half past eleven I've helped Wink into bed and am helping myself to some of her sherry when the phone rings.

'Philippa,' a small cough-voice says. 'It's me.'

'Where are you?'

'I ran into an old friend.'

'Sheila by any chance?'

'Yes.' He sounds surprised that I've found him out. 'Anyway, no need to worry, I'm staying over here as 'It's' coming in.'

A poor excuse if ever there was one.

'It's hardly a hurricane.'

'Yes, but Sheila's made up the spare bed for me now. In Terry's room.'

The thought of Terry's room does something to my insides and I end the conversation with Bob a little curtly.

'You mean 'Justin'.'

'Yes . . . Justin, Terry, whatever he's called.'

'You should have phoned earlier.'

'I'm s — '

Then the line goes dead. If I wasn't still holding the handset, I'd believe I'd put the phone down on him. But I am still clutching it. There is no Bob. Just a crackle. Still, at least I can go to bed now, knowing he hasn't been blown off the planet but into the arms of Auntie Sheila. What has she done with Bernie? Unless Bob really is staying in Justin's bed.

Justin.

That sets my insides off again. Will I ever get any sleep?

But it doesn't matter, does it? I am not going back to school tomorrow. I can have a lie in. Bob isn't even here to ask me how I've got on. So I'm not going to worry about what he thinks.

★ ★ ★

And no. I don't get any sleep. When I eventually switch off the light at around one o'clock, I lie there picking out all the noises: bin lids in the street, the branches of the horse chestnut, the odd clang that could be any number of objects coming loose from their mooring. I switch the bedside lamp on. It flickers every now and then. I stare at the curtains which ripple unnervingly, tossing the Cavalier around on a wave of wind. This is too much.

I get up to check on Wink. She is fast asleep, snoring, her eye mask on. I tiptoe out and make my way to the living room, where the wind seems worse. The windows rattle more insistently and the branches of the conker tree flap more furiously. The wind whistles up through the floorboards; I can feel it round my ankles. Captain isn't happy about all this. He is thrashing around inside his cage. I take off the travel rug and open the door to stroke his head which he usually likes when he is feeling stressed. It works to a certain extent but he still mutters under his breath, 'Don't panic, don't panic.'

'Don't worry, Captain,' I tell him. 'I'm not panicking. Go to sleep.'

The thought of sleep entices me back to bed. I

can hardly keep awake. It has been a long day, what with the children and Mr Donnelly and Christopher Bennett and Bob and 'It'. My legs are dead, my brain numb though I just have enough energy left over to be annoyed with Bob. He should've phoned earlier. He should be here now, making me Ovaltine and keeping me company in the storm.

I read *Spycatcher* for a while, a copy that Wink managed to get hold of somehow. This does the trick and soon my eyelids begin to droop, but every time sleep pulls me under, there is another new noise to try and make sense of. Eventually sleep wins the battle and I am dreaming once again of being that glamorous Russian spy in a Bond film, trapped in a train compartment with 007 himself, when I am slapped wide awake by a heart-thumping, stomach-sinking crash, a sickening mixture of glass shattering, wood creaking and something heavy falling over. For a second I think the train has crashed but then I get a grip and am out of bed, heading for Wink's room . . . maybe she's fallen out of bed . . .

No, she is still there. I can make out her frail body in the darkness. All quiet, all still. She'd sleep through anything . . . the noise must've come from the living room . . .

I'm not quite sure what comes out of my mouth when I open the door. I'm not sure if I am able to say anything at all. It looks like we've been the victims of a cruel and nasty burglary or a direct hit by a bomb. Or maybe I am still dreaming, like Max in *Where The Wild Things Are*. Our living room has turned into the world all around.

Gradually my brain catches up with what has happened. For the wind is now screaming straight at me. There is no glass left in the window. It has been smashed by the horse chestnut tree which has . . . no, no, no . . . fallen right into the room and is pinning the crushed cage to the floor.

Above the furore of the storm, I make out a screechy voice saying 'Shut that door, shut that door,' as if Larry Grayson is present right here in our living room.

Then I spot a flash of red. Red tail feathers. There is Captain in the branches of the tree, as if he is back in the rainforest, like my father. Yes, I am most definitely dreaming.

I am pulled from my shocked inertia by a voice outside in the street.

'You alright up there?'

I can't get anywhere near the window to see who it is so I go down to the shop and switch on the light. Mr Taylor is banging on the door, peering through the glass, his dressing gown billowing all around him, revealing the prize-winning knobbly knees that I never expected to see again.

'You look terrible Philippa,' he says as I let him in. 'Is anyone hurt?'

'No, Wink and I were in bed, poor old Captain's alright, I must've left his cage open, I was so tired, not thinking, he's sat in the tree.'

'Show me,' he says, authoritatively, and he

bolts the shop door saying, 'you can't be too careful ... looters ... ' (He is a *Daily Mail* regular.) And as he guides me back up the stairs, I realise I am shaking.

'Let me call 999 for you,' he says after a moment's surveillance of the great outdoors in our living room. 'You'll need some help clearing this lot up.'

'I'd better phone Bob first.'

'Isn't he here?'

'He's at Sheila's.'

'Ah,' he mutters, saying very little, meaning an awful lot.

Half an hour later Bob is back, looking almost as ruffled as Captain, who is now ensconced in the bathroom, much to his annoyance as he was enjoying his rumble in the jungle.

'I'll just check on Wink,' he says. 'She can sleep through anything that one.'

For some reason I follow him into Wink's bedroom. Just to check. He switches on her bedside lamp and we both notice, Bob and I, at the same time. Her snoring has stopped. Her chest is very still. She's taken off her eye mask and is lying serenely on her back, lids closed but with her favourite blue eye shadow smudged across them. A bit of pink on her lips. Rouge on her cheeks. She isn't asleep though. She has gone. Gone with the wind, leaving behind a droopy-feathered, dust-covered African Grey parrot. And a huge hole in my life that I don't think will ever be filled again.

2006

They say it is a tiny hole. It may repair itself
without surgery. We'll have to wait and see. Wait
and see. Wait. I'm good at waiting. I can do this.
We can do this, you and I. You and I.

16

1992

You've Been Framed

I don't have to go back and face Mr Donnelly and his herd of hooligans. By the time the consequences of the storm are dealt with, and my poor old Wink sent off down the final conveyor belt, it is taken as understood between Bob and myself that I will stay in the shop for the time being. I dance around him as Helena once did, fitting my movements to his. But under the counter sits Wink's ashes so that every day, as I reach for a paper bag, I think of her.

'Bob, we've got to do something,' I say finally, one closing time, picking up the urn and dusting it with my sleeve. 'She can't stay there forever.'

'Alright,' he says, locking up. 'Grab your coat and a torch. It's high tide. Let's do it.'

And we know exactly what it is we have to do because Wink has laid it all out straight in the will that we found in her bedside cabinet. We never knew she was so organised. Or that she was so flush, leaving her savings to Bob and me. For a rainy day.

Which, luckily it isn't today, though the wind is a bit fresh (and hopefully in the right direction).

283

Bob tucks Wink inside his sheepskin coat and we let ourselves out the back, past the chippy and Wink's old house, down into Belgrave Road, past the Chinese, the florists, the hairdressers, the junk shop, Toy Town, the guest houses and the hotels, over the footbridge and along the front, past the Princess Theatre and on to the harbour, all the way around until we find a quiet spot, where we can sit in the dark, on the wall, the waves crashing at our feet.

He takes the lid off the urn and says, 'Didn't she do well.'

Then we take it in turns, dipping our cold hands into the ash, scattering it like bird seed, watching the wind take it up and out to sea. Our Wink.

★ ★ ★

Five years later, I feel I should perhaps be reassessing my career opportunities. Patty and Lugsy have gone, to Canada of all places, Vancouver Island, almost a continent away from Helena (who at least marked Wink's passing with the biggest bunch of lilies Interflora could muster). Sheila dips in and out of Bob's life according to her whims, less of late as Bernie requires more of her attention since his latest bout of heart trouble. Linda, at the last report, has married a naval officer, someone she met through Clive, and is living happily ever after in Plymouth. Cheryl is now a proper doctor with her own stethoscope and everything and has decided to give her Pill the boot as she reckons her fertility is at its ripest at twenty-seven. As for Captain, he is now more than ripe, probably somewhere in his fifties, though the vet thinks he might have another twenty years in him. And Wink was right, certainly longer than any husband could've managed.

At this rate, it could quite possibly take another five years to reassess my career opportunities but everything changes with the arrival of an old friend one Saturday morning in the run-up to Christmas, back home from London for a rare few days holiday. Bob and I are busy serving and sorting out paper bills, so the shop bell is ignored as we aren't expecting any one special. Eventually I look up from Mrs Strickland's hefty magazine invoice that she's decided to settle at long last, and notice a rather swanky woman dressed in a camel coat that drapes to the floor, with her hair Pre-Raphaeliting down her straight back. Her make-up is expertly done, if a little over-dramatic for the streets of Torre. Someone like her should really be entering a shop somewhere in Bond Street or Covent Garden. Which of course she normally would be, as that is her usual choice of shopping venue.

'Hello, there,' she says, the Grammar Girl voice still alive and kicking. 'It's me, Toni.'

'Toni!' Bob and I gasp in unison.

'I was just passing,' she says. 'Thought I'd call in for the *Western Morning News* and a packet of Extra Strong Mints.'

Well, we can't let her go that easily. Bob whisks her out to the back where he prises her coat from her and rustles up some coffee. After a few minutes, she totters back out warming her manicured hands around her drink that Bob has seen fit to pour into the most embarrassingly chipped mug. I am conscious of my own chewed fingernails that are highlighted by fingerless gloves. I try not to think of my scruffy jeans and sweatshirt.

Toni leans against the cigarette display and tells us both about her mum and dad, how Sheila has put Bernie on a strict high fibre diet and makes him walk along the seafront everyday with their new Yorkshire terrier, Coco.

'How's Terry-I-mean-Justin?' Bob stutters — which is more than I dare to.

'*Justin's* still in Camden,' she says, the emphasis on his new name showing her disdain.

'With the Swede?' he asks.

'Do you mean Bente?'

'Maybe.'

'She was Danish. She's gone back to the land of Lego. Got fed up with our penchant for fitted carpets and white sliced bread or something. Or was it Terry she was fed up with, I can't remember. It was a while ago now.'

'Is he alone?' I hear myself enquire, feeling a hot flush of menopausal proportions wash up from my toes to my forehead in two seconds flat.

'He lives alone but no doubt he has the pick of the bunch.'

No doubt.

'Bob,' she says. 'Can you spare Philly for a bit. I fancy a walk down to the harbour and I hate walking on my own. In London you always have

286

somewhere to walk to. Here you can just walk for the sake of walking and it feels a bit weird to be walking alone.'

''Course,' says Bob, slightly taken aback by the lack of varied verbs in an otherwise well-reasoned speech. 'Take as long as you want. I can manage.'

'Are you sure, Bob?' I check. 'It's almost lunchtime.'

'Go,' he says.

So Toni and I put on our coats — her cat-walk job and my kagoul — and set off down the road, the familiar route, past the Chinese, the florists, the hairdressers, the junk shop, Toy Town, the guest houses and the hotels until we come at last to the footbridge, the sea loitering with intent on the other side. We use the bridge to cross over the road, spray covering our faces and hair in a fine layer of dampness and then scurry on, along the front, past the Princess Theatre until we arrive at the harbour, the chink of moorings and the smell of money that has gone missing from a lot of Torquay.

Toni sits down on a bench, staring out at the water that is doing its best to capsize the yachts. I'd rather not sit on something so wet but it seems rude to stand so I keep her company.

'Have you ever thought of getting away, Philly?'

From time to time. More so lately. Seeing Toni walk into the shop has made me think of it again, taking me back to that time in Tip Taps, watching her spin around in her leotards, to the blushes of the squadron leader, the tears in

Sheila's eyes, the envy in my heart from watching her dream of the shiny lights of London. And then again, that time I heard about her buying a flat, taking in a show with Sheila. That feeling of being left behind.

'Yes, I have,' I say. 'I've thought of it. But where would I go?'

'London,' she says firmly. 'Come to London.'

'It's not that easy, Toni.'

'It is. You can come and work for me.'

'What do I know about selling houses?'

'You've been selling since you were six-years-old. The only difference is that property is more expensive than Kola Kubes. Terry's left. He's chucked it all in. Couldn't stand the heat. Times are hard but we have a vacancy. For the right person.' She drags her eyes away from the marina to look at me, pleadingly. 'Phil, you could do it. I know you could.'

'Where would I live?'

'We've got a spare room. We've got lots of spare rooms,' she says a little glumly.

'We?'

'Adrian and me. My partner.'

'Partner?'

'In every sense of the word.'

Adrian. The man who wasn't good enough for our Toni. The hard-nosed money-maker. The man who lived through Black Monday just a few days after Wink had failed to live through the Great Storm.

'What does Adrian think about this?'

'Oh . . . he's fine with it. He's cool.'

'Really?'

'There's nothing stopping you.'

'There's Bob.'

'It's time he let you go,' she says. 'You've stayed long enough.'

And right then, I decide to go. It is London, after all. My birth place. The city Helena taught me was the only place you should live, at some point in your life. The place where I saw a lady turn into a princess. Where I travelled underground with a boy called Raymond. Where Wink was a star.

It is my time to shine. I am going to London!

★ ★ ★

It is much easier than I ever thought in the end. Bob is barely tearful when I tell him. He hugs me hard and whispers 'good for you' into my hair. Then he goes for fish and chips while I brew the tea and when he's back, we eat off our laps in front of the telly, and all is going well until *The Generation Game* comes on. Bruce is back.

'Wink, Wink,' says Captain, sadly.

'It's just you and me, mate,' says Bob, looking at the old parrot perched on his stand. And the look of dejection that passes between them is almost enough to make me forget this whole idea.

'It's what she would've wanted.'

I don't like to ask who he means by 'she': Wink or Helena?

But I like to think that it would be both of them.

'Don't go changing my curtains, mind,' I warn

him. 'Or digging up the backyard. Cos I'll be back. This is still my home.'

★ ★ ★

Toni is waiting for me when the train pulls into Paddington. She helps me with my bags and hails a cab with a finesse worthy of Helena. We pass through rough bits of London and posh bits of London, seedy and smart, cheek by jowl, until we come to Belsize Park with its stuccoed houses and leafy streets. She points out her old flat as we drive up Haverstock Hill and I get a flash of Terry. A flash of more than is good for me.

'Here it is,' she announces, waving her arm at a double-fronted Victorian villa with off-street parking for both her Golf and Adrian's no doubt flash car.

For Toni and Adrian own a house now. She sold her flat and he sold his terrace and, thanks to a re-possession, they were able to afford this huge place, though it was in a right old state when they got it. But now it is virtually renovated. I suspect I am about to enter the pages of *Wallpaper*.

The driver takes my suitcase up the front steps and Toni tips him in a way I can only admire.

'Welcome to your new home,' she says, dramatically, as she opens the smart, glossy black door and ushers me inside.

Toni does the estate agent tour, the whole spiel, leaving me in awe of her acquisitions: original tiled entrance hall with a feature banister and ornate cornicing . . . stripped pine doors to all ground floor rooms . . . stripped pine floors in the spacious knocked-together reception room on one side of the hall . . . on the other, a study with floor-to-ceiling bookshelves . . . a laundry room and cloakroom . . . and a large kitchen at the back with French doors . . . leading onto a patio . . . and a good-sized south facing garden with a reasonable level of privacy.

'It's lovely, Toni,' I manage to say. But what I don't mention is that I am being nibbled at by the green-eyed monster again. Why does she have all this and I have absolutely nothing?

Upstairs, I can only gasp at the stained glass window on the landing, the marble bathroom, the vast master bedroom with ensuite (no avocado here as times they are still a-changing), the two spare rooms that look like they have never been slept in and the smaller box room that is quite clearly destined to be a nursery one day.

Mine is the bedroom at the back of the house, next to the family bathroom with its power shower and roll-topped bath with gold taps where we now stand, facing each other over the bidet.

'You've pretty much got this to yourself,' she says. 'You'll only have to share it with Mum and Dad when they come and visit — which isn't that often. Thank God.' She laughs a forced kind of laugh, one that hides a whole new perspective on the story.

'You've got a lovely house,' I make myself tell her. 'And so tidy.'

It is incredibly tidy. Not a cushion un-plumped

or a bit of fluff on the expensive Turkish rugs.

'I know,' she says. 'Mum would be impressed. But unfortunately I can't take the credit. That should go to Marcia, the cleaner.'

★ ★ ★

It doesn't take me long to unpack. I've hardly brought more than Dick Whittington on his first outing to the capital. The bare essentials. A few clothes that won't overly embarrass me walking those streets of London. Some toiletries. Two pairs of shoes. Slippers. A towel. A pile of books. And Tiger, of course. I tuck Tiger into his new bed and remember the first time I ever set eyes on him, gliding down the conveyor belt to the cheers of the audience and plucked from obscurity by Wink to live on, as a legend. The prize she gave me for supporting her. I always tried my best to do that. But really, she was the one who supported me.

'Philippa!' It is Toni, calling me in her shrill, persuasive voice. 'Come and have a glass of Beaujolais. Adrian's back.'

My stomach is a little anxious as I walk downstairs, the stress of the move maybe. Though as I prepare to enter the kitchen to meet my new landlord, I suspect it has more to do with him.

He is leaning against the Aga when I first see him so I will always associate the smell of lasagne with Adrian, amongst other things — like Beaujolais, of which he has an enormous glass in his hand. He is telling Toni — in his stuffed-up, nasally drawl — all about his day at the office, while she is chopping green stuff for a salad dressing. She is genuinely interested in what he has to say as normally she would be in the office too, but has taken the day off to welcome me. I'm still not quite sure what I've done to deserve her kindness but presumably she is just like her mother, feeling the need to do her bit for me. For poor Philippa.

'Ah,' Adrian barks. 'There you are. Come in, come in, don't lurk in the shadows. Have some of this.'

He fills another enormous glass and shoves it in my hand.

'This is Adrian,' Toni says, 'as if you hadn't already guessed.'

She moves over to him, wiping her hands on her butcher's apron before wrapping her arms around him in what I can only think of as a display of possession. She might be happy to share her house with me, but this is her husband. Hands off. As if he'd look at me in a million years when he has sophisticated, woman of the world, Toni.

'How's your brother?' I ask, taking a huge slug of wine to calm the jitters.

'Terry's still Justin. Still living the bachelor life.'

'Still a loser,' Adrian interrupts.

Toni opens her mouth possibly to dispute this but she gulps some wine instead before turning her attention to serving up supper — a vegetable lasagne and a fancy salad that is a far cry from Bob's Fray Bentos pies and peas. Adrian wolfs his down, talking estate-agent speak to Toni — thankfully pretty much ignoring me. As soon as his plate is wiped clean with his rustic bread, he's off 'to see a man about a dog'. Toni shakes her pretty head at his faux cockney and offers her lips for him to kiss.

'Don't have too many, darling,' she says cheerily as he grabs his jacket from the back of the chair.

'Don't worry,' he snaps. 'I'll still be fully functional.'

Then he's gone and Toni starts lobbing the dishes into the dishwasher, the same way her mother did after the dinner party debacle several years earlier, the night I discovered I was capable of being in love.

'Are you alright, Toni?' I ask.

'Don't mind me,' she sniffs. 'I'm just knackered. Work's been stressful . . . the market, you know . . . I think I'll have a bath. Make yourself at home. Watch television. Put your feet up.'

Then she too is gone and I am left in their large family kitchen, wondering if it would feel any nicer if it were actually filled with a family.

★ ★ ★

My new job isn't much to write home about — so I don't bother. But I do phone Bob with regular updates, so he knows I am missing him, so I know he is still there, in the shop.

I am the lowest of the low in the hierarchy of the office, a sleek estate agents that is somehow surviving against the odds, probably down to Toni and Adrian's partnership which, though I can already see the cracks at home, is new plaster-smooth at work. So while Toni and Adrian are out there, gunning up business along with Mac and Denise, I am left to type up house details and answer the phones.

'It won't be forever,' Toni assures me. 'I have plans for you. Let me work on Adrian.'

Plans? I am only just realising these plans involve using me as cheap labour. And as for working on Adrian, that isn't going to be easy. He thinks he is the bee's knees when actually he is the dog's slime. He swings from morose to manic and treats me like I'm still a child, which is exactly how I feel in his presence. He sometimes ferries me around in his BMW, parking up on double yellows while I race into unmarked doorways with brown envelopes that have to be hand delivered to men with names like Big Mike and Small Dave. He cuts up buses and taxis and likes to show off his car phone and CD player (which is completely wasted on Phil Collins). All in all, he is the sort of man who can't be ignored, who fills up the room when he walks into it, who talks over any conversation. He even manages somehow to take over the thoughts in your brain, like something from the *Twilight Zone*.

In hindsight (a very annoying thing to have), seeing him swing his BMW onto the driveway that first night in London, as he came back at midnight, wild-eyed and weird, should have sent out warning bells. I should have found alternative accommodation straightaway. But I don't do that until the day after Toni reveals her plans to me.

These plans are not quite what I had in mind when she first approached me on the sea front back home. I thought I'd be working my way up to selling houses. But, one evening a few weeks into my new life, Toni reveals the real reason for getting me to London.

Adrian has once again gone off to see his man about a dog which I am beginning to suspect could be a drug dealer as he always comes home with tell-tale eyes (remember I've spent my life in ports and know more than you'd think a West Country girl would know). I am not sure how much Toni knows about her partner but surely she must realise Adrian's stuffy nose is not the result of a permanent cold. (He could do with some Vicks Sinex but I'm not going to suggest it.)

Toni is onto her second bottle of Merlot and almost through a box of Maltesers when she flicks off the telly and turns to me.

'I want a baby,' she says. 'But it's not happening.'

When I don't say anything, she continues.

'I've seen the doctor and there's something wrong with me. My eggs aren't that good. They're getting on a bit. Adrian won't even see the bloody doctor himself. Oh no, he's the big man and can't possibly be firing blanks. So it's definitely my fault.'

I really don't know what to say, thinking about Adrian and all that stuff. It is too much for me to take in.

'So we've reached an impasse. I want a baby but it's not going to happen. So this is where you come in Philly.'

She examines her glossy fingernails.

'Me?'

'I want you to have our baby.'

'What do you mean?'

'I want your eggs and his sperm to get it together.'

'I'm not sleeping with Adrian,' I say, jumping to my feet. 'How could you ask me to do that?'

'No, Phil,' she starts laughing in an almost hysterical way, pulling me back onto the sofa and offering me a Malteser, which I decline as food no longer makes everything alright. 'I mean we use the turkey baster method.'

My stomach sinks. At what Toni is asking me to do.

'No, I can't.'

'I'll pay you. We'll pay you. We'll be there for you all the way through. Please, Phil, you're my only option.'

I find that hard to believe. This sounds like the plan of a mad woman. A desperate one, at any rate. And what about cocaine-fuelled Adrian?

'What does Adrian think?'

'He doesn't know yet.'

'He'll never agree.'

'I can persuade him.'

'You couldn't persuade him to go to the doctor.'

'That's different. This won't affect his pride.'

Pride comes before a wotsit, as Wink would say. I'd like to say it too but my words shrivel up and die somewhere inside me, in that place where I keep the memories of the night I morphed into the Cavalier. The girl curled up on her bed, losing blood, losing her baby, almost losing her life.

'I can't do it,' I tell her, tears in my eyes.

'Please, Philly, please say yes. Look, you only have to try it the once and if it doesn't work, he might be persuaded to go to the doctor's. He might see he's not all he's cut out to be. That it's not all necessarily down to me. There might be something they can do to help us along. Time's running out. Please, Phil.'

'I can't. I'm sorry.'

And then I tell her why. I tell her what happened to me when I was sixteen. I tell her she was almost an aunty. That the father of my baby was Terry. T-J. Justin. (Well, you didn't think it was the bogey boy, did you?)

'Does he know?'

'No-one knows. Only me. And now you.'

'I'm sorry,' she says. 'But that was ten years ago. You're the only one who can make me happy.'

I think of all the times I was her pony, leaping over bamboo canes, galloping and trotting across Uncle Bernie's lawn, his polyester tie around my neck. I think of the evenings I spent in her pink 1970s bedroom — still untouched and waiting for her expectantly back home in Torquay — sitting on her bed surrounded by Pan's People, being experimented on with blusher and lipstick and eyeliner. A living, breathing Girl's World.

I won't do it. Not anymore.

So I tell her: 'You're the only one who can do that.'

★ ★ ★

The next day I phone Joe, who is living his socialist dream in a council flat in Lambeth, working for a housing association. I tell him what has happened. He tells me to pack my bags and get a cab, which is quite possibly the most decadent thing he's ever suggested in his life.

★ ★ ★

I am migrating south, like the swallows and the swifts. South of the river to Lambeth and to a future without a family or a job but with my friend, my Jiminy Cricket, there beside me, nudging me all the way.

2006

And that's where we are now, though the hospital has a slightly more prestigious location than the fifth floor of Joe's tower block. But I don't care about the location, the view, the postcode. I only care about the doctors doing their best for you. Though I am sure the more I hold you, the better you look. And slowly, slowly, unlike your mother (Me), who never had a problem with feeding (the bottles, the bottles), you are starting to get the knack. The let-down reflex kicks in and I feel my womb contract. But deeper still than this pain, is the pain of motherhood. The pain of love.

17

1997

I'm a Celebrity — Get Me Out of Here

Another Christmas comes and goes, followed by another January limping behind, dragging with it the annoyance of expectations for the coming year, like a bit of loo paper stuck to the bottom of a shoe. Loo paper aside, I know by now not to expect too much. But then again, I also know to expect the unexpected.

I've been in London for four years and nearly all of that time has been spent down the road from my birth place, where those honourable gentlemen are getting a little anxious about their seats which will be snatched away from them in a few months time, to be replaced by a new generation of honourable members. I've been living close by to where my mother grew up. Near that park with the rhododendrons where the nannies take their charges to feed the ducks. Not far from where my grandfather could still be living, if he is even alive at this point in time. I've never tried to find out. I've got all the family I want down in Torquay. All the family I need.

Meanwhile I make do with Joe — though four years living with a reformed Socialist who's signed up to the whole New Labour experiment is hard to stomach at times. What has happened to my radical Joe? My heckling-from-the-floor Joe? He's become a social worker, that's what. And secretary of the local Labour Party branch. And older. And possibly wiser though of course I can't be sure of that as I still don't have a political conscience in my possession.

I don't have a boyfriend either. Joe's friends have tried their best but I am not interested in worthy men who think only of canvassing and the 'Project' (which will never be a patch on Lucas' secret one). As far as members of the opposite sex are concerned, the only one of them I am interested in (apart from Mr Bob Sugar) is Joe — my flatmate, who I've lived with ever since that night he rescued me from Belsize Park — not on a white horse but in a borrowed Fiat Panda (he decided against the cab in the end). I am happy sharing a home with him in the back streets of SE1. And I am very happy doing my job.

For a job is something I do have. And although it isn't well paid, it is one I enjoy. Like my mother, I sell books in an independent book shop. But, unlike the stock in Jabberwocky, these books are new. Clean and crisp and untouched, waiting to be devoured for the first time by loving literary customers. I have the whole world of literature around me and still hope I'll be able to turn that key in the lock that will reveal the meaning of life. Here are characters I can relate to, who I can learn truths from: good old Jane Eyre has been joined by Bridget Jones, and the new kid on the block, Harry Potter (whose creator, I discover, was born just two days after me).

But none of these characters are as strong as my boss, who is the latest in a long line of fearsome women to have taken me under their wing. This time it is Evelyn.

Evelyn runs the shop as smoothly as Patty could ever hope to do, but without the sex appeal. Evelyn lives with her life partner, Judith. In their spare time they keep an allotment with regimented rows of vegetables and neatly pruned fruit bushes. Evelyn and Judith like to ply me with freshly-plucked garden produce whenever they can because they say I have a sickly pallor which is probably true as I spend my working day surrounded by books and my evenings watching television. In the summer I often return to the flat with a bag of courgettes or a punnet of raspberries. In the autumn, Evelyn pops a jar of chutney in with my weekly pay packet. In winter I have to make do with sprouts (unfortunately). In the spring I have to go to the greengrocers or the market or even Sainsbury's while Evelyn and Judith spend every spare minute clearing and digging and quite possibly mulching (whatever that is) in order to sow the seeds for the next batch of crops.

January is a fairly quiet time in the gardener's calendar and so Evelyn and Judith visit museums and art galleries on their days off. Judith is a civil servant and has many days off unlike Evelyn and I who seem to live at work (but then I am quite used to that). One Monday morning Evelyn tells me about their

Sunday which they'd spent in the National Gallery.

'When was the last time you went, Philippa?' she asks. 'You really should make the most of this great city of ours.'

On my next day off, guilt eventually persuades me to leave my duvet and to spend at least some of my spare time productively. After a long bath and a forage in the fridge for some meagre lunch (what can you do with a tube of Tartex and a bendy carrot?), I catch the No. 12 up to Trafalgar Square, where Nelson balances on top of his column with a pigeon on his shoulder, the way Captain used to perch on Wink's.

As I climb the stone steps to the National Gallery, I wonder vaguely why it is I am doing this alone. Shouldn't I have found someone to accompany me on cultural outings at this stage of my life? I am thirty-one after all and don't have much to show for it. Whatever I once had, I've somehow managed to lose on the way. I've lost my mother. My surrogate gran. My cat. And several best friends (I did manage to recapture Joe, though I fear I might be losing him again, this time to another man — Tony Blair — rather than the continent of Africa). As for men? I've pretty much given up on the idea of sex as it doesn't lead anywhere that I particularly want to go. But it would be nice to have someone to talk to about all this. It's hard trying to absorb these famous paintings on my own. Paintings I've seen on greeting cards, on book covers, on Athena posters (though I've yet to come across the knickerless tennis girl).

Once I've browsed through the Monet's, the Matisse's, the Gainsborough's and the Bruegel's, I end up back where I started, in front of a huge canvas. I couldn't see it easily when I first arrived as a swarm of people were huddled around it, all of them looking up at it, listening to a guide's interpretation. Now the gallery is quieter, people drifting home, back to crumpets and Darjeeling in front of the television. Back to *Songs of Praise* and the *Antiques Roadshow*. I'm not ready to go back yet. I am actually enjoying my little taste of culture. So I plonk myself down on a bench and gaze up at the scene: *The Execution of Lady Jane Grey*.

I am sharing the bench with a young man, an art student, busy sketching Lady Jane's blindfolded face, working at her mouth, her parted lips. Looking back up at the painting, you can see why those lips are parted: a moment of panic as she gropes for the block. You can see she is being helped in this moment. A kind-looking man gently guiding her to the block. The block where she will lay her pretty head and have it severed from her young body. Then your eyes are inevitably drawn to the ashamed-looking executioner who stands to one side, embarrassed to have such a massive axe in his hand, looking more appropriately dressed for leaping across the stage like Rudolf Nureyev in those red tights of his. And then you are led on to the other two women, her maids presumably, one on the verge of fainting, the other with her back turned, facing the wall, her arms raised in anguish.

It is a horrible, beautiful painting. And so real.

You feel you could reach up and touch the silk of Lady Jane's gown. The sharpened metal of the executioner's axe. The scattered straw on the floor, waiting to soak up her blood. You feel you could step into the picture and rescue this poor girl from her unfortunate end. You want to leap in and push the executioner to the ground. You want to grab Jane in a fireman's lift and carry her to safety. Get her a good solicitor who can prove in court that she's been used by those around her. Those who were supposed to care for her. But you can't. She is already dead. You can't turn back the clock. Though sometimes you want to take out the batteries and stamp on it until it is in a thousand tiny pieces.

'Are you alright?' the student asks me and it is then that I realise I am crying. 'I'd give you a tissue, if I had one.'

'Thanks,' I sniff. I search in my pocket but all I can find is a ball of fluff and a penny. Why aren't I the sort of woman who carries pocket-sized packets of Kleenex?

'Have mine,' a voice says.

I think I must be dreaming when I swivel around . . . for there is Adrian, holding out a handkerchief the size of a small tablecloth. The last person I expected to see in an art gallery when he could be out selling houses.

He is looming over me in a formidable way so I stand up straight and almost manage to look him in the eye.

'Hello, Adrian,' I say, once I've used his hanky. 'What are you doing here?'

'Skiving,' he says. 'Fancy a drink? You look like

306

you could use one.'

I check my watch. Knowing Adrian he means a drink-drink and I've just been thinking about going home for that Darjeeling and a handful of crumpets.

'A bit early isn't it?'

'It's never too early.'

'Go on, then. A quick one.'

So that's how we end up in a wine bar in Soho, one of Adrian's haunts.

'What are you doing out of Belsize Park?' I ask him once the small talk is beginning to run out.

'Having a breather,' he says. 'Toni's doing my head in.'

'Poor Toni.'

'Poor Toni? Don't you mean poor Adrian?'

'You're a big boy. You can look after yourself.'

'That's where you're wrong,' he says, somewhat morosely, swilling his wine round the glass. 'I need someone to take care of me every once in a while.'

'Are you saying Toni doesn't understand you?'

'I'm saying Toni couldn't give a monkey's. There's only one thing she cares about.'

'A baby?'

'You know then?'

And somehow after a significant part of a bottle of Chablis, I tell him about Toni's proposal in her flat all those years before.

'That's why you left?'

'I sometimes wonder what would have happened if I'd stayed. Whether she would have persuaded me. Whether it would've worked.'

'She should never have asked that of you.

She's a woman possessed. And you think she was bad then . . . '

'I take it there's no progress in that department.'

'Well, I've been to the doctor's.' He attempts to stab an olive with a cocktail stick but it flies out of the dish and onto the floor. He stares after it, shoulders slumped. 'Apparently I've got lazy sperm.'

I have to swallow the urge to laugh at the thought of Adrian's sperm pressing the snooze button — which is slightly funnier than the thought of that turkey baster Toni was proposing.

'She wants to go to Romania now. Adopt one of those kids from the orphanages.'

'Gosh,' I say, profoundly. 'That's a big step.'

He rubs his eyes, which are rimmed with red, the kind of make-up Toni might've experimented with on me.

'And you?' I ask. 'Have you got yourself straightened out?' I take his hanky from my pocket as evidence.

'What do you mean?'

'The old snuffy nose.'

'Ah.'

'Well?'

'Yes, I'm sorted.'

'Sorted?'

'I mean, I don't do that anymore. It's all behind me.' He waves his hand vaguely. 'I'm trying to make her happy.'

'And what about you?'

'What about me?'

'Are you happy?'

'No,' he says. 'I'm bloody miserable.'

And seeing him sit there like a little boy, biting his nails, I believe I have it in my power to make him happy. I can do something. Maybe four years ago I could've helped Toni. But I wasn't ready then. Now I want to help Adrian. But in helping Adrian I don't really think too much about how this will affect Toni. How this will affect my life in every way possible.

★   ★   ★

He hails a cab for me later, after we've eaten in some Italian place, dark and dingy in a basement but nice enough tortellini. At the last moment he jumps in beside me and I don't protest. I think he just wants company. He just wants to kill some time travelling in a cab halfway across London and back before going home to Toni. But when it brakes to a halt outside the flat, Adrian gets out with me, paying the driver from a wad of notes stuffed in his wallet.

'How about a nightcap?'

Unfortunately all we have is a bottle of cherry liqueur that Joe's mum brought back from Switzerland when she went skiing some time ago. Adrian is not put off easily and soon tucks in after his initial distaste. I stick to a cup of tea. I have a feeling I might need to keep my wits about me which is difficult after all that over-priced wine chased by those (regrettable) flaming sambucas.

'Where's this Joe bloke then?' asks Adrian, flicking through a copy of the *New Statesman* that he knows can't possibly belong to me.

'At a meeting.'

'With the Trots?'

'They're not Trots anymore. Haven't you heard?'

'Oh yes, I've heard. That's right. They've sold their souls to get into power.'

'I wouldn't know.'

'Still not a political animal, Philippa?' he asks, throwing the magazine down on the coffee table that separates his chair from the sofa that I am hogging to myself.

'Not really,' I yawn. 'I'm more of a fluffy bunny.'

'Show us your tail.' He gets up from his chair and moves my outstretched legs out of the way so he can sit down on the sofa next to me. Close to me.

'Do you mind?'

'Go on,' he says. 'Just one little peek.'

He is edging nearer and nearer to me. And I am not totally against the idea though of course he is married. To Toni. Well, not actually technically married. They've never officially tied the knot. Does that count?

Yes, I think it most probably does, I hear Jiminy Cricket whisper in my ear.

'I think I'd better call you another cab,' I say with some degree of firmness.

'Let me stay here, Philippa. On the sofa,' he adds. 'Pleeease.'

He is obviously much firmer than me because I let him. I fetch a spare duvet and pillow and leave a note for Joe in the kitchen, advising him to steer clear of the lounge till morning.

'Make sure you call Toni,' I say before I shut the door.

That way I can sleep with a clear conscience knowing I've done my best. I've tried to get him to do the right thing. But knowing somehow that he probably won't.

Like Cinders, Joe is normally home before midnight. But, Fate sticks her oar in and entices Joe to spend the night with his almost-girlfriend, a Blair Babe from John Smith House. And as it happens, my conscience must be a little murky because I can't get to sleep no matter how hard I try. Maybe it has more to do with the knowledge that Adrian is lying on the sofa on the other side of the wall, but I do keep wondering what is going through Toni's mind. Whether she is sick with worry that Adrian hasn't come home. Or relieved. I make myself think it is the latter. It's amazing what you can convince yourself if you set your mind to it. If you are desperate enough. And yes, I am desperate. I must be.

★　★　★

In May, Joe and his comrades (who aren't really comrades anymore) find themselves on the winning team for once. Tony is Prime Minister and the days of Tory bashing are done. For now. Even I manage to get my hopes up, my political conscience having finally been pricked — though not my moral one which I am happily ignoring while I carry on seeing Adrian. And I mean 'seeing' in every sense of the word. I am a

311

mistress. The other woman. The phrases *filthy harlot* and *disgusting slut* spring to mind accompanied by the far-off image of a little Margot Fonteyn galloping down the road after her mother, hair scraped back neatly in a bun. Glass tinkling to the floor. Maybe I am my mother's daughter after all. She, who betrayed her friend, Sheila. And me, betraying her daughter. The next generation making a muck-up. But, hey, I think, chin up. As everyone is saying: things can only get better.

★ ★ ★

And actually they aren't bad for a while. Adrian makes the treacherous journey south of the river whenever he can, which is surprisingly often. I don't ask what he tells Toni about where he is, where he is going. She is absorbed with adoption plans. Adrian says she won't even register his absence — though I am not sure that is entirely true. But if he is surplus to requirements, I am only too happy to have what is left over.

★ ★ ★

Apart from the romance in my life, things carry on as before. I still have my job and I still have Evelyn and Judith's allotment offerings. And I still have Joe.

'Isn't it time you got a place of your own?' Adrian asks after one evening when we've had to share a living room with three local councillors and an MP's researcher before discreetly withdrawing to my room to get down to basics.

'I can't leave Joe,' I say. 'He'd be lost without me.'

'You?' he says, kissing my shoulder that he's just uncovered. 'You're a pig. I thought I was messy but you're something else.'

'We can't all afford cleaners,' I say, a cheap dig at Toni.

He stops kissing me, turns away. 'I didn't fall in love with Toni for her cleaning.'

'I don't want to know why you fell in love with Toni, thank you very much.' My voice sounds hauntingly like Helena's, hoity and proud. Adrian turns back to me.

'But I'm not in love with her anymore.'

'Are you in love with me?'

'Maybe,' he says. 'Are you in love with me?'

'Maybe.'

Oh dear. I have a piece of toilet paper stuck to my shoe. One that I know is there but however much I wave my foot about, it just won't go. (And my metaphors have really taken a turn for the worse.)

★ ★ ★

Maybe we are in love, it is hard to say. I know I like being with him. I know he is annoying and arrogant and facetious and a poser and an ex-druggie and an adulterer and a golfer and that he makes me laugh. He makes me feel I am living a life, my own life — not one I've borrowed from a library or read about in the bookshop.

But. There is always that niggle. A niggle that has nothing to do with Jiminy Cricket but that has everything to do with that old fear, the one that has been handed down to me from Helena. The feeling this will all end in tears. That those tears are waiting just round the corner.

★　★　★

By the end of August when Evelyn and Judith are up to their ears in courgettes and spinach and runner beans, this niggle proves to be right. I am in another place metaphorically speaking to where I was at the start of the summer. Adrian would like to get me physically to another place. He's even suggested helping me out with a deposit for a flat.

'East Dulwich is a good area,' he says, 'for south east London. You should try there. It's up and coming. Prices are going to rocket' (etc, etc, estate agent blarney).

But now Adrian is in a different place; he's gone away for the weekend with Toni, to Torquay of all places, staying with Sheila and Bernie and Coco the dog. Even Justin will be putting in an appearance there apparently — if he still calls himself Justin. It could be Beowulf for all I know, it has been that long since I've had news of him.

Joe and I are staying in London with the tourists (not that there are too many in our neck of the woods). We decide to have a lazy boozy Saturday together. We drink beer in the park (the other end from the winos and from little bottles, not cans), sitting on a rug, watching young lads

314

play football and children on the swings. We take a boat trip on the Thames, the only breezy place in the city, and I think of Mr Raby eating his tea at three in the afternoon. We enjoy a long balmy evening in the pub garden, drinking more bottled beer and fighting off the midges. No Adrian, no Blair Babe. Just two best friends.

* * *

I am woken very early the following morning by Joe. He is standing next to my bed in his boxers and I wonder if he is sleep-walking. I have time to notice he has the legs of a rugby player though he wouldn't know what to do with a rugby ball any more than Evelyn would. (She thinks PE should be replaced in the National Curriculum by gardening. 'When have you ever seen an allotment invasion?') Then, I realise he is speaking to me.

'It's the phone,' he says. 'Bob.'

My heart flutters. Why is Bob phoning at this time of day? Something must have happened. Maybe it is Helena. Maybe she is dead. She is dead and I will never see her again. Never get the chance to have a mother.

All these thoughts pass through my brain on the short journey to the phone in the living room next door.

'Bob?'

'Philippa,' he coughs. 'Have you heard? Switch on the radio. The television.'

It can't be Helena. She wouldn't make it to the news. And then I see what has happened. At

315

least I think I can see but it doesn't quite make sense. I must be mistaken.

'Joe! Come here!' I call out. He thuds back in the room trying not to spill two mugs of tea (oh-why-don't-I-love-him-like-a-boyfriend?), a worried look in his eye. I point at the television where we see news footage of a car wreck. In an underpass in Paris. I can hear Bob in tears down the end of the line. The rattle of pills. And I remember how we saw her on that hot day in July. Cheryl with a tea towel wrapped round her head. A newly-wed Princess gliding down the Mall, a halo of sunlight wrapped around hers. And now she is dead. Even Joe, a staunch Republican to the end, is quiet. There is nothing to say. Not yet.

'I'll phone you later, Bob. Take it easy,' is all the words I can put together. Of course I am relieved my mother was not in that car, but I feel strangely moved by what I've seen. And can never guess at what will follow.

'I'm going to phone Sheila,' Bob says before putting the phone down. And my heart drops still further.

★ ★ ★

I stay indoors all that day, in my pyjamas, watching the news updates along with much of the nation, aware that something extraordinary has happened. And nothing can be done to change it. When I watch the CCTV footage of Diana and Dodi leaving the Ritz, I want to tell her to turn back, to spend the night in the hotel,

316

to leave in the morning and to live a long life. But — like poor Lady Jane Grey — it is too late. The clock keeps ticking. The heart of the princess has stopped beating. She's been used by those around her. It was always going to end in tears.

★ ★ ★

At work the next day, Evelyn is not herself. She keeps sighing and blowing her nose and saying '*I can't believe it.*' This is what many people are saying, lining up at the cash point, in the bakery, on the streets, in the shop: I can't believe it.

Later in the week, Joe is at the stage where he believes the nation to be in the grips of mass hysteria, though he has time to be annoyed with the Queen and proud of his Prime Minister, whose honeymoon period is suddenly over. If it is a wave of mass hysteria, Evelyn and Judith are bowled along in it, tugging me with them. Evelyn says she and Judith are going up to Kensington Palace to pay tribute.

'Would you like to come with us? We're going as soon as I've shut up shop. On the bus.'

'Alright,' I say. And I am surprised at how much I want to do this.

So a few hours later, Judith arrives bearing an interesting bouquet of nibbled pinks, some frothy-looking fennel and a few sticks of curly celery.

'I know,' she says in her stuff-and-nonsense voice. 'A pretty poor show, but the best is over.'

'Don't worry.' Evelyn tries to be cheerful. 'I'm

sure she'd approve of the sentiment.'

'Do you think so? She was such a stylish creature. This back to nature approach is more down Charles' street . . . '

'Come on, you two,' I say. 'We can get a candle from that new poncey shop over the road. That'll brighten things up.'

'Splendid idea,' they chorus.

But I'm not sure any of us are feeling particularly bright about the pilgrimage.

⋆ ⋆ ⋆

When finally we arrive in Kensington, we aren't altogether sure how to get to the Palace but it isn't a problem; we follow the people with flowers. I've never seen such a bizarre sight: women I expected, yes, but not all those men in suits — as if there's been a spate of infidelity in the area and this is all they can come up with (is Adrian out there somewhere?).

We are directed by a policeman as to where to line up — an orderly British queue for an extraordinarily un-British show of emotion. We shuffle along reading the notes and poems people have written to their Princess. There are flowers spread out like they've grown into a field. Photos. Candles. The smell of perfume is overwhelming.

We lay down our offering and Judith lights our candle with a match borrowed from an American who is strangely overwrought by the whole process. I am quite shocked to find myself here, crying over a woman I've never met but who I did once get very close to one summer's day. A woman whose picture used to stare out at me from the magazines and papers in Bob's News. A woman who was a mother. Who is now dead.

What would happen if I were to die? Would anyone notice? Who would grieve for me? Who'd light a candle? Evelyn hands me a tissue from her pocket-sized packet of Kleenex. It is just as well everyone else around here is crying because I don't look out of place. I am one of many in a crowd of tearful strangers. But what they don't realise is that I am crying for me. For the bad person I am. For what I am doing to Toni who only wants to be a mother.

Or maybe I am wrong. Maybe they do know. Maybe they are all crying for themselves.

And that is when I decide to end it with Adrian. To walk away from yet another doomed relationship. Jiminy Cricket is telling me I've got to do something.

★　★　★

Unfortunately for me, Joe has been gripped by his own hysteria. It is his turn to be in love. On the day of Diana's funeral, whilst I stand alone on the Mall, he asks his Blair Babe to move in with him and although he would never ask me to leave, what else can I do?

So I find myself flat-hunting for a place just big enough for me and Tiger, using the money Wink left me, put away for a rainy day. For that rainy day has come. That rainy day is pouring

319

down on me, washing my life away down the drain, leaving me broken-hearted, guilt-ridden and abandoned once again.

Surely, surely, from now on, things can only get better?

2006

You will get better. You will get stronger because I am stronger. They say that what doesn't kill you makes you stronger. And this tiny hole will most definitely not kill you. It will heal and mend and your heart will beat strongly, healthily, properly. A persistent rhythm. A good beat. Boom, boom, boom. You are my baby-with-no-name and I love you. It is you I have been waiting for all my life.

18

1999

It's a Knockout

Another funeral. This time it is Bernie's. His faulty starter motor has finally given up, leaving Sheila stranded on the hard shoulder of life. A widow. You might think she would be relieved to be a free woman, free to cadge a lift anywhere, preferably with Bob, driving off into the sunset of late middle age. But now Bernie has gone, she at last reverts to being the devoted wife she was when they first tied the knot all those years ago in Wolverhampton, when Devon was still a place they liked to go on their holidays.

Sheila puts her heart (much stronger than Bernie's) and soul (somewhat confused) into the making of the funeral. Most of Torquay seem to be here, paying their respects, and a good portion of the West Midlands. But these two groups will mix well. It was the sprinkling from London — Toni and Adrian, Justin and me — that is quite possibly a recipe for disaster.

I've attended more than my fair share of funerals but thankfully this one is taking place in another venue, Bernie and Sheila being Roman Catholics. But a funeral's a funeral when all's said and done. It would make a change to be

322

invited to a wedding or a christening. At this rate the prospects of either of these life-enhancing events being staged on my behalf are highly unlikely. Maybe Toni will have more success. She might possibly manage to drag Adrian up the aisle one of these days or even manage to procure a baby from somewhere or other. For they are still together, still a couple of some description, which is surprising given Adrian's apathy but not given Toni's tenacity. (She's had no luck with Romania and is now looking much further afield, to China.)

They are sitting in the front pew next to Sheila. Toni is holding her mother's hand in a rare moment of support, though it isn't quite clear who is supporting who. It could even be mutual. This thought, I am ashamed to admit, disturbs that old green monster, the one who watched Toni pirouetting around Tip Taps in front of a war veteran and a mother in tears. A mother who loved her. Who didn't want her to flee the nest.

Right now, tutus and ballet shoes are a long way away. The only thing on Toni's mind is the father who doted on her, championing her above Terry, her more lacklustre older brother. And there he is, sitting next to his mother, holding her other hand, looking sombre rather than grief-stricken. Justin who is still Justin and might be Justin for good now. You can't go changing your identity for ever (unless you're Madonna maybe). He is forty-four. Well and truly a grown-up though he still looks to me like the teenager who hung around the garage with his mates, giving me Chinese burns. He is a travel writer now — got the travel bug when he was living with his great Dane, doing odd pieces of writing here and there. Turns out he is good at it. Much better than he ever was at selling houses.

Justin has a new girlfriend, Mel, who is very small and petite, almost on a par with Mandy Denning — half my size and twice as pretty with sleek hair and funereal clothes that manage to look fashionable rather than borrowed, like mine. I've had to raid Bob's wardrobe for a black cardigan as I left my jacket in London in the rush to get home. He is sitting next to me now, my Bob, dressed in a new dark suit that actually makes him look well-groomed. Dapper, almost. It has been a long time since he's bought a new suit. The last one had sported big lapels and flared trousers and was worn only twice, both occasions in honour of Wink. It still hangs in the wardrobe amongst his other cardies. 'I'll never get rid of it,' Bob likes to say. 'It's of great historical value.'

Six strapping men lug Bernie's coffin past us and Bob hands over his handkerchief as I am still not in the habit of carrying around a pocket-sized packet of Kleenex. He can no longer ignore my sniffs as one or two unknown people have turned round to find out the source of such grief. And real grief it is. I have to dab at my eyes that are brimming with tears as I realise just how fond of Bernie I was, with his winks and his bamboo canes and the way he scooped me out of my cot one summer evening long ago.

But my grief is nothing compared to Toni's.

Through the hats, I can see her shoulders shaking, her head bowed, Sheila leaning towards her. And Adrian picking up her delicate hand and kissing it — an affectionate gesture, which really works up the green monster into a frenzy as I can't remember him ever doing that to me but then he has special dispensation under these circumstances. He knows how much Toni loved her father. And her grief looks like it will consume her, grief that has no doubt been quickened by the realisation that he'll never be a grandfather. He would have done well in that role. I'm not so sure about Sheila as grandma . . .

'Stand up,' Bob tells me. 'You're meant to be singing.'

He hands me a hymn book, open to (oh-dear-oh-dear-oh-dear) *Abide With Me*. I would probably carry on sitting down, here on the pew — not out of disrespect but from something far more complicated — if it weren't for Bob dragging me to my feet and telling me to get a grip, one of Captain's favourite phrases, though Bob's tone is much kindlier than either the words suggest or how that manky old parrot would express them.

* * *

Much later, when speeches have been made by the priest, by Sheila, by a panel beater from Dudley, we move on to the crematorium as the Pope will now allow Bernie to be cremated like lesser mortals. It is everything you'd expect of such an event though we could do without the final song, *Hold Me Close* (has Auntie Sheila forgotten the significance of this?).

Now we are all back at Auntie Sheila's where I've volunteered to roll up my sleeves and lend a helping hand. I zigzag through the suits and black dresses, offering trays spilling over with vol-au-vents and sausage rolls and egg mayonnaise sandwiches, all of Bernie's favourites, though it has been a long time since he's been allowed to indulge in such fatty foods — not since the high fibre diet which made him into half the man he used to be. Not that it helped. His dodgy ticker had a limited shelf life and was never going to be easily fixed with duct tape or a bit of soldering.

Toni comes into the kitchen but isn't much help either, standing still, staring at the funeral cake that Sheila has decided to bake for her late husband and that now takes pride of place amongst the food on the kitchen table. I don't have the luxury of staring as I have to get the next batch of cocktail sausages out of the oven and impaled onto sticks. (Somebody has to keep these people fed with something to soak up the vast quantities of alcohol being knocked back in Bernie's memory.) Toni pulls herself together enough to refill her sherry glass (which is far too small for the job in hand) and winces at the sight of so much cholesterol all around her.

'I don't know how Mum could make all this food. She should know better.'

'It's just a mark of respect for your dad, I suppose.'

326

She raises her eyebrow — at the word 'respect' presumably.

'A bit late now,' she says, staring out the window at the winter garden beyond. At Coco, Bernie's abandoned excuse of a dog, cocking his little leg against the naked sycamore tree. 'I hope this heart thing isn't hereditary,' she goes on, laying her hand against her silk blouse, feeling her own heart. 'Another reason to adopt anyhow.' She brightens up a bit then, at this glimmer of hope that is always burning out of her reach. But it makes me think of my tiny baby floating around inside me, the size of one of Evelyn's ripe apples — but alas, not ripe enough . . . was that why I lost the baby? Did it have a dodgy, faulty heart? Does Justin? Is there some kind of gene that he carries?

I make my excuses, leaving Toni alone to mope over the cake, and disappear into the garden for some fresh air; the after-life presence of Bernie is oppressive. I can still hear his phlegmy cough following me from room to room. Out here I am able to see the positives of his life: the new greenhouse, the kitsch Alpine rockery, the surgically-pruned rose beds. I'll miss Bernie. He was as good an uncle as any. And I believe he loved my mother in some way, his own way. He certainly loved Sheila. How else would he have put up with her Bob-pinings all these years?

Oh dear. This is all too much. If I were a smoker, now would be the time to reach for a fag and inhale deeply. As it is, I have to make do with a tepid cup of tea and a slice of Dundee cake. But someone else has the same idea: there is Justin sitting on a bench under the sycamore, puffing on a cigar of all things.

It has been a long time since I've spoken to Justin. Now is the moment to put that right. I leave my safe haven behind the pampas and sidle over to his tree. It is damp on the bench. I can feel it seep through the tights and skirt I'm not used to wearing.

'Where'd you get that from?' I indicate to his cigar. 'Was it one of your dad's?'

'No.' He blows the smoke up into the air, away from me. 'Adrian gave it to me. He's handing them out like Ferrero Rocher in there.'

'I bet your mum's pleased about that.'

'She's itching to get out the Febreze. But then she lets Adrian get away with murder for some reason.'

'Really?'

'She thinks he's good for Toni, bizarrely.'

'Really?'

'Yes, really, Philippa. What's with all the surprise?'

'I didn't think he'd be good enough for her — in your mum's eyes.'

'He's grown on her — like staphylococcus.'

'What's that?'

'Bacteria that lives on the skin.'

'Nice.'

He relights his cigar as it isn't handling the breezy weather too well. We sit quietly for a while. I am not really sure what to say exactly, it has been so long since I've been with him. But it is alright. Despite everything.

'I suppose Mum reckons Toni can look after

herself,' he says eventually.

'You don't sound so sure.'

'She's got a lot on her plate.'

'The baby.'

'Yeah,' he says. 'The mythical baby.'

Coco bounces up to us at this point, yapping and jumping up at our legs, snagging my tights. I push him off but Justin makes a point of stroking his tummy, under that ridiculous tartan coat he is wearing. Then Coco spots a magpie (only the one) and chases it without any game plan as to how to catch it. I half expect the bird to turn the tables, pick Coco up by his diamante-studded collar and fly off; the bling round his scrawny little neck is just the sort of thing a thieving bird like that would go for.

Justin takes another puff at the fat cigar, blowing expert smoke rings that would've impressed Miss Goddard's Hiawatha no end. Then he turns his attention to me but in a way that yanks the tablecloth out from a long abandoned feast. He looks up at the house and says: 'Is it over between you two?'

'What?'

'You and Adrian,' he says.

I don't answer.

'He told me.'

'He did what?'

'He got drunk — just for a change — the night you'd finished with him. It all came out. I bloody punched him.'

I must look absolutely horrified because he says (facetiously): 'Don't worry. Toni doesn't know. I never told her.'

I employ a cliché Miss Mothball would have been proud of: 'I never meant it to happen.' Then I add my own take on things. 'Adrian was unhappy. We just sort of fell together.'

'And now?'

'Now? It's none of your bloody business now.'

'She's my sister.'

'She's an adult.'

'I wish you'd bloody act like one,' he says, a little too loudly for my liking, up on his feet now. 'You've got to stop waiting for your mother to come back and sort your mess of a life out. That's down to you.'

A freaky echo of the words I said to his sister, sitting on the bed in Belsize Park. 'You're the only one who can do that.'

He is right. I am the only one.

Adrian chooses this point to come out into the garden and I am tempted to accept the cigar he is offering to me. I am tempted to do anything that will help me ignore what Justin — pacing back and forth on the wet grass — has just said. About my mother. About Helena. So I look at Adrian and I dive straight in.

'Justin was telling me to steer clear.'

Justin stops the pacing. Adrian eyeballs him. 'Of what?' he asks.

'You.'

Adrian puffs on his own cigar, studying Justin through narrowed eyes, shaking his head.

'Nice one,' he says.

I am expecting a big confrontation right now, right here on Bernie's lawn but Justin obviously thinks otherwise.

'Do what you like,' he says, chucking his cigar butt in the pond. 'I'm going in.'

He turns away and there — tripping down the path towards this debacle — is Mel. He strides towards her, the wind rearranging his still-longish hair into strange and weird shapes that gel alone can never do. Hair I once tangled my fingers in. Hair I'll never touch or smell or feel ever again. That is all Mel's privilege now.

'Yeah, go to your girlfriend,' I call after him — quite eloquently, I think, considering the circumstances.

'Grow up, Philippa.'

Grow up.

I remember how I felt the first time he held me, when he was still T-J. My sixteenth birthday. I felt like a grown-up then, like I would never be the same again. And I don't suppose I ever was. But I was a silly child. And him? He was the grown-up. He was the one who should've known better.

Grow up.

But now it is Adrian who reaches for me in a script that could've been written by Miss Mothball or Wink's beloved Danielle Steel:

He takes me in his arms, puts his lips to mine and kisses me as if his life depends on it. As if he will die without me. As if I am the only one that can save him. And it is so good to feel like this. Like I have power at my fingertips. Knowledge in my heart and in my brain. The whole wide world at my feet. The rest of my life in front of me.

'Marry me,' Adrian says.

I can almost hear the birds breaking out in

song, the harps plucked by tubby, rosy cheeked cherubs, the slushy muzak of an airport reunion at the end of a film. But the script is soon crossed out and rewritten by Auntie Sheila who's come out into the garden for her own slice of fresh air and oneness with Bernie's memories. At the sight of such an unlikely and unexpected coupling, she shrieks and flaps like a mother gull and launches herself from the back door. I can make out the immortal phrases *filthy harlot* and *disgusting slut* hurling over the sodden lawn towards us.

And I know, without a doubt, that I've made a choice that will change things for good. That will test every single relationship I know.

'Yes,' I say, turning back to Adrian. 'I will.'

(Oh dear.)

But there is one person I am most concerned for. And that, sadly, isn't Toni, grieving for her father, but Bob who, when he lumbers behind Sheila across Bernie's soggy garden, is slow on the uptake. He looks at Sheila — still shrieking at us — in puzzlement. He looks at Adrian as if he hasn't a clue who he can be. And he looks at me as if he thinks he knows me but can't quite place me. As if this is a case of mistaken identity. That I am still inside, rolling up my sleeves and lending a helping hand in Sheila's kitchen, stabbing cocktail sausages through the heart. But it is his heart I am piercing. His starter motor that will never work in quite the same way again.

'What are you doing?' he asks, dazed.

'Adrian's asked me to marry him,' I announce to the gradually assembled guests which includes the panel beater from Dudley and (oh-please-no) Toni who is unable to speak or object or even cry but who manages to conjure up a look that could be sold on the black market and then wallops Adrian so hard in the face that his feet skid beneath him, toppling him to the ground where he lies quite still, just his eyes blinking.

'Get out,' Bob whispers, standing over him. 'Pick yourself up and get out.'

Adrian picks himself up, with what little dignity he can gather off the soggy grass, and takes my hand, not even bothering to wipe the mud from his Paul Smith suit.

Bob finally turns his attention to me, remembering who I am at last.

'Of all the people in London, why did you have to choose Toni's husband?'

'He's not her husband.'

'It doesn't matter.'

'Yes, it does. He wants to marry me. I'm sorry about Toni, but he doesn't love her.'

'I'm sorry too, Philippa. Sorry you don't know how to do the right thing.'

'Maybe if I'd had a proper mum and dad then I would know. As it is I have to make my own decisions. And I've decided I want a proper family of my own. I want a proper life. I want Adrian.'

'He can't have children. Has he told you that?'

'I don't want children. Why the hell would I want children with the upbringing I've had.'

I might just as well have punched him in the face. And actually, I feel like punching him in the face.

'If you go with him,' he says, 'I'll never speak to you again.'

So what do I do?

I don't punch him in the face. I go.

I walk away, my hand in Adrian's hand, being led up the garden path and out of my old life for what might possibly be for good.

★ ★ ★

Six weeks later I marry Adrian in Southwark register office. He is wearing something casual. I am in a dress, both of us out of our comfort zones. We say our vows in front of a paltry show of friends and family (those of them who'd come). Someone takes a photo on one of those new digital cameras and shows it to me on the little screen. There we all are, a raggedy collection:

Joe with his arm around the Blair Babe (Rebecca), now his wife and mother to a bundle of blue crushed to her voluminous breast.

Cheryl, who's been good enough to drop her dying patients in Bristol and come to London for the day.

Adrian's best man and brother, John, a city banker with novelty tie and matching waistcoat.

Adrian's mum, Pamela, who hates me at first sight. ('I was switched at birth,' says Adrian. 'There's no other possible explanation.')

Adrian's school friend, Will, who's quite clearly always lived in my husband's shadow (I know the feeling).

Evelyn and Judith, wearing matching trouser

suits like they are part of some religious cult.

And — who-would've-thought-it-after-all-these-years — Auntie Nina.

'I heard on the grapevine,' she says, sailing in on a wave of Chanel No. 5, dressed to put me completely to shame.

I am not entirely sure what grapevine this could be though I have my suspicions. At least there is someone to witness my marriage. Someone who knew me when I was a child. Someone who could possibly be proud and shed a tear.

It is only later — in the Crown and Greyhound — that she hands me the card, after several double gin and oranges.

It is from Helena who, of course, is the root of the grapevine planted across the ocean.

Congratulations! it says on the front. You did it!

Well, yes, I certainly have done it though I am not absolutely sure I should be congratulated for it.

And inside, in her finest schoolgirl handwriting, a somewhat cryptic message that I could choose to listen to or ignore:

Don't worry what people think. Follow your heart.

I am not convinced that Helena should be the one to give out advice of that nature. But I do know about broken hearts and dodgy hearts, so I am not really sure I should trust my own to be working properly.

Too late now. I've got myself hitched to Adrian: an adulterer, a golfer, an estate agent, an ex-druggie, a poser and the man I think I am in love with. Whatever being in love means.

'Helena might've ventured across the pond if she hadn't been so ill,' Auntie Nina says.

'Ill?'

'Bronchitis,' she explains with a sigh and a tut. 'She should really stop smoking.' And with that, Auntie Nina extracts a Camel from her very expensive leather handbag and lights up in the manner of a star of the silver screen.

★ ★ ★

We don't have a honeymoon as Adrian and I haven't made the most sensible financial move in marrying each other. He has to get used to living south of the river, in my tiny flat, with no money for a cleaner, no tube station for miles. But in time East Dulwich will grow on him — even if I don't. In time he will set up a sister office on Lordship Lane as it makes sense to keep the business going, leaving Toni to run Belsize Park. But I will not leave Evelyn or the books because at least I know I can spend my days surrounded by other worlds, other people. I can be anyone. Go anywhere. And I can have as many happy endings as I want.

★ ★ ★

For now I have Adrian to myself. In the evenings when he eventually gets home. At night, when he reaches out for me in what I can only describe as desperation. For a little while. But for some reason, when I am in the flat alone, it isn't Adrian I pine for. It is everyone but him.

On January 4th, I am home early from work and I switch on the television. It is *Blue Peter*. They are digging up the time capsule, John, Peter and Valerie. The contents are all mouldy and disgusting and I have a moment of panic thinking about Lucas' chocolate tin buried in Bob's backyard. I know I can't dig it up. I am not allowed back there. I don't have a child of my own. And that might never happen, with Adrian's track record. Which leads me back to Justin, the father of my child that never quite made it. The tiny baby that was in a rush. Too early. And that is when I know I've made a mistake. A big mistake.

Oh sod it.

2006

A big mistake. Are you a mistake? Never, ever. I will treasure you always. Cherish you every moment. The most precious gift I have ever had. More than Lucas, more than Bob, more than Wink or Joe or Miss Parry.

Talk of the special baby unit has stopped. It's completely full up with babies more poorly than you. (Poor things.) Though you, a special baby, are being closely observed. But they are pleased. Really pleased that finally you've got to grips with this feeding and there's no stopping you. With every breath you take, you get stronger and I get more confident that you will do this. We will do this.

19

2005

Runaround

Five years later, I am still married, still virtually-motherless and still not a mother myself, although I have — in the manner of Miss Parry, my Tudor queen — taken on two long-haired cats (Lesley and Valerie) that spend their days lounging around our messy four-bedroomed-Victorian-semi-in-tree-lined-street-with-access-to-local-amenities-and-secluded-garden, leaving a trail of fur that make my husband sneeze. (At least that's what he blames the runny nose on.)

My family is very small at this moment in time. There is no point wishing for a child; that chance came and went over half my life ago. Since we walked out of that winter garden, Adrian and I, we've never bothered with birth control, no point given his track record. Even after several hundred half-hearted chances, not one of his lazy sperm has bothered to get up and go. I sometimes believe that is why I settled for Adrian, knowing I'd probably never have children. Knowing I'd be a useless mother, having been abandoned by my own.

Our childlessness must at least be some

consolation for Toni who is forty-six and still searching the world over for a baby — only now she has someone committed to undertake this quest by her side: Sheila. Toni doesn't need a man apparently, not having re-discovered her mother (oh dear, it's Tip Taps all over again). I am not actually persuaded I need a man either, my old pal Celibacy looking so appealing right now. And if I do need a man, in all probability, it isn't this one.

★ ★ ★

Summertime. I am no longer put to bed in the middle of the afternoon, left behind bars to listen to the wood pigeons and the herring gulls. I am nearly forty-years-old. Forty! What have I got to show for those four decades? A ridiculously expensive house that I 'share' with my hardly-ever-at-home workaholic husband, two lazy fluffballs, a friend who has increasingly less time for me, and a job where I spend my days buried in different worlds to the one I unfortunately inhabit.

I have more than many, but I don't have what I thought I would have at this stage in my life. It isn't the things I've never possessed that worry me — a high IQ, celebrity, breathtaking beauty, power, wisdom and brains — but the things I once had: a small boy with a big voice and duck egg skin, a cat with tiger stripes, a girl with cherry lip gloss from Solihull, a boy called Raymond from Preston, a grumpy old woman in a wheelchair, a newsagent called Mr Bob Sugar, a mother who loved me, a father in darkest Peru, a small bundle of life spinning around inside me. The people I've lost along the way. I'd hoped to find at least some of them again. Even one of them would've done.

'How are you intending to mark your birthday?' Evelyn enquires one morning. It is quiet in the shop and I've been out choosing lattes and pastries. Not easy as so many cafes and delis have sprung up within spitting distance (Adrian was right about it being an up-and-coming area. It has most definitely arrived, along with every type of coffee you can think of). 'Anything special?'

'A quiet night in with a takeaway and a bottle of Sancerre, if Adrian's got anything to do with it.'

She makes a funny sound at the mention of his name. She always makes this sound. A mixture of snort and tut that is quite clearly an expression of contempt for my other half.

'Wouldn't you like a party?'

'I'd hate a party.'

'But why, Philippa? Parties are lovely.'

'No.'

'Why ever not?'

'All the obvious reasons and then several thousand more.'

I haven't enjoyed a birthday party since I was ten and the toast of my school. I'd rather not think about my sixteenth (poor Diana, poor me, I knew it would all end in tears). And now, at this stage of my life, I'd rather not highlight my embarrassing existence to everyone who knows me. I'd rather not be centre stage. That always ends badly.

Evelyn doesn't push it. She finishes her skinny latte in silence, tidying the book mark rack, leaving me to finish sorting out the Crime 3 for 2s. And I presume that is the end of it. A mushroom biryani and a bottle of expensive French wine will do me fine, thank you very much.

So what happens? Shock, horror, twist, Adrian gives me a top present, something I've been wanting for ages, an iPod. But that isn't all. He goes out of his way to alert the nation to my rite of passage and throws a party. Not a thrown-together Bob-style one, but a reasonably well-orchestrated surprise one. Only not as finely-tuned as it might've been which is why I turn up at my fortieth wearing a chavvy tracksuit and dirty Reeboks. Well, how was I to know? He sends me off — unfairly or so I think — to go down to Oddbins for the wine and then on to Bombay Delights to pick up the curry. He says he wants to tidy up and make the place look nice for me — which does strike me as strange but I don't question it. I am happy to get out. To have a bit of a walk. To clear my head at the thought of all those lost years.

By the time I arrive back at the house, a long evening of television viewing laid out before me, there they are, lined up in the hallway and on the stairs: everyone (bar Dr Cheryl) who was at our nondescript wedding, some neighbours, plus a flock of estate agents, and — no-please-no — Toni.

'Surprise!' they chorus.

There is a delayed stunned silence as they take in my Reeboks and I take in their glamour before people return to the lounge armed with their glasses and nibbles, all except Toni, who remains in my hallway, reflected in the mirror Adrian and I bought in Greenwich market in the days when we used to spend Sunday mornings together, instead of being separated by golf. Toni and her reflection both look radiant in their matching expensive biased-cut long strappy dresses with immaculate accessories straight from the pages of Vogue. They are sipping Champagne and holding hands with two beautiful African men called Adebayo.

I step in front of the mirror in an effort to break the illusion. I can only handle one Toni at a time (and even one is pushing it).

'Hello, Toni,' I say graciously.

'Happy Birthday, Philippa,' she says. 'Hope you don't mind me coming. Adrian thought it was time we made up.'

'Did he?'

'I see him all the time so it's a bit weird I never see you.'

'Well, that's the Thames for you. It might as well be the Atlantic.'

Adebayo laughs politely and I like him for trying. But 'like' is not the feeling I have for Adrian who's forced me into this situation. He knows I hate surprises, ever since the one he sprung on me in Bernie's soggy garden. The marry-me one that I was suckered into without thinking. The one that cut me off from Bob, (oh,

343

Bob, where are you now?) and today he's invited Toni here. Ms Tip Taps herself. His ex, his business partner, his once-cohabitee. Toni, who runs the north London office, while he takes care of the south. Toni, who he sees all the time, talks to everyday. Toni, who he is now riveted to, laughing way too loudly at her jokes, her witticisms that are far more sophisticated than anything that tumble out of my mouth. Toni, who my husband is quite clearly comparing to me, looking with envy at the beautiful tall man at her side with the voice of a Shakespearian actor.

I make my excuses and move away from the clique. Someone shoves a glass of pink bubbly in my hand which I make short work of as I stand in the doorway of the lounge which is surprisingly full of people who've made the effort to come to my party — only a few of whom are dear to me.

Over in the bay window that gives onto our leafy street sits Joe on our sofa, gorging on a slice of garlic bread and chatting to Rebecca while she breastfeeds their third baby, Gabriel. Joe waves at me, a little ironic comrade salute, then shouts 'Happy Birthday!' a little too loudly, earning him a turn-to-stone look from Rebecca as Gabriel pops off the breast to search for the source of his father's heckling voice.

Leaning against the mantelpiece are the flock of estate agents who've taken off their ties in an effort to appear casual though I can tell by the veins throbbing in their temples that they are still at work in spirit. Once upon a time Toni would have been over there with them, joining in, but

344

right now she and Adebayo brush past me through the doorway and move elegantly into our lounge where they stand together, up close and personal, on our very expensive Persian rug, talking intimately — something I haven't done with anyone in a very long time.

Further along, next to the gate-legged table that has been opened up to accommodate all the bring-a-bottles, stands Evelyn and Judith who've added their homemade blackberry wine to the collection, potent wine which has somehow found its way into my glass and will soon be hurtling through my bloodstream, searching out my brain cells and destroying them one by one.

Evelyn and Judith have been trapped against the gate-legged table by an earnest neighbour who is lecturing them on the kindest way to deter the slugs from decimating their crops. If Auntie Nina was *compos mentis* she could tell them that there is one sure fire way of killing slugs and that is with a pair of kitchen scissors. But Auntie Nina is down the other end of the room, sitting at the piano playing Gershwin with the gusto, if not the finesse, of Liberace.

I decide that unless I want to join Auntie Nina for a duet I should fill my stomach with some food and that is when I come across Adrian, leaning against the Aga (mark two), a bottle of Evelyn and Judith's witch's brew in his hand, deep in thought.

He looks up as I come in, takes a glug from the bottle.

'Happy birthday,' he says, filling my glass from the same bottle he's just drunk from and which he is now lifting in a toast. 'Cheers.'

'Bottoms up,' I mumble in return, wishing my bottom felt more pert in this baggy tracksuit.

'Shall I get changed?' I ask him.

'Don't be daft,' he says. 'This is you, Phil.' He indicates my scruffydom. 'Why make yourself look all fancy when you're not? Everyone likes you just the way you are.'

I ignore the Billy Joel (no change in his musical taste) and decide now is as good a time as any to take up smoking and grab a Camel off Auntie Nina who's wandered into the kitchen with a half-drunk bottle of Harvey's Bristol Cream in her hand. And it is barely ten past eight. Auntie Nina hands me her silver lighter and Adrian watches me in amazement as I have a coughing fit, though he doesn't say a word; he doesn't get a chance. For once Adrian has met his match in Auntie Nina who's sat me down at the table.

'What a shame Helena isn't here,' she muses. She is about to say something else as she looks at Adrian but then her words get lost in a haze of smoke and nostalgia (a dangerous pair).

'Isn't it,' I agree though I know the one person Auntie Nina wants to be here, can never be. For he is still a speck of stardust floating around waiting for his mother to join him one of these days — which won't be too long judging by the way she is knocking them back.

'I must circulate,' Adrian announces. Then he leaves us to it.

Auntie Nina takes my hand in earnest. We are alone at last with our favourite ghost. But we

346

don't really make the best of it. Instead, Auntie Nina decides to commune with him by putting her head on the table. I manage to extricate my hand, enabling me to stuff my face with Pringles whilst finishing off Auntie Nina's cancer stick.

Then I remember the iPod in my pocket and plug in my earphones. During *Dancing Queen*, I feel my mobile vibrate; a text message from Dr. Cheryl wishing me Many Happy Rtns which seems doubtful from where I'm sitting. I light up another of Auntie Nina's cigarettes and lose myself in *Super Trouper*. After a while, through the smoke screen, a face materialises, one I'm not expecting to see. An uninvited guest.

'Happy Birthday, Phil,' the guest mouths, a man who's celebrated his own special birthday not so long ago (half a century!). I haven't seen him in ages, not since Bernie's funeral, though I often lie in bed upstairs at night, staring at the pattern in our handmade curtains, remembering a note squeezed into my hand in his sister's bijou bathroom across town. The best night of my life that led, a few months later, to the worst. The Cavalier holding the oxygen mask to my face. The squeaky trolley. The splatter of sick on a lino floor.

'Alright, Justin,' I say, taking out the earphones. 'I wasn't expecting you.'

'I don't suppose you were,' he says cryptically, taking in Auntie Nina slumped at the table, the cigarette stub that I post into an empty can of Stella, the shiny new iPod. 'I came all the same.'

He delves in his big dispatch rider type bag

and pulls out a brown paper package, tied up with string.

'For you,' he says.

Inside, when I eventually manage to untie the knot, is a *Blue Peter* annual. A vintage one, 1971. Unfortunately Auntie Nina decides this is the moment to pull herself together, and sits back up, breathing rather heavily. She spots the annual and immediately thinks of her lost boy with his messy hair and his voice that cried out across Torquay and, so it would seem, from the Other Side.

'Lucas,' she whispers, trance-like. 'This is from Lucas.' She grips Justin's arm and says, 'Oh, thank you. Thank you for bringing this. Do you have any other messages?'

I look at Justin, willing him on.

'Ye-es,' he stalls.

I kick him.

He goes on. 'He told me to tell you . . . he misses you.' (At this point Auntie Nina starts to wail at the thought of her small boy hopelessly calling out for her in the dead of night.)

I will him on some more, kicking him a little harder.

'And he says . . . not to worry about him. He's fine.'

'Thank God,' she says. 'Thank God.' And she leaves the room with a fresh glass of sherry and a serene smile on her painted lips.

'That was nice,' I say when I hear the piano cranking up again in the distance.

'What? Fooling a drunk woman her dead son's just contacted her from beyond the grave?'

'Don't say it like that. You put her mind at rest. Gave her a little nugget of peace.'

'Maybe,' he says, helping himself to some killer wine (which is definitely not for wimps). 'What about you? Have you found peace?' He asks this like he really wants to know the answer.

'Not especially. Have you?'

'Not especially.'

He takes the tube of Pringles off me and shoves a stack of them in his big gob, washing down the remains with more blackberry wine. Then he says it: 'Have you heard from Bob?'

'Not a word,' I say, slightly taken aback that he should bring this up now, but still . . . the sound of his name . . . 'How is he?'

'Why are you asking me?'

'Your mum's no doubt got her claws into him.'

'He's not exactly resisting.'

'Maybe not. But the whole of my life all I can remember is your mum chasing my . . . Bob. He's given up the fight.'

'It doesn't matter now,' he sighs, slumping back into the chair. 'Dad's dead.'

'I know, I'm sorry.'

'What for?'

'Your dad, you know, being dead.'

A small smile works its way around his lips at my discomfort.

'I liked him, alright?'

'Did you?' he asks, surprised.

'He had his moments.'

'I must've missed them,' he says, tipping the last of the crisps into his mouth. 'I don't feel a lot when I think of him. I don't feel like I've lost much at all.'

'You should try being me. I've lost pretty much everyone along the way.'

'You've picked up your fair share too.'

'Adrian? Is that how you see it?'

'It doesn't matter how I see it. It's how you see it.'

'I wish I'd never set foot in that garden that day. Never sat under that tree. Never said yes to . . . all this.' I sweep my arm vaguely around me, taking in the Aga, the table, the Dualit toaster, the cupboards full of Champagne flutes and Dartington glass. 'I wish I'd stayed in your mother's kitchen doing the dishes.'

That's when he looks at me, straight-faced. Not a smile, not a sneer, not a hint of desperation but something else, something I can't put my finger on.

'Give us your iPod,' he demands. And then he extracts something else from his bag. 'You probably need some proper music on there but this'll have to do. It is a Monkees CD. The Best of.' He proceeds to move over to my PC on the desk in the corner of the room and burn it or something onto my iPod. Just like that. Then he plugs the earphones back into my ears and I get a blast of *Daydream Believer* which he lets me sing along to for longer than is polite.

'Fancy some fresh air?' he asks eventually, when he can stand no more.

And I can't help but remember the time his sister dragged me away from Bob in the shop, down to the harbour, where we sat on a wet bench and she asked me to come to London. Little did she know what would happen there.

'Yeah, let's get out of here.'

And I walk out the kitchen door, into the muggy July evening, Justin right behind me, a long way from that garden of our childhood where we played ponies and bad guitar-based rock. From the bottom of this garden, we look back at the house where I live with Adrian, the man I took from his sister. We can make out the shapes of the party guests within, moving in the twilight. Shadow puppets acting out their feelings: joy, celebration, drunkenness, lust, loss and love. The last thing I glimpse before I lead Justin down the garden path of our secluded garden towards the summer house is my husband, upstairs in our bedroom, drawing the curtains whose pattern still eludes me. I spent the whole of the first summer in that room, after work, stripping off layers of wallpaper, relining and painting. I did it all on my own. Now he is there without me, his familiar shape bending towards a woman. A woman he's never stopped loving. Two shadow puppets acting out their own play of betrayal.

In the glorified shed, in the darkness, I can smell the nicotiana that I planted up in terracotta pots and have to banish thoughts of Helena. And Adrian. There is only this second. This moment. There is only now.

I tangle my fingers through Justin's hair, something I thought I would never do again as long as I lived. Adrian might be my husband and I might be very stupid, but lying on the wooden floor with Justin is possibly the only thing that will keep me sane. That will remind me I was a person. That I won't blow away on a gust of wind. Really, it is the only thing I can do.

★　★　★

Three weeks later I make another trip to the chemist. But this time I do the test myself. I do it in the comfort of our own bathroom, wee on a plastic strip and wait for a little blue line to appear in a little window . . . yes, there it is. Before I have time to take this in, to comprehend the full consequences of what this means, there is a knock at the front door. I am too much in a fuddle to leave it, to wait for them to go away in order to contemplate the stick in my hand, so I rush downstairs and fling the door open. There is Auntie Nina.

'I'm going to have a baby,' I blurt out.

'Are you, darling? Well, that's lovely news. Congratulations.'

She comes in for a cup of coffee. Very strong coffee because she would actually prefer gin. She sits at the kitchen table, polished and restored once again since the spillages of blackberry wine at the party. She listens to me gibbering away and then she asks in her straight-to-the-point way: 'You're getting on a bit, Philippa, aren't you, to be having a baby?'

And there is that niggle, which my excitement can only just contain.

'Forty's young these days. Forty's the new thirty.'

'Well, your mother and I were from a different generation. We had our children young. Not that it did us any good.'

Nina sips her coffee then she says: 'I'm glad you went for the cream tiles. Cream will never date. Just you see, your little one will be all grown up and you still won't need to change them.'

I am finding it hard to listen to Nina. I want her to go now. I want to be alone with the stick. Alone. Because its implications are only now beginning to sink into my thick brain.

When she's drained a second cup, I see her to the front door where she tells me to take care, a phrase she uses with its true meaning. Then she adds: 'Make sure that husband of yours does some running round after you for a change.' I know she doesn't think highly of Adrian. Not many people do. She grips my arm as if she's about to say something, then she lets it go in exchange for a Camel.

I watch Nina get in her car — the way they teach young girls at finishing school — and drive off, with a slightly unnerving squeal of tyres. The smell of burning rubber makes me rush inside and be sick. Or maybe it's this speck of a baby making itself known.

As I lean back on my heels on the bathroom floor I feel suddenly weak and want Auntie Nina back. My hormones are making me as fickle as Helena. I don't want to do this on my own like the last time. I have a house and a husband that I've procured through irresponsible means, leaving me with no other family. I should give it my best shot and try and make it work otherwise what does that decision say about my judgement? What has the last five years all been about? And where is the alternative? Where is Justin in all this? On his latest travel venture . . . Sofia . . . Budapest . . . Prague . . . Timbukbloodytu. He walked away that night. He kissed me afterwards and asked me if I'd be okay. There was a pause when I could've said no, I won't be, take me with you but instead I thought of Toni. I thought of Auntie Sheila. I thought of Bob. There was no way I could leave Adrian, Toni's once-partner, to take up with her brother. *Of all the people in London.* So I said, yes, I'll be fine. And he walked out of the summer house, walked back up the garden path and disappeared into the bushes. He left me in that moonlit garden, alone. He walked away.

I will tell Adrian the miraculous news tonight. That should be enough to make him see sense. To get over Toni once and for all. He need never know I know. She need never know I know. It can all be brushed away, swept under the carpet. Worse things happen at sea. (Thank you, Miss Mothball. Today I need your clichés more than ever. I can't think beyond my next word).

★   ★   ★

Bad plan. It just delays the inevitable. The shock of my announcement makes Adrian marvel at the miracle that he's pulled off, you would think single-handedly. I do nothing to dampen his incredulity, his satisfaction. But the initial impact soon fades as the future begins to make itself felt. As I start going to Mothercare and buying baby accessories off eBay. Over the coming months, while I grow fat and heavy, Adrian grows aloof and uncaring. He says ante-natal classes are for women which doesn't inspire great hope that he'll be any help at the birth. In fact I don't think he will be there at all. We might as well be living back in the sixties. I might as well be part of that generation for all the progress that has been made.

And do I confront Adrian with all this? No. I say nothing. I do nothing. I don't want to upset my baby. I want to be a good mother. I *will* be a good mother.

★   ★   ★

When I am eight months pregnant and washing up is something that has become as trying as swimming the Channel, Adrian breaks the news to me. He doesn't stand by the Aga brandishing a glass of wine. He sits himself down at the kitchen table and puts his head in his hands. I have a vision of Auntie Nina but Adrian is not drunk. He is not stoned. He is as sober as a judge. As sober as my grandfather who I've never met, but who I've heard — on that busy old grapevine — has recently died and will never ever be able to pass judgement on me. On my life. For that is now down to Judge Adrian, my husband. And he is on the verge of condemning our marriage to the bin.

355

'It's over,' he says. 'I'm in love with Someone Else.'

He thinks I don't know. He thinks I am stupid. They both think I am stupid. Well, maybe it is them who are stupid. Maybe I know more than they do. Or maybe I don't. Maybe I know nothing.

★ ★ ★

He is at work when my waters break. I consider phoning him but dismiss that idea out of hand. I consider Joe but he has his own family now and his wife would hardly go a bundle on what I am asking. So there is no-one. I call a cab and hide the pain in my voice as I'm afraid they won't want me in one of their cars but ten minutes later an Irishman from Mayo is standing on my doorstep. I could kiss him if I weren't doubled over. He half-carries me to the cab (he has the arms of a weight lifter, fortunately) and then speeds off over the humps of East Dulwich, through Camberwell and down the Walworth Road, heading for St Thomas'. I wish now I hadn't gone all nostalgic and chosen the hospital of my own birth. I should've gone for King's, a darn sight nearer. Still, the Hail Marys reassure me somewhat, the thought that this is out of my control now. No going back even if I wanted to, which I quite possibly do.

Michael, the cabbie, swings into the ambulance bay and nabs a porter who comes running with a wheelchair when he hears the noise I'm making. Then there are lifts and corridors and lino and I try, really try, to block out the splat of sick echoing at the back of my mind. The sirens flashing and wailing across Torquay. The Cavalier who went off in a huff years ago.

Finally I am in a delivery room. The bumps and sways of the journey have dilated my cervix nicely and I am virtually ready to push. That is when the peace descends. A moment of calm transition between full dilation and giving birth. I remember my iPod. I ask the midwife, Fran, if she'll get it out of my bag. And then I listen to The Monkees. And then I start to cry.

Come on, Philippa, get a grip. You're nearly there.

And then there's an overwhelming, all-encompassing, you just-can't-fight-it need to push. All the stuff you hear about melons and grapefruits and all the rest of it is absolutely true. Three agonising, skin-splitting pushes later and she is placed in my arms. A baby girl. Small and wet and a little bit blue.

You are here. You have arrived.

20

2006

I Love Lucy

'Hi Phil.' A cheeky grin is the first thing I see when I wake up — having managed a measly twenty minutes kip — followed by a whiff of prawn cocktail crisps.

'Hello, stranger. How are you?'

'I should be asking that,' Joe says, offering me a crisp. I am famished so I take a handful. That's my Joe, always thinking of bar snacks. The first person I called with the news. The first familiar face to come and see me. Us.

'What took you so long getting in touch?'

'Oh, you know.' And no, of course, he doesn't know, but lovely Joe doesn't push it. Instead he is transfixed by you. Lovely you.

'How's the little one?' He peers at my baby asleep in her tank. 'What's her name?'

'Not sure yet. I was thinking of Maggie maybe.'

'What?'

And in that word, the spark of fire in his eye, I see my old Joe. My Jiminy Cricket about to remonstrate me for my lack of political conscience.

'I'm joking,' I say. 'Did you lose your sense of

358

humour along with Clause Four?'

He laughs, to prove he hasn't, then he picks you up, an expert now, having three children of his own. Whatever happened to the man who thought there were enough children in the world? He fell in love. He grew up. As we all must do one day. As I am finally beginning to.

★　★　★

Evelyn and Judith turn up bright and early the next morning, laden with fresh produce — mostly bought from the greengrocers as not much is happening fruit-wise on the allotment. You, my baby-with-no-name, are in the middle of a squawking session, little face all red and cross. Judith takes control, grappling you from my arms and looking like she means business.

'Let Judith try,' Evelyn says, sitting me down in the chair, turning her attention to this new, somewhat bewildered mother. 'Are you getting your five portions?' she asks, taking in my pallor which I know — from the odd glance I've caught in the glass doors on the way to the loo — is a whiter shade of pale.

Judith carries on rocking, stroking your hair as if you were a cat. I feel a twinge of guilt for Valerie and Lesley who've been taken in by Evelyn and Judith in preparation for this time.

'Don't worry about them,' Evelyn instructs. 'They're fine. They've got their fluffy paws firmly ensconced under our table.' And she indicates the intricate pattern of fur decorating her expensive cashmere cardigan. 'Judith and I have decided we're cat people. Now, have a banana. The last thing you want is to be constipated with everything else going on down below.'

Indeed.

'What do you think of her then?'

'She's really rather lovely,' says Judith. But she could do with a name.

'I know. But I don't feel ready to give her one yet. I've got to get it right. It's so final.'

'Well, make sure you give her a decent middle name. That way she can always change it when she's older.'

'Alright. I'll think about that one too.'

I don't have a middle name. Philippa has always been enough on its own. But Someone Else does. Terry Siney does.

Oh, Terry Justin Siney. Where are you now?

★   ★   ★

Yet another visitor. It is still too early for Auntie Nina to have knocked back her first drink of the day so she is quite chirpy as she totters in, stooping to kiss me on both cheeks, a floppy pink bunny under her arm. 'For your little one,' she says. 'Where is she?'

She sees you then, in the cot, sleeping the way babies are supposed to sleep.

'Oh, Philippa,' she says. 'Helena would be charmed.'

There is silence then, at the mention of her name. But names are on Nina's mind.

'What are you going to call her?'

'If she'd been a boy it would have been Lucas.'

360

'Darling, how sweet of you to think of him.'

'I always think of him.'

'Do you?' she asks, wandering over to the window and peering at the office blocks. (I'd hoped for a river view, the Palace of Westminster, when I booked in here but all I got was a lousy grey-scape.) 'I sometimes think I imagined him. That he never existed at all. That he was all a dream. A fairy tale.' She reaches up her sleeve for a hanky, her chirpiness dissolving, and comes and sits on the bed. 'That's why I left Torquay. Why I've never gone back. I suppose I thought it easier to leave him behind.' She blows her nose. 'That was wrong of me. He was my son and I left him all alone.' She starts to cry and I put my hand on her arm.

'I'm sorry, Philippa,' she says, a little while later after she's taken deep breaths, had a glass of water and composed herself. 'This is supposed to be a happy time for you and I'm dragging up the past. You see . . . I loved him so very much.'

'I know you did Auntie Nina. And you shouldn't worry about not seeing him. I used to visit him a lot when I lived in the shop. I'd tell him all my secrets.'

'You did?'

'Of course. He was my best friend.'

'My Lucas,' she breathes.

And I want to cry too but I am a grown-up now. I am a mother.

'So, Philippa, what have you got in mind?' Nina asks, brightening a little as she takes in your pretty face.

'What do you mean?'

361

'A name. You really must decide.'

Decide . . . yes . . . she is right. I have to decide.

'Lucy,' I say. 'I will call her Lucy. That's as close as I can get.'

And maybe, one day, when she is bigger, she'll have a crop of messy hair. A shouty voice that will sing out across the streets and pierce my heart with a shot of love.

'You are Lucy Wink Smith,' I tell my daughter. 'And I love you.'

(So much for the sensible middle name but what else can I do?)

★ ★ ★

Finally he comes back and finally I let him in.

'How is she?' Adrian asks, tentatively, his usual cock assurance a little limp. He avoids close contact with me, edging around the room, eventually ending up by the cot, looking sheepishly at the contents within (ie. You).

'She's feeding a bit better today,' I say, meaning: I've been managing perfectly alright without you.

'Good.' He ignores the subtext. 'That's good.' He scoops Lucy out of the little cot and rocks her gently. Maybe he is using her as some kind of human shield as he is about to set the record straight.

'Go on, then,' I say. 'Enlighten me. Who is it?'

'Haven't you guessed?'

'I think so.'

'Someone who wants a baby more than

anything in the world,' he says.

'Toni.'

He nods his head, carries on rocking you back and forth, back and forth, jiggedy-jig, jiggedy-jig.

I feel sick.

'I'm sorry, Phil,' he says. 'I guess I never stopped loving her. Not really. I thought it would work, you and me, but when you told me you were pregnant, I didn't feel like I was supposed to. Not for long. It felt wrong somehow. Like it should've been Toni with the growing belly, the wind, the heart burn.'

'I'll give you heart burn.'

But how can I feel anger at what he is saying? Of course it shouldn't have felt right. I deceived him. Deceived him into thinking it was his child. That I'd given him a miracle. When all along it was Justin. For the second time in my life, it is Toni's brother who's come up trumps. Bingo. Happy Birthday. Surprise!

'It's not your baby,' I say.

'I know you're mad with me Phil, but you're going to need me. And Toni will do her bit. You know she will.'

'No, it's not your baby.'

'You needn't worry we'll take over. Of course, it's your baby.'

In the words of Morrissey, it's time the tale were told. Oh dear. Take a deep breath, Philippa Smith, and tell him.

'It's Someone Else,' I say, looking him in the eyes, which are sad and full of the burdens of life and finally . . . realisation.

'You mean . . . '

'You didn't hit the jackpot. Someone Else did.'
'Who?'

He pins me to the bed with his astonished stares, waiting for my answer so I give it to him.

'I thought I'd keep it in the family. It's her brother. It's Justin.'

'That loser?'

'Yeah, that loser. Terry. T-J. Justin. He's the father of my baby. He's the daddy. Which makes Toni an auntie. That should be some comfort to her, eh? She gets you back and she gets a niece into the bargain.'

We don't get much further because my bodyguard, Fran, muscles her way into the denouement, dispersing my astonished, gobsmacked husband with efficiency as lethal as tear gas. I hear her telling him I need my rest which seems like a luxury that will quite possibly be out of my reach for good. After that there is the squeak of footsteps, the heavy thud of a door. Then the comfort of Lucy's breathing. The beating of her heart. That's all I need.

★　★　★

The next day we have another visitor. Not the visitor I was hoping for, but one I knew would come. And now she's in front of me, standing still and awkward, all nasty thoughts are dissolving into a messy pile of emotion.

'Hello, Philly,' Toni says. 'How are you?'

'News travels fast.'

'When it's this important yes, it does.'

She drinks you up, your smallness, your

babyness, and within seconds Toni's eyes are wet and shiny and my own emotions are on the slippery slope.

'She's your niece. Did you hear that too?' I try to make my voice kind, try to care enough about how she must feel in all this.

'Yes, I heard. I'm so pleased. Pleased it's not Adrian's. Pleased for you. For Justin. Pleased this one made it all the way.'

I hold you up and Toni reaches out and takes you, a precious parcel, holds you close and smells your head. She sits down with you on the bed next to me so I am subjected to a waft of perfume that transports me back to the house with all the empty rooms in Belsize Park, the flat on Haverstock Hill with the bijou bathroom, Toni's teenage bedroom of the pink shagpile and woodchip, honing her make-up skills. The young girl trotting down the road, Margot Fonteyn hair. The tinkle of glass on the shop floor.

'Are you going to tell Justin?' she asks, after a while.

'I couldn't bear the look on his face,' I say quietly, because I sound stupid, a wimp.

'Don't you think it's about time he knew? About both babies?'

'Are you mad?'

'No, I'm stark raving sane. Tell him. Stop being a martyr.'

A martyr? I am not a martyr. Or am I? Is that what I am doing? Why am I so set on doing this myself, dealing with it all on my own? Maybe she is right. Maybe he should know about both

365

babies. No. I can't tell him. He'll think I am being a child, that I still haven't grown up. But why should I care what he thinks? Of course I care what he thinks. I've always cared what he thinks, ever since I was a little girl leaping over Bernie's bamboo canes . . .

'Are you alright, Philly?'

'Will you tell him for me?'

'It's something you should really do, Phil.'

'I can't.'

She shrugs. 'If that's what you want, I will. It's about time he settled down.'

'He'll never settle down. Not with me at any rate.'

'Do you want him to?'

'I've always wanted him to.'

And, not surprisingly, she asks: 'Then why the bloody hell did you marry Adrian?'

Good point.

'Lots of reasons. Stupid reasons. All the wrong reasons . . . I'm sorry.'

'So you should be.' She smells Lucy again, to keep her on the straight and narrow. 'It happened. Can't change that. And I suppose I should be apologising too. For taking him back.'

'Yes, you are supposed to be saying sorry. Adrian is actually technically my husband. I'd almost forgotten.'

'Sorry.'

There is an ocean of silence in which we thrash about, trying our best to get back to dry land, then I catch hold of you, my little bobbing life-raft . . . well, Toni hands you back to me after planting a kiss on your little boxer nose.

'Lucy might make him settle down,' she says, ever the optimist.

'We can manage on our own.'

'You need a family.'

'She's my family.'

Toni gets up to leave, but can't quite bring herself to go.

'Do you remember Diana?' she asks.

'Ye-es,' I say, unsure where she is going with this.

'Then you'll know there's no such thing as a happy ending.'

And I remember that day, early Sunday morning, Joe waking me up with a mug of tea, his rugby player legs. Bob in tears on the phone. The underpass in Paris. And the week that followed.

'But we still have to aim for it,' Toni goes on. 'Adrian's my happy ending. Not your archetypal happy-ever-after ending, a little 21st Century, but an ending all the same. With a chance of some happiness attached to it.'

'And I've got Lucy.'

'Yes,' she says, 'you have. But it would be nice to have someone else too, wouldn't it? Someone else to share it all with.'

She leaves us then and makes a very important phone call to her mother, who is a great aunt of sorts but, more importantly, a grandmother — news that will take Sheila completely by surprise. Toni then tracks down Justin on his mobile, in Warsaw. Tells him she is an auntie.

Then it is Sheila's turn to break the news, working the grapevine. She goes to the shop and tells Bob he is a grandfather. I don't know what look passes over his face but I sense that in that moment I am forgiven. I am his daughter once again.

★ ★ ★

It is left to me to tell Helena and I finally pluck up courage early the next morning, while you are still sleeping and there is comparative hush in the vicinity. I get my hours mixed up and realise too late that it is in actual fact the middle of the night in Toronto. But the phone is picked up and above the crackly line I can make out a faint, husky voice murmuring a panicky *Hello?*

'Congratulations!' I say. 'You did it!'

'Philippa? Is that you? What exactly have I done?'

'Become a grandmother!'

'No, I'm not . . . really . . . am I? Tell me.'

So I tell her. I tell her everything.

'Terry,' she murmurs, bemused. 'Who would've guessed?' There is a pause where all I can hear is the crackly line . . . or is it her wheezing chest?

'I'd come and see you if I could.'

'Why don't you?'

'I've got emphysema.'

'I thought that's what old coal miners got.'

'And old smokers.'

Oh dear. Emphysema. That doesn't sound too good. I don't go into detail about Adrian or Justin nor any of the other things I really should be saying, like *why were you such a rubbish mother?* Not right now.

'It was good talking to you,' I mumble. 'I just wanted you to know.'

'Thank you, Philippa. I'm so glad for you. Take good care of that little girl of yours. What's she called, by the way?'

'Lucy,' I say. 'She's called Lucy. It's the closest I could get to Lucas.'

'Lucas,' she breathes and I realise the crackles are definitely down to her. 'Well, you'll know soon enough then. You'll know what this has all been about.'

'I'm sorry?'

'I've gotta go. Orville's calling. We'll speak soon.'

And she is gone.

As I put the phone down and contemplate crying, who should walk in but a slightly older, slightly balder Bob, fresh off the Paddington train, carrying a bunch of Andy's wilted roses.

'I've come to stay for a bit,' he says, kissing me on the cheek as if he's just back from a therapy walk on the moors. 'If you'll have me.'

My Mr Bob Sugar.

21

2006

Bob's Full House

You are three months old. You are small and doll-like but your eyes do not click shut when you lie down; they flutter closed and then I can see the shell-skin of your lids that reminds me why I chose your name. And your heart? It's beating well, stronger and stronger.

We live on our own, you and I, getting on like a house on fire (whoops, memories of Wink), in the big four bedroom house in East Dulwich. Adrian has crossed back over the River Thames to old familiar territory, the double-fronted Victorian villa where he and Toni are living together again. They are soon to go to Africa, several months ahead of Madonna, to acquire a baby. But Toni and Adrian will do it with the help of Adebayo, quietly and without fuss. They will bring home a plump little orphan girl with no family to her name. She will live happily in Belsize Park surrounded by people from all four corners of the globe in a family house that has been crying out for her for years. In a house that has finally become a home, its cavernous kitchen finally filled with noise and mess that even Toni's cleaner won't keep on top of so that, to Auntie

Sheila, it will look like that burglar has returned at long last.

You and I, on the other hand, are now ready to leave this cosmopolitan city behind, heading west to the place that is part of my very blood and bones. We are leaving Paddington and its huge iron and pigeon-splatted glass canopy, my own little girl wrapped in a yellow shawl on a warm August morning. A shawl I bought because it reminds me that Helena once swaddled me in a similar one (haven't I learnt anything?) which was passed onto Andy, his burial shroud.

We are not alone on our journey. We have someone to escort us across the capital and through the Underground. Someone to help us onto the train. To help stow the luggage on the overhead rack. To hold Lucy while I eat my egg and cress sandwich. That someone is Bob.

We are taking the train as Bob no longer drives; his nerves are not up to it these days. I myself have given my Laguna to Joe and Rebecca who need a second car with their kids' schedules and no money.

'You have a political conscience after all, Phil,' he says as I hand him the keys.

'You obviously don't have an ecological one,' I retort, quick off the mark for once. 'Fancy owning two cars.'

Valerie and Lesley, the fluffballs, are so happy with Evelyn and Judith that they are staying put. So I needn't worry about them curling up in the cot or triggering asthma attacks. I'll do anything to keep you safe. To keep you with me.

The rest of our worldly goods — rather more

than Helena and I owned — are following on in a removal truck. The house in East Dulwich has a For Sale sign (guess-which-estate-agent?) nailed to a post in the front garden. For now, we'll be living with Bob, at the shop, the only place in the world I want to be.

★ ★ ★

'A new start,' says Bob as he spots me gazing wistfully at the white chalk horse on the hill at Westbury.

'A new start,' I agree. I make a bold move and reach into the pocket of his cardigan where I know I'll find his bottle of pills. 'You don't need these anymore, not with me looking after you.'

He frowns, uncertain how exactly I plan to do that when I already have plenty to keep me occupied.

'Have you heard from Sheila?' I ask, changing the subject.

'She's picking us up from the station,' he says. And when I don't respond to this, he adds: 'I should've told you.'

The last time I saw Sheila was on Bernie's soggy lawn, running full pelt at me, shrieking like a mother gull protecting her young. Protecting Toni. I'm not exactly looking forward to seeing her now, with my own maternal instincts kicking in. Kicking off. But she has to meet you sometime.

'She's pleased,' Bob says, sensing my anxiety. Which is bordering on terror. 'Really pleased.'

'Is she?'

'She just wishes Justin would come home.'

'He will be soon.'

'He will?'

'I had a letter. Here, have a look.'

I rummage in the changing bag and pass it to him, a much longer affair than the note scrunched into my hand on the eve of my sixteenth birthday. Not in his unjoined-up scrawl but typed on his laptop in a hotel somewhere in Eastern Europe. I've read it over and over, each time hearing his Brummie twang, hardly daring to believe the words I never thought I'd hear. Showing them to Bob might make them come true.

```
Dear Phil
   I could send you an email only
somehow a letter seems more right.
Don't ask me why. More formal, I
suppose. More important.
   Toni's told me all about Lucy.
She told me she was an auntie and
it took me a while to work the
rest out. And she told me
something else. That this wasn't
the first time. Phil, you
should've said. All in all I've
made a right mess of things. I'm
selfish and restless and always
think I know best. I thought
you'd be better off with Adrian,
even though he's a mardy pillock.
But you had a home, a job, a
life, security — all the things
```

you craved ever since your mum left you all those years ago. I was wrong. You were wrong. You had all those things in Torquay. All I had to do was put my hand up and you could've had the full set. The missing link. But I kept on moving. Kept going to those foreign places that were just about as far away from you as I could go. Because I thought you'd never say yes. I thought you'd laugh in my face.

I'm coming home in a few weeks. I don't know what I'll find when I get there. But I hope you'll let me through the shop door. I hope you'll let me hold our daughter. Please let me hold you and make it right. My homecoming queen.

Terry.

And there, in that final word, that name, I decide I will.

★ ★ ★

Sheila is waiting for us on the platform as we get off the train, the anxious grandmother, desperate to get her hands on you, stunning in your yellow shawl.

'She's gorgeous, Philippa. Absolutely lovely.'

'Hold her,' I say, passing you over.

As the train pulls out of the station, I fight the

feeling I am in an old film, *Brief Encounter* or *The Railway Children*, though there is no steam, no red bloomers, just the August sunshine, but the emotion is swirling all around, the three adults wondering where all the years have gone, wishing Bernie and Wink had lived to see this day.

Before leaving, I take one last look up the track, letting the breeze brush over me, breathing in the sea air. I am home. We are home.

★ ★ ★

Sheila drives us, slowly and very carefully, to Bob's News. 'I'll call back later,' she says. 'Give you a little time to settle in.'

As her Volvo disappears, Bob and I are left standing outside the shop.

'You won't recognise the place,' he says. 'I've made some alterations.'

The alterations include a new till, a new line in healthy snacks, (*How are they doing? Not very well*) and a new lowered false ceiling thus dispensing with the need for fingerless gloves in winter. Out the back, the kitchenette has been upgraded to one of B&Q's finest. And out in the yard, Andy's rose bush is flourishing. Then we go upstairs . . . which is a revelation! All the woodchip has been stripped off and replaced with smooth new plaster painted the colour of the sky over Torquay on a good day. Which makes a change from the old beige. A job lot so every room has been done over. The living room, the bathroom,

Bob's room, Helena's room, every room but one: mine, which remains the same with the wallpaper of bluebells that match the Cavalier's eyes so well. And there he is, the old swashbuckler, hiding in the pattern, lying in wait until bedtime tonight when he will be astonished at what I've brought home.

'Why didn't you do my room?' I ask Bob.

'I thought you'd want to be consulted.'

'You never wanted to see me again.'

'Let's not be reminded of all that.' He straightens a picture on the wall, Adam Ant in all his glory. 'It's over now. You're back home.'

'Yes,' I say. 'Back home.'

I should feel a little bit sad, disappointed, that my life has come to this, living back home at my age (nearly forty-one!) but I just feel relief. And the best thing about my room is that now I will share it with my daughter who will sleep in a cot purchased by her grandmother, Sheila. Not a lick of lead paint to be found.

★　★　★

Later, after Sheila has called back and we've consumed one of her cottage pies made especially for the occasion, we sit around the living room, Captain preening himself on his perch, the television off, the window open, so we can hear the gulls and see the twilight sky that was once partially obscured by an unstable horse chestnut tree.

'Helena would be proud,' Sheila says, holding you, stroking her little fingers. She is content, her granddaughter, gazing up at Sheila's shock of badly dyed hair.

'I need you both to do something tomorrow,' I announce grandly, for we are on the brink of a most historical event.

Bob and Sheila swap a look, wary at what I am about to suggest. I have no idea at this moment that tomorrow this wariness will be justified.

★   ★   ★

Tonight I will not draw the bedroom curtains. I don't want the Cavalier scaring my little girl. There is plenty of time for them to get acquainted. For now I want to watch the stars, those I can pick out of the sodium glare of the great metropolis of Torquay. I want to think of your namesake up there, a special speck of stardust watching over you. Watching you grow up.

★   ★   ★

You wake me bright and early for a feed and a nappy change and for once I manage to leap out of bed rather than crawl. Today I am on a mission. I've waited a long time to be qualified for it. Over thirty years. Now I am a mother I can go in the backyard and dig up the Time Capsule.

Breakfast is a quiet affair. Sheila has stayed over ('saves me going home and back again as you want me here tomorrow, Philippa'). She and Bob eat their magic muesli which I notice has worked its way into the pantry. I make my way through half a loaf of Hovis, breastfeeding being hungry work, even with apprehension swirling round my stomach. What if everything has gone mouldy, like on *Blue Peter?* What if I find it all too sad, just as I am beginning to get a grip on my new life?

★ ★ ★

Bob's latest shop assistant, Karen, is a genuine Devonian who, when her husband lost his dairy herd to foot and mouth, was sent out to earn some money while he diversified and did a PGCE (he couldn't do any worse than me). So Bob and Sheila are free to come out the back.

We stand in the yard, Bob and I, a trowel apiece. Sheila sits in one of three deckchairs, cuddling you, saying how pretty you look in her new (ridiculously puffy and lacy) summer dress and matching mini sunhat that she bought as a coming home present.

'Mind Andy,' Sheila warns as we start digging.

'Don't worry,' I reassure her. 'He's nearer the rose bush.'

The unidentifiable shrub has grown considerably over the years and Bob and I are having some trouble with woody roots but after a while, as my muscles begin to ache (even though they are in pretty good shape from baby-carrying), Bob's trowel finds some resistance. Something hard.

'A stone?'

'No,' he says. 'I think this is it.'

'It's not soggy then?'

'No. I wrapped the tin in polythene when we dug it up before. Things were getting damp.'

'You did? But you weren't supposed to look.'

'*You* weren't supposed to look. And you didn't. You fainted, remember. We had to lug you inside and lie you out on the sofa. I felt I'd missed my vocation as an undertaker that day.'

'I don't remember as a matter of fact. Not much anyway. Only that I woke up and missed Andy's fur beside me.' There is a pause before I ask: 'So did you? Did you look in there?'

'Yes,' he says, sombre, smearing some dirt across his forehead in an effort to wipe off the sweat forming there.

I am worried now, seeing the wariness creeping back. Why did I have that last piece of toast?

Bob gets back to the matter in hand and pulls the tin from the earth. After a moment's hesitation, he brushes the clumpy red soil off the top of the polythene with his soft shop-boy hands, and removes the tin. Then he stands up and presents it ceremoniously to me. I sit down with it on a deckchair, the one Helena used to sunbathe while I splashed about with a washing-up bowl of soapy water. The smell of Fairy liquid mixed with sunshine. Rainbow colours dancing on the water. Bubbles floating in the air. Crushed red geranium petals at my feet . . .

'This is it then,' I say, prising the rusty lid off with a screwdriver that Bob has fetched from the lean-to.

Yes, this is it. Lucas' life in a box, a chocolate tin, lined with Helena's misplaced Laura Ashley blouse. I handle each of the items in turn, most of them pretty well preserved, though smelling of a potent cocktail of dead air and sweet memories:

A set of decimal coins.

A set of stamps.

A Beano.

A Monkees single, *Daydream Believer.*

A lock of glorious messy hair.

That *Blue Peter* annual.

A school photograph. Our class, squashed together, some of us cross-legged on the playground floor, others on benches, sitting or standing depending on size: Miss Mothball, Mandy Denning, Christopher Bennett, Lucas, in his bobble hat. All the other children whose names I can half-remember or who I've completely forgotten. Children who could now be dentists or tax collectors or traffic wardens. Who could even be dead, like Lucas . . . And there, above my Thing Two, is a little fat girl called Philippa, not looking at the camera at all, but looking down at her best friend in all the world.

And here are the things I put in at the last moment, my booty from the outside loo: one of Andy's whiskers, a gold button, some shells from the beach, plus a lock of my own frizzy hair that has baffled hairdressers from here to London.

And now. At the bottom, in a plastic wallet, is another photograph I don't remember ever seeing, though there is something vaguely

380

familiar in the faces that stare out at me down through the years. A Polaroid photograph. A plumpish, big-boned woman, maybe in her forties for she has crow's feet and slightly matronly hair, wearing what was known as a bed jacket, sitting on a chair with a baby, a bonny newborn, in her arms. The background is institutional . . . a hospital . . . you can make out a metal bed to one side . . . Who are these people? Why are they in Lucas' Time Capsule?

I flip the photo over and there in beautiful schoolgirl handwriting are the words that one day I was meant to read. *Elizabeth and Philippa, August 6th 1965, St Thomas', London.*

That is me, as a baby, one week old, the first time I've seen me so small. Maybe it is wishful thinking, but I am pretty sure I can make out you, Lucy, in there. And at last I get to see my grandmother, who died so long ago. She got to hold me after all, just as Sheila is holding her new granddaughter in the deckchair. Maybe she was sick in the hospital when I was being born. A death and a birth. They often go hand in hand . . . But how did this picture get in here?

Images beat about in my head: Helena coming into an empty dining room. Bare boards and dust. A forgotten marble. *That's where my Laura Ashley blouse got to.* Helena's slender hands as she gave me the tin. The Secret Project. She knew all about it. She must've slipped the photograph into the box before I buried it. All those years ago . . . Why didn't she just give me the photo? Why bury it in the garden?

We sit quietly out here in the yard, listening to

381

the shop bell in the background, the low hum of chatter floating through the back door, Karen's gossip, the pip-pip-pip of the new modern till. A seagull freewheels overhead, ever hopeful for scraps, then vanishes, leaving an almost reverential hush. As if this is a moment of revelation. And surely it is, for Bob has disappeared briefly inside and reappeared with a battered old letter. A faded blue Basildon Bond envelope that he places in my hand.

'I rescued it from the tin when we dug it up, you know, Lugsy and I.' He gestures at the hole in the ground. 'After you fainted, Wink and I sorted through everything as we could see they wouldn't last forever. Just as well really — we didn't imagine we'd have to wait this long.' He nods over at you, attempting a joke that doesn't seem at all appropriate right now.

'Go on.'

'So we saw this photograph which Wink put in the plastic cover. But it's the letter that tells the whole of it. The bigger picture, as it were. And I've kept it inside because if it got ruined you might never find out. What Helena wanted you to know, once you had a child of your own. So you'd understand. She wanted you to be a mother when you read this, that's why she buried it. That's why Wink and I rescued it.'

'And did you read it?'

Bob blushes. 'I'm afraid so, yes.'

Nothing, not even Bob's build-up, prepares me for what I read, as I sit on the deckchair, the box in my lap, the letter in my hand. The longest letter Helena has ever written me.

Dear Philippa,

By now you should be a mother. You should have seen the photograph of you as a baby sitting on Elizabeth's lap. And now is the time for you to know the story behind this photograph. The truth.

Picture it: Elizabeth, wife to a judge, mother to Helena, is diagnosed with breast cancer. It is 1964 and her chances of survival are not good. She is forty-two, a woman who should be in her prime. She feels she has done nothing with her life, other than support her husband and entertain on his behalf. Her daughter, Helena, has been packed off to boarding school in Wales so Elizabeth doesn't even have the satisfaction of being a proper mother to her. And now she is facing a death sentence, each second ticking by reminding her that she has not even begun to live.

Now go back a few years. Helena is eight-years-old and the judge has decided to book a fortnight's holiday for the three of them in Torquay. Maybe he is thinking for once of his wife and daughter — on the other hand, it could be his golfing handicap. They stay in the Palace Hotel, where there is a young waiter who happens to take a shine to mother and daughter who frequently dine alone. He has no family of his own and he enjoys chatting with intelligent, witty Elizabeth and giving extra dollops of ice cream to pretty, bright Helena. On their last evening, after Helena has been put to bed and her husband retired to the hotel bar for the duration, Elizabeth has a stroll around the Palace grounds and who should she bump into but the young waiter, having a sneaky cigarette. He shouldn't be out there but something made him seek the fresh air, other than the opportunity for an undetected smoke. They pass the next two hours deep in conversation and though they are from different worlds, different generations even, they find they can talk about nothing and everything. Elizabeth remembers what it is like to be young and for that reason, the next day before they leave the hotel for the final time, she slips a piece of paper into the waiter's hand. On the paper is written her address and telephone and the instructions that if he ever finds himself in London he must look them up. She doesn't suppose for one minute he will, but the gesture seemed romantic to her and she was only too happy to go along with this whim for once.

Nine years later, that is exactly what he does. He calls the number and Elizabeth answers straight away as if she knew it would be him. She has recently received the bad news and is wondering how she will get through the next few months, worried about leaving Helena alone with the judge, she can be so moody, he so hot-tempered. When the young man suggests a trip to the cinema, she can't help but laugh. Such a youthful thing to do. And so romantic. So she finds herself saying yes, and that is how they end up going to the pictures watching a matinee showing of Goldfinger. He meets her outside with a single red rose. She hardly recognises him, he is well and truly a man now, about thirty, and not in his waiter's uniform, but in a smart, dapper suit. They enjoy themselves so much, slipping back into their once familiar ways, that they agree to go again the next afternoon. And the next. By the fourth showing, they know all the words, all the hammed up orchestral manoeuvres, and their relationship has passed from friendship to something altogether different so that they find themselves booking into a quiet, exclusive hotel in the West End where one afternoon of passion results in Elizabeth falling pregnant, despite the new-fangled coil that she has fitted to ward off this very thing happening on the rare occasions she and the judge share the marriage bed. She is filled up with cancer; the last thing she wants is a baby. The waiter goes back to Torquay without ever knowing about the baby or the cancer, promising he will be back in a few months. Unfortunately it takes him rather longer than that as he has a nasty case of shingles and when he does eventually return, he phones the house in Dulwich only to be informed that regrettably the judge's wife has passed away. What he isn't told is that she refused what treatment might have prolonged her life in order to save her unborn child.

Elizabeth took a brave, possibly stupid decision and told the judge of her indiscretion and the consequent pregnancy. The judge, rather than making a song and dance about it and divorcing his dying wife, which wouldn't go down well in society, arranged a private adoption, though it would be a miracle if Elizabeth lasted long enough for the baby to be born at full term. But there was something about her resolution that made the judge prepare for the eventuality.

When the time came, the judge was unable to confine his wife at home as she was too ill. He booked her into a private room at St Thomas' hospital where a strict sister was up to speed and utterly professional (if a little sergeant-majorly). On July 29th 1965, Elizabeth gave birth to a baby girl who she named Philippa. She was born clutching the coil that had failed Elizabeth but that was a symbol of the miracle that she was. It had been agreed between the parties concerned that Elizabeth would nurse her baby for ten days — that was the only demand she made and the judge in a rare moment of weakness agreed. After that, Philippa would be handed over to her new life. Her new identity.

But before that happened, when she — you — were a few days old, against my father's orders, I snuck into the hospital and I met my baby sister — well, technically half-sister. You had this frizzy hair and big eyes that seemed to look in amazement at everything around you. But at the last minute, I couldn't let you go. So I told my mother — our mother — that I would bring you up as my own. I would take you away to a place where no-one would ever find us. Elizabeth agreed — what mother wouldn't want to keep her two daughters together? — and, before any papers were signed, she instructed her solicitor from her hospital bed — and what would turn out to be her death bed — to set up a trust fund that would pay an income into my account every month until you turned eighteen.

So, Philippa, it was all arranged. A few days later, when you were a week old, I came to the hospital for normal visiting hours to see you both. The last time she held you, our mother, she was smoothing your hair. I took a photo on a Polaroid borrowed from a happy father down the corridor before she kissed you goodbye and handed you over to a nurse for feeding. Then she kissed me goodbye, whispering thank you, and slipped her ring onto my finger before going to the loo as agreed. I took her place in the chair. When you were brought back winded and pink, I cradled you in my arms, telling the young nurse that I would watch you until Elizabeth returned. I asked if it would be possible for a cup of tea, I was parched due to the hot weather. She promptly disappeared. I wrapped you up in a yellow shawl smuggled in with me in my Harrods bag which I had also stuffed full with nappies and baby cream from Elizabeth's bedside locker. All my other worldly goods were squeezed into my vanity case which I'd kept out of sight under the bed. Then as if Fate had arranged it, a man in a pinstripe suit wandered, lost, into the wrong room. I asked him if he would be a gentleman and help me out, knowing we'd have a less suspicious exit with a man in charge. I smiled sweetly and he said of course and carried my bag while I held you close. We walked out of that hospital, you in my arms, into the hot August sunshine. The start of our new life.

That is the truth behind the photograph. The rest you must ask Bob. I pray he is still there to tell you.

Your loving sister,
Helena.

Helena's words float before me and I wonder if my mind is playing tricks. Did I really just read that? Bob has sunk into the third deckchair, his head back, his eyes closed so I can almost believe he is sleeping.

Helena is my sister.

I take a closer look at the photograph, at my real mother, Elizabeth. I can see her hair that has been brushed back into a bun but what I didn't spot before was the frizzy tendrils that had escaped. I see her big, wide

387

shoulders and, even though she is sitting down, I know her legs are long. I see the ring on one of her fingers. It is hard to make it out but I know it is the one I wear on my own finger. The one Bob gave to me on my sixteenth birthday, left behind by Helena.

Helena is my sister.

Why did she want to take me on? She was too young. She couldn't cope. She should've let me go. And why did my real mother agree to it? She must've known exactly what Helena was like. Shoes, lipstick, handbags. Who would she turn to for help?

'Why didn't Elizabeth just sign those papers?' I ask Bob whose eyes are open now, fixed on the blue sky. A vapour trail. Anywhere but me. 'I could've had a proper family.'

'She was your family.' Bob swings his eyes to his knees, rubs his chin so I can hear the scratchiness of the whiskers he has yet to shave. 'And what is a proper family exactly?' he asks, a little philosophically for my liking.

'I don't know.' I have to think about this. There must be someone I know who has a proper family. 'Cheryl's!' I say triumphantly, like I've banged the buzzer on a television quiz. 'Cheryl grew up in a proper family. And look at her. She's a doctor. I could've been a doctor with a family like that.'

'No, you couldn't,' he says, gently. 'You were hopeless at science.'

I remember Nathan and me in the back of Doug's mini. How he'd lose me with his talk of molecules and genetics. Maybe I should have listened more carefully.

'Can you think of anyone else?'

I couldn't think of anyone else.

'That's not the point,' I say, my argument somewhat defeated. 'Helena should've told me all along. Why pretend?'

'She wanted a new life. She didn't want anyone to know who you were in case your grandfather came looking. He was a judge. He knew people. He could've made her come back to London. Got rid of you. She loved you.'

'Why did you go along with it? You've known for years.'

I can see Sheila biting her lip, clutching you — in your own innocent world, unaware of the drama in the yard, eyes closed, fingers twitching. Sheila grips Bob with an expression that says quite clearly and simply: *Tell her.*

That is when Bob starts crying, right there in the deckchair in the backyard, proper tears, runny nose, the whole works, causing a great big hammer to swoop down from the sky and whack me on the head . . . Of course! Oh, God . . . why have I never seen it?

'It's you,' I say. 'You're the waiter. The man in the dapper suit. You're the one.'

'Yes,' he says, rummaging for his handkerchief. 'I'm sorry.'

'But how . . . '

He doesn't answer my question directly. Instead, in his own roundabout Bob way, he tells me the story he should've told me long ago.

'Helena found me,' he says, as if he were a stray cat, a misplaced pair of white gloves. 'Your first day of school, do you remember? She'd got a new job as an admin assistant at the Palace. Her first day and it hadn't gone too well. In fact it was awful — she'd had a nasty encounter with one of the managers. But she did have a moment to make some enquiries, of a woman in the office who'd been there since before time began. She asked about the waiter who'd befriended them all those years before. Elizabeth had told her what had happened in London and Helena could remember me quite clearly, all that extra ice cream. The woman remembered me too. She came in the shop from time to time and told Helena where to find me. So she collected you from school and came on down. The moment that shop bell rang and she appeared, I knew there was something special about her. I offered her a job and she accepted.'

'Did you know who she was?'

'I hadn't a clue. I never guessed in all the years she lived and worked here. Not for one second.'

'So when did you find out? When you buried Andy?'

'No. Actually it was before then. In Canada.'

'Canada?'

'That day I was in bed sick. She called by while you were out shopping. She told me everything. That I was . . . you know . . . I was your father. That she was Elizabeth's daughter. She said she was sorry she'd never told me. She couldn't explain why. Who can explain that?'

There was a silence while we both think about this.

'And then, I'm afraid, I made a bit of a fool of

myself,' he goes on.

'Oh?'

'You see . . . something happened . . . just the once . . . one night not so long before Orville came to Torquay . . . '

'You and Helena? I had no idea . . . well, I knew you'd always fancied her but Helena . . . '

Bob tries to hide his blushes in his hands.

'Well, she was adamant nothing more would happen. That she wasn't in a position to take up with me. But it was only in that motel room that she told me why. Her mother. Elizabeth. That she was ashamed. It felt all wrong. Because of Elizabeth. And you. All too messy. The generations mixed up. So she grasped the chance that Orville offered her and she thought she was doing the right thing by you. Leaving you with your father. But she never said. Never told me the truth. That was her biggest failing.'

'But you didn't make a fool of yourself. She must have gone along with it.'

'No, I mean in the motel room.'

'What did you do exactly?'

'I told her I loved her. That I'd loved her ever since she came in the shop that day, after a job, with you at her side. I loved you both and I wanted us to be a family. I begged her to come back to Torquay. To bring Wes. But after my grand speech all she could say was: 'I can't leave Orville.' I did what I could: I protested, digging a deeper hole for myself. 'He'll find someone to look after him,' I said. 'He's tough.' But she said, 'No, I mean I can't leave Orville because I love him.' That's what she said. And she killed that

391

small hope I had. That me being your father would be enough to bring her back.'

'So the pills . . . when we got home . . . that's why you needed the pills.'

'I loved her so much. I begged her but she was adamant. She said she could never leave Orville. And nor could Wes. And then I made myself think of Wes. How you and I, we'd seen it for ourselves, that young lad rushing home from school so his dad wouldn't be alone.'

Yes, I remembered. A boy in a dodgy hat kissing Orville Tupper on the head, making us coffee, sweet and kind.

You begin squealing, insistently, in a way that can't be ignored.

'I think she wants a feed,' Sheila says.

I get up and relieve her. You quieten enough for me to hear Bob sniffing. Sheila is watching him, concern in her eyes, as he stands up to his full five foot nine, (I think old age has stolen that extra half inch from him) but he is looking at me and I hear him say the words I've always wanted to hear. Words I've always wanted to believe. The impossible is true. It has been true all along.

'You're my daughter,' he says.

★ ★ ★

Later we stand together out in the yard, you and I, while I snip, one-handedly, two roses from Andy's bush.

'Come on, Miss. Let's go for a walk.'

I put you in the pram — also donated by Grandma Sheila — and push you up the road past Wink's old house, past the chippy, to the Bone Yard where I buried the silver jubilee coin and shared a bottle of Pomagne with Christopher Bennett.

Nothing much has changed. The same yews, cedar and pretty stone church. The granite crosses, the carved angels. They have stopped burying the dead here. Lucas was one of the last to have this peaceful spot as his final resting place. Peaceful when there aren't kids playing hide and seek. Though he'd like that. He and Albert Morris. They'd like the sound of children's voices bouncing round the graves like a game of pinball.

We find the spot — a little overgrown but not as bad as I feared — and I lay one of the roses down by the headstone. No, nothing has changed. Lucas is still dead. Still seven-years-old. But I've come back, bringing you with me.

'Here she is,' I announce. 'Lucy.'

Then I tell him that *Doctor Who* has been resurrected. I tell him that there are stickers and cards and all sorts of TV tie-ins. I tell him about *Blue Peter* — that there is a myriad of young trendy presenters and it is as good as ever. That there are all sorts of channels these days, even ones devoted solely to children's programmes. Then I tell him about you. That I am determined you will lead a happy life. I will make sure of that. I tell him about Helena. I tell him that the young pretty woman who was such good friends with his mummy, wasn't who we thought she was. She wasn't a bad mother, after all. She was my sister. And she loved me. Finally, I tell him

393

about Bob. That he was a waiter in a former life. That he was in actual fact my father. He was never in the jungle. He was here, in a sweet shop in Torquay, all along.

A shadow falls over the grave. I've never been scared here, not since that first day when we thought Albert Morris was chasing us through the giant rabbit hole but I spin round quickly — just in case.

It is Bob.

'I'm sorry,' he says. 'For giving up on you. I should never have done that. I could blame the pills — they make you do strange things. But I won't. I blame myself. I should've told you the whole truth. If I'd done that then maybe you wouldn't have made such a mess with Adrian.'

'Aren't I allowed to make a mess?'

He can't find an answer to that. There is no answer.

'I've got Lucy,' I say, after a bit. 'She's what matters in all this.'

'Never forget it,' he says.

'I won't,' I said. 'I'm her mother. I love her.'

★ ★ ★

We visit Wink's small memorial stone over in a quiet corner by the wall. Her final resting place is flying with the gulls over the harbour but I lay a rose for her too and remember her sitting with her gammy leg on my lap, coming home from London in the back of Linda's Maxi, regaling Larry facts about his childhood . . . born out of wedlock . . . put in a foster home . . . and then it comes back to me, the other crucial fact that Wink was telling me, the one I'd blocked from my mind or simply forgotten: He'd been brought up by his foster sister. A sister who he'd thought of and referred to as 'Mum'.

My Wink.

I show her you, the jackpot, the one that runs rings around Tiger and Captain. The one that will shine above all others.

'Look what I've got,' I say. 'Didn't I do well?'

★ ★ ★

Two weeks later, Someone Else turns up on my doorstep. Terry Siney. For now, as his letter to me suggests, he is plain old Terry again.

'You never escape your roots,' he says, in his best Brummie accent. 'However hard you try.'

'I know,' I say. 'Look at me. Back behind the counter serving sweets.'

'You're my roots, Phil,' he says. 'In the words of Barry White,' he sniffs, embarrassed, 'You are my everything. You and Lucy, that is.'

2007

To celebrate your first birthday, the fact that your little heart is mending all by itself, we are going on holiday. There is no need for anyone to pop down to the travel agents in Castle Circus because your daddy gets given free flights all the time as a travel writer, especially one as in demand as him. He has managed to wangle four tickets and — with Sheila safeguarding the shop, Coco, and Captain — Bob is coming with us. We are going to Canada!

★   ★   ★

You are not keen on the take-off, grabbing your little ears and squealing. But once we are up there, flying, you are happy on your daddy's lap, yabbering away to Tiger in your arms. I even manage to sleep for a bit but dreams of our lost baby tell me this is not a good idea. I need to keep those old useful wits about me for in a few hours we will be in Toronto where I will see my sister, your Auntie Helena.

★   ★   ★

It is Bob's turn to hold you on his lap. He sings you a lullaby, if you can call *Goldfinger* a lullaby.

I look at Bob's fingers and imagine them entwined in Elizabeth's hands. Their brief, snatched moments together. My parents.

Like Dick Whittington, Bob went to London in search of gold. And he found it, though he never knew it. Perhaps now, flying over Iceland, he will realise the gold is in his fingers. His granddaughter.

Oh dear. Tears are waiting just around the corner but now I have Terry who reaches into his pocket for a packet of Kleenex. I will marry this man.

* * *

As the sun rises over the Great White North, we suck on lollipops and try to distract you from your ears in the moments of our descent. We are the last to get off the plane; there is no hurry. We have waited long enough.

Not least Helena, a widow now since Orville passed on a few months ago who, when we finally make it through to Arrivals, is waiting in a wheelchair, a tank of oxygen on one side, Wes on the other. They brighten as they spot our strange little grouping. Wes pushes Helena towards us and we meet halfway. I bend down to kiss her on the cheek, and I whisper: 'Nice to see you.' 'To see you, nice,' she whispers back. And we get a glimpse of how we would have lived together as sisters if that is the way Life had taken us. But instead we are here and there is no point questioning it. It is what it is.

Wes clears his throat and announces: 'Welcome to Canada!' Then he gives me a hug and

397

says, 'Good to see you, Aunt Philippa,' which makes me feel all sorts of things like old, happy and excited to be here.

He is a tall man now and, when he bends down to pick up one of our suitcases to put on the trolley, there is the start of a shiny bald patch on top of his head . . . so, just for a moment, I wonder . . . that night of passion in the shop before Helena met Orville Tupper . . . is there another secret waiting to be told?

Nothing would surprise me. Nothing in this funny old game called Life.

But the one certainty in all of this is that I want to play the game with these people here, making a riotous noise in the deserted Arrivals hall. As I watch them making a fuss of you, kissing you and cuddling you, I know that I want to play the game as best I can.

And I want to play the game with you.